The Ex Next Door

Jo Platt was born in Liverpool in 1968 and, via the extremely winding route of rural Wiltshire, London, Seattle and St Albans, she is now happily settled in Bristol with her husband and two daughters. She studied English at King's College London before going on to work in the City for ten years. In 2000 she escaped into motherhood and part-time employment, first as an assistant teacher in a Seattle pre-school and then was a Bristol-based secretary to her husband.

Also by Jo Platt

JO PLATT
The Ex
Next Door

CANELO

First published in the United Kingdom in 2023 by

Canelo
Unit 9, 5th Floor
Cargo Works, 1–2 Hatfields
London SE1 9PG
United Kingdom

A CIP catalogue record for this book is available from the British Library.

Print ISBN 978 1 80436 323 2
Ebook ISBN 978 1 80436 322 5

Cover design by Head Design

Look for more great books at www.canelo.co

Printed and bound in Great Britain by Clays Ltd, Elcograf S.p.A.

1

For Gerry and Tony, with love.

Prologue

From the moment we met, Elliot and I had a shared sense that we were meant to be. A chance encounter at a London art exhibition left us mutually smitten and, swept along by an intensity of feeling, we had moved in together within weeks. In the months that followed, every major step forward occurred without debate or dissent and, for over two years, I felt only deep affection and a certainty that we would be together for the rest of our lives.

Looking back, it was hard to pinpoint exactly when things started to change, largely because the deterioration in our relationship – or at least in my experience of it – had occurred so gradually. But what I did know was that the decline had gone hand in hand with a growing anxiety on my part about the fact that I was not the only woman in Elliot's life who found him attractive.

Not that women finding him attractive was anything new. It was just that it hadn't bothered me before, because it hadn't felt like it had anything to do with us as a couple. But for whatever reason and, as I said, at a point that I have never since been able to determine, I began to feel insecure about it, and also increasingly inadequate when, for example, he mentioned certain female work colleagues.

I would occasionally, casually mention my insecurities to him, but he would always just laugh them off, in an incredulous and dismissive kind of way, which was actually quite reassuring – but only temporarily. Over time, my anxieties slowly built, eventually becoming tinged with suspicion.

It was a suspicion which peaked three Fridays before Christmas – the night of Elliot's office party, when he texted me at around midnight to say that he was going to the home of his colleague, James, for drinks and that rather than disturb me in the early hours, he was going to stay over. I could hear female voices in the background as he made the call and I told him not to worry about disturbing me, I would rather that he came home. He had laughed at that, told me I was sweet and that he'd see me in the morning.

By the time he turned up the next day at around lunchtime, I was distraught with wholly unsubstantiated concern as to what he might have got up to. Nevertheless, I resolved to play it cool, feigning an interest in the trivial details of his evening, but all the while keeping an ear out for any mention of another woman.

'Was the restaurant good?' I asked.

'It was OK,' he replied, from his stretched-out position on the sofa. 'But not great.'

'And how was James? Did his wife mind you crashing back there? How many of you went?'

'Only four.'

'And she was OK with that? Haven't they got a toddler?'

'They were asleep and we kept a lid on it.'

'Did Andrew make it, or did he bail?'

'He bailed. As usual.' He yawned and stretched lazily.

'How about Harvey?'

'He was there for a bit.'

'And Rachel? She's usually up for a late night.'

'Yes.' He extended a hand towards the coffee table and picked up a magazine.

I controlled my breathing, my stress levels rising further with the confirmation that he had spent post-party time with Rachel Letts, a woman who, in my opinion, was amongst his most ardent admirers, seeking him out at every work event to which I'd tagged along.

His phone buzzed and, as he removed it from his pocket, I craned my neck in an attempt to see the screen from my position in the armchair beside him. I glimpsed a capital 'R' and a lower case 'h' in the sender's name.

'Anything important?'

'No.' He yawned for a second time.

'Who was it?'

I was aware of a snap to my tone and there followed a pause, during which Elliot hauled himself into a sitting position and turned towards me.

'Are you OK, Esme?'

I blinked, as if confused. 'Yes. Why?'

'Because you seem tense.'

'Because I asked who texted you?'

He frowned and then held the phone out towards me. 'Richard.'

I stared at the name, clearly visible at the top of the screen, and nodded dumbly as Elliot returned the phone to his pocket.

'And you're positive everything is OK?' he asked gently.

I forced a smile. 'Positive,' I said, moving from my chair to the sofa and kissing his cheek, frustrated with myself over an irrational and constantly resurfacing jealousy that I just couldn't seem to quell. 'I'm glad you had a good evening.'

After that, we had drifted on for exactly one more week, until the day of my own work Christmas party, at which I drank far more than I could handle. As a consequence, I elected not to go home and instead spent the night at the flat of my newish colleague, Owen, and his girlfriend, Taya, who lived within staggering distance of our final-destination club.

I sent Elliot a single-line text at around two a.m., telling him where I was, and then promptly fell asleep.

Whether in my drunken state I had intentionally mirrored his behaviour of the previous week, I couldn't say. But there was certainly no sort of connection between the two events in my fuzzy, aching head as I walked into the kitchen of our flat the next morning.

'Hi,' he said, offering me a small smile as he looked up briefly from the newspaper, open on the table in front of him.

'Hi.' I checked the kettle on the hob and then turned on the gas beneath it. 'God, I'm so in need of caffeine,' I groaned and flopped down next to him, leaning in for a kiss.

'Hang on,' he said, laughing and shifting in his seat. 'Why don't you tell me what happened last night first?'

'What do you mean?'

'You didn't come home.'

'I stayed over at Owen's. I texted you.' I frowned and rubbed my forehead. 'Didn't you get it?'

'I got a text at three in the morning to say that you were getting into bed at the house of some guy I've never met. That's not really an explanation of how that situation came to be, is it?' His tone was light and reasonable, as if bordering again on laughter, but to me, the implication felt the opposite.

My frown deepened, as the dull pounding in my head began to strengthen. 'You know I work with Owen. I've mentioned him lots,' I said. 'And sorry, but are you asking me if I had sex with him last night? Because I don't remember asking if you shagged Rachel Letts when you decided not to come home last Friday.'

He didn't look at me, but his smile fell away and his jaw tightened. 'I was at James's,' he said quietly, 'as you know.'

I looked at him, hesitating over a response, before weeks and months of slowly building paranoia won the day. 'So you claim.'

I couldn't quite believe I'd said it, but there was definitely catharsis in the accusation and, for a moment, I felt more in control of the situation, and of myself, than I had for an awfully long time.

The kettle whistled and he stood up, turning off the gas. 'I think it's best if I go, Es,' he said calmly. 'Call me when you're prepared to talk through what happened last night and we can think about where we go from there.' With that, he left the kitchen and, after packing a large suitcase, the flat.

For the first couple of hours after his exit, I was furious at what I saw as his hypocrisy, arrogance and lack of trust. But as the day wore on, and a sleepless Saturday night segued into a miserable Sunday morning, I became increasingly uncertain of the moral high ground and was desperate for him to call so that we could indeed talk things through.

Of course, I could have called him. I could have apologised for my stubbornness, reassured him that nothing whatsoever had happened with Owen and told him all about Owen's lovely girlfriend, who had brought me tea and toast when I awoke.

But I didn't. Instead – and in spite of wanting him back and missing him to an almost unbearable degree – I let all his doubts linger and I let our relationship end.

And although I would stop short of saying that I was haunted by that decision, there was no doubt that more than once over the years without Elliot which followed, I certainly wondered at it.

Chapter 1

Four years later – April

I was just about to turn the second lock on the gallery door when Lloyd knocked on the window of his shop, mouthed something incomprehensible and then, in response to my confused expression and slight shrug, came outside.

'I *said*, Esme,' he began, his beaming pink face already shiny with sweat, despite it being only seven degrees and eight a.m., 'I've got some lovely chops in today.'

'Ooh.' I kept my eyes locked firmly on his, while trying to ignore the wiping action of his hands down his blue-and-white striped apron. 'Sounds good.'

'I'll keep some for you – and for David too.' He nodded towards the gallery. 'The laddie nae in yet? Nae aboot the hoose?' he asked with a chuckle, a reference to my business partner's Scottish roots and accent which, for some reason, Lloyd found endlessly entertaining.

'Well, if he is in, he's locked me out,' I replied, holding up and jangling the keys. 'But as you well know, he's pescatarian these days, Lloyd. So you've really got to stop trying to force-feed him meat.'

He tutted disapprovingly. 'The bloke needs to get some iron down him. He looks like the Dingle Dangle Scarecrow.'

I laughed and looked up from the door. 'I'll tell him you said so.'

'Not me.' He shook his head. 'That's what my missus said after she popped in to pick up that swirly glass bowl thing from him last week. Said he looked really peaky.'

'Gwen said that?'

'Yep. Tall and stringy like the Dingle Dangle Scarecrow. Don't get me wrong, she still thinks he's a good-looking guy and says that if she was ten years younger...' He rolled his eyes. 'But she thinks he's lost weight over the past couple of months.' He looked down and patted his rounded stomach. 'Maybe I should ask him for tips. I've been piling on the pounds and now Gwen wants me to go to Monday running club with her,' he added miserably.

'Would that be so bad?'

'Er, yes, it would,' he said, in an *of course* kind of way. 'All the blokes run like the wind and look like The Rock.'

'Rubbish. My dentist is a member and he looks like Alan Carr.'

'Hmm...' He seemed unconvinced.

'You should do it. You could invite David along to help him build some muscle and lose the scarecrow look.'

He laughed. 'I'll think about it. But right now,' he continued, jerking a thumb over his shoulder, 'I'd better get back to sorting the back room.'

He nodded a farewell and disappeared back inside, while I did my best not to think about his cream-tiled back room – of which I had only ever caught a glimpse – and about what 'sorting' might constitute in a butcher's shop. David hadn't always been pescatarian and I wondered if working next door to a butcher – albeit an absolutely lovely one – for the past two years might have had at least as much to do with his decision not to eat meat as the influence of his vegan girlfriend, Sophie. I further wondered how long it might be before I, too, could no longer look a pork pie or a Sunday roast in the eye.

I pushed open the gallery door and went inside. The sound of David talking on the phone immediately reached me from the back of the shop.

So he *had* locked me out.

I dumped my backpack on the counter and made my way through the gallery to the workshop, repositioning a row of three small ceramic birds and a largish bronze hare as I went.

'You locked me out!' I began accusingly on reaching him, only to discover that he wasn't alone. Jasmine (Jazz to her friends) Dean — one of the local artists who sold her work through us and, it had to be said, one of the few to whom I hadn't massively warmed — was there too.

'Oh, hi, Jasmine, I didn't realise you were here. Sorting out some more framing for your show?' I nodded towards the samples of varying width and colour that David had laid out on the bench in front of him.

She smiled, toying with a tightly coiled, white-blonde curl that had escaped from the colourful scarf, tied land-girl style, around her head. Floral DMs and a khaki jumpsuit, unbuttoned to reveal a red bandeau top, completed the look.

'Hi, Esme. Yes, David's just helping me out with the latest prints. He's *so* incredibly patient.'

'OK,' I nodded. 'So do you have more prints? Or are we talking about the ones we looked at last week?'

'I'm afraid they're the ones from last week,' she said, biting her lower lip, in pretence of guilt. 'I really, *really* loved the frames you pushed for those, and I'm ninety per cent sure I'm going to stick with them. You've got such a great eye that I'd be bonkers not to, but I just thought I'd take one more teensy-weensy peek at the options and ask David's advice, before absolutely, definitely deciding.'

I glanced at David, who left it a moment before looking at me. The delay was, I knew, an encouragement for me to take a breath before responding.

'How very wise of you to get a second opinion,' I said, in a saccharine tone to match her own. 'And I can relate, because I always dither neurotically over the framing of my own work.'

Her eyes narrowed and David cleared his throat. 'So, Jazz, you're thinking maybe the lighter oak now?' he asked, his matter-of-fact Edinburgh tones oozing businesslike calm and reason.

'Well, I just wonder if you're right about the more subtle grain and lighter colour complementing the blue tones a little better than the ones Esme...' She hesitated with theatrical awkwardness and placed a hand on her chest. 'Better than the ones *I* chose last week.'

I suppressed a sigh, smiled politely and then left them to it, contorting my face into a snarl as I turned my back and returned to the counter to set up the till.

She left about five minutes later, looking doe-eyed up at David as he held the door open for her and offering me a cheery wave as she exited.

I returned the wave, baring my teeth into a grin.

'My, my, she was up early,' I said, as the door swung shut behind her.

David didn't respond, instead walking over to the counter and beginning to flick through the waist-high rack of prints alongside it. 'Just looking for something to replace...' he murmured absently, looking briefly over his shoulder at an empty space on the far wall.

I turned my head to the window and watched as Jasmine held up a hand in thanks to the driver of a white van who had screeched to a halt to let her cross the street.

Returning my attention to David, I addressed the top of his head of dark hair as he continued to flip through the prints. 'Did she just happen to be passing? I mean, how did she even know anyone would be here?'

'I bumped into her over the weekend,' he said. 'I thought we had one of Anthony Gilbert's prints in here, didn't you?'

'Having sleepless nights over the frames I'd suggested, was she?'

He stopped flipping, but it was a moment or two before he looked up. When he did, his slim features were arranged into an expression of pure patience. 'I'm sure you're not going to take it as a personal insult that the woman changed her mind about the shade of a wood veneer.'

I took a breath in preparation for enlightening him regarding the myriad of micro-aggressions and provocations I felt Jasmine directed my way every time she set foot inside the gallery, the most recent being her accusation that I had 'pushed' my frame preferences. But I knew he'd think me petty, so resisted the temptation.

'Lloyd says you look like the Dingle Dangle Scarecrow,' I said instead.

His eyebrows twitched slightly before he lowered his head and resumed his search of the prints. 'That's... interesting.'

'He and Gwen think you're in need of some iron.'

'Noted.'

'He's got some chops if you want them.'

He nodded in surprised approval. 'Makes a pleasant change from the offer of haggis. Especially as I know he doesn't even stock haggis.'

'You should call his bluff next time,' I said, opening drawers in search of a till roll. 'Good weekend?'

'Passed without incident.'

'Mine too – ooh, other than that I've *finally* got a next-door neighbour.' I opened the front of the till and inserted a newly discovered roll.

'Seem OK?'

'Not met her yet, but she looks very glam from a distance; like she could stand in for Holly Willoughby or Tess Daly. I saw her wheel a suitcase inside on Saturday, but we haven't spoken.'

'And how's the house? Are you feeling settled?'

My shoulders sagged slightly at the thought of the semi-detached, red-brick Victorian cottage – a mile and a half west of the Clifton Suspension Bridge – which I'd been calling home for the past three weeks. 'Well, it beats the Premier Inn, and the village location is great for walks, but it's very Airbnb. Still can't wait to get back to the flat. Not that the repair works on

that are going to be finished anytime soon,' I added despondently, suppressing a shiver at the recurring mental image of an
upended claw-foot bath.

'Here it is.' David pulled a pen and ink of the Wills Building
from the rack and held it at arm's length. 'Black, two-centimetre
frame? What do you think?'

'Perfect.' I smiled, grateful and unsurprised that he'd opted
not to pursue the topic of my current living arrangements. The
insurance company had been great about everything, and I was
of course very grateful to have escaped into a newly refur-
bished, tastefully furnished cottage, following the destruction
of my Redland flat. But without my furniture, photographs
and artwork – all of which were either in storage or had been
laid waste by a devastating combination of cascading water and
rubble – the cottage was very much a house, not a home, for
me.

David studied the print in his hands for a moment longer,
then walked towards the workshop, pausing as he reached the
open door.

'Dingle Dangle Scarecrow?' he asked, looking at me over his
shoulder. 'Like the nursery rhyme?'

'That's the one.'

He nodded and looked thoughtful.

'Of course, *I* don't think you look like the Dingle Dangle
Scarecrow,' I said.

'No?'

'Shoes are all wrong.'

He glanced down at his feet.

'And you'd have to keep your mouth shut because, as you
know, scarecrows aren't Scottish. But physically...' I shrugged.
'I guess I can see it.'

'Well, that's my day made.' He offered me a cool stare,
followed by a quietly amused smile. 'Coffee's made,' he said,
heading off.

I watched him go, reflecting on the fact that not once, during
our entire three-year business association, had David's exhibited

emotions ever seemed to extend beyond a small, closed range of *quiet amusement* and *barely perceptible irritation*.

Not that that was a problem: quite the opposite, in fact. He was yang to my yin and most of the time our very different personalities actually felt like a plus. He was calm, calming and an excellent strategist. But his more considered approach sometimes left him at risk of missing an opportunity to connect with a new artist or customer. Whereas I, with a more instinct-based approach and a tendency towards impulsiveness, was more adept at landing a catch.

The scraping of a stool across the workshop floor brought me back to the moment and I moved from behind the counter, picking up my backpack on my way to fetch the coffee. I'd made it as far as the hallway between the kitchen and the workshop, when I caught sight of David, sitting at his bench and staring at a largish block of roughly hewn wood.

He looked up, suddenly aware of being watched.

'Work in progress?' I asked.

'Just something I might hack away at over lunch,' he said dismissively, with a characteristic refusal to take his sculpture seriously.

'Well, I'd love to see it when it's finished — and I'm sure all of our customers would too,' I added at volume, continuing into the kitchen before he could shoot down the suggestion. Despite his, in my opinion, considerable sculpting skills, he had so far stubbornly refused to put any of his work up for sale in the gallery.

Once in the kitchen, I placed my bag on the table next to the coffee David had already poured for me and reached inside, taking out a pencil and the red, leather-bound sketchbook which served as my journal. Sitting down, I flicked through the pencil drawings, and occasional watercolours, which filled the cream-coloured pages, until I reached the next blank sheet. Gazing thoughtfully at it for a moment, I tapped the pencil against my lower lip. And then, after a first sip of coffee, and a final glance towards David and the workshop, I began to draw.

Chapter 2

I didn't rush to call on my new neighbour, assuming that we'd probably run into each other by chance at some point. But when the days ticked by with no further sightings of her, and only occasional footsteps on uncarpeted stairs to confirm that she hadn't decided that two miles was too far to go for a pint of milk – and immediately moved out – I decided that I really should knock and say hi.

The opportunity came a week after I'd first spotted her, when I heard the clank of a gate and saw her jogging up the path to her cottage dressed in workout gear. With some curiosity, and an urge to get the now overdue pleasantries over with, I picked up the boxed trinket bowl I'd brought home with me from the gallery and, judging myself to look just about present-able after a morning spent sketching and painting, I hurried next door.

By the time I got there, she'd disappeared inside, but returned to answer the door within seconds of me releasing the heavy, brass, fox-head knocker and affixing on my face what I hoped was a welcoming and politely interested smile.

'Hi,' she said, still flushed and mildly breathless from her recent bout of exercise.

'Hi, I'm Esme, I live next door,' I began, taking in the golden, mid-length hair, the tight-fitting pink vest-top and the black cropped leggings. A grey sweatshirt, tied loosely around an enviably slim waist, completed the ensemble.

Other than surreptitiously looking her up and down and guessing at her age – early thirties – my only other immediate thought was that it didn't matter that she was currently pink and a bit sweaty: she appeared toned to a degree which would have put a personal trainer to shame and groomed to a degree which made me want to rush next door and reach for the hair straighteners.

But instead, I settled for running a self-conscious hand through my hair – which I now couldn't recall even brushing after my shower that morning – and ploughing on. 'I suppose I should say that I live next door *for now*,' I clarified, smiling broadly. 'It's only temporary, while my flat in town is repaired. It flooded when my neighbour's water tank exploded. The ceilings fell in and a bath landed on my bed, so I had to move out.'

I was well used by now to news of my domestic disaster being met with wide eyes and gaping mouths. My new neighbour's expression, however, remained totally Zen. 'Oh my goodness, how absolutely awful!' she exclaimed, sounding horrified while appearing completely unperturbed. 'Poor you.'

'Yeah, it wasn't great, but everyone escaped unhurt, so that's the main thing.'

'I'd be in absolute bits,' she said, with a lack of animation that would have made her the perfect life-model.

'It's fine. The insurers are sorting everything out and, in the meantime,' I glanced next door, 'I get to live here. Anyway, I just wanted to pop round, say hi and give you this. You know, to say welcome to the neighbourhood.' I handed her the box. 'I have a small gallery in Westbury Park and this is a piece by a local potter.'

'Wow, that's so lovely of you – and this is so beautiful,' she said excitedly, opening the box and taking out the bowl. 'I'm Morgan, by the way, and I'm so sorry, but I'm just back from a run and about to hop in the shower, otherwise I'd invite you in. Plus, the house is a tip.' She shook her head, as if in apology or dismay, and then somehow managed to convey the idea of a smile, without actually moving the corners of her mouth upwards, instead curling her plump upper lip to expose a few, bright-white teeth. At that point it occurred to me that her lack of facial movement was probably down to an overfondness for injectables, rather than a profound equanimity of spirit.

I offered her a more conventional smile in return. 'Oh, that's OK. I'm actually in the middle of something myself,' I said, tugging at my outsize blue shirt which was spattered with acrylics of every colour.

'You're an artist?'

'Only on the side. I mainly stick to selling other people's paintings.'

She nodded and did the smiling-not-smiling thing again. 'How wonderful. I'd love to see some of your work.'

I waved a hand. 'Oh, it's not very good, but you should definitely drop by the gallery. As I said, we're in Westbury Park. I'll let you go and have your shower now, but I'll shove a card through your door later. And maybe we could have a glass of wine or a coffee another time, when you're more settled in.'

'That would be *so* nice,' she sighed. 'My partner has to commute to London several times a week, and works long hours locally in between, so I'm often home alone. He was straight into the Bristol office this morning. On a Sunday.' She tutted, her eyes narrowing slightly and her nose wrinkling, which I took as an attempt to signal dejection, disapproval or possibly irritation – I wasn't quite sure which.

I tutted my empathy and then took a step back, deciding that I was quite looking forward to finding out more about Morgan, her frozen features, her abs of steel and her absent partner. She seemed friendly enough and besides, there was something very freeing about the idea of getting to know the person you lived next door to, safe in the knowledge that should they turn out to be boring, bullshitty or an out-and-out nutter, you'd be moving on in a short while anyway.

'I'll let you get on,' I said. 'Bye.'

'Ooh, wait a moment.' She gestured over my shoulder with the expression of someone staring at a particularly boring spreadsheet. 'Here he comes now. I can introduce you, if you like – or another time, if you're in a hurry to get back to your painting. If he decides to put the car in the garage, it'll take him *forever*. It's quite a tight squeeze.'

I turned to see a silver convertible slowly pulling up the lane and then turning onto the short, gravelled drive running alongside Morgan's cottage. As the car came to a halt outside a gabled garage, I raised my hand to shield my eyes from the sun and squinted at the windscreen in a failed attempt to see the driver. After a moment, he emerged: tall, lightly tanned, almost as fair-haired as Morgan, and casually dressed in jeans and a grey T-shirt. He raised a hand briefly in our direction without looking up and then walked around the car, opening the passenger door and reaching inside to retrieve a document wallet from the front seat, before closing the door and turning to walk towards us.

I think we must have recognised each other at precisely the same moment, because his step faltered and his lips parted slightly in an expression of silent surprise – or horror – just as I experienced a sensation not unlike being immersed in a bath of ice.

'El, this is Esme – she lives next door,' said Morgan brightly, as I stood with my back to her, staring at the new arrival, my mouth dry. 'She's come round to say hi and to give us this little bowl. Isn't that kind of her?'

'El' looked past me towards her. 'That was kind,' he agreed, blinking twice before turning his attention to me. 'Elliot,' he said, holding out his hand.

I looked up at him, my face now as expressionless as Morgan's. 'I'm covered in paint,' I said, keeping my hands determinedly at my sides.

He raised the extended hand to his head and scratched his ear. 'Decorating?' he asked.

'Painting pictures.'

He nodded and managed a half-smile, but didn't speak.

'Yes, Esme's an artist,' said Morgan. 'I'm so jealous. I'd love to be more creative.'

She said something more, but I wasn't listening now, instead focusing entirely on a need to be gone. I waited until she stopped speaking, before turning somewhat mechanically towards her. 'I must let you go. But it was so nice to meet you. Bye.'

Then, without so much as a second glance in his direction, I edged past Elliot Chase – my ex and the one-time love of my life – and returned next door.

Chapter 3

I settled myself into one of the black leather chairs in Cass's empty salon and waited for her to return from the kitchen with the coffees we regularly shared at the end of the working day – either in her salon or in the gallery next door. Cass was a shameless gossip, a good listener and an unedited sharer, which made her the perfect pick-me-up and provider of perspective, whenever a personal or professional cloud appeared on my horizon. I really hoped she could work her magic that evening.

I turned for a moment and stared out into the now-deserted street, before rotating back to gaze at my reflection in the oblong mirror in front of me. How, I wondered, did today's Esme Green compare with the four-years-younger model? That was the last time Elliot had seen me in person. I supposed he might have stumbled across me in one of the few carefully angled and lit images I had posted on social media. But my photographic online presence was deliberately small – microscopic, really – and besides, those pictures were hardly preparation for the Sunday-afternoon-covered-in-paint version of me.

Or maybe, like me, he had unfollowed, or muted, all social media accounts potentially capable of delivering a painful reminder of our relationship. I'd done that as part of a determined effort to forget and move on. Neither of which I was sure I had yet fully achieved.

I tugged at a section of my shoulder-length, highlighted, brown hair. It was a good cut and colour – excellent even. I worked next door to a hairdresser who gave me a sizeable discount, so I'd have had to go a long way to avoid a decent haircut. But I didn't always look after it or style it as I should, and my heart sank, not for the first time, at the thought of the stained work shirt, unironed cargo pants, make-up-free face and untidy bonce I had sported during my first encounter with my ex in over four long years.

And what about the rest of me?

I leaned forward, resting my elbows on the glass shelf below the mirror and cupping my face in my hands, scrutinising my reflection. Was it so very different at thirty-four to what it had been at thirty?

Well, I still had cheekbones and a healthy BMI. That was something. But although I may not have piled on the pounds, I'd definitely gained some shadows under my eyes and, now that I looked closely, some very definite frown lines. Maybe, like Morgan, I should have started on the Botox by now. And maybe jogging around the block a few times a week wouldn't have been a bad idea either because, overall, there was no denying that I looked stressed, knackered, pale and wan.

I pinched my cheeks between thumb and forefinger in an attempt to force some colour into them. Did I always look this crap these days? Or was my current appearance the rather more recent result of my ex-partner moving in next door and the accompanying recognition of a small, but quite terrifying, sense of regret?

'What are you staring at?' Cass placed a large white mug down next to me before lowering herself into a chair, identical to and next to my own, and placing her coffee on the dark-grey tiled floor. 'And have you been squeezing zits? You look like Kev's granny when she's been at the sherry. You've got great skin; leave it alone. Unless you're worried about those pores. Is that it? Because Terry can sort those out with a hydrafacial.'

'Pores?' My frown lines deepened further and my eyes crossed as I focused first on my forehead and then my nose. 'Have I got a pore problem?'

'Of course you haven't. All I'm saying is that if you *do* want a facial, Terry'll knock a third off. Now, sit up and let's have a bit more detail about what happened on Sunday with your ex, starting with: is it all just a bloody enormous, totally unbelievable, coincidence or did he plan it?'

I picked up my mug and turned towards her. Her expression was one of intense interest, hands folded, waiting for me to reply. She was dressed conservatively today, in a sleek, wrap-around black dress and black mid-heeled boots. If it hadn't been for the glossy asymmetric cut, dyed a fiery red and highlighted with a single, bold blonde streak at the front, she could have easily passed for a psychiatrist.

I shook my head. 'He's not the kind of obsessive or senti-mental weirdo who would go to the trouble of tracking me down and moving in next door. Plus, he looked just as stunned as I was.'

'So, it's fate then.'

'Fate?' I frowned, surprised at her uncharacteristically dramatic turn of phrase and unable to tell whether she was being serious. 'There's nothing meant-to-be about this as far as I'm concerned, Cass. All that's happened is that my ex has, by coincidence, moved in next door. Simple as.'

She looked unconvinced. 'He pretended not to know you. That doesn't sound very simple. That sounds like he's complic-ating stuff from the word go.'

'I did the same,' I pointed out.

'Following his lead, though.'

I shrugged. 'Maybe. Or maybe it was a mutually panicked reaction. In any case, I expect he went straight inside and told her all about me.'

'But you don't know that for sure?'

'I don't,' I admitted, taking a first, cautious sip of my coffee. 'Because I don't have any contact details for him, and I'm not going to look him up and start a conversation.'

'Fair enough, but tell me a bit more about him. When did you two get together?'

'Almost eight years ago, at an exhibition in EC1.' I remembered the evening vividly. Elliot's employer – a merchant bank – was sponsoring a show that I, in a very junior way, had helped to curate. Elliot had been funny, charming and direct, telling me that I was fun and fascinating and that he wanted to take me to dinner, preferably the next evening. For the first and only time in my life, I had been swept off my feet in a way which slightly flew in the face of my feminist instincts, but which, nevertheless, I had loved.

'And how long is it since you broke up?'

'Sorry?' I blinked, as Cass dragged me back from my moment of nostalgia. 'Oh, four and a bit years.'

'And were you the dumper or the dumpee?'

I rolled my eyes.

'What? I'm just trying to get up to speed,' she said. 'But hey, we can talk about my problems instead, if you like. Number one is that Lloyd dropped some pies off for me just before closing, which was great. But clients can be a bit funny about a butcher in the salon. And, you know, Lloyd does have that smell about him sometimes: Lynx mixed with dead stuff.' She lowered her coffee to her lap. 'Do you think I should say something to him? Or maybe to Gwen, next time she's in?'

'Gwen would understand, but I think Lloyd would be pretty hurt,' I said doubtfully.

She heaved a sigh and her shoulders dropped. 'Yeah, you're right. I can't say anything. So,' she smiled and saluted me with her mug, 'that's that dilemma solved. Now, shall I go on to my next problem, or do you want to carry on filling me in on yours?'

'Do you have another problem?'

'Well, I could big something up.' She looked around the salon. 'We've lost another brush,' she offered. 'I think it's that dodgy teen I got in to wash hair as a favour to my cousin, Vanessa. She's the one who works with all the hitty kids at school. He had a big bulge in his skinny jeans when he left here on Saturday, and if he didn't have a whole load of sample sachets down there, then he needs to see his GP. I've thought about frisking him before he leaves each evening, but Ness says that's not allowed.'

'Shocker.'

'I was surprised too,' she said, sounding disappointed, but shrugging resignedly. 'Anyway, back to you. Tell me all about this Elliot. You know you want to.'

I heaved a sigh, but she was right, I did. I had an awful lot to get off my chest and the burden of keeping it to myself felt crushing. Nevertheless, I thought it best to spare her all but the most essential of details.

'He dumped me – sort of,' I said.

'Sort of?'

'He walked out and asked me to call him so that we could talk it through, but I never did.'

'You must have seen him after that, though.'

I shook my head. 'All further communication was through friends. He arranged to come and collect his things while I was away for the weekend and then we served notice on the flat. We haven't seen or spoken to each other since – until Sunday.'

Cass's eyes widened. 'Wow, that's pretty extreme, Es,' she said, puffing out her cheeks. 'And there wasn't even a tiny bit of you that wanted him back?'

'Oh, I definitely wanted him back. I was absolutely devastated.'

'But you didn't *ask* him to come back?'

'No.'

'Interesting decision,' she said, her eyes narrowing in thought. 'Do you wish you had?'

I felt myself tense at the crunch question I'd asked myself more than once over the past four years, usually about ten seconds after extracting an increasingly crumpled sketch of Elliot from the bottom of my T-shirt drawer. It was a drawing torn from my daily journal, moments before I had consigned the rest of that year's edition – plus the previous three – to the bin on New Year's Day, three weeks after Elliot exited my life. It was the only image of him, photographic or hand drawn, that I had allowed myself to keep and, interestingly, it was the only lost possession over which I had cried, when water had destroyed my Redland flat four years later.

'I don't know,' I replied, too terrified to consider the possibility that almost half a decade ago I had made the mother of all mistakes, from which I would never fully recover. 'I try not to think about it. I just accept the fact that I didn't call him and leave it at that.'

'Good girl.' Cass nodded approvingly. 'But what was he like? What were the two of you like, before it all went tits up?'

'He was thoughtful, good-looking and very popular, and, in the end, I found that hard to handle. I became paranoid – possessive – and that spoiled things, as you might expect.'

She frowned, as if confused. '*You?* Paranoid and possessive? I can't imagine that. You've never been that way with any of the blokes you've introduced me to.'

I shrugged. 'Well, that's how I was with Elliot.'

'Really?' She shook her head, her expression serious. 'I'm so surprised, Es.'

There was undeniable disappointment in her tone, for which I couldn't blame her. I wasn't exactly a fan of possessive women either. It was a trait which, in my experience, went hand in hand with neurotic insecurity and a tendency to view all remotely pleasant female company as a threat.

I tried to reassure her. 'I hated feeling that way, and I've never felt like that before or since,' I added, deciding to stop short of sharing the dawning realisation that I'd never felt as serious about anyone else as I had about Elliot, before or since.

Could it be that, post-Elliot, I was someone who instinctively shrank from closeness? From commitment? After all, a number of perfectly acceptable men had crossed my path since Elliot: Harry the physio; George the builder; Ted the potter... But none of those relationships had felt as if they had long-term potential. I had never seen any of them as let's-buy-a-house-and-make-babies material. And now I wondered whether, subconsciously, I had decided that me and men with long-term potential were an unhealthy mix. It wasn't a great thought.

Cass meanwhile was still trying to compute. 'So he must have done something terrible to make you feel like that? Did he cheat on you?'

'No, but that didn't stop me wondering about it,' I said miserably. 'He was just very attractive, in an all-round kind of way, and women responded to that.'

'By trying to shag him? And he didn't tell them to piss off?' she asked, still clearly desperately in search of a defence. She was such a good friend.

'Women flirted with him,' I agreed, 'but not many – not in front of me, anyway – and he dealt with them politely.'

'Politely? What does that mean?'

'It means he didn't tell them to piss off, but made it clear that he wasn't taking it seriously. He turned it into a joke.'

'That sounds like he was joining in to me. I hate that.'

I smiled sadly and returned my mug to the glass shelf. 'Look, I've had plenty of time to think about this and the problem was mine, not his.'

'Just doesn't sound much like you,' she murmured sceptically.

'Good,' I said, 'because looking back, it definitely wasn't the best version of me.'

'So what now? You're just going to try to avoid him until you can go back to your flat?'

'I guess so. Hopefully, that shouldn't be too difficult. Morgan – that's his girlfriend – said he works away a lot.'

'And what was she like?'

I slumped slightly in my chair. 'Pretty perfect-looking. She clearly looks after herself: lots of exercise, lots of...' I paused and pointed to my face, 'treatments. Her expression didn't change throughout our entire conversation.'

Cass tutted. 'It's like Terry always tells his clients here: less is definitely more. Remember the time I went OTT with the Botox just before Mandy's wedding and ended up looking like Ming the Merciless?' She laughed and I attempted to join in, but we both knew that my heart wasn't really in it.

'It must have been such a shock,' said Cass gently, leaning forward and patting my knee. 'But it sounds like, fingers crossed, you might not see anything more of him.'

'Yes,' I said quietly, 'it does.'

'But what if...' She paused to brush something invisible from her dress, as if distracted in the middle of an inconsequential question. 'Would you be bothered if you *did* bump into him?'

I didn't answer and she looked up. 'Bothered?' she repeated. 'At all?'

I nodded slowly. It was a possibility that I had already thought through. 'Bothered. Very.'

'But you do still want to bump into him?'

'I don't know. Depends on the outcome.'

She smiled. 'And what's your best outcome? A handshake and putting the past behind you or,' her smile broadened, 'his perfect girlfriend moving out and the landlord knocking through?'

'You're dreadful.'

'Just answer the question!'

I turned in my chair and gazed again at my reflection, still blotchy from my attempts to give myself a healthy glow. 'I think maybe my preferred outcome is actually that we don't bump into each other.'

'Hmm, well, I won't push you on that,' she said. 'But if you should see him in the lane, just remember three things. Firstly, you're starting from scratch. You'll both have changed, for better or worse, and you'll have forgotten an awful lot of stuff about each other, good and bad. Secondly, you're strong, sexy and successful, and can have any man you want—'

'Oh, for God's sake.'

She placed a finger to her lips. '*Any man you want,*' she repeated emphatically. 'So just make sure you're wanting the right one. That's *very* important. I thought I'd got the man I wanted when I got Geoff the chef at twenty-seven and, boy, was I wrong. OK, so his cooking was great, but the service was crap, if you know what I mean. I thank God – or whoever – every day for my Kev walking into my life three years later. He may not be able to boil an egg, but he can certainly—'

'Yes, I know you're very sexually fulfilled, Cass,' I interrupted, keen to avoid a rundown of Kevin's expertise in the bedroom. 'What was point number three?'

She looked at me disapprovingly. 'I was actually talking about Kev servicing my *emotional* needs, if you must know.'

'Were you?'

'Let's just say he's an all-rounder.'

'Well, you've been together ten years, so I guessed he must be,' I said. 'Anyway, come on, point number three and then we can forget all about my new neighbours and talk about something else.'

'Oh right, yes, well point number three is actually the most important one of all. Just remember that whatever happens with Elliot – small stuff, big stuff, juicy stuff...' She leaned forward, reaching out to place a hand on the arm of my chair and lowering her voice conspiratorially. '*Especially* the juicy stuff... You just be sure to tell your Aunty Cass all about it.'

Chapter 4

At the time of making the assertion that I didn't want to see Elliot, I wasn't sure whether I was being entirely honest with Cass – or with myself, for that matter. An increasing tendency over the following days to linger at my garden gate, inspect the front-garden shrubs and, one week later, to wash the windows of my home for the first time in… well, ever, could certainly have led some people to conclude that maybe I wasn't all that averse to 'bumping into' him after all.

Not that it mattered. Because for three weeks after our initial, shocking reunion, I saw nothing of Elliot, and my only sighting of Morgan was one Tuesday evening when the tinkling of glass alerted me to the recycling being put out. That sent me running with indecent haste to the living room window to see who was toting the green box, only to feel undeniably deflated on discovering that it was her and not him.

After that, I couldn't pretend anymore. Despite finding the idea of a second encounter with my ex genuinely terrifying, I was, like a moth to a flame – or a lemming to a cliff edge – inexplicably drawn to it.

What I hadn't realised, until it actually happened, was that I wanted said encounter to take place at my convenience and on my terms, when I was prepared for and seeking it. What I *didn't* want was to be slapped in the face with it, just as I was about to shut up shop, at 5:30 p.m. one rainswept Wednesday evening in late May.

Lloyd had just popped in with a venison and Stilton pie and we had retreated to the small kitchen next to the workshop, so that I could put it in the fridge and also hand over a gift for his wife, Gwen, whose forty-sixth birthday was the following day.

'Just don't drop it,' I said, as he took the gift from me and cupped it gently in his large, work-worn hands.

'Ooh, is it fragile then?' he asked, smiling down at the smallish blue box, tied with a white satin ribbon.

'Yes, it's a—'

'No, no, don't tell me,' he said hastily. 'I like to enjoy the surprises with her.'

'In that case, I'll just tell you that it's glass and something Gwen was admiring in the gallery a few weeks ago.'

'Bet she'll love it, Esme.' He beamed down at the box, his cheeks glowing pink.

'Fingers crossed,' I said. 'But what have you got her?'

'A Dyson.'

'Yeah, right,' I laughed, elbowing him gently. 'Come on, what have you really got her?'

'A Dyson,' he repeated, now looking up. 'One of those wall-mounted ones. She's been talking about buying it for ages, but I said *no way*, because our old Hoover isn't broken. But all along, I'd already got her one.' He winked at me, laughing at his own cunning. 'I've had it hidden in the shop for weeks and I'm taking it home tonight. Can't wait to see the look on her face tomorrow morning.'

I frowned slightly, wondering whether or not to voice a concern that wanting to purchase a cordless vacuum cleaner was not at all the same as wanting to be gifted one. But in the end, I decided against it, on the basis that I didn't want to pointlessly burst Lloyd's bubble, and besides, having been married to Gwen for fifteen years, he knew her much better than I did.

'Sounds like you've put a lot of thought into it. She'll spot that and really appreciate it,' I said, more to reassure myself than to compliment him, as I led the way back into the empty gallery, David having left early for a dental appointment.

'Hope so,' he said, as we came to a halt by the till. 'For the past few birthdays she's picked out something for herself because she said I had too much on my plate to run round fussing over her. But I've really missed surprising her. I mean, you should have seen the look on her face the year I got her a crosshead, twin-handled mixer tap. And then again, the year after, when I surprised her with the aluminium flat-top side-gate. Fitted it in the night, I did – in the rain, by torchlight,' he added proudly. 'My trick was to keep my ears open all year round for things that were bothering her, like the condensation in the double-glazed utility room window, or the leaky hose pipe. I'd store all her heart's desires up in here.' He chuckled and tapped the side of his head. 'And then... bingo! On her birthday she wakes up to a new window, a new hose, a new tap...'

'That's really great,' I replied distractedly, beginning to log off the till, while wondering how long the pie Lloyd had given me would keep. I was just about to ask him, when Elliot walked in.

The shoulders of his dark-grey jacket were damp from the rain and he looked slightly uneasy as he lowered a now-folded umbrella, his attention caught by Lloyd. I watched as he took in the striped pinny, white coat and navy-blue trousers. 'I'm looking for...' he began, before spotting me. 'Oh, there you are,' he said, his expression neutral.

I neither spoke nor moved. It wasn't a conscious decision to remain silent but, with hindsight, I'm pleased that I did. Because if I had at that moment tried to say anything – anything at all – the resultant babble might have earned me a straitjacket and a blue light.

After a second or two of complete immobility, I offered him a nod, in lieu of words, and while we continued to look at each other, with neither of us saying anything at all, Lloyd ended what I assumed must have been an increasingly uncomfortable silence for him.

'Well, I er... had better go and get the Dyson, Esme. I've got my wife a Dyson for her birthday,' he said to Elliot, with genial inclusivity.

I switched my focus determinedly to Lloyd, only vaguely aware of Elliot's reply, which involved a halting reference to Gwen being an extremely lucky woman.

'Bye, Lloyd,' I said quietly.

'Bye,' he beamed and then, after a polite but slightly uncertain nod towards Elliot, he left, the door slamming noisily behind him as it was caught by a gust of wind.

I started at the sound and then turned to Elliot.

After a slight pause, he smiled – a little sadly, I thought – and said, 'I didn't know we'd be next door. Obviously. I mean, I thought you might still be in Bristol. But it's a big place and besides, I never thought you'd pick a village over the city.'

At last, I found my voice. 'It's fine,' I said hoarsely. 'Don't worry about it. It's only temporary.'

'Same for us. Just a short let.'

He offered no further explanation and, not feeling in a position to ask for one, I simply nodded.

'So I thought maybe we could go for a drink, or a coffee,' he said. 'Now, if that's not too short notice? It might make living next door to each other less awkward over the weeks to come. What do you think?' He concluded the suggestion with a smile that I had never expected to see again and which, I realised with some unease, I had missed.

'We can go another time, if right now doesn't work. I'm away from tomorrow, but back Saturday,' continued Elliot, clearly – and mistakenly – putting my lack of immediate response down to a packed social calendar.

'I'm just trying to remember what I'm doing this evening and over the weekend,' I said, frowning up at him, my attempts at clear thinking under significant threat, not only from his mild manner and hesitant smile, but also from nostalgia run wild. I was in dangerous and uncharted territory, for which I was neither equipped nor prepared. Consequently, a conversation with him at this very moment might not be such a great idea.

On the other hand, there were several points in favour of taking him up on his offer to talk everything through without delay. I didn't see how we could possibly comfortably live next door to each other without first clearing the air, and wouldn't it be better to clear it sooner rather than later? I might feel unprepared for – not to mention physically sick at the thought of – a one-to-one, but at least if we went that evening, I would have only the time it took to cash up and lock up to angst about it, rather than hours, days or weeks, if I requested a deferral. Besides, rejecting the suggestion without a convincing excuse might appear churlish and lead Elliot to suspect that I wasn't entirely over our break-up, and that was the last thing I wanted – even if it happened to be true.

'Now is best,' I said, with as much conviction as I could muster.

'Great. I passed a pub up the road.' He glanced towards the window. 'Would that do?'

'If you mean The Cambridge Arms,' I replied, 'that's fine. I just have to sort out a few things here. Meet you there in half an hour?'

'That works,' he said, turning away to open the door. 'See you later.'

Chapter 5

Elliot was sitting in the corner of the bar farthest from the door and was halfway down a pint by the time I arrived at The Cambridge, rather later than expected. Cashing up hadn't taken long, but I'd decided that I needed to take a breath before setting off. His effect on me thus far had been unsettling to say the least and I wanted to make sure that it was Esme Green, the thirty-four-year-old, independent, thoroughly grounded business owner on show this evening, not a babbling idiot, desperate to find meaning in the nothing-but-coincidental reappearance of an ex.

I bought myself a lime and soda, and went to join him.

'Hi,' I said, giving myself a few extra seconds of composure time by avoiding eye contact until I had pulled out a chair and sat down. 'Sorry, that all took longer than expected.'

'No problem,' he replied, shaking his head and returning his phone to his jacket pocket. 'I had a couple of emails to send anyway.' He looked at me and smiled. 'Look, I'm so sorry about all this, Es,' he said, sounding exhausted. 'I mean, I'm not sorry about seeing you. It's great to see you, obviously. I'm just, you know, sorry about *this*.'

It was a gentle and apologetic opener, to which my instinctive response would have been a reciprocal smile and a light expression of regret that I hadn't got in touch sooner. But wary of a dynamic that I didn't understand, a man I recognised but no longer knew, and personal feelings in need of protection, I did neither of those things. Instead, determined to think through every response before articulating it, I picked up my drink and took a sip.

'It's fine,' I said airily. 'It's just a shame that it came as such a shock to both of us, or we might have handled things better in front of Morgan. You've explained things to her, I take it?' I asked the question as casually as I could, while focusing on keeping my hand steady as I returned my glass to the table.

He didn't answer immediately and when I looked up, he quickly lowered his eyes to his pint. 'I haven't actually, which I know is really stupid of me. I should have said something right away, but she started talking about work and the conversation moved on.' He looked up and grimaced apologetically.

'And you didn't move it back?'

'No.'

I wondered if some further explanation would follow and, when it didn't, I began to experience some low-level resentment – and higher-level hurt – at the thought of perhaps being an episode in Elliot's history which he felt a need to airbrush.

'I know I should have said something to her,' he said. 'I don't like the idea of having to pretend that we don't know each other.'

'I don't like it either.'

'I know. And I'm sorry.'

I frowned. Was that really as far as he was going to go with this? Mournful looks and a repeated apology? Why couldn't he just explain to Morgan who I was? Was our relationship really such an emotionally traumatic, no-go area for him?

Or maybe emotions had nothing to do with it. Maybe it was all a lot simpler and more superficial than that. Maybe his past relationship with the wrinkly, mega-pored, unkempt woman next door was all just a little bit too embarrassing for him to publicly acknowledge. Maybe it didn't sit well alongside his current ability to snare the super-fit, immaculately groomed, non-surgically-enhanced model of girlfriend he so clearly preferred these days.

Whatever his reason, I decided that I didn't want to hear it.

'It's not for long. I'm sure we'll manage,' I said, my tone clipped. Curt was, I decided, way better than crushed.

'I wish I could introduce you to Morgan properly.'

I shrugged. 'There's no law that says you have to acknowledge me to her. The main thing is that I'm now completely clear how I have to behave if I bump into you in the lane. How about I pretend to forget your name – call you Keith, or something – just to keep it convincing?'

He closed his eyes and heaved a sigh. 'You're upset and I don't blame you.'

'I'm not upset,' I said, clearly upset.

'Seriously, Es, it's not a case of not wanting to acknowledge you. It's just…' He hesitated and there followed a lengthy pause before he spoke again. 'You know what, you're right,' he said at last. 'At least we know how we have to behave. And yes, call me Keith. Because that would be really funny,' he added, sounding crushed, not curt.

His tone marked a moment of misery for me, of a depth I hadn't felt in years, and I reached for my drink, hiding a swell of emotion behind my glass. I glanced at the door, desperately wanting to leave but too afraid of outing myself so unmistakably as a woman who hadn't managed to emotionally detach from a relationship which had ended over four years ago.

'So, how's work?' I asked. 'And life in general?'

His eyebrows flickered upwards and his expression seemed to harden slightly. 'Great, actually,' he said. 'I feel like I'm exactly where I want to be. Lots of challenges professionally, but feeling relaxed personally. It's a good combination.' He offered me a brief smile, before returning his attention to his beer. 'And you? How long have you been working in the shop?'

I bristled at his use of *shop* and pursed my lips to stifle a snapped response.

'We've had the *gallery* for over two years now,' I said, after a moment. 'I'm the co-owner.'

I was pleased to note a twitch of surprise. He clearly hadn't expected me to have experienced any sort of career advancement in his absence and, judging by the difficulty he was now having raising a smile, he wasn't enjoying the fact that I had.

'Your own business?' he said. 'Great. And your business partner, what's their background?'

'Corporate high finance,' I said lightly. 'He was extremely successful, but tired of the grey tedium and dull superficiality of it all, and wanted a more colourful, creative and personally involved kind of life. You know, getting out there, meeting the people his work impacts and attempting to enhance lives, rather than sitting on his arse in an office, crunching numbers, looking for cash cows and destroying livelihoods at a distance.'

There was no ignoring the resentment in my tone as I concluded the thinly veiled attack on Elliot's own career. He, meanwhile, was back to looking crushed and I regretted my bitter little speech as soon as it was out.

'Good for him,' he said quietly. 'Good for both of you.'

'Yes, we're very happy and fulfilled,' I said, feeling just about as far from that as it was possible to be.

He nodded slowly and then raised his glass. 'To you,' he said, draining the contents.

'And to you,' I returned miserably and a little breathlessly. It felt as if someone was hollowing out my chest with an ice-cream scoop.

'I'd offer you a lift home, but I'm off to Temple Meads,' he said, thereby removing any doubt as to whether a second drink might be on the cards.

I shook my head. 'It's fine. I'm on my bike, hence the soda. Besides, rolling up in a car together would rather give the game away, wouldn't it, *Keith*?' I said, attempting a light laugh.

I was pretty sure that I had intended the comment as a mood lightener and not another barb, although admittedly I hadn't analysed my motives closely enough to be certain. But it didn't matter. Whatever my actual intention, Elliot assumed it to be negative and I watched as his expression shifted from hurt, back to something bordering on anger.

'I'm sorry,' he said, getting to his feet, 'that I can't stay until you've finished your drink. But I'm pleased that we've managed to clarify a few things. Maybe I'll see you outside the cottages at some point, but if I don't, good luck with the shop.'

I looked up at him, strangely grateful for his repeated use of *shop*. It freed me from any guilt I'd felt at snubbing his apology and dissing his job.

'Bye,' I said simply, deciding to avoid any attempt at either situation retrieval or upping the ante.

His response was a silent nod, and as I watched him turn and walk away, with my feelings of emptiness increasing, it occurred to me that despite now living next door to each other, Elliot and I were currently farther apart than we had ever been.

Chapter 6

Until I saw Lloyd the next morning, I hadn't actually thought it would be possible for anyone to be looking more miserable than I felt. He was inside his shop and pricing up his window display, skewering little white cards, attached to little metal forks, into various sausages and cuts of meat, with the expression of a mortuary worker tagging corpses. I paused on the pavement and watched for a moment, waiting for him to look up and wondering whether his traumatised expression might be down to sudden-onset veganism.

Having run out of cards, he at last glanced up, but not before heaving a sigh so profound that his chest visibly expanded a good three to four inches with the effort of it. On seeing me, he raised a hand but – for the first time that I could remember – he didn't seem able to raise a smile to go with it. Not that I minded; it freed me from having to attempt to look at all upbeat myself.

Making his way to the door of his shop, he hauled it open and stepped out onto the pavement.

'Morning, Esme,' he said quietly. 'You in early as well?'

I checked my watch and was surprised to discover that it was still before eight. I hadn't bothered to put the radio on that morning, nor paid much attention to the kitchen clock.

'I guess so. I just wanted to be up and out and doing something today. What's your excuse?'

'Well, Gwen woke early for her—'

'For her birthday! Yes, of course!' I exclaimed, smiling at last. 'So you're in early and going home early? Has she opened her presents yet, or is she saving them for this evening?'

He shook his head slowly and then lowered it, staring miserably at the pavement. 'Didn't have a great start to the day, to be honest with you, Esme.'

'Why not? What's happened?' I asked, reaching out and placing a concerned hand on his arm. 'Gwen's all right, isn't she?'

'Yes and no. She's well, but she's not herself at all.'

'What do you mean?'

'Well...' He inhaled deeply and wiped a hand across his face before continuing. 'I gave her the Dyson and when she unwrapped it, she laughed and laughed. She couldn't stop laughing, actually. So I joined in and everything was great for a moment. But then, suddenly...' He paused again, swallowing hard, raising his eyes to the sky and blinking rapidly. 'Suddenly, she started crying and when I told her that I'd never seen someone so moved by a vacuum cleaner, she unclipped the duster attachment...' At this point, he stopped staring at the sky and lowered his gaze to look directly at me. 'The long one with the oblong hole. The one for venetian blinds and the like. Not the round one for corners.'

'I know the one.' I nodded rapidly, encouraging him to continue, but at the same time fearful of what might be to come.

'Well, she unclipped that,' his head drooped once again, 'and threw it at me. Really, *really* hard.'

I gasped and put a hand to my mouth.

'And as you know, Esme, Gwen plays netball, so her hand-eye co-ordination is really excellent,' he continued dejectedly, yet also with unmistakable pride. 'Fortunately, I ducked and the attachment missed me. However, she did take out my Institute of Meat Marketing award, and now the glass is cracked and the frame all chipped, where it hit the grate.'

'Oh no, Lloyd, I'm so sorry,' I said – and I meant it. Why on earth hadn't I expressed some doubt the night before? I felt as if I was at least partly to blame for the miserable start to his, and to Gwen's, day.

'Yes and then she locked herself in the bathroom and wouldn't talk to me and wouldn't come out. It's all on camera,' he added forlornly, reaching into his apron pocket and extracting his phone. 'I'd propped it up on the bedroom fireplace to catch her reaction. Fortunately, the duster attachment hit home slightly to the left of it, or I might have been looking at getting a new Galaxy too.'

'That's all just so awful.' I moved my hand from my mouth to my forehead, my guilt deepening, even as I wondered what would be a decent length of time to wait before asking Lloyd if I could see the footage. 'And have you tried messaging her since?'

'I have,' he said solemnly. 'I have asked her what the matter is. I did wonder if it might be…' He paused and mouthed the word *hormones* silently at me. 'And it also crossed my mind that now she's nearer to fifty than forty, she might be worried about ageing, putting on weight… things like that.'

'You didn't ask her if it was any of those things, did you, Lloyd?' I asked, with a certain amount of dread.

'I did. I know how important it is for women to talk about their feelings and the menopause, Esme.'

I looked at him for a moment, knowing what I had to do, but distressed at the thought of taking a sledgehammer to his heart. However, it being perfectly clear that hinting was not an effective means of communication with Lloyd, I cut to the chase.

'The problem is the Dyson.'

'What?' he spluttered, his eyes widening and circling in bemusement. 'But… but how can that be when she definitely said she wanted—'

'She wanted the Dyson,' I cut in, 'just not for her birthday.'

'But she said she wanted—'

'She wanted a *treat*,' I said flatly. 'Not a necessity.'

'But it wasn't a—'

'Yes, I know that strictly speaking you already had a fully functioning vacuum cleaner but, *please*, Lloyd,' I said, again placing my hand on his arm, 'please, please just take it from me that in Gwen's eyes, the Dyson is a necessity and not a treat.'

Clearly still struggling to compute, he turned slowly towards the shop window.

'And let me tell you right now,' I said. 'Pies are not a treat either.'

'Even the—' he began, slowly raising a finger to point.

'Even the organic ones,' I said patiently. 'If you're stuck for ideas, treats include, but are not limited to: flowers; fizz; fashion; beauty treatments; weekend breaks and jewellery. My advice would be that the minute Andy arrives in the shop, you go and buy some flowers and champagne, and then go home and take it from there. Tell Gwen that you've thought it all through and have realised where you went wrong and that you're taking her out to dinner tonight. Oh and tell her that she's beautiful.'

Lloyd nodded along, while still staring at the window. 'OK, Esme,' he said quietly. 'And thank you.'

I shook my head. 'I should have said something yesterday.'

'So you never thought the Dyson was a good idea?' he asked, suddenly turning towards me and achieving the impossible by looking even more stricken.

'I thought it was brilliant that you had put such a lot of thought and preparation into it,' I replied, attempting positivity. 'I just wasn't one hundred per cent sure that a Dyson had the wow factor to work as a birthday present.'

'You know, now you've got me looking back and wondering about the tap and the hose,' he said, his expression one of crushing, dawning realisation. 'Did they have the wow factor, I'm asking myself. Maybe Gwen didn't think *they* were treats either. Do you think that's why she asked me to stop buying birthday presents for her?'

'Morning.'

I turned, grateful to be rescued from Lloyd's epiphany by the arrival of David.

'David! Great to see you!' I beamed, hitching my bags up onto my shoulder and giving him a relieved, one-armed hug. 'Yes, so sorry, I'm coming now. Was just having a quick catch-up with Lloyd.'

'There's no rush. We're both early.' David smiled amiably, while also frowning slightly at my arm around his waist. 'How are you, Lloyd?' he asked. 'And how is Gwen? Did she like her present?'

'Actually, Lloyd's just rushing off to sort out a few more birthday surprises for Gwen. Isn't that right, Lloyd?' I added, while gesturing to David to hurry up and open the door.

'It is. I'm going to give her lots of unnecessary things, David,' said Lloyd, sounding slightly dazed.

David looked at me quizzically.

'In we go,' I said briskly, ushering him inside. 'Pop in later or message me, Lloyd, to let me know how you get on. Bye!'

I followed David inside, closing the door behind us and leaning against it.

He turned and raised an eyebrow. 'I take it the Dyson wasn't a winner.'

'He'd told you about it then?'

David nodded. 'I passed him outside as I was leaving yesterday and he mentioned it. I didn't have time to get all the details, but I assumed he'd be supplementing it with other stuff.'

'Well, he didn't. And as for it being a winner, it didn't even make it to the starting blocks,' I added wearily, walking to the counter and dumping my bags down heavily on the floor next to it. 'The worst bit is that even when Gwen lost it big time and started throwing bits of it at him, he *still* didn't get it.' I leaned back, resting my elbows on the counter and staring up at the ceiling. 'Dear God, what a shitty start to the day,' I murmured.

He didn't reply and when I looked at him, his expression was serious.

'You seem to be taking Gwen's disappointment over the Dyson pretty hard,' he said. 'Anything else wrong?'

I shook my head and sighed. 'No, no, I just didn't sleep great.'

'You're sure?'

'Yes, I'm fine,' I said, bending to retrieve my bags.

'Only, you seem a little low.'

I left my bags where they were and straightened up, struck by his comment. Typically, our daily exchanges tended to revolve around art, books, politics and, of course, the gallery. I couldn't remember us ever having a *No, really. How are you?* moment before. Even when David's grandmother had passed away, and my home had been destroyed by several thousand gallons of water, neither of us had pressed the other to go beyond a firm assertion that we were 'fine'. So David asking for additional confirmation that all was well felt like a bit of a turn-up for the books.

Keen not to let a wholly unexpected – but very welcome – opportunity to offload about Elliot go, I had just got as far as, 'Well, you'll never believe this…' when David was distracted by something to my left and looked away.

Following his gaze, I turned to see Jasmine crossing the road and heading our way: a blonde, curly-haired raincloud, primed and ready to make a bad day worse.

'David!' she exclaimed, bouncing through the doorway. 'Sorry to crash, but I just wondered if you'd be around after work tomorrow. I'd like to drop off some more pieces for the showing next week and I think I might want to swap a couple of the paintings out.'

He didn't immediately reply, and she smiled and put a hand to her curls, which today were bobbing about, wild and unrestrained. 'Oh my God, you're staring at my hair. I'm such a bedhead this morning, and look at this,' she added, tugging at a cutesy floral tea dress, which she'd teamed with yellow kitten-heels, topped with red bows. 'I look like a tea towel, don't I? But I just grabbed the first thing I trod on. I'm leading a class in thirty minutes and overslept.'

I was tempted to interrupt and ask, firstly, why it wasn't *me* she wanted to run the swaps past, as I was the one co-ordinating the showing, and secondly, why she hadn't dropped by another time or, better still, messaged rather than calling in personally, if she was running late.

But deciding that I really didn't have the energy to buy into any of her crap that morning, I settled for a gentle cough instead.

She whirled around, hand on chest. 'Oh, Esme! I didn't even see you and you're standing right there. Seriously, I am so, so not with it this morning. I am *definitely* in need of a quiet night in. Know what I mean?'

She laughed and then quickly returned her attention to David, thus depriving me of the opportunity of informing her that actually no, I didn't have a clue what she meant because, now that I thought about it, an awful lot of my nights had been 'quiet' and 'in' since going rural.

I walked to the other side of the counter, with a view to distracting myself by unboxing some pieces which Douglas Muirhead, one of our much less irritating artists, had dropped off the day before.

Jasmine, meanwhile, was still gushing. 'So, David, can you stay a tiny bit late tomorrow? After closing, I mean. What time is the latest I could pop in? What's your...' she giggled girlishly, 'bedtime?'

I looked up sharply, in time to catch her biting her lip. Was she flirting with him?

The gallery door opened and all three of us turned towards it, David and Jasmine smiling as Cass entered.

'Hi, all,' she said, raising a hand and then turning breathlessly towards me. 'Sorry to bother you, Es, but I've forgotten... Hey, Esme, over here.' She clicked her fingers rapidly above her head. 'Are you listening to me?'

'Yes, of course, no problem,' I said distractedly, while straining to hear David's response to Jasmine's *bedtime* line.

'Well, look at me then,' said Cass, leaning over the counter, taking my face between her hands and turning it towards her. 'And not at them,' she added in a murmur. 'What's going on?'

I frowned, releasing my head from her hands and nodding towards Jasmine.

'She's flirting with him,' I whispered angrily.

Her eyes flicked left and she tilted her head backwards slightly as we both listened in.

'That's just *so* great of you,' Jasmine was saying. 'I'll bring a bottle of wine with me, as a thank you. Ooh and I'll try *really* hard not to stay and help you drink it. Not making any promises, though,' she laughed.

Cass looked at me. 'Yes, you're right, she's coming on to him,' she said, matter-of-factly. 'Now, like I said, sorry to bother you, but I need the spare keys to the salon. I've left mine at home.'

'That's just so out of order,' I muttered.

She blinked. 'Hey, and how many bloody times have *you* forgotten *your* keys?'

'No, no.' I shook my head and wrenched open a drawer under the counter. 'I mean it's out of order for her to be all over him like a rash. And now,' I added in a hiss, looking up and throwing a hand in Jasmine's direction as she followed David into the workshop, 'she's found an excuse to drag the poor guy out the back. I thought she was supposed to be pressed for time.'

Reaching into the drawer, I took out Cass's keys. 'There you go,' I said sullenly, handing them over.

She took them from me, saying nothing, but smirking slightly.

'What?' I asked, putting a hand to my nose. 'Is it my pores?'

'Your pores are fine... ish,' she said. 'I'm just wondering why you're so pissed off about Shirley Temple chatting up David.'

'Because he's very happy with Sophie, of course!' I exclaimed, slamming the drawer shut. 'I really can't stand women like Jasmine. Why can't she bog off and find her own relationship, rather than trying to mess up someone else's? There's just no excuse and he's clearly not comfortable with it.'

'Says who?' asked Cass, her eyebrows raised. 'He looked perfectly happy to me with the attention. Let's face it, he's probably used to it. Besides, he's single, so you can untwist your knickers.' She smiled affably and held up the keys, before popping them into a pocket of her skinny jeans. 'Thanks for these. You're a life-saver.'

'Hang on.' I lunged at her over the counter, grabbing her arm. 'He's not single.'

'Ow!' she exclaimed, rubbing her arm. 'You grip like a lobster!'

'Sorry.' I hoisted myself further across the counter in an attempt to reach and stroke her arm. 'But David's not single,' I repeated quietly, glancing towards the workshop. 'He's with Sophie.'

She batted away my hand and rolled her eyes. 'Keep up, Forrest. Him and Sophie split up two haircuts ago.'

'What?'

'Yeah. My Mandy cuts her hair and got the full story – not that there was much of one. No big rows, no cheating; he just called time on it. Mandy said it's been really difficult to cut Sophie's hair the last couple of times, cos she's in bits and keeps hiccoughing and putting her head in her hands. That reminds me, I meant to run something past you. You know I give her a discount because David works next door? So, now they're not together anymore, do you think it'd be OK for me to start charging her full price?'

I stared at her, stunned that at no point in the past two months had David thought to mention to me that he and Sophie were no longer a couple. Surely I'd asked after her in that time. I was convinced I had. In fact, I was certain that he'd told me she'd changed hospitals and was now working at the Bristol Royal Infirmary. Did he really not think an add-on of: 'Oh, and, by the way, I've dumped her,' might have been pertinent to the discussion?

'Nah, you're right,' said Cass, waving a hand. 'I can't do that to her. Definitely not while she's still in mourning, anyway. I'll wait till she stops hiccoughing. Bye, then. I'll be round tomorrow for a drink at six!'

'I can't believe he didn't tell me...' I murmured as she exited, and David and Jasmine re-emerged from the workshop.

'Esme will go through them,' said David. 'She's the expert.'

'Oh, I know,' beamed Jasmine. 'She is wonderful with the pricing and positioning side of things. But you connect with my art on such a *personal* level, David, and that's at least as invaluable to the process as knowing who to invite and what to charge. David and I are just saying what an excellent salesperson you are, Esme,' she continued more loudly, walking towards me. 'I'm always so grateful to you for your help.' She sighed lightly and then smiled up at David. 'I have to go. But I'll see you tomorrow evening.' With that, she turned and headed for the door, offering him a last look over her shoulder as she exited.

'I can take the pictures from her tomorrow night if you want to go home,' I offered, as soon as the door had clicked shut behind her. 'I've got nothing else on, other than my catch-up with Cass.'

He looked up from an intricately carved wooden photo frame he was inspecting. 'It's fine.'

'I just meant if, you know, you wanted a break from it.'

'From what?'

I retrieved the cardboard box of Douglas Muirhead's clay sculptures from under the counter and set about removing the parcel tape from its edges. 'I feel bad that you step in to deal with her so much of the time, even when it's stuff I should be handling.'

'It's not a problem,' he said, turning and walking to the back of the gallery. 'Coffee?'

'Please,' I said, watching him go and feeling hugely dissatisfied with the exchange.

He disappeared and I returned to picking at the parcel tape, marvelling at the fact that Mandy the hairdresser who, as far as I knew, had never even spoken to David was more up to date with his personal life than I was. Surely, having worked with me day in, day out for two years and known me for three, he should feel able to tell me that he'd split up with his girlfriend. Just like I shouldn't have to think twice about telling him that my ex had moved in next door, for that matter.

Our lack of deep personal exchanges had never really bothered me before, but now that I thought about it, it didn't feel quite right that he and I were clearly failing to share even the very basics of our lives beyond the gallery. I mean, Lloyd and I rarely spent more than ten minutes at a time in each other's company, but just that morning he had confided in me that his wife had tried to assault him with a domestic appliance.

Tiring of my lack of progress with Douglas's box, I reached into a large earthenware pot on the counter and took out a pair of scissors, musing that, on the upside, work was still a *much* more pleasant and relaxed environment than home, where I was currently doomed to spending months living in fear of running into Elliot every time I ventured outside.

I stabbed the scissors into the box, running a single blade slowly down a length of tape, slitting it open with satisfying ease, before prising the cardboard flaps apart. Then, reaching inside, I carefully released each of the small, but painstakingly detailed, wildlife sculptures in turn from its bubble-wrap shroud, my mood lifting with every reveal.

However, my expression darkened and I frowned down in confusion as I unwrapped the final, and by far the largest, of the four pieces, wondering at first if Douglas had wrapped and delivered someone else's work by mistake. But as I turned the piece over in my hands, there on the base were his engraved initials.

I shook my head and smiled. Douglas, it seemed, was a bit of a dark horse.

Chapter 7

'So, remind me again why we're drinking this round here, rather than in the gallery?' asked Cass, toasting me with her Friday gin and tonic, and looking around the salon.

'Because...' I said, pausing to take a sip from my glass, 'David's staying late for Jasmine, isn't he? And we can't talk with them there.'

'Ah yes, sorry, I'd forgotten. But don't you want to keep an eye on her? You know, in case she tries to take advantage of him?'

I rolled my eyes. 'As you well know, I was pissed off with her yesterday morning only because I didn't realise he'd split from Sophie. Actually, I wanted to ask your advice about that,' I continued, leaning forward in my chair. 'Do you think I should ask him about Sophie? You know, check how he's coping?'

'Coping with the attractive woman throwing herself at him, you mean?'

'Seriously, Cass, should I?'

'No.'

'Really?' I pressed, dissatisfied with the abruptness of her response. 'Only, it struck me today that maybe I should try to talk to him a little more about stuff that goes on outside work. You know, introduce a bit more personal chit-chat. Nothing intense – just what's going on at home, who we're hanging out with, that kind of thing. I feel bad that I never *really* ask him how he is. He could have all sorts of stuff to deal with that I know nothing about, and I thought mentioning Sophie might be a way of getting the ball rolling.'

'Still, no,' she said, shaking her head emphatically.

'Why not?'

'Because if he hasn't talked to you about it, he doesn't want to talk to you about it.'

'But maybe he *does* want to talk to me about it, but thinks that I'm not interested, or don't care. Plus, it'd be nice for me to tell him about some of the things going on in my life – especially right now. But if he doesn't think he can reciprocate, I'll just end up looking needy.'

'Hate to break it to you, but that horse bolted looooong ago.'

I sighed and slumped in my chair.

'Oh for God's sake, I'm joking,' she laughed. 'But what makes you think Dave might suddenly want to open up to you, Oprah? That's just not who he is, is it? You've said before that you knew that from day one.'

I didn't reply, aware that she had a point. I'd had all sorts of preconceived ideas about what David would be like when we'd been introduced by a friend from my uni days three years earlier. At the time, I'd been managing the Bristol branch of a nationwide gallery chain and selling my own, rather angst-ridden, artwork on the side. Meanwhile, David – my friend had told me – wanted to give up his massively well-paid City job – something complicated and boring involving *speculative algorithms* – and open an art gallery, having developed a passion for wood-sculpting and recently completed a framing course.

I'd politely nodded along to David's inspiring backstory of wealth and privilege, while trying to hide a growing cynicism regarding a loaded thirty-something who wanted to swap his suit for sandals and opt out of the rat race, having decided that he wasn't a money-hungry bastard after all, but a creative in search of a simpler life. Although not so simple, I noted, as to involve giving up a second home in Cornwall.

To me, his gallery idea had seemed to have all the hallmarks of a passing-phase vanity project, and the man himself all the hallmarks of a complete tool. However, not wanting to appear

49

ungrateful to a very well-intentioned friend who'd been kind enough to recommend me to David as a potential manager for his gallery, I had agreed to a meeting – during which he quickly proceeded to pull the rug out from under every negative expectation I had of him.

Because David Erskine wasn't, it turned out, a mouthy former-corporate, existing in a moneyed bubble and unable to relate to the harsh reality of actually having to earn a living. Neither did he appear shallow, patronising, unconsidered or reckless. He had, he explained – with no hint of ego or pretence of expertise – a longstanding passion for art, and wanted to invest and work in a creative industry, in a small-scale and locally supportive way. Most importantly, he wanted to be personally involved and present day-to-day, hence the development of his framing skills, a service which he planned to locate in the gallery premises.

My immediate, and ultimately lasting, impression of him was that he was a thinker: intelligent, focused, measured and informed. OK, so he wasn't a natural gossip – and hadn't gone with me when I'd attempted to lighten the mood with a limerick about bankers – but a serious nature wasn't always a bad thing, I had told myself, and besides, I wasn't in need of a kindred spirit or cinema buddy. I simply wanted to be part of a business start-up.

Cass was right: David wasn't someone who would be at all comfortable sharing or listening to personal angst, and the idea of pressuring him into doing so suddenly seemed both selfish and ridiculous.

'Besides, there's no need to tell Dave all your seedy stuff,' said Cass, 'when you can tell your Aunty Cass instead. Come on,' she coaxed, 'I've been dying for an update about your drink with Elliot.'

'I updated you on the night. It was shit,' I said miserably.

'Three crappy little WhatsApps don't count as an update. I need he-said-you-said level of detail. And hurry up, because Kev's going to have the curry ready for seven.'

'I thought you weren't going to let him cook again after he set the oven gloves on fire.'

'Delivered… ready… Same thing. Spit it out. What did Elliot say?'

I took another gulp of my G&T. 'I'm not sure what else there is to tell. You already know that he didn't tell his girlfriend about me.'

'Yeah, but you didn't say why not. Didn't he explain?'

'Not really. He just said that the conversation with her had moved on too quickly.'

'Bollocks it did. There's more to it than that.'

I nodded. 'I'm pretty sure he's embarrassed.'

'Embarrassed of what? Of you?' she exclaimed, with flattering incredulity.

'Yes, of me. Of our relationship.'

'Double bollocks,' she scoffed. 'But I'd love to know what the real problem is. You haven't seen him since?'

'No, thank God. I'm just keeping my fingers crossed that one of us moves out before that happens.'

'Are you really, though?' She sounded sceptical.

'I honestly am, Cass,' I insisted wearily, leaning an elbow on the arm of the chair and resting my chin on my hand. 'I can't think of anything that can be said or done to make things better, but I think it's just about possible that things could get even worse if we run into each other again. We were both quite upset by the end of our last conversation.'

'Have you thought about dropping him a line to clear the air?'

'We didn't swap numbers, and googling him and then messaging him would make me look like a stalker. And *very* needy.'

'It would.'

'So that's that then.'

'Maybe.'

We sat in companionable silence for a minute or two before she said, 'Oh my God, I know what I meant to tell you. I had Lloyd's Gwen in here this morning.'

I gasped and sat up. 'Was she all right? I haven't seen Lloyd since yesterday morning. I went into the shop today, but Andy said Lloyd wasn't coming in and he was so busy that I didn't feel like I could ask for details.'

'Well, I know why he wasn't in…' she said teasingly.

'Please tell me everything's OK.'

Her smile disappeared, replaced by a frown. 'What's with all the desperation? What do you know?'

I shook my head. 'No. You tell me what happened today and then I'll fill you in on the prequel.'

'OK,' she said, not looking entirely satisfied with the plan, but relenting nevertheless. 'Well, when I saw Gwen, she'd been to have her nails done on Whiteladies Road and then Sara squeezed her in here for some foils – all courtesy of Lloyd, for her birthday.'

Relief flooded through me. 'Oh, thank God.'

'And that's not all. This afternoon they were heading off to the Cotswolds for… wait for it… for a spa weekend.' She guffawed loudly. 'Both of them! This is Lloyd we're talking about! On a spa weekend! Can you imagine him in a bathrobe and a turban?'

I put a hand to my mouth. 'I could cry for them, I really could,' I said, feeling genuinely emotional.

'Hey,' said Cass, waving her glass at me and frowning again, 'what do you know that I don't? Come on, let's hear this prequel.'

–

I arrived home about an hour and a half later, clambering off my bike and wheeling it down the side-path to the back garden. My Friday night drink with Cass had, as usual, been a mood-boost and by the time I'd headed back to the gallery to fetch my bike,

I was feeling pretty good. And my mood had further improved on discovering the gallery empty. I hadn't been looking forward to the prospect of another conversation with Jasmine and I was pleased that David obviously hadn't had to endure her for too long either.

Locking my bike in the shed at the end of the cottage's long narrow garden, I unbuckled my helmet and headed back to the front door, crouching low to pluck a few weeds from the borders as I went. Consequently, Morgan spotted me before I spotted her.

'Hi there, Esme!'

I stood up to see her waving from behind the waist-high, grey-stone wall that divided our gardens. She looked just as depressingly attractive as she had during our last encounter, although this time jeans and a white shirt had replaced the sports gear.

I could tell that she was attempting a friendly smile, to the extent that her frozen features would allow, but my preference would still have been to offer her a quick 'hello' and leg it into the house. Any and all desire to get to know Morgan had immediately evaporated on realising that she was Elliot's partner, but it was obvious from her position at the wall that she was keen to talk.

'Hi,' I said, reluctantly walking over to join her. I glanced anxiously towards her cottage, checking for any additional signs of life.

'Just finished work?' she asked.

'I squeezed in a quick drink with a friend afterwards,' I replied, my eyes continuing to dart from her face to her cottage and back again. 'Have you two been home long?'

'Oh, Elliot's not home. He won't be back until Sunday morning.' She sounded despondent at the prospect, while I cheered up considerably at the news.

'So he's away?'

She nodded. 'I was going to ask if you fancied coming in for a drink.' Her mouth stretched into a quasi-smile, her unwrinkling eyes staring out of her head with all the warmth and expression of a couple of ping-pong balls.

I pressed my lips firmly together in order to prevent the escape of manic laughter and a loud, 'No way!'

'That's so kind. But the thing is…' I began, before hesitating and racking my brains for an excuse. I had been so accepting of the fact that neither Elliot nor I wanted anything more to do with each other, that the offer of a drink from his partner was not a scenario I had worked through, and I felt thoroughly unprepared for fending it off.

'Sorry, I'm hesitating because I'm torn,' I began again. 'I'd love a drink, but I've actually got a lot of stuff – work stuff – to wrap up. I have to get it all done tonight, because I've no time over the weekend. I'm working tomorrow, which is something I don't usually have to do because we have rotating cover-staff. But I have to tomorrow because someone's sick, and then I'm out all day Sunday, so I only have tonight to get everything done.' I came up for air, taking a deep breath, uncomfortably aware that my response had been unnecessarily and suspiciously detailed, with a distinct air of panic about it.

'Don't worry,' she said quietly, her body language conveying extreme disappointment in a way that her face could not. 'It was just a thought.'

Guilt welled up inside me, but I knew that there was just no way I could put myself through an evening of conversation with Elliot's partner over a glass of wine. Not only would any refer- ence to their relationship be a dagger to my soul and a crushing blow to my self-confidence, but I'd also have to spend the entire time watching every single word I said. Plus, I couldn't imagine Elliot being over the moon when she told him that we'd spent the evening together.

'Another time would be great, though,' I lied.

'How about next Friday?'

Dear God, she was keen.

'Er...' I took out my phone, attempting to look as if I was genuinely considering the possibility. 'Let me just check...' I tapped unseeingly at the screen.

'I hope you're free. Elliot will be away again and I'm only working in the morning. I'm a personal trainer and I'm temping at three different gyms at the moment...'

A personal trainer, I thought bitterly. Well, that explained the abs and zero per cent body fat.

'...so there's no chance of an after-work, end-of-week drink with anyone,' she continued. 'I just hate being home alone at the best of times, but a Friday night somehow seems particularly sad, doesn't it?'

'Yes,' I said dejectedly; my own misery having nothing whatsoever to do with the prospect of a Friday night on my own, and everything to do with the fact that I knew there was now nothing for it but to accept her offer of a drink and then pretend to be working late – or dying – when the time came.

'Next Friday sounds great...' I began resignedly, before looking up suddenly from my phone. 'Oh, but I'm afraid I can't,' I said, fighting to keep the excitement of discovering a genuine excuse from my voice. 'We have a private viewing and sale at the gallery. How stupid am I? I'd forgotten all about it.' Despite my best efforts, I was smiling with relief and just hoped that it was coming across as apologetic. 'I'm so sorry I can't make it.'

Her shoulders drooped and although she couldn't quite manage to look hurt, she definitely wasn't trying to look happy either.

'But I wonder if instead...' I continued, keen to remedy the awkward social situation and rising tide of guilt in which I was currently drowning, while running through my very limited options. 'I wonder if you would like to come along to the exhibition.'

She immediately brightened. 'Really? Are you sure?'

Obviously, I wasn't at all sure, but it was too late now. 'Yes, come along. There'll be a small crowd, plus a complimentary glass or two of Prosecco.' I unzipped a side pocket of my cycle bag, took out a business card and handed it to her. 'Here's the address of the gallery. The exhibition is from seven till ten.'

'Thank you,' she said. 'Thank you so much.'

'Not at all,' I smiled, waving away her thanks and congratulating myself on a solution which, even when examined in more detail, wasn't a terrible one. I had avoided the intimacy of a one-to-one drink, but at the same time left Morgan with the impression that I wasn't avoiding her. I could introduce her to a few people at Jasmine's show and then check in with her occasionally during the course of the evening. Who knew? She might even buy something! And if Elliot didn't like the fact that she was spending the evening at my gallery, well then he could come up with a way to dissuade her. If he managed that, then fine. I didn't care either way. The important thing was that I'd managed to be neighbourly and avoid hurting someone's feelings in extremely difficult circumstances. The rest was up to them.

'Well, enjoy your busy weekend,' said Morgan. 'I hope it's not too tiring.'

'I'm sure I'll survive,' I replied genially, before heading inside, with a certain sense of triumph, to pour myself a glass of wine and set about cooking supper.

Chapter 8

'Knock, knock,' said Lloyd, half-opening the gallery door and leaning inside.

'Lloyd!' I exclaimed, coming out from behind the counter and beckoning him in with both arms. 'How are you? Cass told me that you and Gwen went on a spa weekend. How was that?' I looked him up and down, my eyes coming to rest on his beaming face. 'My God, your skin looks *amazing*. Your pores are microscopic.'

'We had a couple's facial,' he said. 'They cleanse you, then they exfoliate you and then they massage you.'

'Ooh, very nice.'

'Gwen said it was her best birthday ever – apart from when I gave her the side-gate,' he smiled. 'But I knew I'd never top that.'

I searched for any hint of irony in either his tone or expression, but finding none, I simply nodded. 'You peaked early with that one.'

'And how was your weekend?' he asked.

I hesitated, wondering how truthful to make my account. My Friday night sense of triumph had been extremely short-lived and swiftly followed by a Saturday of forced labour – thereby giving one of our weekend staff an unexpected paid day off – and a very wet Sunday, mostly spent avoiding all the windows in my home, lest my next-door neighbour should spot me giving the lie to my 'fully booked' weekend. I was, I realised, going to have to start planning my leisure time more carefully for the next few months and accept more of the dinner invitations I had taken to turning down since moving out of Bristol, on the basis that I didn't always fancy driving or cycling into town for a teetotal night out.

'It was good, thanks. But what have you got there?' I continued, swiftly changing the subject and pointing to a brown paper package clutched in his left hand. I fully expected it to contain steak, or similar.

'It's my Institute of Meat Marketing award,' he said, as if that was all the explanation necessary.

'OK and…?'

'It's the one…' He hesitated awkwardly, clearing his throat. 'It fell off the—'

'Oh, yes, it needs reframing,' I interrupted, holding out my hand.

'I know it's not a standard size,' he said, handing it over.

'Not a problem. Would something like that do?' I pointed to a frame on the wall behind me. 'It'd be…' I tapped at a calculator on the desk, '£7.96 with your discount, and David will cut you a complimentary mount to make the certificate fit.'

'Thanks, Esme. And thanks for, you know, pointing me towards a spa,' he added a little shyly.

I waved a hand. 'I just threw a few vague suggestions at you. You're the one who got it spot on and, I should add, looks ten years younger for it. Cass has been trying to get me to have a facial for ages and, looking at you, I'm definitely going to book myself in for one now.'

He laughed and then looked over his shoulder as the gallery door beeped, heralding David's arrival. 'Ah, here's the wee tall man, now. Take the low and slow road to work today, did we, laddie?'

'Aye, my birlinn was late across the loch this morning,' said David good-naturedly.

Lloyd frowned. 'Your what?'

'My birlinn,' he repeated. 'It's a boat.'

'Oh, well, I never knew that. You learn something every day,' grinned Lloyd, rubbing his hands together in the manner of a man newly energised and eager to crack on. 'And with that happy thought in my head, I'll be off. Thanks again, Esme,' he said, nodding in my direction.

I watched, lifted by his mood, as he exited and sauntered next door, pausing for a moment outside his shop to lift his face towards the June sunshine.

'I picked up some more printer ink over the weekend,' said David, now unpacking the contents of his backpack onto the shelves under the counter. 'I realised we were low on Friday night.'

'Is a birling an actual thing?' I asked, as he stood up and zipped his bag.

'It's *birlinn* and yes, it is – or was – a sort of Hebridean longboat.'

'Oh, OK. Will commit that to memory, in case I ever get a chance to be on one of those nerdy quiz shows.'

'Has the kettle boiled?'

'Not yet. Too busy chatting to Lloyd. He dropped something off for you.' I held up the brown paper package.

'Steak?'

I shook my head. 'A certificate. Can you cut a mount for it, so that it fits an A4 frame?'

'Will do.' He took the package from me and headed for the kitchen. 'Coffee?'

'I'll make it,' I said, following and, despite my Friday-night conversation with Cass, considering asking him about Sophie. 'You have a seat,' I said, as we reached the kitchen, 'and tell me about your weekend.'

'Yesterday was a washout, wasn't it?' he said, opening Lloyd's parcel. 'How was yours?'

'I ran into my neighbour and invited her to Jasmine's exhibition.'

'I'll look forward to meeting her. How's the guest list coming along?'

'It's looking good, but...' I hesitated for only a moment before taking the plunge, 'that reminds me. Is Sophie coming?'

I posed the question casually, while switching on the kettle, my back deliberately to him. 'Shall I add her to the list?'

I wasn't sure whether I imagined a slight pause.

'Not this time,' he replied, sounding perfectly relaxed.

'OK,' I said and then, deciding to give him another chance to get personal, 'I haven't seen her for ages. Why isn't she coming on Friday? Is she working?'

This time, there was a quite definite and prolonged silence, and I turned towards him, ready to engage – ready to listen to whatever issues or anxieties he might wish to confide.

'Institute of Meat Marketing?' He was staring down at the certificate in its cracked frame, his expression one of total confusion. 'And you said that Lloyd displays this at home?'

I heaved a sigh and turned back to the kettle as it switched itself off. 'In his bedroom, apparently.'

'Really?'

'Really.'

I finished making the coffee and handed him a mug. 'There you go.'

'Thanks.' He placed the certificate to one side and looked thoughtful for a moment. 'Sorry, what were we talking about?'

'Sophie not coming to Jasmine's show.'

'Oh yes, the show. You must be getting on well with your neighbour if you've invited her along.'

Disappointed by this, possibly deliberate, diversion of the conversation, I shrugged. 'I wouldn't go that far. It just seemed the right thing to do. I think she's feeling a bit lonely and she's on her own on Friday, so...'

He smiled and picked up his coffee. 'That was kind of you.'

I hesitated, wondering whether to confide that it wasn't kindness but a fear of intimacy which had motivated me to invite my neighbour to a busy exhibition, rather than into my home, because she coincidentally happened to be my ex-partner's new partner – a fact to which she remained oblivious. I could also add that my ex-partner and I were now on *extremely* bad terms and doing everything possible to avoid sight or sound of each other – which was tricky, not only because we shared a party wall, but also because his new partner seemed to have taken a shine to me, no doubt due to the slim neighbourly pickings on offer in our village.

In the end, I decided that if David didn't want to talk to me about Sophie, even in response to a direct enquiry, then the chances of him wanting to hear about *my* relationship woes were slim to nothing. And actually, maybe that was no bad thing. There was, after all, no obvious benefit to either of us in offloading. What would that achieve, other than to bring negative experiences into an otherwise happy workplace? Besides, Cass was right, if I ever felt an irresistible urge to offload during office hours, I had her just next door and positively gagging for detail.

'I don't know about kind,' I said, picking up my coffee and heading back to the gallery. 'Like I said, it just seemed like the right thing to do in the circumstances.'

Chapter 9

Douglas Muirhead looked first at me and then, rather more uncertainly, down at the three clay sculptures on the counter in front of us. He'd turned up at four thirty in response to my voicemail suggesting that he pop in for 'a quick chat' sometime, not realising that we were shutting up shop an hour earlier than usual that evening to give ourselves extra time to prepare the gallery for Jasmine's exhibition.

'I'm in your way,' he said meekly, his slow, soft tones strangely at odds with his six-foot-three, sturdily built frame; like a rugby player lip-synching to Penelope Wilton. 'I should have called first. I could come back next week.'

'No, no,' I said. 'I'm pleased that you've dropped by. I've been wanting to tell you how much I love these.'

I looked down at his bordering-on-twee, but skilfully made, wildlife sculptures: a little hedgehog, nestling amongst fallen leaves; a mole, peeping out from a newly formed mound; and a squirrel, sitting up on its haunches, its head cocked to one side, its fur appearing almost soft to the touch. Douglas's attention to detail was something else and I knew he would have taken hours of painstaking care over each piece.

'They'll be snapped up. You've already built up a little bit of a following, you know, Douglas. People are asking after your work by name, and David and I think we should definitely up the price.'

'Gosh.' He ran a hand across the top of his head, which was covered in a mop of golden curls, his already large eyes anxiously widening further, so that he now resembled a giant toddler. 'Do you really think so, Esme?'

'I really do,' I continued, nodding enthusiastically. 'These pieces,' I laid a forefinger gently on each in turn, 'are immediately recognisable as your work, which means they will sell themselves. But what I really wanted to talk to you about was this one.' I reached under the counter, bringing out a sleeping male nude, which was around three times the size of the largest of the other sculptures. 'This one is much edgier than the other examples of your work we currently stock, isn't it?' I said, placing it on the counter.

'I'm so sorry,' he replied, taking a pair of small round glasses from a green canvas backpack at his feet and putting them on, his voice now barely above a whisper. 'I never actually intended for him to escape the house.' He bent low, so that his face was just inches from the piece as he gazed intently at it. 'I wrapped him up months ago because, you know, sometimes you just don't want to look at a piece, do you? And then, last week, I stupidly put him in the box instead of the large badger. I had no idea. I'm so sorry to have bothered you with him.'

'Oh, Douglas, not at all,' I replied quickly, keen to avoid him mistaking comment for criticism. 'I'm so delighted that we've had a chance to see this other side to your work. It's very different, but that doesn't make it any less brilliant, interesting or marketable. It's actually David's favourite of the four,' I added, picking up the piece again and turning it thoughtfully in my hands. In contrast to the others, it was decidedly stylised, its limbs lengthened and twisted beyond realism.

At that moment, David himself returned from the back room, carrying two of Jasmine's paintings. 'Hello, Douglas,' he said, smiling. 'I didn't hear you come in.'

Douglas raised a perpetually anxious hand.

'David, I was just saying how intrigued you were by this figure,' I said, holding it up.

'Indeed I was.' He stooped to rest Jasmine's pictures against the wall. 'Your wildlife work is wonderful, Douglas, and this darker piece is just as skilful.'

Douglas smiled shyly, while blinking rapidly, clearly delighted, but also apparently a little overwhelmed by David's approval.

'Yes, so what we've got to think about now,' I said, placing the human figure carefully back down on the counter, 'is how best to market this alongside – or maybe not alongside – your wildlife work. Assuming you want to market it, that is. I know you said you boxed him by mistake and I do understand that some pieces can feel a little too personal to share publicly.'

Douglas appeared to consider the matter for a moment and then shook his curls. 'No, I would really like to sell him, Esme. Very much indeed.'

I clapped my hands. 'Brilliant. Well, let me just have a little bit of a think about how best to do that, and can I ask whether you have any other pieces like this one? They don't have to be in exactly the same style. Just anything that is, as David put it, a little *darker* than the wildlife figures.'

He looked at the figure and nodded slowly. 'Yes, yes, I do. He's actually part of a... well, kind of a set.'

'Better and better,' I beamed, glancing at the clock on the far wall of the gallery, suddenly aware of time marching on. 'Would you be able to pop those over to us, whenever you're ready? No rush. Maybe when you drop off the next wildlife pieces? Then we can talk some more about how best to push forward with this.'

Douglas looked, I thought, a little emotional. 'Thanks so much. You're such an encouraging person, Esme. You *and* David,' he added, glancing towards my colleague, who was now balancing on a step-stool to hang one of Jasmine's oils. 'I'm so grateful for your guidance – and who would have thought that such feelings of light and positivity could come from a place of such darkness?' he added in a murmur, his smile adopting a slightly fixed quality as he lowered his eyes to the countertop.

'We're just delighted to be working with you, Douglas,' said David, climbing down and joining us. 'And if you're not too busy this evening, why don't you come back in a couple of hours or so and enjoy a glass of wine with us at Jasmine Dean's showing tonight? Doors open at seven.' He held out his hand.

Douglas turned to him, his eyes shining as they shook hands. 'I'm a little nervous of crowds,' he said, bending to pick up his backpack, which clanked as he did so, 'but that is so very kind of you.'

'That sounds heavy,' I said, nodding at the bag.

'I'm used to the burden, Esme,' he replied and then, after another brief round of pleasantries, he left.

David closed the door behind him, turning the hanging wooden sign to 'closed' as we watched Douglas pause at Lloyd's window, his eye apparently caught by some prime cut or other.

'I really like Douglas. He's so talented but so self-effacing, and that latest piece of his is a real revelation,' I said, watching as he continued to gaze at the meats on offer. 'I just don't feel like I've quite met the real Douglas yet.'

'Yes, he does seem like a man with hidden depths.' David returned to the far side of the gallery and started to remove more pictures to make way for Jasmine's work.

'A man of many layers and with a sweet centre,' I mused. 'Like a jam puff with specs. And hair.'

'That's exactly what I thought,' said David.

'Really?'

He climbed down from the step-stool. 'No, not really. I can't actually think of another person on the planet who would have come up with that simile.'

'Well, thank you,' I said, smiling to myself and setting about bubble-wrapping Douglas's sculptures for weekend storage. 'I'm going to take that as a compliment.'

Chapter 10

I always enjoyed our evening exhibitions. We held just four or five a year and, of course, in comparison to the much larger events I had helped to put together as a bit-part player in a London gallery team, they were extremely small-scale and decidedly provincial in feel.

But hand in hand with small-scale and provincial came intimacy and warmth. And that, plus the excitement of a local artist at having an evening devoted solely to their work – often for the first time – made the Westbury Park shows at least as fun and rewarding as anything I'd been involved in in Notting Hill, Battersea or Kensington a decade earlier.

But as I considered Jasmine's faux generous offer to 'pop out to Waitrose and get some really interesting nibbles' – a mere ten minutes before we were due to open the door to invited guests – I had a horrible feeling that this was going to be one Westbury Park exhibition that I wasn't going to enjoy very much at all, for three fundamental and immutable reasons. Firstly, I was going to have to spend the entire evening promoting Jasmine. Secondly, I was going to have to do that in the company of Jasmine. And thirdly, I really couldn't stand Jasmine. What's more, I was pretty damn sure that Jasmine didn't care much for me either.

She had arrived half an hour earlier than expected 'to help', despite the fact that I always told our artists to think of the show as a party at which they were the guest of honour and to leave all the boring stuff – hanging pictures, lining up wine glasses, et cetera – to us. This, of course, had more to do with keeping them out of our hair than wanting them to feel special, as even the most accommodating of artists were prone to becoming neurotic pains in the arse when it came to the presentation of their work – myself included.

Jasmine, however, had bounced in at six fifteen, declaring that she couldn't bear the thought of us 'slaving away unaided'. She had then proceeded to congratulate David on everything from his artistic eye to his on-point footwear, while obliquely questioning my every decision, from the font used in the typed descriptions of her work to the selection of light bites – the latter query culminating in the extremely last-minute offer of a quick trip to Waitrose.

'Wow,' she said, clasping her hands together as I placed the last of the upturned champagne flutes on a long, cloth-draped table at the back of the gallery, 'everything looks fabulous. Thanks, Esme. I feel just so special this evening.'

She ran a hand along the white tablecloth and smiled down appreciatively at the wines, soft drinks and four silver trays, soon to be loaded with light bites.

For a moment my resentment towards her subsided and I smiled back, ready to set aside her earlier criticisms as minor and down to nerves.

And then she hit me with it.

'Those trays are so lovely, but they look quite weighty. I hope you won't be back and forth too much reloading them.'

I looked down at the trays and then back up at her. 'Don't worry, I won't be back and forth at all. Four trays of nibbles will be quite enough. It's the booze they'll fill up on and that's good for sales.' I laughed lightly, hoping she might leave it there – but no.

'Really?' She frowned, as if puzzled. 'I always get the munchies when I have a glass of something.'

'That's interesting,' I said, suddenly wishing I had a glass of something to throw over her and pausing for a moment to review my menstrual cycle. Yep, as suspected, my progesterone levels were in the ascendency.

'So how about I pop to Waitrose and get us a few little extra somethings? Some really *interesting* nibbles,' she continued, checking her watch. 'I would only miss the first twenty minutes or so of my exhibition and I honestly, honestly, don't mind. I mean, I definitely don't want *you* going, although I suppose David is here to manage things if you did go,' she added, with a smile and a head tilt, as he returned from taking a phone call in the workshop.

I focused on my breathing. Her offer to nip out, as ridiculous and insincere as it so obviously was, was actually rather tempting, as it would have removed her from the gallery for half an hour. However, we couldn't – as she well knew – open the doors without the star of the show present and, besides, to have sent her to Waitrose would have felt too much like an admission of a catering error on my part, and my progesterone levels simply wouldn't allow that.

'Most people will be here to feast their eyes, not stuff their faces,' I said, trying to sound pleasant rather than pissed off, failing miserably and not really caring.

Her smile froze a little, before suddenly regaining its warmth as she looked up and over my shoulder.

'I was just saying how wonderful everything looks, David,' she said softly. 'And how very special I feel.'

'Marvellous,' he said, glancing at me and pointing towards the gallery door. 'I wonder if we have an early guest, or maybe she's just window shopping. Recognise her?'

I turned to see Morgan, wearing a perfectly fitted cream dress and a faceful of expertly applied make-up, peering with intense interest at an item in the window.

'That's my neighbour,' I said, unexpectedly grateful for her arrival, which provided a welcome distraction from Jasmine and effectively drew a line under the light-bite debate.

I hurried to the counter, where I retrieved the blackboard announcing Jasmine's private showing and carried it outside.

'Hello, Morgan!' I said, positioning the board on the pavement.

'Oh, hi.' She turned from the window. 'I'm so sorry I'm early, but it's hard to judge the journey time from the village, isn't it?'

'It is,' I agreed, despite never really having had a problem with the logistics of the trip myself. 'But we're only a couple of minutes away from seven, so don't worry.'

'I was just looking at the sweet little hedgehog,' she said, pointing to Douglas's piece, which I had hurriedly unwrapped and made space for half an hour earlier, just in case he decided to be brave and join us.

'Do you like it?'

'I *love* it. It's so detailed.'

'It's by Douglas Muirhead. He takes such care over his work. Unsurprisingly, it's hugely popular.'

'If you could keep it for me, I'll tell Elliot that I'd like it for my birthday,' she said. 'It's next month.'

'Oh, right.' I made an immediate and conscious effort to reposition my smile, which had dropped at the mention of Elliot's name and the thought that he might be forced to call into the gallery to pick up the gift. But I clearly wasn't fast enough.

'Is that a problem?' asked Morgan hastily. 'If it is, I can pay for it now.'

I shook my head, frustrated at my continuing inability to manage my feelings, even after all this time. 'It's not a problem *at all*, and I'm delighted that you like it. Douglas's pieces do tend to sell really quickly, so I'll put it to one side right away. I've got some more examples of his work in the back room, but I'll show you those another time. Jasmine Dean,' I added in a conspiratorial whisper, while indicating the blackboard bearing her name, 'might get a bit upset if I start showing off another artist's work this evening.'

She laughed, making a recognisable attempt at a smile, which I assumed meant that the Botox was wearing off, or that the fillers were breaking down, and I found myself hoping that she wouldn't bother topping them up just yet. Despite the unfortunate circumstances of our relationship, I couldn't help warming to Morgan, and one consequence of that was that I really wanted her to stop turning herself into a waxwork.

'And talking of Jasmine,' I continued, turning towards the door, 'let's go inside and I'll introduce you to her. She can show you some of her work while I get you a glass of Prosecco. I might even have one myself, you know, just to take the edge off.'

–

Maybe it was because I'd held out such very low expectations for the evening, but when I checked my watch and saw that it was nine thirty, I was genuinely surprised by how time had flown and by how relatively infrequently I'd wanted to throw stuff at Jasmine.

And my lack of ill will wasn't the only good news of the evening, because the night was also proving to be a great commercial success. All of the originals I had selected had sold and my chosen prints were also selling well, both framed and unframed. Meanwhile, the fact that we hadn't sold any of the three disappointing oils, which Jasmine had insisted on swapping in, was yet another – admittedly churlish and unprofessional – plus point in my book.

'We're having *such* a good evening,' I said excitedly to David, as he came into the kitchen with a box of used glasses and placed them next to the sink.

'We are,' he agreed. 'It's a good crowd – including your new neighbour,' he added, as I took a bottle of Prosecco from the fridge and handed it to him.

'You've chatted?'

'She worked in Edinburgh for four years, so we have things in common.' He popped the cork and returned the bottle to me.

70

'I didn't know that. I know nothing about her really,' I said a little guiltily. 'And I feel bad that I haven't paid her more attention this evening, but it's been so busy. Jasmine has invited way more people than she told us about.'

He began to rinse the glasses. 'Well, they got their wallets out.'

'True,' I admitted. 'But they're also knocking it back pretty quickly, so I'd better get in there with this.' I held up the bottle and headed for the door. 'I must try to have a quick word with Morgan, if she's still here.'

'She was talking to Douglas when I last saw her.'

I paused in the doorway and turned back towards him. 'Douglas is here?'

'He arrived about half an hour ago and installed himself behind the counter. I pointed him out to Morgan and she went to talk to him.'

'That was nice. I hope she told him that she's reserved his hedgehog. He'd be over the moon about that.'

'He would. Look, I'll just finish these and then I'll be back in there.'

'Great. See you in a minute,' I called, hurrying back to the packed gallery to find Jasmine, her back towards me, holding court with several friends in front of one of the three unsold oils.

'Yes,' she said, 'I had a gut feeling that this one wasn't right for tonight, but I had to allow myself to be guided by Esme.' She sighed and shrugged resignedly, before leeching up the hastily offered reassurances and compliments of her friends.

I joined the group, tapping her on the shoulder. 'Top-up?' I asked, through slightly clenched teeth.

'Oh, Esme,' she said, starting slightly, 'I didn't see you there.'

'Drink?' I repeated the offer, tightening my grip around the neck of the bottle.

'Er, yes, please,' she said, holding out her glass and at least having the decency to look a little awkward. 'I was just saying... um...'

I looked up at the catastrophe of colour behind her and decided that I had a choice. Either I could embarrass her in front of her friends, by reminding her that I had strongly recommended against including the piece in the show – and, in the process, kill any chance of a sale – or I could promote both her and the awful painting.

'I hope you're not being critical of yourself and second-guessing your talent,' I said, nodding up at the picture, as I filled her glass. 'It's so difficult to be objective about your own work, and I would argue that you shouldn't even try to be. Your work is at its best when it is a wholly immersive process and that is only possible if you retain complete subjectivity. This landscape is actually a stand-out piece, because you have painted instinctively, venturing outside your comfort zone, with considerable success. It's unique amongst your work, which increases both its artistic and its investment value. Any buyer with a broader experience of your art and an understanding of the market will recognise that. Now, would anyone else like a top-up?' I asked without pause, smiling at the group. Three glasses were immediately proffered and, having spotted Morgan standing on her own by the gallery door, I filled them up and moved on – without throwing anything other than a final glance at Jasmine, and feeling rather proud of the fact.

Morgan saluted me with her glass as I approached.

'Hi,' I said. 'I'm so sorry that I haven't managed to catch you this evening.'

'I've had a great time,' she replied, glancing over her shoulder towards the street. 'I met Douglas Muirhead. He was very sweet.'

'He is. I'm pleased you got to meet the man behind the hedgehog.' I held up the bottle of Prosecco. 'A drop more?'

She shook her head, placing a hand over her glass. 'Thanks, but I've had loads and my ride will be here any moment.'

'You've called a cab? I could've given you a lift home. Although that probably wouldn't be till around eleven, I guess.'

'Thanks, but Elliot's coming for me.' She turned away again, which was just as well. There were only so many times I could get away with my face dropping like a stone at the mention of his name before Morgan noticed that something was up. 'He was supposed to be away until Sunday, but something has been cancelled. So I get a ride home, which is why,' she continued, returning her attention to me and holding up her glass, 'I felt able to have a little more of this than I usually would. The thing is,' she lowered her voice and leaned towards me, 'I actually get very anxious about meeting new people and a bit of this,' she tapped the near-empty glass with a perfectly manicured nail, 'really helps.'

I took a deep breath, desperately trying to focus on the woman in front of me currently confessing her vulnerability, rather than on the overwhelming need to escape her company before her boyfriend turned up.

'I'm exactly the same,' I said, trying to reassure her in as few words as possible. 'I think most people are. But you never look at all anxious to me,' I concluded quickly, without adding that she never looked particularly happy, sad or excited either. 'Now, I have to go and fill a few more glasses, so come with me and I'll introduce you to—'

I gestured over my shoulder and went to turn away, but Morgan placed a gentle hand on my arm. 'You're so interesting and self-assured, Esme. I never have anything to say.'

I turned back towards her, forgetting all about Elliot for a moment and frowning at her with concern. Was she really that lacking in self-confidence, or just a lot more inebriated than she looked?

'What? Of course you have things to say,' I insisted. 'Just two minutes ago David was telling me how much he'd enjoyed talking to you about Edinburgh. I think you've made his evening.'

She looked up and something in her eyes indicated that if she could have smiled, she would have. 'He's kind.'

'He's a good guy,' I agreed. 'Hey, and here he is!' I exclaimed, as he came to stand beside me. 'Are your ears burning?'

'Always,' he replied, 'but I've come to ask where the framed print for Charles Hardwick is.'

'Oh, right,' I said, delighted to be handed an excuse to be gone. 'He wanted to take it with him this evening, didn't he? It's wrapped and in the workshop. You chat some more to Morgan, while I go and fetch it for him.'

'No rush,' he said. 'He's not going until he's finished his drink. I just wanted to be able to lay hands on it when the time came.'

'Hmm, well, I think it's there,' I said, trying to sound doubtful, 'but maybe I should go and—'

Sadly, that was as far as I got, because just at that moment Elliot walked in and, as we were standing immediately next to the door, all chance of escape was lost.

'Hi,' he said, sounding a little breathless and glancing briefly in my direction before smiling at Morgan.

She reached a hand up to his shoulder and leaned her head against his upper arm. 'Hi,' she said. 'Thanks for coming to get me.'

'No problem.' He continued to smile, but I could tell that he was uneasy. 'We'd better make a move because it's all residents' parking around here.'

David spoke up. 'You're fine. There are no restrictions from five p.m. Friday through to nine a.m. Monday.'

I wanted to whack him with my bottle.

Elliot looked at him, pausing slightly before nodding his acceptance of the information.

'David,' I said, working to keep my voice level, and grateful for the cover of background chatter and laughter, 'this is my neighbour, Elliot, Morgan's partner.'

'Hi, Elliot. Great to meet you,' said David, with the merest trace of a frown.

'David is Esme's partner, El,' explained Morgan, her words bleeding into each other slightly, as the Prosecco hit home. 'He's

74

from Edinburgh.' She looked up at David. 'You must both come to dinner with us some time. We'd love that, wouldn't we, El?'

'Of course.'

'So why don't we fix a date now?' she suggested, nudging him.

'Maybe not now, because today has thrown all my schedules out,' said Elliot, still – God knows how – managing to maintain a smile. 'But we'll definitely have to pencil something in soon.'

I stared at him, my resentment towards him and his total mismanagement of the situation growing by the minute. He really had to sort this out, because I didn't think I could take another week, let alone several months, of dodging invites and lying by omission to a woman who, I increasingly felt, could do with a local friend – and who needed to be told as soon as possible that that local friend could not be me.

Morgan, meanwhile, had moved on to hedgehogs.

'...so beautiful and delicate. Esme's put him to one side for me,' she said, as she placed her arms around Elliot's torso and squeezed. I felt like crying.

'Why don't I go and get it now?' I said, hastily handing the wine bottle to David. 'Save you coming back. We can sort out payment any time over the phone.'

Without waiting for approval of my suggestion, I turned and walked quickly through the crowd of browsers, buyers and singularly annoying artist, to the workshop. Once there, I leaned against David's workbench, closing my eyes and taking several deep breaths, while telling myself to get a grip. All I had to do was get the hedgehog, hand it over and they'd be gone. All related matters could be considered and dealt with another time. Now was not the moment to start analysing my problems and reviewing my options.

I took a final deep breath and opened my eyes to discover Elliot standing just a few feet from me, his expression one of contrition mixed with despair.

'Don't you *dare* say you're sorry,' I hissed, straightening up, anger proving a handy distraction from misery. 'And what the hell do you think you're doing coming back here?'

'It's OK,' he said quietly, holding up his hands, as if in surrender. 'I just asked to use the bathroom.'

'It is *not* OK. None of this is OK,' I growled, walking to the back of the room, opening a cupboard and taking out the boxed hedgehog. 'Now, take this,' I said, returning and thrusting the box towards him, 'and then go home, tell your girlfriend the truth and move house.'

He reached out for the box, but instead of taking it from me, he placed his hand gently over mine and left it there.

I looked down at his hand and tried to say something, but couldn't.

'I know it's up to me to sort things out,' he said.

Then he removed his hand from mine, took the box and returned to the gallery.

Chapter 11

I closed the gallery door behind the last of the departing guests and rested my weight against it for a moment, lowering my head and pausing to collect both my thoughts and my feelings.

The night had been an unequivocal success. We had sold all but two of Jasmine's originals and multiple copies of her prints, and yet I couldn't recall feeling quite so miserable in years. All I wanted was to go home, go to bed and cry – preferably all weekend. Oh, except that I didn't really want to go home, because home was currently just a dividing wall away from the cause of my misery.

With enormous effort, I straightened up, contorted my features into a more cheerful expression and walked to the far end of the gallery, where Jasmine was standing, talking to David in hushed tones.

She stopped as she heard me coming and turned towards me, raising her half-full champagne flute in salute as I approached.

'Cheers, Esme. I was just saying to David what an amazing evening it was and that it's entirely down to you two. I'm so very, very grateful to you both.'

Perhaps due to my emotionally damaged state, I found myself disproportionately moved by the unexpected display of humility and had to clear my throat before replying.

'At the end of the day, Jasmine, you paint beautiful pictures that people want to buy,' I said croakily.

'Hear, hear,' said David. I wanted to turn and offer him a smile, but didn't seem able to summon up the energy.

Jasmine, by contrast, looked ready to run a mile in her cutesy, flower-covered heels as she glanced up with satisfaction at the third-rate landscape she had insisted upon including in the show. It was now bearing a small, red, circular sticker, indicating that it had, against all odds – and following protracted negotiations with a prospective purchaser, during which I had bullshitted shamelessly and flattered endlessly – eventually sold.

'You know, I was just saying to David how hard you tried to persuade me not to show this one,' she began, smiling sweetly and gesturing upwards with her glass, 'but I knew it would sell. Funny, isn't it, artist's intuition? You know how I hate being a bother, but I'm so pleased I was stubborn with you over it.'

I frowned, genuinely wondering if I had lost concentration and misunderstood her. 'I'm sorry, are we talking about *this* picture?' I pointed at the landscape.

She turned towards me. 'Oh, you are kind, but don't pretend. I know that I was disgracefully pouty over it. I find it so hard to be assertive and it took all my courage not to give in,' she added, blinking coyly up at David. 'I so lack self-belief, as you know, but I just knew that this was the right painting, at the right time.'

I looked at her, still for a moment and not quite believing what I was hearing, and then I took a deep breath. 'OK, well, I think it's time for you to piss off now, Jasmine,' I said lightly, walking past her and snatching up a half-empty bottle of Prosecco from the cloth-covered table as I went.

'Esme...' David sounded like my dad the first time he heard me swear: just as appalled and just as disappointed. I was surprised how much it stung.

'Sorry, Esme, what did you say?' Jasmine's childlike, faux-confused tone was intensely irritating, but at least it distracted from the pain of David's disapproval. I stopped walking and turned to face her.

'I advised you several times not to hang the painting because, quite frankly, it's just not very good.'

She made a noise like a startled lamb and David said, 'Stop,' now sounding more like a court order than a concerned parent.

I didn't pause for breath.

'You insisted on swapping it in and then, when it failed to sell – along with those two other inferior ones you like so much over there,' I jerked a thumb over my shoulder, 'you told your mates that you'd never wanted to show it in the first place and that it was all my fault. Nevertheless, I came to the rescue by bigging up and selling the crap painting for you. And yet now you have the quite unbelievable nerve to claim the credit. Well, I've had it up to here with you,' I said, waving my bottle high in the air. 'And that's why, in case you genuinely didn't hear me the first time around, I would like you to *just... piss... off.*'

With that, and with tears teetering on the brink of my lower lids, I stomped off into the workshop, swinging my bottle and slamming the door behind me.

By the time David appeared about ten minutes later, I was perched on a stool and a third of the way down my second glass of Prosecco, having necked the first, while seeing how many of David's framing and sculpting tools I could name – none – and trying not to think about Elliot, as trying to forget about him clearly wasn't an option for me at this point.

David stood unspeaking in the doorway and, in the end, without turning towards him, I said, 'I thought you'd gone. I'm just going to finish this and then I'll clear everything away. No need for you to stay.' I reached for the bottle of Prosecco on the workbench next to me, upping the level in my glass in order to emphasise a preference for drowning my sorrows, rather than entering into a conversation.

'I'll give you a lift home,' he said simply, his tone flat and disappointingly uninquisitive. 'You won't be able to drive after that.'

'I'll get a cab.'

'OK.'

He turned and left, and a moment later I heard the clink of glasses and the scraping of a table, as he began to clear the gallery in readiness for opening the next morning.

I closed my eyes, heaved a sigh, wearily hauled myself off the stool and went to help.

For the next half-hour – and in complete silence – we cleared the tables, rehung pictures and repositioned 3D pieces which had been temporarily relegated to the workshop. Then, as David swept the floor, I went into the kitchen to finish rinsing the hired glasses, ready for return.

I had just downed my tea towel and returned to nursing a glass of wine, when he entered the kitchen and sat down opposite me.

'That was totally unacceptable,' he said. 'On every level.'

'In your opinion,' I replied, staring unblinkingly at my drink. 'In *my* opinion, it was a long time coming and thoroughly deserved.'

He said nothing more, but when I looked up, I saw that his expression was dripping with just as much disapproval and disappointment as his tone had been forty minutes earlier. After an unbearable silence of at least five seconds – possibly six – I slumped forward, resting my head in my hands.

'I'll call her tomorrow and eat humble pie until I'm sick.' I looked up at him miserably. 'I'm sorry. It was really unprofessional of me and unfair to you, and I will put it right.'

He leaned back in his chair and ran an exhausted hand through his hair. 'I think it'll be fine,' he said. 'Not that I want to dissuade you from the humble pie. I think you should definitely follow through with that. But she's gone away in a good mood.'

'Really?' I asked doubtfully.

'Really. It was a very good night for her, Esme,' he said, his tone steady and reassuring. 'And that's entirely down to your expertise and planning. No one else could have sold that landscape this evening and Jazz knows that, even if she can't quite bring herself to acknowledge it.'

I smiled at him, grateful for the validation, and was just about to bat back some reciprocal praise, when he pushed back his chair and stood up.

'Come on,' he said, beckoning to me. 'Grab your jacket and I'll give you a lift home.'

–

The fifteen-minute drive to the cottage was spent in pretty much complete silence – a situation that would usually have bothered me, as I generally found conversational gaps of any length a breeding ground for insecurities and paranoia.

But that particular evening, my head was too uncomfortably and irresistibly full of Elliot – not least, the image and sensation of his hand resting on mine – to even notice the lack of conversation, let alone worry to what extent I might have been to blame for it.

It was only as we pulled up outside my home-of-the-moment and David said, 'Here we are,' that I started slightly, experiencing mild guilt, at having been such an uncommunicative passenger, and strong concern that David might still be preoccupied with my earlier rant at Jasmine.

'Thanks so much for the lift,' I said, unbuckling. 'And again, I'm really sorry about what happened with Jasmine.'

'It's fine,' he replied, sounding, to my relief, genuinely unbothered. He gestured towards the cottages. 'So, is that you on the left?'

'Yes, that's me,' I nodded, realising that he had never actually seen the house before. 'I really should have people round, but I suppose it's just felt a bit too temporary for that. You know, like inviting friends back to your room at the Travelodge.' I turned to exit the car. 'God, I really can't wait to get back to my flat.'

'At least you've got decent neighbours.'

I paused with my hand on the door.

'Or at least Morgan seems nice,' David continued. 'I didn't really get a chance to talk to Elliot. Is he OK?'

'He's hardly ever here.'

He nodded, still looking towards the house. 'Yes, I got that impression from her.'

'We don't have to go to dinner with them, you know,' I said suddenly. 'If Morgan follows through with her invite, I mean.'

'I do realise it's not compulsory.'

'What I mean is, I'm not desperate to go and I don't want you to feel that you have to come along to keep me company during an awkward evening.'

'Why should it be awkward?'

'Well, I...' I paused, hovering on the brink of telling him everything: that my neighbour was my ex, that it hadn't been a good break-up and that things had just got a whole lot worse.

But once I started with the explanations, where would I stop? Would I also tell him that when Morgan had hugged Elliot, I couldn't breathe, and that when he had touched my hand just a few minutes later, it had felt like a rush of oxygen to my lungs?

Wouldn't it be better to just keep it all to myself, sit it out and wait for the day, a few short weeks down the line, when a big white removal van would pull up outside our cottages and, quite literally, make it all go away?

'It's just that I don't really know Morgan,' I said, 'and I was worried that you might think that I was keen to go and so you should come as a favour to me.'

He took a breath as if about to say something, and then let it go and took another. 'It hadn't occurred to me that you might need help. Despite your occasional tendency to go off-piste, I actually think of you as reasonably socially adept. I wouldn't have a problem coming along. I liked Morgan and I don't want her to think that I didn't.'

I nodded. He was, as I had told Morgan just a few hours ago, a good guy.

'OK, well, I'd better go,' I said, at last opening the door and climbing out of the car. 'But thanks for the lift, and for not losing it with me. I'll sort things with Jasmine over the weekend, I promise.'

'I know you will. See you Monday.'

'See you.'

I closed the door, raised a hand as he pulled away, and then opened my garden gate and walked up the path.

As I reached the porch and glanced upwards, I thought I saw a face at an upstairs window next door. But I couldn't be sure and, as much as I wanted to, I didn't look again to check.

Chapter 12

'If it wasn't for that quite unnecessary squiggle,' the woman waved a tanned right hand, heavy with gold bracelets and an impressive diamond eternity ring, towards the upper left-hand corner of the abstract acrylic, 'I'd pay full price. But as it is, I just don't think I can. It's quite superfluous to the piece.'

I stood next to her and gazed thoughtfully up at the painting, my thoughts now centring primarily on how I could free myself from the entitled, middle-class, middle-aged piece of work to my left, who had insisted on torturing me for the past half-hour with her negative critiques of almost every piece in the gallery, and who was now in danger of crashing closing time.

I was sure she had money to spend, but I was at this point losing all hope of her actually spending it, and I wasn't sure how much more of her pompous haggling I could take.

'It would do for the guest room, *if* we could agree, say, a twenty per cent reduction. Do you see?' She lowered her head and looked at me over the top of her oblong, tortoiseshell spectacles. 'Perhaps you could run and get your boss so that he and I can discuss the price. I think I saw him back there somewhere.' She glanced in the direction of the workshop.

'I'm actually the co-owner,' I said politely. 'My partner has already left for the day but, in any case, I'm responsible for pricing the pieces. I'm *so* sorry that I can't offer you a discount on the painting, but it was hung only yesterday and I'm confident that it will sell quickly, at the asking price. If you'd like me to show you something more within your price range…' I added, unable to resist poking the snake with a stick.

'It is not at all a question of affordability!' she snapped. 'It is a question of worth and I am struggling to agree with your assessment of this painting's worth.'

'Because of the squiggle... yes... I understand,' I said benignly. 'Of course, we could remount it for you, so that the squiggle is obscured.'

She blinked rapidly at the offer.

'Widening the mount by less than two-centimetres at the top would do it, and none of the other detail would be lost,' I continued. 'I'd be willing to arrange that for you at no extra cost. If you'd like to go ahead, I would need a thirty per cent deposit now and the remainder upon collection.'

She continued to blink. 'A deposit?'

'As I said, I'm confident of selling the piece in its current mount and frame. So I'm afraid I can't withdraw it from sale, and remount it, without a deposit. But do feel free to go away and think about it. Here's our card.' I smiled, taking one from the small Perspex holder on the counter and handing it to her. 'It's been so lovely to meet you.'

She took the card from me, clearly experiencing some degree of inner turmoil over what to do in the face of a dismissal which she couldn't resist, without capitulating over the purchase. But after a moment, and rather redder in the face than when she had first walked in, she swept past me and into the street, almost bumping into Lloyd coming the other way as she did so. He saved the situation with a last-minute body swerve, which I thought rather impressive for a man of his rotundity.

'Someone's in a hurry to be gone,' he said, laughing over his shoulder as he entered. 'I'm afraid you've lost a sale there, Esme.'

'Nah, she'll be back,' I said, 'or on the phone to me before the week is out. I tell you, Lloyd, some people's lack of art appreciation is so depressing. You'd think that was a piece of wallpaper,' I sighed, gesturing upwards to the abstract, 'rather than a unique visual representation of someone's feelings. If all she wants is an accessory for her guest room, she should go to John Lewis and buy a bloody cushion.'

'I know. I feel just the same about my sausages,' he said despondently, shaking his head.

I looked at him doubtfully. 'You do?'

'Oh, yes. I had a customer in yesterday, buying multiple cuts, and at the end he looks up from his list and says, "Oh, and maybe some sausages."'

He paused significantly, looked at me and then shook his head a second time. '*Oh, and maybe some sausages.* Just like that – as if all sausages were the same and he didn't really care one way or the other if they weren't. No respect for variety, craftsmanship or flavour whatsoever. It grates on me, Esme, because quality sausages are as individual as you or me.'

The corners of his mouth drooped downwards and he hung his head, like a mourner at a sausage funeral.

I took the opportunity to roll my eyes and then decided to move the conversation on. 'That's so distressing, Lloyd, but how are things with you? Good day? Anything I can help you with?'

He looked up and grinned. 'Yes, yes, there is actually,' he said excitedly. 'We're having the lounge re-carpeted next week, and the sofa and chairs arrive the week after.'

'That's nice.'

'So...' He delved into a back pocket of his navy trousers, taking out a piece of card and two fabric swatches, which he placed on the counter next to us. 'This is the wall colour, this is the sofa fabric and this one is the chairs',' he said, indicating each in turn. 'And the carpet is sand,' he concluded, looking at me expectantly.

'Lovely. Really lovely.'

His eyes lost none of their expectation.

'I'm sorry, Lloyd,' I said, frowning, 'did you want my help with something?'

'Well, with picking out some pictures, of course.'

'Oh, I see,' I nodded slowly. 'So, you want me to colour-match some art to your room?'

'Yes, please.'

'To accessorise the room with art?'

'Yes, please.'

'Like I might help you to pick out a cushion?'

'Do you do cushions?' he asked, looking round. 'Because that would be great.'

I inhaled deeply and exhaled a sigh. 'No, sorry.'

He waved a hand. 'Not to worry. Just the prints then.' He leaned towards me conspiratorially. 'They're a gift, from me to Gwen. A totally *unnecessary* gift,' he added with a wink.

'Brilliant. But are you sure you wouldn't like her to be involved in choosing the prints?'

He shook his head. 'No. I want it to be a surprise and I know she'll love anything you pick.'

I looked at him doubtfully, but he was clearly set on the plan, and I had to admit that it was a big step up from the Dyson debacle. 'OK, but if she's not sure about them, just bring them back and we'll swap or refund.'

'Thanks, Esme,' he said, 'you're a pal. I'd like three, please: framed. About so big,' he said, indicating a size with his hands. 'Up to sixty quid a pop; modern but nothing, you know, too weird.' He pointed up at the abstract. 'For example, that's not for us. Looks like he's spilled his poster paints a bit there.'

'Yes, and what's with that squiggle, upper left?' I murmured, making a note of his preferences on my phone. 'OK, so,' I continued more loudly, 'I'll have a think about this overnight. I might have a couple of other questions, but then I'll come back to you with a few prints for you to look through whenever you get a moment.'

'Oh, no need for that,' he said magnanimously. 'I trust you entirely.'

'Well, if you're sure. Can I keep these?' I asked, picking up the swatches and the piece of card.

'Of course,' he beamed and then checked his watch. 'And now I'll get out of your hair. It's almost six.'

'Not a problem,' I smiled. 'It's always lovely to see you. I was thinking the other day, actually, that I haven't seen Gwen for ages. I've been really bad at getting together with people since I moved out of town.'

'Well, you'll be back soon. I bet you're looking forward to moving back into your flat.'

'I so am. The cottage is great but...' I hesitated for a moment. 'But it's not home.'

'Of course.'

'I tell you what, the next showing we have here, you and Gwen must definitely come. She really enjoyed the Sharon Marshall one, didn't she?'

'She did,' he said, making a move towards the door. 'She loves a bit of culture, does my Gwen, and I love free booze.' He laughed at the thought and then left, heading back towards his shop and executing his second body swerve of the half-hour, this time in order to avoid Elliot coming the other way.

There was a polite exchange of apologies, followed by Lloyd glancing over his shoulder, just in time to make intrigued eye contact with me as I stood in the gallery doorway, no doubt wearing a shell-shocked expression to go with the mixed sense of anticipation and horror, which was becoming quite the norm whenever Elliot appeared unexpectedly – an occurrence which was definitely on the up.

Including the possible face-at-the-upper-window sighting, this was the sixth occasion I'd seen him in the three weeks that had passed since Jasmine's show, the others all being chance brief encounters outside the cottages. On each occasion, we had managed a civil 'hello', but nothing more.

I stepped back, holding the door open for him, as he approached and entered.

'Hi,' I said, immediately turning away, walking to the other side of the counter and taking a business card from the holder, 'and have one of these. It's got my mobile number, the gallery email address and our website on it. It'll save you coming here, out of your way, if you have something to say and, to be honest, I'd much prefer it too.'

I held out the card and looked up at him. His head was tilted downwards towards my outstretched hand but, even at that angle, I could tell that he wasn't looking great. His shoulders were sagging, as if hung with weights, and grey circles underlined his eyes.

'OK.' He took the card from me, staring down at it. 'I just came in to pay for the hedgehog and to ask if you had anything else by Dougal Minehead.'

'You see,' I said brightly, 'in future, you can do that kind of thing online – and his name is Douglas Muirhead, by the way.'

He looked up. 'If you have anything else by hedgehog guy that'd be great. I want to get Morgan a couple more, or maybe even three, for her birthday,' he said, unsmilingly, 'otherwise there's not much of a surprise. But if you want me to leave, I'm happy to come back when Damien is here.'

'It's David. And are you deliberately misnaming everyone?'

He nodded slowly. 'I am, actually.'

I smiled in spite of myself and as he smiled back at me, in obvious relief, I again wondered what had stopped me making that call all those years ago. Maybe if I had, we'd now be smiling at each other across a breakfast bar, or sitting side-by-side on a sofa in our shared home, rather than engaging in tense conversation across a glass-topped counter.

'We've sold Douglas's mole, but his squirrel is still up for grabs and he dropped off a badger at the weekend,' I said, pointing to a display stand behind him. 'That's a much larger piece.'

'I love them,' he said, without turning around. 'Add them to the bill.' He took out his wallet and handed me a debit card.

I took the card and inserted it into the reader, entering a total and then passing the machine to him. 'Thank you,' I said.

'Have you got time for a drink?' he asked, eyes still lowered as he entered his pin. 'There's something I'd like to explain.' He looked up and returned the card reader to me. 'If you'll let me.'

I tore the two receipts from the reader and handed one to him. 'I just don't want to feel any worse than I do right now.'

'Well, I know it's not a competition, but I don't think I could,' he said quietly.

I thought for a moment and then nodded miserably. I felt the same: a nadir had been reached.

'OK, I'll come,' I said resignedly, because, after all, what did I have to lose?

Chapter 13

Neither Elliot nor I wanted to return to The Cambridge so, at his suggestion, we instead agreed to meet at seven at the small, white-rendered pub, a stone's throw from our cottages. The extremely local choice surprised me at first, until he explained that Morgan had gone to Wales for a long weekend with friends. Neither of us suggested a drink at home – both, I assumed, balking at the idea of meeting anywhere other than completely neutral territory.

I arrived early, driving straight to the pub from the gallery and resisting a significant urge to go home first, reapply my make-up and change my clothes. I had told myself there was neither a need for, nor indeed a point to, that. My relationship with Elliot was water so far under the bridge as to be out to sea, and my sense of self-worth was no longer impacted by his opinion of me emotionally, professionally or physically. I didn't care what he thought and I had nothing to prove to him.

But despite this stern lecture to self, I was quietly grateful that I hadn't chosen to cycle to work that day and therefore wasn't quite the level of sweaty mess I might otherwise have been. Because I wasn't actually one hundred per cent sure that, in those circumstances, I wouldn't have nipped home for a quick shower and freshen up.

For his part, Elliot was fifteen minutes late, mouthing apologies when he spotted me from the doorway of the quiet bar, and then hurrying to get himself a beer.

'I hung around at the cottages for you,' he said, when he finally joined me and sat down at our small corner table. 'I assumed you'd drop the car back. I guess I should have texted,' he added, 'now that I finally have your number.'

He made it sound like a goal achieved and I realised that that felt worryingly good.

'It's fine,' I said, relaxing a little and feeling grateful for the head start with my glass of wine. I had decided on the drive from Westbury Park that a lime and soda just wouldn't cut it on this occasion.

'So...' He took a sip of beer and then placed the bottle on the table between us. 'Shall we just skip the "how are you/how is life" stuff this evening?'

'Gets my vote. Ideally, I'd like to go straight to the part where you tell me that Morgan knows that we were in a relationship and doesn't have a problem with it. Or, failing that, your moving date.'

'Sadly, I can't tell you either of those things.'

I sighed, but knew that I was now beyond being angry. I was simply too emotionally exhausted by the situation for that.

'OK, well, how about you just tell me whatever it is you want to tell me, and then I'll decide whether *I* need to fix a moving date.'

'Of course you don't.'

'I said *I'll* decide whether I need to fix a moving date. But anyway,' I picked up my glass and leaned back in my chair, 'the floor is yours.'

He shifted slightly in his chair, took a deep breath and then addressed the table. 'I want you to know that I'm doing my very best not to hurt anyone – neither you nor Morgan. I know that's probably impossible, but just know that the mistakes I've made, and the things I've handled badly, had that at their root. I have been trying to navigate a difficult situation with as little upset caused to the people I...' He paused and looked up at me. 'I'm trying not to hurt anyone.'

I did, I realised, believe him. 'OK.'

He cleared his throat and returned his attention to the table. 'When I first saw you at the cottage, I was shocked, obviously.

But more than that, I realised – and this is what made everything which followed more complicated than it should have been – I realised immediately that I had been wanting to see you for a long time. A very long time.'

His voice caught and he took another sip of beer, as his words sank in like little drops of calm. He had missed me. Never once, in over four years of intermittently gazing at his crumpled, sketched image – usually when I was at my most sentimental, maudlin or pissed – had it occurred to me that that might be the case.

I raised my glass to my lips in an attempt to hide both my face and my feelings, as my initial sense of calm was, without warning, washed away by a tidal wave of something worryingly akin to regret over what might have been.

Elliot, meanwhile, was still talking. 'I didn't want to acknowledge how I felt and, because of that, I didn't want to acknowledge you to Morgan – not in that moment. Even so, I might have gone inside and talked to her about it all, if she hadn't immediately said how attractive you were and asked whether she should be worried that we were living next door to a bohemian artist. I can't remember exactly what she said, and she laughed as she said it, but she...' He looked up and when he spoke again, his tone was more controlled. 'I knew that there was part of her that meant it. She's not a confident person. She's insecure in a way that I didn't fully appreciate when we first met and I don't want dismissiveness or insensitivity on my part to ruin a relationship that is so important to me. Not again.'

Now I met and held his gaze. But unsure what to say in response to what seemed like a declaration of both past and present affection, I kept quiet.

'So, I kept quiet,' he said. 'I didn't tell her that I knew you and that we had been in a relationship. Instead, I moved the conversation on and I haven't moved it back. If it was ever a conversation I could have had with her, it's not one that I can have now. Not without risk. She would wonder why I hadn't told her right away and assume that I had something to hide. And then I'd lose her, Es.'

There was an unmistakable desperation in his tone and he paused to take a steadying breath before continuing.

'So, the alternative is just to get through the next month or so. I know this isn't your problem and that it's particularly difficult for you because she really likes you. I also know you well enough to realise how uncomfortable that must be making you feel. But it's just the odd conversation with her over the garden wall and maybe a drink with her another time, and that's it. I'll do my best to stay out of your way and, before you know it, we'll be gone. We're here only because Morgan didn't like the idea of living in London. I said OK to Bristol, on the condition that I could make the commute to London work. Obviously, I can't,' he added quietly, 'and I've already told her that.'

I felt my body, along with my spirits, droop. Suddenly, even blinking felt like an effort. I had gone to the pub that evening believing that it would be absolutely impossible for me to emerge feeling any worse than I did already, but I had been wrong. I had gone from being tortured by the close proximity of an ex, from whom I increasingly believed I had never moved on, to being tortured by the close proximity of an ex who, it was now just possible, had never quite moved on from me either, but – and here was the tragic rub – who was now asking me to help him to preserve his current relationship.

I honestly didn't know whether to laugh – manically, obviously – or cry.

So instead, I shook my head and managed a sad smile. It seemed like a good compromise.

'It's fine,' I said quietly. 'I'm not going to say anything to upset Morgan or spoil your relationship. She seems very nice and you're right, it'll soon be over.'

'I'm sorry, Es.'

I stared into my glass of wine. 'Me too.' I wasn't quite sure what he had been apologising for, but it felt good to reciprocate.

Neither of us spoke for quite some time after that, and it was only when Elliot stood up to get a second round of drinks that I realised he had been holding my hand across the table.

Chapter 14

As I cycled to work the morning after my second pub meeting with Elliot, it occurred to me that the two hours spent in his company had changed precisely nothing. He still lived next door, our past relationship was still publicly unacknowledged and Morgan was still blissfully in the dark.

Not that I could blame him entirely for the miserable status quo. After all, I had willingly signed up to it, on the basis that I couldn't think of an alternative which wouldn't jeopardise his relationship with Morgan, or make our currently uncomfortable situation even more so.

So as I wheeled my bicycle wearily through the gallery courtyard and into the workshop, it seemed to me that things were destined to trot on as awkwardly and unsatisfactorily as they had to date, until one of us – either Elliot or myself – moved out.

I had just taken off my backpack and was about to unbuckle my helmet when my phone pinged twice. Continuing the unbuckling process with one hand, I reached into my jacket pocket with the other and took out my phone to discover Elliot's name on-screen for the first time in over four years. The event was significant enough for me to still be staring at my phone and clutching the chinstrap of my bicycle helmet when David entered from the gallery a few moments later.

Aware that he was speaking to me, I slipped my phone into a pocket and pulled myself together.

'Hi,' I said, taking off my helmet and placing it on the workbench.

He didn't reply and when I looked up, he raised his eyebrows questioningly. 'So, where are they?' he asked.

I shook my head. 'Sorry, where's what? I didn't hear the original question.'

'Douglas's sculptures. You've moved them, and there's a voicemail message from a customer who saw the badger yesterday and wants it.'

'Oh, right. They sold. If you give me the customer's number, I'll call them back,' I said briskly, hoping that the conversation was at an end and that he would now leave, so that I could read Elliot's message.

'Who bought them? They were here when I left just after five. It wasn't that woman who was giving you the art lecture, surely?' He smiled affably and at any other time I would have taken the opportunity to vent about her, but today I just wanted to be alone.

'No, not her,' I said hurriedly, picking up my helmet and backpack, and walking past him into the hallway. I hung up my things on the pegs next to the kitchen door and headed into the gallery. It was only as I reached the counter and went to take out my phone that I realised David was following.

'Douglas's pieces are selling well, aren't they?' he said. 'The woman who came in yesterday lunchtime had specifically come to see his work and it's not the first time that's happened. It's something to think about.'

'It certainly is.' I crouched down, pretending to look for something beneath the counter, but actually responding to a sudden urge to be out of sight and take a few deep breaths.

'Everything all right down there?'

I sighed and stood up. 'Yes, yes,' I said brightly. 'Everything's fine.'

'Just checking, because I was fully expecting at least a five-minute rant from you this morning about your final customer of yesterday.'

'Oh, you know me. Water off a duck's back.'

He raised a single eyebrow and there followed a moment's silence before he said, 'Coffee?'

'God, yes please,' I said, smiling with relief, my hand returning to my pocket, as he walked away. 'That'd be great.'

'Oh, and…' He stopped, turning back towards me.

'Yes?' I was aware of my tone being rather more high-pitched than usual, as I gripped the edge of the counter and stared at him, in an attempt to prevent my eyes from rolling back in my head.

'I saw Jazz yesterday evening.'

'Did you?'

'She told me that you'd sent flowers and a card.'

I nodded rapidly. 'Yes, yes, I did do that. A few weeks ago.'

'She was very appreciative of the apology and the trouble you'd gone to.'

I shrugged but said nothing, not remotely interested in anything to do with Jasmine or in anything at all, for that matter, except the text message – still unread – on my phone.

'Great.' David turned and, at long last, left the gallery.

I exhaled and took out my phone, staring again at the notification, fearful of, but also excited by, the feelings which the small grey square with white lettering had elicited. Then, aware that David could return at any moment with my coffee, I unlocked the screen and read the message.

> Heading to London for the weekend, but wanted to say thanks again for listening last night and for understanding. I wish things were different, but our lease is up soon. Feel free to count the days.
>
> x

'Coffee,' said David, placing the mug down on the counter and making me jump.

'Thanks.' I returned my phone to my pocket.

'So, who bought the sculptures?'

I looked up sharply, paranoia making me wonder if the question was a loaded one. Did he somehow know that I had spent the previous evening alone with my neighbour, in a pub, hinting at our unsatisfactory past and openly discussing our rather sticky present?

But his expression was one of simple interest, with no hint of suspicion or accusation.

'My neighbour,' I said.

'Ah yes, Morgan's quite a fan, isn't she?'

I hesitated for only a moment. 'Yes, she is.'

He nodded and then headed back towards the workshop.

I watched him go and, as he disappeared out of sight, I leaned heavily against the counter, thinking again about Elliot's text, its expression of regret and the dawning realisation that his departure wasn't, in fact, something that I was now entirely looking forward to.

And I knew then that I had been wrong about last night; it had changed everything.

–

It was a long day, during which absolutely everything – from David's implacability to a visit from Lloyd, during which he lamented the waning popularity of the faggot – had irritated me beyond all belief and reasonableness.

Not wishing to let loose my irascibility beyond the bounds of the gallery, I opted out of Friday night drinks with Cass, citing a headache, and instead headed home on my bike, channelling all my frustration into forcing the pedals round with an aggressive determination which would have made Victoria Pendleton look like an unmotivated slacker.

As a consequence – and thanks also to having expended what little energy I had left in hurling colourful abuse at a careless four-by-four driver – exhaustion was definitely winning over emotional distress by the time I dismounted outside the cottage.

All I wanted was to go inside, have a glass of wine, shove something in the microwave and go to bed – all without thinking about Elliot. It was a tactic of distraction and denial which, deep down, I knew I wouldn't be able to maintain throughout the weekend, let alone for an indeterminate number of weeks. But this, I told myself, was a situation which could be managed only in bite-size chunks, and dealing with the Friday evening chunk was enough for me, for now.

The fact that there were multiple lights on in the cottage next door registered with me only as I returned to the front garden after putting my bike away. On noticing them, my heart sank. I had been counting on at least forty-eight hours free from timing my entrances and exits to avoid Morgan. But clearly, for whatever reason, she'd decided to abandon her long weekend away.

My shoulders drooping, I was just wondering whether I should call Cass and ask if I could come and stay for the weekend, when I heard Morgan's front door open and then slam shut. Definitely not in the mood for conversation, I pressed my back flat against the wall of the cottage, before crouching low and shuffling crab-like the short distance to the porch. There I remained, hiding behind its half-height walls, while searching various jacket pockets for my keys and listening for any sounds of movement next door.

Hearing none, I switched to all fours and leaned cautiously forward, peering out from the edge of the porch, first towards next-door's garden and then into the lane. Finding the coast clear, I stood up quickly and began a fumbled, slightly panicked attempt to insert my key into the lock.

'Need a hand?'

Letting out a shriek and dropping the keys, I turned to see Elliot standing alongside the porch, smiling broadly.

'Oh, for God's sake!' I put a hand to my chest. 'What do you think you're doing, creeping around like that? You terrified me.'

He frowned, as if confused. 'You're accusing *me* of creeping around, when you're commando-crawling across a garden, as if you're in a suburban edition of *SAS: Who Dares Wins*?'

'I was looking for something,' I snapped, bending down and snatching up my keys. 'And besides, you're not even supposed to be here. Neither of you are,' I added in a whisper, as it dawned on me that the conversation wasn't one either of us would want Morgan to overhear.

He shook his head. 'It's just me. Morgan is still away. I cancelled tomorrow, because…' He paused and then shrugged. 'Well, I just did. But maybe I should have updated you.'

I removed my helmet and shook out my hair. 'You don't have to update me about anything. Just don't skulk around, scaring me. How on earth did you get from there,' I pointed to his porch, 'to here, without making a sound?'

'I saw you hiding – incompetently – and climbed over the wall. I thought it would be funny to surprise you. But clearly, I misread the room. My apologies,' he added, with a bow.

'Yes, well, maybe I'd be able to see the funny side if I wasn't so totally knackered,' I muttered, turning to put my key in the lock, 'and hadn't just been nearly run off the road by some stupid woman, the height and colour of an Oompa Loompa, who could barely see over the steering wheel of her white four-by-four.'

'I'm sensing annoyance.'

'An off-road vehicle, designed to show the dirt!'

'It does seem something of a contradiction.'

'Whose genius idea was that and how utterly, utterly vacuous do you have to be to buy one?'

'So a drink is out of the question then?'

Struck silent, I remained facing the door, my hand on the key, while the question sank in. After a moment or two, leaving the key in the lock, I turned to face him.

'What do you think?' he asked, his expression now serious.

'I think that spending time in your company makes me feel worse, Elliot. I keep thinking that's an impossibility, and then discovering that it's not.'

He nodded slowly. 'Good to know.'

'I'm sorry.'

He placed his hands in his pockets and shook his head. 'No, no, it's perfectly understandable. I move in next door, reminding you of a relationship you'd left behind and would rather forget. And then, to make matters worse, I burden you with my current relationship issues and ask you to be complicit in deceiving my partner. To be honest, if I could avoid spending a Friday night with me right now, I would too.'

'Would it sound too clichéd to say it's not you, it's me?'

'I'm afraid it would.'

'OK, I won't say that then.'

He smiled and jerked a thumb over his shoulder. 'Well, I'm going to go next door and cry now. You have a good evening and, you know, if you find yourself in need of being brought low tomorrow, I'm here all weekend.'

'I'll bear that in mind.'

'And if you did decide to drop by,' he continued, walking towards the gate and addressing me over his shoulder, 'there need be no excavation of the past, no over-analysis of the present. We could just be two neighbours who'd rather have a glass of wine together than alone, discussing their days, their commutes, the state of the nation and their favourite restaurants and, who knows, maybe finding common ground and friend-ship.' He raised a hand as he opened the gate and stepped out into the lane. 'Again.'

I watched him go, waving in return, while wrestling with my feelings and teetering on the brink of calling him back. Then I looked away, turned the key in the lock and went inside.

Chapter 15

It didn't take long the next morning for me to realise that if I wanted to think about anything other than Elliot that weekend, I had to busy my mind and my body and, most importantly of all, get out of the house. So after a late-ish breakfast, during which I twitched at the sound of every stair-creak and door-slam from next door, I phoned Cass, asked whether she was free that evening, and whether it would be OK for me to come round and stay over.

She had agreed immediately, without requesting any further information, and had given me the option of arriving early afternoon. I thanked her but explained that I was going for a swim and then shopping, and would be round about seven thirty, if that was OK, adding that a takeout was on me. She battled over the latter and, in the end, it was agreed that I'd bring booze and a dessert, and that Kevin would sort the rest.

I'd put down the phone, relieved that I now had a Saturday evening and Sunday morning plan in place. I also determined to start pulling my finger out and booking in friends for dinner and going out more, so that I wouldn't have to exist in a state of tension every weekend for the foreseeable future.

Post-breakfast, the day went surprisingly well. I heard Elliot drive off at around eleven, which meant that I was able to leave for my swim at midday without any furtive checking of the front garden. I then enjoyed a late lunch out, following which I shopped till I dropped, treating myself to a floral blouse, a cream linen dress and a pair of suede wedges, which I'd wanted forever, but could never quite come up with a reason for buying.

Fortunately, a helpful sales assistant had agreed that huge pores, plus an ex moving in next door with his new size 6 girlfriend, were easily enough justification for making the purchase – and for buying the protective spray too.

All in all, the day could have been a lot worse, and as I arrived back at the cottage at six fifteen and started smushing meringues, raspberry liqueur, fresh cream and red berries into a two-minute Eton mess, while staring dreamily at my shopping bags on the kitchen table, I was actually feeling pretty good.

Three-quarters of an hour later and I was just struggling to close the front door, and trying to stop my overnight bag – from which two bottles of wine and a large, red Tupperware box were protruding – from slipping off my shoulder, when my phone rang. Unable to answer it, I pulled the door shut and teetered down the gravel pathway to my car, placing my bag in the passenger footwell and then climbing in the driver's side.

I had adjusted my new blouse and was buckling myself in, when I remembered the missed call and decided to check my phone. Leaning an elbow on the passenger seat, I began to excavate the contents of my bag, finally locating the phone under my pyjamas, but not before it had begun to ring again. I saw Cass's name on-screen and took the call.

'Hi, Cass. How are you?'

'No change. I just wanted to tell you where I'd left the key.'

'The key for…?'

'For the house.'

'Whose house?' I frowned into the phone.

'You haven't played my message?'

'I haven't had a chance. Is everything OK?'

'Yes. I'm in A & E and—'

'A & E?! What's happened?'

'Don't panic, I'm absolutely fine. Feeling really good actually. I went for a massage this morning. One of my customers recommended this woman in Filton who—'

'Tell me about the massage later. First tell me why you're in A & E.'

'Oh, OK,' she said, sounding a little put out by the interruption, 'but it's really no big deal. Kev's just had a cooking mishap. Nothing serious.'

I heaved a sigh and closed my eyes. Kevin had a poor reputation in the kitchen, having scalded, sliced and even grated himself on numerous occasions in his attempts to prove himself the culinary equal of Cass's only other serious boyfriend, Geoff the chef. But this was the first time his efforts had landed him in hospital.

'I thought, when you said he was going to sort dinner, that he was buying the takeaway,' I said. 'I didn't realise he was going to have another go at haute cuisine.'

'I know, I know.' She sounded suddenly exhausted. 'But he'd bought himself a new chef's hat and wanted some pictures for Insta. Those éclairs Geoff sent round for my birthday last year still play on his mind. I should have binned them really, but they were amazing, weren't they? Do you remember the strawberry ones, Es?'

I suppressed a second sigh. 'Yes, I do, and they were very delicious but, more importantly, how is Kevin? What's he done this time?'

'Grater again,' she said, in a tone now hovering between exasperated and bored.

'How on earth did he end up in hospital? Did he just keep grating?'

She laughed loudly. 'Can you imagine that? Ha, ha, ha, ha! Him grating away until his fingers were nothing but—'

'Er, yes, I can imagine it actually,' I said, cutting in, 'and it's making me feel sick. Are his fingers very badly grated?' I asked with a shudder.

'Nah. He did a thumb and two fingers, and then stuck loads of the blue kitchen plasters he'd bought for the photographs on them. Then he wrapped cling film around them, because he said that's what they do on *MasterChef*. But I said, "No, Kev, on *MasterChef* they use special condoms." Anyway, he wouldn't put condoms on his fingers and then he couldn't bend them because of all the cling film, and he lost his grip on the casserole dish – the massive cast-iron one I never use because it's too heavy. Long story short: suspected broken foot.'

I winced. 'So they're not positive it's broken,' I said, with very little optimism.

'They say we have to wait for the X-ray but, put it this way, remember the guy on *Britain's Got Talent* who broke the world speed record for making balloon animals?'

'Yes.'

'Well, Kev's foot looks like the poodle.'

'That doesn't sound great.'

'No. But you know the real tragedy of it all, Es?'

'Kevin's inability to walk?'

'No, the real tragedy is that when I stuck a finger in what was left of his beef bourguignon, it actually tasted really nice. Best thing he's ever made by a long way.' She heaved a despondent sigh, before continuing more briskly, 'But, anyway, the key is under the green recycling bin. You order in some food and we'll pick up the tab.'

I took a moment to compute the suggestion. 'Cass, I'm not going round to your house to eat dinner while you and Kevin are in A & E.'

'Why not?' She sounded genuinely confused.

'Because you and Kevin are in A & E.'

'So? I'll see you later tonight – or in the morning.'

'It's a really lovely offer,' I said, touched by her kindness, 'but you know what A & E is like. You two will want to do nothing but slob and sleep tomorrow. We can sort out another evening for dinner.'

'Are you sure? I feel like we've really screwed up your Saturday night.'

I laughed. 'How can you be feeling bad for me when I'm in my cosy cottage and you're stuck in A & E? I'm absolutely fine here and looking forward to a rain check – and to seeing Kevin's poodle-foot, of course. Is it really that bad?'

'Honestly, Es, it's so big and round. I could draw a face on it and call it Wilson.'

'Well, give him my love.'

'I will and Es…' she began, before hesitating for a moment. 'If you change your mind, you know, about coming round, the key's—'

'Under the green recycling bin. Yes, I know. And thank you,' I added, 'for being such a good friend.'

'Look, I've got to go,' she said, suddenly sounding breathless. 'They've started wheeling him somewhere and I've gotta catch up. But I'll text you when we're home and, if you fancy it, come over then.'

She hung up and I slowly lowered the phone to my lap, staring at it for a moment before transferring my gaze to the bulging overnight bag in the footwell and wondering what to do next. Despite my protestations to Cass, I was very reluctant to return to the solitude of the cottage, a solitude thrown into greater relief by an awareness of readily available company next door.

It was several minutes before I resignedly hauled both the bag and myself out of the car and walked slowly to the garden gate. There then followed only one brief further moment of hesitation before I opened the gate and made my way up the path towards the front door.

It opened before I'd even made it into the porch, causing me to come to an abrupt halt.

'Car trouble?' Elliot offered me an easy smile and leaned nonchalantly against the doorframe, his arms folded. He was wearing a pale-grey shirt and jeans, the latter spattered with mud at the hem. His blond hair looked like it hadn't seen a comb all day and a light shadow of stubble covered his chin. The overall effect was undeniably, depressingly attractive.

I frowned, but didn't reply.

'Guilty,' he said, holding up a hand, 'of being a nosey neighbour. But in my defence, I live in a village where the only person with whom I am on speaking terms is my next-door neighbour. There's nothing on telly, I don't fancy reading a book and I've already walked twelve miles today. So watching my sole local acquaintance sitting in a stationary vehicle for ten minutes actually passes for entertainment. I've come up with several explanations for your intriguing behaviour, including a flat battery and first-date nerves.' He smiled mischievously.

'I was supposed to be spending the evening with friends, but I've just found out that one of my hosts is in A & E.'

His face fell and he stood upright, his hands dropping to his sides. 'God, I'm sorry, Es. Are they OK?'

'He's fine. Just a suspected broken foot.'

'So maybe not completely fine, then?'

'I guess not,' I admitted. 'He also grated his hand pretty badly, but he does that a lot so...' I concluded the sentence with a shrug.

Elliot nodded. 'Doesn't count.'

'Anyway...' I paused for a deep breath, looking down at the bag hanging from my shoulder. 'I have wine and I have dessert and I...' I looked up. 'I wondered whether you'd like to share them with me.'

His eyebrows rose slightly and he appeared to consider the offer. 'From what you've said, it seems that I'm very much your Plan B – your second choice – for tonight. Am I right?'

My gaze lowered to his muddy hems. 'You are right,' I said quietly, aware now of the blunt insensitivity with which I had put my proposal. I wondered how I'd feel if our roles were reversed and decided that I'd probably be closing the door in Elliot's face right about now. 'I'm sorry, I didn't mean to make you feel—'

'No, no,' he said, interrupting and grinning broadly as I looked up. 'I'm hugely flattered. I honestly thought I'd be *way* further down the list than that. Do come in.'

He flourished a hand and, as he stepped backwards, I walked the short remaining distance to the front door and stepped inside.

Chapter 16

I hung the tea towel on a hook next to the oven gloves and retrieved my glass of wine from the fashionably gnarled kitchen table. Then, making my way to the living room, I lowered myself onto the grey-checked sofa, which was identical to my own next door.

In fact, every item of furniture, and every fixture and fitting – not only in Elliot's lounge, but also in his kitchen – was identical to those in my own temporary residence. It was a familiarity which definitely helped to lessen the awkwardness and uncertainty of our first evening together in four and a half years.

Sitting at the same faux-aged table, looking at the same range, fridge and cupboards had created a comforting, albeit false, sense of this not being my first evening in Elliot's current home. The company was, of course, also far from unfamiliar, and after a slightly shy and stumbling start, during which Elliot had asked me if I ate meat and I had noted with mild surprise that he required glasses to follow a recipe, we had quickly fallen into the practical roles of head and sous chefs that we had taken it in turns to fulfil when we were a couple.

By the time we had finished the Eton mess, the only indicator that our relationship was rather more distant than it had once been was the conversation – which flowed without a break. In the past, we would have been comfortable with silences: but not anymore. Now the chat was constant, as well as determinedly light and in-the-moment, stemming almost entirely from what we had each been up to that day, including exercising, shopping, cooking, reading and work – with neither of us apparently having any appetite for delving into the past, enquiring after old friends or sharing future plans.

All in all, the evening had been surprisingly relaxed and uncontroversial, and as Elliot joined me in the living room, wine glass in hand, and sat down in the beige calico armchair next to the sofa – a twin of the one next door – he, too, appeared completely at ease.

I glanced around the room. 'Everything is absolutely identical, you know. The tables, the blinds, the curtains, the cushions... They clearly couldn't be bothered to come up with more than one scheme.'

'I guess they were thinking short-term corporate lets and weekend breaks,' said Elliot. 'They probably didn't anticipate the neighbours popping round for dinner.'

'Guess not,' I murmured, now scanning the walls, 'but even the artwork is the same, which is a bit of a shame.'

'So why don't you hang some of your own?'

I turned to find him smiling mischievously. 'Or do you sell it all?' he asked.

'I paint solely for pleasure these days. I have no need to sell my soul.'

He shuddered, as if disgusted. 'God, the very idea of tainting art with monetary gain.'

'That's not fair,' I laughed. 'Obviously, I don't think that selling art devalues it or I wouldn't be running a gallery. It's just that, in my case, the pieces I'm most proud of happen to be the most personal, and the idea of having to show, or explain...' I frowned, a couple of glasses of wine making me more willing to talk, but much less articulate. 'Never mind. I know it's stupid,' I said, addressing my concluding remark to the fireplace.

'It's not remotely stupid. It's perfectly legitimate and it's how you've always felt.'

He spoke quietly and I turned to find him staring into his glass of wine. His comment was the first spoken acknow-ledgement that evening that we shared a past. Up until that moment, a written transcript of our conversation would have suggested that we were nothing more than recently acquainted neighbours, eager for company and happy to discuss the trivia of our days, but with no interest in going beyond that.

But Elliot's reference to my feelings, past and present, had ended the charade – and we both knew it.

'Sorry,' he said, looking up. 'I didn't—'

'It's fine,' I interrupted, before he could say anything more. 'Hey, and look,' I continued a little breathlessly, gesturing upwards with my glass to the heavy wooden mantelpiece above the stone fireplace, 'at least those are unique to your place. I don't have any of Douglas's pieces next door.' I managed a smile and stared at the badger, hedgehog and squirrel as if transfixed, reluctant to look again at Elliot.

'No.' The word was emitted as a sigh. 'They're not to my taste either, but Morgan loves them. She found them in the bottom of my wardrobe and didn't want to wait until her birthday to put them on display. I wouldn't be surprised if she orders some more from you.'

I nodded rapidly and cleared my throat. 'Fabulous,' I said, the mention of Morgan only making me feel worse. I looked away from the sculptures and over my shoulder, in an attempt to hide my rising discomfort from Elliot and on the pretext of scouring the room for further objects of interest. But all I actually managed to do was spot several further reminders of Morgan which, until that moment, I'd either missed or determinedly ignored.

Through an effort of will, I kept my smile in place as my eyes drifted from a photograph on the bookcase – showing her fit, fresh and smiling on a beach – to a discarded cream silk scarf and several silver bangles lying next to it. I turned again and my attention was caught by a fitness magazine on the coffee table in front of me. A Post-it note curled upwards from its cover, with an instruction to *Check out page 37* scrawled in a hand other than Elliot's. And as I inhaled deeply, in an attempt to regain my recently departed sense of calm, I realised that I could smell her perfume. The woman was everywhere – even in the air.

Coming here had been a mistake. I saw that now. It had been fine, fun even, while the conversation had remained firmly rooted in the now. I had very much enjoyed the first part of my evening with the charming and handsome man, and the accompanying frisson of an attraction barely acknowledged. The two of us – emotionally isolated from the past and socially isolated in the present – worked fine. But that small, acutely painful, reference to the past – to *our* past – coupled with a myriad of reminders that Elliot was now someone else's partner, represented a cold, hard reality that I just couldn't bear. I didn't want to be reminded of what Elliot had been to me and neither did I want to think about what he now was to someone else. It was too much.

'I'd better be getting back,' I said lightly, leaning forward and placing my glass on the coffee table.

His head jerked towards me and he blinked, as if waking from sleep. 'Why? No, don't go,' he said quickly.

I smiled and rose to my feet. 'I've got to. I'm really pooped after my swim and my mega-shop.'

'Look, Es,' he said, standing up, 'we both know that you're not leaving because you're tired. Let's at least be honest about that.'

I stopped smiling and we stood together, unmoving, in the first extended silence of the evening.

He spoke first. 'I'd like you to stay, not so that we can rake over the past. I'd like you to stay because I enjoy your company and because I know that the chances of me being able to enjoy your company – like this – ever again are slim. So don't go, not just yet, and especially not like this.'

I shook my head. 'I'm sorry, Elliot, but this is your home, and more to the point, it's Morgan's home.' I took a breath, as my voice threatened to catch. 'I forgot that for a couple of hours, but suddenly this doesn't… It doesn't feel neutral to me and, more importantly, it doesn't feel right. So,' I turned and picked up my bag from the end of the sofa, 'I'm going to go.'

Hitching the bag up onto my shoulder, I walked past him to the front door.

'Hang on,' he said, reaching out and gently catching hold of my arm. 'You're absolutely right. We shouldn't be here. But if something as simple as changing our location means that I get to spend another couple of hours talking to you about – oh, I don't know...' He ran a hand through his hair. 'Maybe what it's like for me sitting in an office every day, crunching numbers, looking for cash cows and destroying livelihoods at a distance.'

'That sounds incredibly familiar.'

'I know. I noted down your comment for ease of reference, whenever my self-esteem levels are getting just that bit too high.'

'Elliot, I—'

'Or we could stick to village gossip. I mean, who are all those angry pensioners who walk down the lane en masse every Sunday lunchtime? Are they some sort of geriatric protest group?'

'They're leaving church.'

'See? That's just the kind of local knowledge you can share.' He paused. 'While we sit...' he nodded towards the window, 'in the neutral pub at the end of the neutral road. Neutral like Switzerland,' he added softly. 'Where's the harm in that, Es?'

I sighed. Maybe he was right. The prospect of a bit more idle conversation in a pub did seem pretty harmless, and besides, I was as keen as he was that what had been a predominantly positive evening shouldn't end on a negative note.

'OK,' I said. 'I'll come to the pub. But just for an hour, because I am genuinely knackered. Swimming really takes it out of you.'

'As does walking in thick mud,' he said, picking up his keys from a window ledge, as we reached the front door. 'By the time I got home this afternoon, my calf muscles—'

He was interrupted by the buzzing of his phone, and appeared frustrated as he took it from his back pocket and looked at the screen. 'Sorry, it's my new graduate assistant, Joshua,' he said, texting a reply. 'Great guy. Just a bit too keen. He's working when he should be relaxing. There. Done.' He placed the phone face down on the window ledge and opened the front door.

'You're not taking it with you?' I asked, stepping outside.

'I'm not,' he said firmly, following and pulling the door shut behind us. 'Josh and I could do with some space. It'll do us both good.'

Chapter 17

I was already running late for work on Monday morning, when the sound of Morgan slamming shut her front door, just as I was about to leave home, triggered a further delay.

I had watched Elliot head off about ten minutes earlier, from behind my bedroom curtains, and as I now stood in the living room and gingerly peeked out, I saw Morgan hovering, somewhat distractedly, in her front garden. She wasn't someone I was desperate to run into at the best of times, but after a Saturday night spent with Elliot, during which we had very much enjoyed each other's company – albeit entirely innocently – I felt an increased reluctance to see her.

That being the case, I returned to the kitchen where I remained for exactly three minutes, before once again returning to peer from the living room. Annoyingly, Morgan was still on her pathway, at first frowning up at her cottage and then suddenly transferring her attention to mine. I quickly darted down below window height to avoid being seen, but after a few moments of feeling increasingly stupid, I took a deep breath, stood tall and braced myself for an encounter.

To my enormous relief, by the time I had put on my jacket, picked up my bags and exited, she had gone. On the downside, I was now running very late indeed.

'Sorry, David,' I called, crashing through the gallery door and dumping my bags and coat on the floor behind the counter. 'I was waylaid.'

'No problem,' he said calmly, entering from the back rooms and placing three framed prints on the counter in front of me.

'These are the pictures for Lloyd. I've texted him to say they're ready.'

'Oh wow!' I picked up one of the oak-framed prints, each of which David had mounted in a pale grey-green. 'They look great, don't they? I just hope Gwen likes them,' I added a little anxiously. 'I'd really love Lloyd to stay in her good books for a while.'

'I'm sure she'll love them. Good weekend?'

'Yes, thanks,' I said absently, examining each print in turn.

'Your neighbour dropped by earlier.'

I looked up sharply. 'Morgan was here?' I asked, filled with sudden paranoia.

He shook his head. 'Elliot.'

After a flurry of blinks, I attempted nonchalance. 'Didn't he realise that we don't open till nine?'

'He came to return your storage container. He said you left it behind on Saturday night. It's in the kitchen.'

I tensed, certain that David must be wondering not only why Elliot had my Tupperware, but also why he should choose to return it to my place of work, rather than to the cottage just next door to his own.

'You know, someone did knock this morning,' I began, keen to pre-empt any enquiry, 'when I was in the shower. That must have been Morgan. She probably didn't want to leave it on the doorstep and thought that if Elliot was driving past the gallery, he could drop it off, to save her coming round repeatedly.'

I took a breath and smiled, uncomfortably aware that my explanation regarding the return of the tub was as boring as it was inaccurate and unnecessary.

'OK,' said David with apparent, and not unreasonable, disinterest. 'Well, so long as it's found its way back to you. Oh and Elliot said that you make a mean Eton mess, by the way.'

'Did he?' I bent down to retrieve my bags and coat from under the counter. If I was starting to show any physical signs of anxiety to go along with the internal ones, I preferred that

David shouldn't see them. 'I'll go and put the box in my bag, so I don't forget to take it home,' I said, emerging from behind the counter and heading for the kitchen, while keeping my back to David. 'How was your weekend?'

'Pretty good.'

He said something more, but I had reached the kitchen by that point and wasn't really listening. 'Fab!' I called, picking up the red plastic container and experiencing a small sense of disappointment at finding no note attached. But then what was Elliot supposed to say? What did I want him to say? *You forgot this*? *Saturday was great*? *I miss you*?

Frustrated at my own ridiculousness, I hastily shoved the box into my tote bag, dumped my things in the hallway and returned to the gallery, just in time to see Lloyd entering from the street.

'Hello, both,' he said, jovially. 'Just popped in to see my pictures.'

'They're on the counter,' said David, gesturing from the far side of the gallery, where he was now hanging a print.

Lloyd rubbed his hands together eagerly. 'Can't wait to see them,' he beamed as I joined him.

'Well, I just hope you – and Gwen – like them,' I said, arranging the prints on the counter, in the order I would have hung them on the wall. 'What do you think?'

He gazed down at them, appearing quietly moved. 'I love them. They're perfect, Esme. Thank you.'

'Aw, it's a pleasure,' I said, delighted by his reaction. 'They're leaf studies, obviously. By a guy called George Brooke, who lives out in Long Ashton. I just love them and I was thinking about how much Gwen enjoys her autumn walks in Ashton Court when I chose them.'

'Yes and the best thing,' he replied, now looking up, 'is that the colour of David's mounts is exactly the green of the cushions Gwen bought over the weekend. How lucky is that?'

I took a breath, forcing myself to remain calm in the face of his appalling lack of art appreciation, while making a mental note to diss a sausage in front of him at the very next opportunity. 'Very lucky indeed,' I said, through slightly clenched teeth. 'I'm *so* pleased that the mounts match the cushions, because that had been my primary concern.'

'Mine too. And now, Esme,' he continued, leaning forward conspiratorially and lowering his voice, 'Gwen wants me to ask you about this new man of yours.'

'What?' I was unable to keep the snap from my tone as I glanced over Lloyd's shoulder, just in time to see David taking an uncharacteristic interest in a conversation of which he was not officially a part.

Lloyd winked. 'The bloke who keeps dropping by to see you. The one I met around the time of Gwen's birthday and who was with you last Thursday. He was here again this morning, wasn't he?'

I felt my face begin to burn as David walked towards us. 'That's Esme's neighbour, Lloyd,' he said. 'She had dinner with him and his partner on Saturday, and left something behind. He dropped it off this morning.'

'Doh,' said Lloyd, slapping a hand to his forehead. 'I thought because he kept calling round at closing time that him and Esme were an item, David! I told Gwen that he looked smitten.'

I smiled weakly. 'He's just my neighbour.'

Lloyd chuckled. 'Gwen won't be at all surprised I got it wrong. She's always telling me that I wouldn't understand body language if someone punched me in the guts and kicked me in the goolies.'

I forced a laugh, while imagining myself doing just that to him.

'Anyway,' he sighed, pointing at the pictures, 'these are great. Can I take them now?'

'How about I wrap them up for you and drop them round a little later,' I said, working hard to keep my tone light. 'I wouldn't want the frames to get scratched.'

'Right you are, Es – David,' he said, nodding at my colleague and beginning to walk away. 'Pleasure doing business, as always.'

As the gallery door shut behind him, David turned to me, raising an eyebrow. I remained silent, bracing myself for the inevitable enquiry regarding Elliot's out-of-hours visits to the gallery.

'What a relief that the mounts match the cushions,' he said, with a nod towards the prints and an entertained glance in my direction.

I rolled my eyes, crouching to look for the bubble-wrap. 'I should have put a bloody cushion in a box-frame for him,' I muttered.

I stood up to find David smiling. 'The prints are a perfect choice,' he said, turning and heading for the workshop. 'You've got a great eye and Gwen will love them.'

I watched him go, feeling grateful, not for the first time, for the equanimity and quiet support of my business partner, and also now feeling a little uncomfortable at the thought of having needlessly misled him, even if only by omission, about my Saturday night activities. He might have no interest whatsoever in the fact that Morgan had been away for the weekend, and he would no doubt think me ridiculous for clarifying matters relating to the movements of a large, red, plastic tub, but, for whatever reason, I felt a need to set the record straight. So, after only a brief hesitation, I made my way across the gallery and towards the workshop.

I had just reached the door into the hallway, when my phone pinged. I stopped walking, took it from my pocket and, experiencing mild but unmistakable pleasure at the sight of Elliot's name on-screen, I opened his text immediately.

Sorry about this morning. Thought you'd be at the gallery. Found your container in the dishwasher yesterday and wasn't sure what to do with it so shoved it in the car. Hope Darren didn't think it was odd that I dropped it off. And yes, I am deliberately misnaming him. But seriously, thanks for letting me be your Plan B. Not sure I deserved it – not sure I deserve you – but thank you. x

The sound of metal hitting the workshop floor caused me to start and lower my phone. I stood for a moment, aware that Elliot's text had somehow left me feeling both empowered and slightly out of control. The sense of a renewed connection, of a shared understanding between us, and of being valued, was great. But I was also aware that the line between closeness and complicity was rather fuzzy, and I wasn't entirely sure on which side of it I was currently standing. In short, my emotional responses were confused to say the least, and after a few seconds of staring into space and trying to remember what I was supposed to be doing next, I returned to the safety and stability of the counter and began to bubble-wrap Lloyd's prints.

Chapter 18

'So what's the state of play with him?' asked Cass, stretching out in the armchair and waving her Friday night gin and tonic towards the front door of the cottage.

'Who?'

'You know who,' she said, tutting. 'The ex next door.'

'Oh,' I swirled my drink and then leaned forward, placing the glass on the coffee table, playing for time.

After lengthy consideration, I had replied to Elliot's text of the previous Monday with two emojis: an eye-roll and a smiley face. I would have preferred to respond with actual words, but my attempts at that had resulted in the kind of overthinking that I was keen to avoid. Our Saturday night together had been a fun evening, spent in entirely innocent and light conversation, and I didn't want to spoil that by picking it apart.

So in the end, I had given up on sentences and sent the emojis instead, to which Elliot had responded with a smiley face emoji of his own and the non-news that his London train had been delayed due to signal failure. I had then reciprocated with the non-news that we'd run out of bubble-wrap and that the nearest post office had also run dry. It was an inane exchange of first-world problems, made significant only by the fact that it reopened a door on daily communication, which had closed years ago and which I had thought sealed shut forever.

Over the next four days, that communication had continued via texts which never exceeded a sentence or two. Thus, I had learned that Elliot was spending all week in London, that he had visited the Tate Modern for the first time in years and that he had been pooped on by a pigeon outside Monument tube station. In return, I had informed him of a slow puncture in my rear bicycle tyre, that Lloyd now stocked haggis, and that we would shortly be taking delivery of a field mouse and a vole from Douglas Muirhead. It was a gentle to-and-fro of uncontroversial life updates, but each brief message had, for me, marked an incremental improvement in our relationship and brought with it an increasing sense of pleasure that Elliot and I were back on speaking terms.

But it was an upturn which, I now realised, I wasn't yet ready to share – even with Cass.

'Haven't seen either of them all week,' I answered truthfully, my mood dipping slightly at the incidental reference to Morgan. 'But tell me about Kevin. Are you sure he's OK on his own this evening? That foot fracture sounded pretty nasty in the end.'

'Oh, he'll be fine,' she said dismissively. 'I've stayed home all week and waited on him hand and single foot since Saturday. I didn't mind at first, but when he called me to come and change the TV channel for him yesterday, because he couldn't reach his crutches and didn't want to crawl across the lounge, I realised that I'd been way too soft on him. He can bum-shuffle perfectly well to the loo in the night and hasn't fallen off it since Wednesday, so I'm sure he'll manage OK for one night without me. He practised getting upstairs before I left and so long as he always falls forward and not back, he's fine. Plus, I've hung his mobile in a bag around his neck for emergencies.'

I looked at her uncertainly. She wasn't painting an entirely reassuring picture. 'What about getting dressed and undressed? How does he get trousers on and off over his cast?'

'He's got my palazzo pants from Zara,' she said absently, looking round the living room. 'Elasticated waist and really long. You know, I *really* like this place, Es. It's so peaceful and quiet. I really think I could do rural.'

'It's OK, I suppose,' I said grudgingly. 'The village is pretty and the walks are nice, but if I need a pint of milk I have to go into Clifton, and sometimes it feels just a bit *too* quiet. I don't know,' I shrugged, 'maybe I'd feel differently if I wasn't here on my own.'

At that, she stopped scanning the room and looked at me. 'Are you OK?'

'Yes, why?'

'Well, you sound a bit… what's the word?' She paused for a moment. 'Forlorn. Yes, forlorn. Are you lonely? Do you want me to set you up with someone? Kev's carpenter mate, Chris, split up from his wife a year ago and he's lovely; right side of forty, no kids, no pets, no allergies and taller than you. Bit shy in company, but I'm sure you'd bring him out of himself.'

I took a breath. 'Well, as ideal as Chris sounds—'

'Thinning hair, but getting a transplant.'

'OK, so as *almost* ideal as Chris sounds… I think I'll leave it for now, thanks. I'll start dating again when I'm back in my own place.'

'But don't you need some company here? Now?'

'Not desperately, no.'

'Hmm,' she said, looking unconvinced. 'Well, you certainly sounded a little bit desperate on the phone last Saturday morning.'

'Did I?' I reached for my drink. 'I think I was just aware that I hadn't been getting out and about much at the weekends. That's the other thing about being here. I feel like everyone else is living it up in the big city while I'm stuck in the sticks.'

'If you're stuck, it's cos you can't be arsed. It's only a mile to Clifton.'

'It's at least two and it feels like ten,' I said sullenly.

She frowned, as if dissatisfied. 'So why not let me set you up with Chris? Or with someone else, if the idea of him doesn't do it for you. I know a guy who owns an artisan bakery in Stokes Croft. He's late forties, but ageing like George Clooney. *Full* head of salt-and-paprika hair.'

'Salt-and-paprika?'

'Used to be a ginger.'

'Add him to the list along with transplant man and I promise I'll hassle you for their numbers when I'm back in Redland.'

'And away from Elliot.' It was a comment muttered under her breath.

My eyes narrowed. 'What was that?'

'Nothing,' she chirped. 'Just talking to myself. Let's change the subject. How's Dave? Sophie's still—'

At that moment she was interrupted by a hesitant knocking on the front door, at which we both mouthed a silent, 'Ooh.'

'Whoever could that be,' whispered Cass excitedly, checking her phone, 'at eight fifteen on a Friday night, two miles from Clifton?'

'Don't know,' I replied. 'It is a bit of a weird time to call round, isn't it?'

'Peek through the letterbox, before you open the door,' she whispered as I got up and made my way to answer it. 'Check if they've got a shifty-looking crotch. You can tell a lot from a crotch.'

Opting to bypass the crotch-check, I opened the front door a few inches and peered outside.

'Hi, Esme,' said Morgan cheerily, leaning to her right to make eye contact with me through the crack in the door. 'Sorry to bother you.'

'No, no, it's fine.' I opened the door fully and rustled up a smile, despite being hugely disappointed to see her. 'Is everything OK?'

'Yes, but we've run out of milk and I wondered if I could borrow some. I'll replace it tomorrow.' She didn't quite smile, but I was used to that by now and I could tell from the curl of her upper lip that she was making a real effort.

'Sure,' I said, stepping back, 'come on in and I'll get you some. This is my friend Cass,' I added, as we walked through into the lounge.

'Hi,' said Morgan, stopping next to Cass. 'Sorry to disturb your evening.'

Cass waved a hand. 'Don't worry. You gave us a little bit of excitement. We wondered whoever could be calling, didn't we, Es?'

'Yes,' I said, continuing into the kitchen, 'I'd just been saying to Cass how quiet it is around here.'

I reached into the fridge, snatching the two-pint carton of milk from the door. It was all I had and we'd have nothing for breakfast, but I didn't care: I just wanted Morgan gone.

'Here you go,' I said, returning to the lounge and smiling as I handed over the milk.

'Thanks, and yes,' she said, taking it from me, 'it can get a little lonely around here sometimes, can't it?' I heard a catch in her voice – as did Cass.

'Are you all on your own tonight, Morgan?' she asked. I groaned inwardly at her instinctive and irrepressible kindly concern.

'I wasn't supposed to be, but my partner got held up in London, which is fine,' she said, sounding like it wasn't even remotely fine. 'He'll be back tomorrow.'

I focused on the carton in her hands, not wanting to look up in case something in my expression gave away the fact that I was already fully aware of Elliot's schedule, thanks to an exchange of texts several hours earlier.

'Oh, that's a shame, isn't it, Esme?'

I turned to Cass. 'Sorry, what?'

'I said it's a shame that Morgan is *all on her own* this evening.' She looked at me and widened her eyes.

I suppressed a sigh and gave in. 'Look, why don't you stay for a drink, Morgan?' I extended the invitation with a lot less enthusiasm than I could have mustered.

'Oh, I couldn't crash your evening,' she said, brightening, obviously delighted.

'Don't be silly,' tutted Cass, getting to her feet before I could say *Oh dear, what a shame* and usher anyone to the front door. 'I'll get you a drink. What is there, other than gin, Es?' she asked, disappearing into the kitchen.

'Red or white wine,' I called over my shoulder. 'And there may be a couple of beers in the bottom cupboard, to the left of the fridge. What would you like, Morgan?' I asked, turning back towards her.

'Are you sure, Esme?' she asked quietly. 'Truth is, I didn't really need the milk. It was just an excuse to get out of the house for a five-minute chat, because I was feeling a little low. You know how it is. But I feel bad crashing your time with your friend.'

And it was at that point that shame overwhelmed me. Here was a friendly, entirely inoffensive woman, seeking company and conversation on a Friday night and what was my reaction? To shove her out of the door as fast as humanly possible. And why? Because she had the temerity to be living with my ex.

'No, no, the more the merrier, honestly,' I said, this time digging deep for some warmth. 'Now, give me that back,' I said, reaching for the milk, 'and let's go into the kitchen and swap it for something stronger.'

—

'Yes, I was *sooo* delighted, Morgan,' said Cass, slowing her speech in an attempt to avoid stumbling over her words, 'when Esme's gallerly... gall-er-y opened next door. And I was *even more* delighted when I discovered it was owned by a woman.' She was sitting next to Morgan on the sofa and leaned over to nudge her affectionately. 'Because, you see, we businesswomen have to stick together and support each other, don't we?' She hiccoughed quietly, winked at half speed and then tapped the side of her nose. 'Because no other bugger will.'

'I'm *co*-owner, Morgan, with a thirty per cent stake,' I corrected, sipping from my latest drink. I had moved on to white wine about an hour or so earlier and I wasn't sure exactly how many top-ups I'd had since then, but it was at least two fewer than Morgan, and Cass was in a whole different league. 'Originally, David interviewed me as a manager for the gallery.

He was going to lease a place in Clifton, and wanted me to source local art and help run the place. But once I heard his proposal, I thought, *I want a piece of that!* I knew I'd have to remortgage, which was a bit scary, and I knew Clifton rents would be too much of a stretch for me. So I suggested Westbury Park to him and said I wanted in. I was sure he'd say no, but he didn't and, three years later, Erskine and Green are doing very nicely, thank you.' I saluted her with my glass.

Cass sat up and pointed at me. '*You* are so bold, Esme Green. That's just one of the things I love about you. And hey! When I talk about unsupportive buggers, I want to be *veeeeeery* clear that I do not include your lovely Dave in that category.' She leaned towards Morgan. 'He's lovely, lovely, *lovely*, except,' she confided in a whisper, 'he's also a heartbreaker. Isn't that right, Es?'

'He's definitely broken Sophie's heart,' I sighed, pulling a sad face.

'Who's Sophie?' asked Morgan, sounding a little slurred. 'Not the artist at the show?' She paused, as if for thought. 'No, that was Jasmine, wasn't it?'

My lip curled involuntarily at the mention of her name. 'No, no, Sophie is David's ex. She's really nice and still not over him.'

'And it's costing me a bloody fortune in discounts,' muttered Cass, reaching for the gin.

'He seems so sweet,' sighed Morgan. 'I can see why you'd definitely be upset if you had him and then lost him.'

I nodded thoughtfully. Morgan was right: you'd be kicking yourself if you'd let a catch like David slip through your net. No wonder Sophie's recovery was proving such a slow one.

'He's minted too,' said Cass, nudging Morgan. 'But sh–sh–*shhhhhh*.' She placed a finger to her lips. 'He doesn't like anyone knowing. I only know cos Esme told me. She's so liss looped… loose lipped.'

Morgan looked at me. 'And you two never…?' She let the question hang.

I had just raised my glass to my lips and now snorted into my wine. 'David and me?' I laughed. 'God no. I mean, he *is* great, but we're *really* different. I'm not his type *at all*.'

Cass shrugged. 'Different can work,' she said, yawning. 'But,' she turned to Morgan, her nose wrinkling, 'they just bubble along, with Dave calming her down whenever she loses her rag, and her getting wound up cos he's not a sharer.'

I frowned, not entirely happy with her summing-up of the relationship. 'You're making me sound like a toddler.'

'He was so kind to me at Jasmine's show,' said Morgan, smiling to herself. 'He really knows how to make you feel interesting. Plus, he's got lovely eyes,' she added.

'Careful now, Morgan,' said Cass, grinning and wagging a finger, 'you're already taken.'

Morgan laughed, as my face fell. I was definitely capable, I realised, of enjoying her company, so long as I wasn't forced to make any connection between her and Elliot. But the moment I saw her in the context of *him*, she was much harder to bear. I knew it wasn't fair or reasonable. But I couldn't help it.

I stood up and Cass caught my eye. 'All OK, Es?' she asked, offering me a wobbly smile. She was drunk, but she still knew something was wrong, even if her insight into exactly what that might be was dulled.

'Great,' I said. 'Just going to get a glass of water.'

'Hmm.' She eyed me uncertainly and I feared she might press the point, when she was distracted by a question from Morgan about highlights.

I escaped into the kitchen, and had just taken a glass from the cupboard and turned on the tap, when my phone pinged. Taking it from my pocket, I was surprised, but not unhappy, to see a text from Elliot.

In bed or still up?

I tapped out and sent a two-letter response:

> Up

Placing my phone on the table, I turned back to the sink. A second later, remembering that Elliot's girlfriend was just metres away and unaware of my ongoing correspondence with her partner, I snatched up the phone and hurriedly began to type.

> Can't chat. Mor

'Need the loo,' said Morgan, appearing suddenly in the doorway. 'Is there one down here?'

'Yes, yes, there is,' I said breathlessly, shoving my phone into a pocket and nodding towards the back of the kitchen. 'Through the utility room.'

'Same layout as ours,' she said brightly.

I smiled twitchily as she passed, before filling my glass with water, downing half of it in an attempt to calm down and then returning to the living room, where Cass was obviously now having some difficulty staying awake.

She blinked and sat up with a start when I put my glass down heavily on the table and lowered myself into the armchair. 'I've had too much to drink,' she murmured.

'No shit, Sherlock.'

She frowned. 'What's the matter with you all of a sudden?'

I shook my head. 'Nothing. Sorry. I think I'm just ready for bed.' I looked at my watch and turned towards the kitchen. 'Do you think she'll head home soon? It's gone midnight.'

'She seems really nice, Es,' said Cass. She sounded apologetic.

I looked at her and felt ashamed – yet again – of my attitude towards Morgan. 'Yes,' I acknowledged quietly. 'She is very nice.'

'Bit difficult to read with the, you know, with all the stuff...' She pointed to her face and pulled her mouth taut. 'She definitely keeps a lot hidden. Hey, her and Dave would make a good pair, wouldn't they?' she added, smiling.

I attempted a smile in return, but it was a pretty poor effort and Cass leaned forward to pat my knee. 'I know I'm pissed,' she said gently, 'but I'm not stupid. I do get it,' she added, flopping back on the sofa.

I gazed across at her, realising that she had been right earlier: I was forlorn. Even when sitting with one of the best friends I'd ever had, I felt lonely and alone, increasingly haunted by a growing sense of regret and missed opportunity.

I had just taken a deep breath and was about to attempt speech when, for the second time that evening, our conversation was interrupted by an unexpected knock at the door – this one much less tentative than the last.

'Shit,' said Cass, sitting bolt upright, suddenly alert. 'Now that's *proper* scary. Don't answer it, Es.'

'I can't just ignore it,' I protested, standing up. 'Someone might need help.'

'The crotch! The crotch! Check the crotch!' she hissed, frantically flapping a hand at me as I walked past her to the door.

I turned, rolling my eyes at her, but made sure to put the chain on the door before opening it, just the same.

'Hi, Es.'

I gasped, quickly slamming the door shut and fumbling to take the chain off, before opening it wide.

Elliot was laughing. 'I'm sorry, but your face,' he said, pointing, his laughter fading into a smile. 'Sorry,' he said, 'but Morgan texted earlier to say that she's staying over with a friend tonight, so I got on a train and...' He hesitated. 'I just thought I'd see—'

'Yes, she's here,' I said stiffly, finally regaining control of my vocal cords. 'Morgan's here.'

I recognised a fleeting panic in his eyes, before he recovered himself with remarkable and admirable speed.

'Yes, I wondered if she might be when I saw your light on,' he said more loudly. 'I just thought I'd check. I hope you don't mind.'

'No, that's fine. Come in. Go straight through.' I stepped back to allow him inside.

He walked past me and into the living room, where Cass was now quite literally on the edge of her seat, eyeing him with interest.

'Hi there,' he said, raising a hand.

'Cass this is Elliot, from next door,' I said, fighting to remain calm and focusing on the space between them in order to avoid eye contact. 'Elliot, this is my friend Cass. She owns the salon next door to the gallery.'

'Great to meet you, Cass,' he said.

She looked him up and down, whether appreciatively or appraisingly I couldn't tell. 'Likewise, Elliot,' she replied, and thankfully left it at that.

'El!' exclaimed Morgan, emerging from the kitchen. 'What are you doing here? I thought you were in London until tomorrow.'

'I decided to get the late train. I texted to find out where you'd gone, but you didn't reply.'

'I was taking a break from my phone.' She appeared to be attempting a smile, but flushed slightly as she spoke, her tone tense.

Elliot, by contrast, looked relaxed to the point of falling over. 'Well, I've found you now, so how about accompanying me home?'

Morgan turned to me. 'Thanks so much for letting me stay and drink all your booze, Esme. You're the best neighbour. I'll be sure to return the favour very soon.'

I stared blankly at her, as feelings of guilt, resentment and regret over my hidden – and increasingly confusing – relationship with Elliot threatened to overwhelm me. Aware now of a slight, but uncontrollable, tremble in my lower lip, I realised, to my horror, that tears were suddenly a very real possibility.

Elliot laughed. 'Poor Esme looks slightly stunned at the prospect of more alcohol, Morgan. Just how much have you guys had to drink this evening?' He nudged me gently with his elbow. 'Don't worry. It'll be fine, Es.'

I blinked and took a breath. 'Yes. That'd be great. Thanks, Morgan,' I said haltingly.

'And so lovely to meet you, Cass,' she continued brightly, clearly oblivious to my increasingly fragile emotional state and Elliot's abbreviation of my name. 'I know where to get my highlights done now.'

Cass grinned up at her. 'Absolute-erly. And remember, there's a ten per cent discount for new customers.'

'We'd better get going.' Elliot smiled down at Morgan. 'It's late and we've got a long walk home.'

She and Cass laughed dutifully, but I couldn't oblige and instead trailed them to the front door in silence. Elliot opened it and waved Morgan through with a broad smile, before turning back towards me, his smile falling away. We held each other's gaze for just a second and then he was gone, the door clicking shut behind him.

I slowly refastened the chain and then stared at the door, giving serious consideration to lying down, throwing a coat over myself and going to sleep. I had neither the energy nor inclination to go upstairs, and the welcome mat would, I decided, offer adequate insulation from the flagstone floor.

I was just wondering which coat to choose from the row of hooks beside the front door, when I became aware of Cass gently taking my hand and leading me on a rather winding route back to the sofa. 'Now sit,' she said authoritatively, flopping down and taking me with her.

After that, she didn't say anything more and we simply sat, my hand still in hers, side-by-side, in silence. When I turned to look at her a few minutes later and saw that her eyes were closed,

I assumed that she'd fallen asleep. But as I made an attempt to disentwine my fingers from hers, she spoke again.

'He's *really* good-looking,' she said, without opening her eyes.

I looked away, gazing at the empty calico armchair – the twin of Elliot's. 'I know.'

'What was he doing here?'

I sighed heavily. 'He came to fetch Morgan. Remember?' I replied, with just a hint of exasperation.

'I'm pissed, Es, not stupid.'

I turned to find her with her eyes now open, looking up at me. 'He came for Morgan,' I repeated quietly, this time without the exasperation.

She nodded slowly. 'OK,' she said, sitting up, leaning sideways and giving me a hug. 'But just remember: you are strong, sexy and successful—'

I laughed and pulled away from her. 'Oh shut up,' I said, slapping her lightly on the hand.

'I'm serious! Strong, sexy, successful and you—'

'Can have any man I want. Yes, I know.'

'Well, it's true,' she shrugged. 'But,' she added, her smile fading a little, 'just make sure you're wanting the right one.'

I swallowed hard and gave her another hug. 'You've said that before.'

'Because it's worth repeating.' She patted me on the back and then stood up. 'Now, I'm off to bed. I'll leave you to put everything in the dishwasher, because I'd only smash stuff.'

'You would.'

'Night then.'

I watched as she began to make her way to the staircase and, when I was satisfied that she was steady enough on her feet to make it safely up to bed unassisted, I leaned back on the sofa and closed my eyes.

Elliot's fleeting visit had left me emotionally concussed. I was already well aware that my relationship with him – as with

Morgan – was comfortable only outside the context of their relationship with each other, with any casual reference they made to one another always feeling like an unexpected slap in the face. That was unpleasant, obviously, but it was just about bearable and something I could cope with, while I had to.

But seeing them together, being with them, as a couple, in the same room, was *not* bearable. When Elliot had taken her hand to lead her home, my urge had been to run, to retreat – not just from the room, but from the cottage and the entire situation. And I now felt certain that the longer that situation went on, the worse it was going to get.

'Es!'

I opened my eyes and looked towards the stairs.

'Yes?'

'Don't you go falling asleep on the sofa, you slob!'

I hauled myself to my feet. 'I'm just clearing up!' I called, gathering the glasses and feeling a pang of guilt at keeping secrets from a friend as good, and as kind, and as close as Cass.

Because whatever I'd told her, I knew without a doubt that Elliot had not come for Morgan that evening. He had come for me.

Chapter 19

I was surprised, but relieved, to find Douglas Muirhead waiting for me when I arrived at the gallery on Monday morning. I hadn't much been looking forward to a first-thing coffee with David, during which I might have had to feign laughter and smiles over my evening with Cass. Not that David would have ever pressed me for fine detail, of course. But he knew that I was spending Friday night with her, so an enquiry regarding what we'd got up to would have been likely and I just wasn't sure that I'd have been able to deal cheerfully with that.

But Douglas being there removed the problem, allowing David and I to completely bypass the topic of Friday night – and the weekend in general – and immediately direct all our focus and attention onto our artist.

'Douglas!' I exclaimed excitedly, on seeing him. 'What a lovely surprise. Have you brought in some more pieces for us?'

He blinked rapidly, clearly overwhelmed by my enthusiasm. 'I… I… have, Esme,' he said haltingly. 'The wildlife pieces and also… also some more human figures. I just hope you like them.'

'Oh, I bet I will,' I replied, dropping my bags and nodding towards the large cardboard box on the counter. 'Is this them?'

'It is. David's gone to make coffee and I was just about to unwrap them.'

'Fabulous. I'll get you some scissors.'

'It's OK, I've got my own,' he said, bringing his right hand from behind his back and revealing an outsize pair of silver scissors, which he slowly raised to shoulder height.

'Ooh!' I laughed. 'They're *huge*, Douglas! And they look *very* sharp. Pleased to see that you're holding them point-down.'

'They are sharp,' he agreed, smiling at the scissors. 'I take them everywhere with me.' Glancing down at the green canvas backpack at his feet, he added, 'You never know when you might need to cut something, Esme.'

'Yes, I guess it's always good to be prepared,' I said brightly. 'Anyway, you get slashing while I go and dump my bags and fetch the figure we already have. I'd like to look at it alongside the others.' I picked up my belongings, hurrying to the back of the gallery and down the short hallway beyond. 'Hi, David!' I called. 'Just getting Douglas's piece from the workshop.'

'Great!' he shouted from the kitchen. 'I'll be in with the coffees in a minute.'

'Fab!'

Retrieving Douglas's repackaged sculpture, I returned with it to the gallery. 'Here he is,' I said, holding the bubble-wrapped figure aloft, as I walked towards him, 'but you're going to need to use your scissors on him too.'

'OK, I've already unwrapped the others.' He gestured diffidently towards the counter, where now sat four clay sculptures. Two of them – a vole sitting on a small log and a mouse with its front paws resting on a half-eaten apple – were what I had come to think of as classic Douglas. The other two were, however, quite different, and dramatically so.

'Wow,' I said, bending to examine the larger of the two: a long-haired woman, dressed in a torn, flowing robe, seated on a simple straight-backed kitchen chair, her feet bare and her face buried in her hands. 'Douglas, this is extraordinary,' I breathed.

'You like it?'

'I do. Very much,' I said, picking it up. 'The lengthened limbs – the style in general – pair it nicely with the sleeping figure.' I gestured towards the supine sculpture which he was currently unwrapping. 'She has an attitude of such agonised despair. You don't need to see her face to know that.'

'*Agonised despair.*' Douglas nodded thoughtfully. 'That's exactly what I was trying to depict. Along with a recognition of karma at play, of course.'

'Coffee's up.' David joined us, placing a tray on the counter. 'These pieces are amazing,' he said, looking at the sculptures and handing Douglas a mug.

'Thank you, David,' whispered Douglas, clearly struggling with his emotions as David bestowed the double kindnesses of a compliment and a coffee.

'Aren't they wonderful?' I enthused, replacing the female figure on the counter. 'We were just talking about this one and her attitude of *agonised despair*. There's definitely a stylistic and thematic connection between the three.' I picked up the final piece, a male nude in the foetal position, the figure's face once again hidden, this time by its arms which covered the head, as if for protection. 'You said they were a set, didn't you, Douglas?'

'I did,' he replied quietly.

'Can you tell me a little bit about that one?' David pointed to the contorted, sleeping figure in Douglas's hands. 'Does it have a title?'

'It's *Father*,' Douglas replied, now smiling broadly, delighted by David's interest and ongoing approval. 'And he's dead, by the way, Esme,' he added softly.

I looked up at him. 'Who's dead?'

'*Father*. You thought he was sleeping, but he's dead.'

'Oh…'

There followed a brief, but very definite, pause, during which it crossed my mind to ask whether *Father* was simply the title of the piece, or also a description of its subject. But artistic curiosity now being outweighed by the pressure of time and a vague sense of the heebie-jeebies, I decided that I was OK with not knowing.

I cleared my throat. 'Right.'

'And that is *Mother*,' continued Douglas, indicating the seated woman. 'The cowering figure is *Sibling 1*. It's a family project, you see. I've got *Sibling 2* at home. That's a rather larger piece, in wire and Modroc – life-size, in fact.' He smiled slowly in a way that just five minutes earlier, as he had gazed at his little vole, had seemed affable and charming, but which now struck me as just a tiny bit Norman Bates.

'Are you planning…' I paused to take an extra little breath, '…to show us *Sibling 2*?' I asked uncertainly.

'No, no,' he said, still smiling. 'I wasn't originally planning on sharing any of them, of course. But *Sibling 2* really is just for me. He'll never see the light of day.'

I glanced at David to see if he, like me, was beginning to experience any disquiet regarding Douglas, his sculptures, and the extremely large and very shiny pair of scissors he was currently holding. But David appeared as sanguine as ever, with his expression, as usual, giving nothing away.

'Thank you so much for entrusting us with these, Douglas,' he said benignly.

'Er, yes, thank you,' I echoed, returning my attention to the pieces. 'We'll have a big think about pricing and positioning, and then I'll give you a call. We won't do anything without clearing it with you first.'

Douglas drained his coffee, replacing the mug on the tray. 'Thanks so much, Esme and David,' he said, shaking our hands in turn. 'I'm so very grateful for your kindness. There is no darkness here,' he added in a murmur.

'Pleasure is all ours,' smiled David.

'Absolutely… absolutely,' I said absently, distracted by a clanking sound as Douglas returned his scissors to his canvas backpack, and then by further jangling as he hoisted the bag onto his shoulder. Clearly the scissors weren't the only metallic items he carried around day-to-day on a just-in-case basis.

'I won't keep you any longer,' he said, straightening up and turning towards the door. 'I know you're busy.'

'I'll be in touch, Douglas,' I said. 'Tomorrow, or Wednesday at the latest.'

He nodded, raised a hand and then exited onto the street, pausing on the pavement outside Lloyd's and gazing down at the window display.

'He always stops at Lloyd's, doesn't he?' I mused. 'That's never really struck me before.'

'What hasn't?' asked David.

'Douglas liking dead stuff.'

'Or maybe just pies.'

'And isn't it amazing the difference the title of a piece can make?' I turned to the human sculptures on the counter. 'Discovering that these are a family unit is quite transformative.'

'So, are you thinking what I'm thinking?' asked David.

I looked over my shoulder at him. 'That Douglas has a backpack full of butcher's knives and a basement full of dead relatives?'

'Or...' he said, raising an eyebrow.

'Or that we should give Douglas an evening showing of his own and use it to emphasise, through juxtaposition, his two contrasting styles? Make it both a fascination and a selling point?'

He saluted me with his mug. 'We're just *so* in tune.'

'I know,' I said. 'Weird, isn't it? We think so differently when it comes to, say, judging politicians by their hair, or being patient with *really* annoying people, and yet when it comes to other things, like...' I paused for a moment and looked around, '...well, like this place, for example, we are actually very in tune.' I smiled. 'I find those rare crossovers in our personalities and attitudes rather comforting. Do they terrify you?'

'Very much so.'

'I knew they would,' I said, returning my attention to Douglas, as he finally tore himself away from the butchered flesh and began to walk slowly up the road, only to return almost immediately for one last look at Lloyd's window. 'God, David, you don't actually think he...?'

'No, Esme, I actually don't,' he said, joining me by the window and handing me a mug of coffee. 'But if you're really concerned, why don't you—'

'Suggest that he invites his family to the showing?'

David saluted me for a second time. 'Terrifyingly in tune,' he sighed. 'Terrifyingly.'

Chapter 20

Douglas's visit got the day off to an unexpectedly good start. His work, although admittedly slightly unnerving, was also genuinely exciting, and the possibility of putting a little show together gave David and I lots to discuss whenever we had a moment to spare.

We decided that I should put the idea to Douglas and, if he wanted to go for it, ask how long he thought he would need to produce enough pieces to make it worthwhile. It had occurred to us both that he might have more than one sculpture at home which he was reticent about sharing due to a lack of self-confidence, and we agreed that I would talk that, and everything else, through with him the next day.

But although Douglas, and work in general, were helpful distractions from my Elliot issues, they didn't prove a complete diversion, primarily due to the fact that Elliot and I were still messaging.

His first text on the subject of his unexpected Friday night visit to the cottage had landed just twenty minutes after I closed the front door behind him, and it had been unsurprisingly apologetic.

> Sorry. That was stupid and selfish of me. I saw an opportunity to say hi and didn't think beyond that. x

I had fallen asleep without replying and woke the next morning to three more texts, each offering a further apology and again bemoaning his stupidity and thoughtlessness. In response, I'd again resorted to the trusty eye-roll emoji, before telling him that I would be staying with Cass for the rest of the weekend. It was a plan upon which Cass had insisted, saying that Kevin would be incredibly hurt if I didn't pay him a visit and draw a penis on his cast. But I knew that what she really wanted was to keep me out of the cottage and under her watchful eye, for as long as possible. Not that I put up a fight. I didn't want to spend the weekend a stone's throw from the happy couple any more than she wanted me to.

By the time I got home late Sunday evening, Elliot's texts had lost all of their angst, which in turn served to lower my own anxiety levels and we soon reverted to swapping inanities. I actually found the exchanges calming, save for the few occasions when I wondered how close-by Morgan might be while he was texting. And the disquiet I felt at those moments served as a reminder that thinking about Morgan and Elliot in the same intellectual breath was definitely something to be avoided.

So it was particularly unfortunate that at 4:45 p.m. on Monday, I should happen to be laughing at a GIF from Elliot at the exact moment that Morgan entered the gallery. I had gone to fetch a vase from the back rooms to replace a window-display item sold earlier in the day, when I heard David greet her warmly by name. My stomach lurched with guilt and paranoia, and I was grateful that I at least had a minute or two to compose myself before he called to me from the gallery.

'Esme, Morgan's here. Are you free?'

'Oh, yes, sure. Will be with you in a moment.'

Aware that my hands were shaking slightly, I put down the vase and forced myself to take several slow, deep breaths. Then, when I thought that I was as calm as I was ever going to be, I went to join them.

'Morgan,' I said, hoping that the slight quake in my voice was detectable to me alone. 'What a nice surprise.'

She looked up from her conversation with David. 'Hi! I just stopped by for a quick browse on my way to another class. I've been doing some one-on-one Pilates in Redland.'

I nodded, praying that was true and that she hadn't in fact come to confront me about the exact nature of my relationship with her partner, or to punch my lights out. She was a petite woman but also, I was very aware, extraordinarily fit and I had no doubt that she could take me out any time she fancied.

'Elliot told Morgan that we had some more of Douglas's work in stock,' said David, with a quizzical look in my direction. 'Apparently, you spoke to him about the pieces.'

My eyes widened and my mouth dried as I tried to recall exactly when I'd told Elliot about Douglas's new sculptures. I also wondered why on earth he'd decided to pass on details of that conversation to Morgan.

'He said you mentioned it when he stopped by to pay for the little hedgehog,' said Morgan.

'Oh, yes, that's right! I did!' I laughed with relief, while also wanting to cry a tiny bit. 'We do have a few more pieces, but sadly they're not up for sale yet.'

'Yes, David was just explaining to me that you hope to have another show.' Morgan looked up at him with obvious warmth.

I nodded, trying not to overthink her visit while drawing a panicky blank regarding what to say next, in case I put a foot wrong.

'It's Morgan's birthday very soon,' said David.

I kept going with the nodding. It felt safe and uncontroversial.

'Yes,' she said, her eyes still fixed on David, 'it's a week Saturday and I wanted to invite you both for dinner at the cottage.'

I stopped nodding and wished that I had brought the vase to be sick into.

'You've been so kind since we moved in,' she said, now turning her attention to me. 'So when Elliot asked me what I would like to do for my...'

She carried on talking while I focused entirely on staying put, rather than leaving the room, which was what every fibre of my being was at that moment urging me to do.

'…couldn't think of anyone I'd rather spend my birthday with this year.' Morgan concluded her speech with an expression closer to a smile than I had ever previously seen her achieve. In fact, I was pretty sure she was beating my own current attempt.

'Well, what a…' I stopped talking and, aware that my voice was starting to change pitch, I cleared my throat and began again. 'That's so kind.'

'It is,' said David. 'I'd love to come. Thank you.'

'And, of course, if you'd like to bring a plus one?' She looked up at him enquiringly.

He hesitated for a moment, glancing at me before answering. 'No, it'll just be me, if that's OK?'

'Of course it's OK!' she laughed. 'But are you *absolutely* sure?' She was obviously having a really hard time believing that he was single.

'I am,' he said, 'and looking forward to it already.'

He turned to me and I nodded violently. I was going to have to extricate myself from the invitation somehow, but that would need a cooler head than I currently possessed.

'Would you like to bring someone along, Esme?' asked Morgan.

'No, it'll be just me.'

'Well, I can't wait.' She clapped her hands together in satisfaction, with no querying of my decision to come alone. Clearly, me being single was immediately believable. 'I'll tell Elliot.'

I winced internally at her reference to him. 'Right, well, thanks so much,' I said. 'I just have a few things to sort out before we close. Would you like to keep browsing? I drove in today, so I could give you a lift home—' I coughed, choking on the offer. 'Sorry. I could give you a lift home, if you're happy to wait half an hour.' I put my hands behind my back, screwing them into tight fists and holding my breath, as I awaited her answer.

'Thanks, but it's OK. I have the car – and a few more classes to teach before I go home.'

I felt myself relax. But the moment was very short-lived.

'There was just one other thing I wanted to talk to you about, though, Esme,' she continued uncertainly, casting an awkward glance in David's direction. 'But, you know what, it's more personal stuff and you're at work, so…'

'Why don't you two go and sit down, while I finish up in here?' said David kindly. 'We're two minutes off closing anyway.'

'Thanks, David,' I said hoarsely, wishing I had a sick-filled vase to empty over his head. Resigned to whatever uncomfortable conversation was to come, I beckoned Morgan to follow and led her into the kitchen. 'Have a seat,' I said. 'Coffee or tea? We've got decaf, or some herbal stuff, if you fancy that.'

She shook her head, now looking as downcast as I felt. This, I decided, was going to be bad.

I sat down opposite her. 'I'm not really in the mood for anything either,' I said quietly.

She didn't reply, instead clasping her hands on the table in front of her and picking anxiously at a perfect nail.

I forced myself to leave the silence uninterrupted and after a moment she said, 'I don't want to put you in a difficult position or embarrass you, Esme, but I'd really like to ask you something. It's just rather awkward.'

She looked up and I nodded acceptingly. 'Go ahead.'

'The weekend I was away…'

I shifted in my chair, uncomfortable at the thought of having to get a story straight. 'Yes?'

'Cass said that you were supposed to spend the Saturday night and Sunday with her, but that you didn't – because Kevin had broken his foot.'

I gazed at the table and nodded again, now feeling strangely and inappropriately calm as I stood on the tracks, waiting to be hit by the freight train of accusation. 'That's right.'

'So you were at home?'

'Yes, I was.'

'Did you see Elliot?'

I looked up and took a deep breath.

'The thing is, he told me he was at home,' she continued, before I had a chance to speak. 'He said he was at home the entire weekend, but...' She hesitated and bit her lip. 'But I'm not sure whether to believe him. All I know for sure is that he wasn't in London, which is where he originally told me he was going to be.'

I hesitated, adjusting to the new dynamic. Morgan, it seemed, wasn't here to accuse me of anything. I wasn't on trial; I was being called as a witness.

'He's telling you the truth,' I said firmly, now feeling much more at ease in the dock. 'He was at the cottage on Friday night, because he said hi when I got home. On Saturday, I saw him in the evening and he said he was tired because he'd been out walking during the day, and he was very muddy.'

'And did you see anyone else with him that weekend?' she asked, her voice now barely above a whisper.

'I didn't,' I said, satisfied that my account had been an entirely factual one.

She visibly relaxed and put a hand to her face.

'You must think I'm dreadful,' she said, suddenly appearing close to tears.

'No, no, I don't think that at all,' I replied quickly, anxious to reassure her and realising that Elliot had been right: she was highly insecure. 'But he told you the truth. He was at home.'

She heaved a sigh. 'I'm so sorry.'

'It's fine,' I insisted. 'You're bound to be feeling unsettled at the moment; new home... new city... new job.'

'You're so kind,' she said quietly, a tear now escaping, 'and so clear-thinking. I wish I could be more like you.'

I reached across the table and squeezed her hand, touched by the compliment and giving myself credit for putting my personal feelings to one side, in order to support her. OK, so the precise nature of my relationship with Elliot was under wraps, but we had done nothing wrong and the secrecy was solely to protect her feelings.

'Oh, don't be silly. We can all feel a little chaotic, or insecure, at times,' I said, with the benevolent superiority of the top nun giving Maria a pep talk in *The Sound of Music*. I resisted an urge to conclude the sentence with 'my child'.

She nodded. 'I try to stay rational and reasonable, but that feels so hard to do right now.'

I smiled sympathetically. 'Because you're in a state of flux and under a lot of pressure.'

'I just keep overthinking everything.' She paused and sniffed, reaching into the pocket of her hoodie and taking out a tissue. 'For example, on the Saturday I was away, I messaged in the evening to ask how Elliot's day was going. He didn't reply for an hour or so, but eventually he said it was going fine. So then I asked what he'd been doing, and he said he'd been walking and that he was tired and wanted to take a break from his phone. He said that I should stop messaging and make the most of being with my friends. I kept telling myself that it was good advice and I tried to feel OK about it, but it still felt like he was pushing me away. Then, when I called him to say good night, he just didn't pick up at all. The next day he said he'd left his phone out of reach, which just isn't like him.'

'Right…' I murmured, beginning to feel slightly less great about myself.

'And since then,' she continued, dabbing carefully at her eyes before returning the tissue to her pocket, 'it feels like he's on his phone a lot more than he used to be. I tell myself it's work, but his body language seems to say something else – as if he's hiding something.' She looked up at me, brow furrowed. 'I sound paranoid, don't I? Especially when you've just told me that he was being completely honest with me.'

I couldn't bring myself to reply. In under sixty seconds, I had gone from basking in the self-satisfied glory of being a supportive female role model, to being confronted with the inescapable truth of the matter – namely, that I was the cause of Morgan's insecurity and thus the very opposite of a woman's woman. I wasn't Reverend Mother. I was Baroness von Schraeder.

'I'm heading off now.' David stuck his head around the door.

'Oh, me too, me too,' said Morgan, blinking rapidly and standing up. 'I'm filling in at the David Lloyd gym in Long Ashton from six thirty,' she added, checking her watch. 'I've just got to pick up the car. It's still in Redland.'

'I'm walking that way if you fancy a bit of company,' said David.

She looked up at him and, despite her recent distress, again managed something extraordinarily close to a smile. He clearly had quite an effect on her. 'That'd be nice.'

'Brilliant,' he replied, before raising a hand in my direction. 'Night.'

'Night.'

'Bye, Esme,' said Morgan, walking towards the door. 'And thanks for the chat. You've made me feel so much better about everything.'

I smiled uncertainly as she and David disappeared into the hallway, before my face fell and I sat unmoving, except for a slight start when the gallery door slammed shut.

Then I took out my phone and texted Elliot, while I was sure that nobody was monitoring his body language.

Chapter 21

'So, basically, *I* am the problem. In fact, *this* is the problem. Being here with you, right now, is the problem,' I insisted, tapping the table as Elliot and I sat together in the darkest corner of an almost deserted wine bar.

In response to the slightly panicked – but mostly miserable – text I had sent him after Morgan left the gallery, Elliot had suggested that we meet around the corner from his local office to talk everything through. The offer, and the prospect of an opportunity to offload, had come as a huge relief and I had immediately leapt at it. But as I sat opposite him, just over an hour later, and concluded my account of the conversation with Morgan, I decided that maybe it hadn't been such a great idea after all.

He shook his head. 'You are not the problem, Es. And us sitting together and having a quiet...' He paused and looked around. '...a *very* quiet drink together isn't the problem either.'

'So where does she think you are right now?'

He shrugged. 'Probably at work.'

'And if she finds out you're not and asks where you were? What then? You'll lie and she'll suspect that you're lying, and then hate herself for what she thinks is paranoia.' I groaned and put my hands to my face. 'And I'm part of that.'

He leaned forward, taking my hands in his and lowering them gently to the table. 'You have done *nothing* wrong.'

'It doesn't feel like that. She's upset because—'

'Because she thinks I lied to her about where I was a couple of weekends ago and because she doesn't know who

I'm messaging every single minute of the day. I didn't lie to her and I don't think she should need to see all my texts and emails in order to be able to trust me. That's not how a relationship should be. Have I been dishonest with her? Of course I have. I have pretended not to know you and I hold my hands up to that. But that is all I have done and, in my defence, I did that because I didn't want to make her feel insecure – or rather, I didn't want to make her feel any more insecure than she already does... *than she has always felt.*' He sat back in his chair and sighed. 'We are *not* responsible for her insecurities, because they are nothing new. I have tried to bolster her self-confidence and self-esteem from day one and, when that didn't work, I have tried to protect her from anything that I thought might hurt or upset her. Maybe that was the wrong approach, but *you* haven't done anything wrong other than try to support me. Believe me, Es, I wish I hadn't dragged you into this and I would do anything right now to make it all go away for you.' He took a breath and picked up his glass. 'Including going home tonight and telling Morgan everything, if that's what you want me to do.'

I placed my elbows on the table and rested my head in my hands. 'I don't know, Elliot,' I said wearily. 'Maybe that would be best. Maybe just being completely honest and explaining that all you ever wanted was to protect her feelings is the right thing to do.'

He didn't reply immediately, but when he did, he sounded exhausted. 'Absolutely,' he said quietly. 'I'll do whatever you want.'

'Just explain that you missed an early opportunity to be upfront with her because you were worried about upsetting her.'

He nodded. 'Yes. It's what I should have done from the start. I've just ended up overcomplicating everything. I'll keep it really simple going forward, and answer all her questions openly and honestly. There's nothing to hide.'

I drank my wine, while running through a few of those question/answer scenarios in my head.

'What if she asks for more detail about the weekend she was away?' I asked hesitantly. 'I know it was just a casual dinner at home and then drinks in the pub, but I could understand if she felt let down by me, as a woman, for not mentioning it to her. Especially when she was so upset in the gallery this afternoon.'

'So if she asks me whether we've spent time together since she and I moved into the cottage,' he began uncertainly, 'would you rather that I didn't tell her the truth about that?'

'Is she likely to ask you that?' I asked, aware of a slight increase in heart rate. 'Do you think she'll want to ask *me* that sort of question?'

He paused for a moment, clearly reluctant to answer. 'I think she might, Es. When we first started dating, she looked up my most recent ex on social media and got in touch with her. I thought the vetting was funny at the time and I was absolutely fine with it, but Morgan is a devil for detail and, as I said, needs lots of reassurance. So yes, I think ideally she'd like to talk it through with you. But it needn't be a problem,' he added hastily. 'I'll just say that you'd rather not discuss any of it with her. I'm sure she'll accept that.'

'But then I'll look guilty.' I was aware of my hand shaking as I raised my glass. 'Whatever happens, I'm going to look like a terrible person.' I took a large swig of wine. 'Because I am a terrible person.'

'That's simply not true,' he said gently, again taking my hand. 'You mustn't worry. I will explain to Morgan that I put you in an impossible position by asking you not to tell her about us. And I'll make it very clear to her that the pub visits and dinner were my idea.'

'Elliot, I knocked on your door with dessert and two bottles of wine!' I exclaimed. 'It's not as if you held a gun to my head!'

'OK, so I'd actually forgotten that you brought dessert, *but,*' he continued quickly, 'you came round only because I'd asked you to go for a drink the night before. I'll emphasise that I was the driving factor in it all.'

I put down my glass. 'This is going to ruin your relationship with her, isn't it?'

'Of course not,' he replied, but with a distinct lack of conviction.

I closed my eyes. 'It will,' I said, now unable to raise my voice above a whisper as I tried to keep a lid on my emotions. 'Morgan is going to ask you for every single detail and it won't matter that it was just a text about bubble-wrap, or a drink as friends, or a spoonful of Eton mess. What will matter is that you didn't tell her anything about it for weeks and weeks, and neither did I, and *that* will ruin your relationship.' I opened my eyes and drained my glass. 'How long have you got left on your lease?'

'Around a month.'

I replaced my glass firmly on the table 'Don't tell her anything. It was a stupid idea.'

'But I hate to see you unhappy.'

'Well, an angry, distraught woman on my doorstep certainly isn't going to cheer me up, is it?'

'Es...'

I waved a hand. 'A month is fine. I can do a month.'

'But then you're stuck coming to dinner on her birthday.'

'God, yes, I'd forgotten that.' I laughed humourlessly. 'Well, maybe I can get sick on the day.'

'Yes, David and his girlfriend will still be there to make up numbers.'

'Except that he hasn't got a girlfriend. They split up.'

'Oh, so it'll just be him?' He paused uncertainly for a moment, before attempting positivity. 'Not a problem,' he said brightly. 'It'll be fine with just the three of us.'

'Forget it.' I shook my head. 'I can do a month and I can eat birthday cake. That's better for Morgan, and for us, than the alternative.'

He hesitated, before nodding acceptingly. 'OK, but if there's anything I can do to make things easier on the night, let me know.'

'Maybe act like I'm not there?'

He smiled sadly. 'I've been trying to do that for the past four years, Es,' he said quietly, 'without much success.'

I stayed silent, choosing not to tell him that I felt the same. I wasn't sure where that conversation might lead, but I suspected that it would be nowhere happy or helpful.

He must have decided that it wasn't a thread he wanted to pursue either, because after a moment he said, 'Talking of birthdays, I don't suppose I can buy yet another of hedgehog guy's pieces, can I? I'm running out of time and can't think of anything else to surprise her with on the day. And she *really* loves those things.'

'Yes, she asked about them this afternoon, actually. I told her they weren't available yet. They've got to be priced and then we're holding on to them because we're hoping to put together a show for Douglas quite soon. Not within the next month, though. So I'm afraid Morgan'll miss out on that.'

'Look, Es, I just want to—'

'But I guess I could talk to David and Douglas about pricing tomorrow and if you'd like one of the pieces, you can have it,' I interrupted, anxious about what he might – or might not – have been about to say next.

'Thank you.'

'I've got some photographs of his new work, if you'd like to see them.'

'No,' he smiled. 'But yes.'

'I think you might find them more interesting than you expect. We've recently uncovered a very different side to Douglas.'

'Different as in…?'

'A slightly unsettling preoccupation with death and despair.'

'Hedgehog guy?' he queried, his eyebrows raised.

'Hedgehog guy,' I replied, nodding.

'You're right, I'm interested,' he said, looking towards the bar. 'But I'm also apprehensive and in need of another drink to steady my nerves. How about you?' He looked at my empty glass.

I shook my head. 'I'm fine.'

'Not even a small one?' he asked, standing up.

I hesitated for a moment and then, because I suspected that this might be my last drink alone with Elliot for an awfully long time, I said, 'Actually, a red would be great. Thanks.'

Chapter 22

'Jesus, I'm only asking what you're going to wear tomorrow night,' said Cass, fetching some ice from the fridge for her gin and tonic before returning to the small kitchen table. 'Don't be so tetchy about it.'

'It just felt like a very loaded question,' I said, lowering my voice and glancing towards the gallery where David was cashing up. 'It sounds like you think I'm going to dress to impress – which I'm not.'

'Hmm,' she said, smirking and raising her eyebrows sceptically.

'I am not!' I insisted.

'Oh, of course I know you're not. As if I'd think you're the kind of woman to go after someone else's man.' She laughed dismissively. 'I'm just trying to lighten the mood. You've been miserable about this ever since she invited you.'

'Yes, well, it's not like it's going to be my most comfortable evening ever, is it? Watching my neighbour get cosy with my ex.'

'She doesn't strike me as the type who'd touch him up over the main course,' said Cass, tutting at the idea. 'And you got on really well with her when she came round for drinks. The only difference this time is that he's going to be there too. And he won't want anything to kick off, so I'm sure he'll be civil. Just let him chat to Dave.'

'I'm not worried about anyone being uncivil,' I said, swirling my gin. 'I can just about handle it when I see them separately and we stick to talking about work and the weather. But seeing them together is different. I just wish she knew about my relationship with him, because you tread carefully when you meet your partner's ex, don't you? You rein it in.' I looked to Cass for understanding, but instead she frowned and her lips thinned – a sure indication of disapproval. 'What?' I asked, holding out my hands. 'What? What have I said?'

'You told me,' she began slowly, 'and I quote, that it was "shit" when you and Elliot went for a drink a couple of months ago.'

'Well, it was.'

'But now you say that "it's fine" when you see him separately. It's almost as if you've been for more drinks since the "shit" evening you told me about.'

'How's Kevin's foot?' I asked.

'Come on then,' she said, putting down her glass. 'How many times have you been out with him?'

I sighed. 'A couple of. Three at most. And we were just catching up. Nothing happened.'

'Nothing down there, maybe,' she said, pointing between her legs. 'But what about up here?' She tapped the side of her head. 'That's why you were all breathless and shifty when he came round to your place looking for Morgan, wasn't it? Looking for Morgan, my arse,' she added. 'I knew something was off.'

'Nothing whatsoever is off, except the fact that tomorrow I have to attend a birthday party that I'd rather swap for a dental appointment.'

'Well, you signed up to it, so you're just going to have to suck it up,' she said unsympathetically, picking up her glass and waving it. 'Just remember that whatever goes down, I need to hear all about it. Oh, and before you start sighing at me,' she added, leaning back in her chair and sipping her G&T, 'I want to hear all about it so that I can help you work through any issues, *not* because you've landed yourself in a really, really interesting situation, in which I'm really, really interested. Hey, Dave,' she continued without pause, turning in her chair as he entered the kitchen, 'I'm just saying to Es that I want to hear *all* about your dinner with her and her— ow!' She bent down and rubbed her shin. 'That really hurt!'

'Sorry,' I said casually, looking under the table. 'I must have caught you when I crossed my legs.' I widened my eyes at her and mouthed, 'He doesn't know, *remember*,' as David walked past us to the sink and began to wash his hands.

'Yeah, so, anyway, Dave,' she said, frowning at me. 'I hope you have a really nice time with Es's...'

I glared at her.

'...*neighbours* tomorrow night,' she concluded, with a wink in my direction.

'I'm sure I shall,' he said, drying his hands on some kitchen roll.

'I want *all* the beef on Monday,' continued Cass. 'What you ate, what you wore, who said what, details of any and all awkward moments...'

I narrowed my eyes at her. 'You know, I'm really not sure that there's going to be anything at all interesting to report, Cassandra.'

'Oh, I bet there will be, Esme,' she replied. 'I mean, I know you've had a few drinks with Morgan, but you and Dave know next to nothing about either of these people, do you? They could be spies or swingers for all you know. That's what happened to my Nanna Pat when she went to her new neighbours' housewarming.'

David looked over his shoulder at her. 'So what were they? Spies or swingers?'

'Well, swingers, *of course*, Dave,' she said. 'They wouldn't have been very good spies if Nanna Pat had rumbled them over a sherry, would they? She wasn't the sharpest. She told me she thought the car keys in the bowl were some sort of raffle.'

'A car raffle?' he echoed, frowning.

'I know,' she sighed. 'Sad, isn't it? I said to her, "You don't pick the *prizes* out of the hat in a raffle, do you, Nanna? You pick the *winning tickets.*" But as I said,' she tapped the side of her head, 'Nanna Pat: not the sharpest. She thought her slippers were guinea pigs towards the end. Gave them names, made them porridge, that kind of thing.'

David looked at her for a moment, opened his mouth as if to say something and then, clearly thinking better of it, turned to me instead. 'Dinner is at eight tomorrow, isn't it?'

'Yep. Fancy coming to me at seven thirty for a quick pre?'

'Thanks, but I'm in Bath, so I might be pushed for time.'

'OK.'

'What are you doing in Bath?' asked Cass.

'Eating... walking... That kind of thing,' he said. 'The weather's supposed to be good, so we thought, why not?'

'Sounds great, but who's *we*?' she asked. 'Who are you going with? Here, Dave.' She patted the chair between us. 'Pull up a seat, have a drink and tell us all about it. There's loads of gin.'

'Thanks,' David screwed up the kitchen roll and dropped it into the pedal bin, 'but I'm out this evening.'

'Ooh, who's that with then? Is it the same person you're going to Bath with?' asked Cass eagerly. 'Male or fema—'

'And I'm late,' he continued, checking his watch and exiting. 'Have a great weekend, Cass. See you tomorrow, Esme.'

'See you!' I called.

'Yeah, whatever,' muttered Cass sullenly, as the gallery door beeped and then slammed shut. 'God, you weren't exaggerating when you said he wasn't a sharer, were you? How can he be late?' She tapped her phone. 'It's only just after six. Who's he meeting?'

'Don't know,' I shrugged. 'But if I had to guess, I'd say a charity worker, an artist or a hedge-fund-trust-fund type. Most of the people he mentions seem to fall into one of those three categories.'

'Well, whoever it is, I'm pretty sure it's not Sophie,' sighed Cass, 'because she was back blubbing all over Mandy's chair *again* at the beginning of the month. She's getting worse, apparently, and Mandy's run out of for-God's-sake-cheer-up stuff to say to her. So I've said I'll cut her hair next time. I'm gonna give her the whole you're-strong-and-sexy-and-can-have-any-man-you-want spiel. Because, I tell you, the woman needs to stop crying before she's dust. Plus, I'm fed up of giving her discounted colours and cuts.'

I lowered my drink and frowned at her. 'Wait a minute, you told me that *I* was strong and sexy and could have any man I wanted.'

'That was *totally* different,' she said, shaking her head.

'How?'

'I wasn't trying to get out of giving you a discount.'

'Well, it doesn't matter anyway because I don't want a man. I'm better off on my own.'

'Oh, stop getting all Italia Conti,' she said, leaning across the table and giving my hand a light tap. 'The right guy is out there. You're just not looking for him.'

'If you say so.'

'Look, I know I wind you up about the ex next door, but I get that it must be difficult,' she said more gently. 'Really difficult. And you seem to be handling it pretty well. Although...'

I looked up at her. 'Although what?'

'It's just...' She pulled a face and shifted in her seat. 'Mightn't it be better to explain the situation to Dave before you go to dinner tomorrow? I'm a bit surprised you haven't already.'

'What?' I exploded. 'You're the one who said that I shouldn't tell him anything!'

'I know, I know,' she said calmly, topping up her glass with gin. 'But that was ages ago, and before he was about to spend an entire evening with you and your ex. Situations change, Es. You gotta keep up.' She clicked her fingers. 'Change. Adapt.'

I closed my eyes and allowed my head to fall backwards. 'Oh my God, it's going to be awful.'

'Now, don't get upset.' She moved onto my glass with the gin. 'It isn't going to be awful; it's going to be fine. I just wonder if Dave knowing what's going on might help things go more smoothly.'

I looked at her wearily. 'I suppose I just thought I'd find the whole thing easier if he wasn't sitting there, you know, judging us – and, more specifically, judging *me*.' I put a hand to my forehead. 'But maybe you're right. Maybe I should call and tell him.'

She looked thoughtful for a moment and then shook her head. 'You know what? Don't listen to me: you're right. You're gonna feel bad enough about hiding stuff from Morgan and pretending not to know Elliot, without Dave knowing what you're up to and being all shocked and disappointed in you. *Plus*, you're probably going to have to tell loads of out-and-out lies tomorrow night and it'd only spoil Dave's evening if he was forced to be in on that. But then again...' She paused and frowned. 'I guess the problem with *not* telling him is that you're actually lying to him too, and that might make you feel *even worse*. *And*, he might pick up on one of your lies and contradict you, and turn everything to shit by accident. Hmm...' Her eyes widened and she shook her head. 'God, it's really difficult, isn't it?'

I stared at her across the table. 'Thanks, that was all really helpful. I now feel so much better about everything.'

'Hey, I'm a hairdresser, not a bloody magician.'

I closed my eyes for a second time and heaved a sigh.

'You know, you'll laugh about this one day,' said Cass, leaning across the table and punching me lightly on the arm. 'I promise.'

'Yeah, probably around the same time I start making porridge for my slippers.'

She laughed and picked up her drink. 'Poor Nanna Pat.'

'So what happened with the swingers in the end?'

'She picked out a Fiat Uno, owned by a technical librarian named Don. They had a lovely time, apparently.'

My jaw dropped as I placed my glass down heavily on the table. 'She didn't...' I said, feeling scandalised.

'He took her to the local pub and bought her a Babycham to cheer her up, after she realised that she hadn't won his car. Then he dropped her home.'

'Oh, bless.'

'They stayed friends – just friends, but good friends – even through the slipper days. Neither of them was one to judge.'

I smiled. 'That was nice.'

'Yep, so let that be a lesson to you, Esme Green,' said Cass, saluting me with her glass. 'Good things can come from even the dodgiest of evenings.'

I nodded, desperately wanting to believe that something good could come from dinner with the neighbours, but not quite able to shake the conviction that right now, even an addled grandma and a swinging librarian had a better shot at a happy outcome than Elliot and I did.

Chapter 23

I stared into my open wardrobe, feeling more anxious than I had in a long time about what to wear. I hated that anxiety, and the sense it brought with it that Cass had been right when she had implied that I wanted to impress, or compete, or something equally as distasteful. I had spent most of Saturday morning trying to suppress all concerns regarding looking my absolute best, but by seven p.m. I had given up trying to pretend that I didn't want to look as attractive as possible – and was berating myself for not having shopped for new clothes or taken Cass up on her last-minute offer of a haircut.

I would have loved to have been able to write off my determination to look good as a laudable sense of self-worth and a desire to reflect my inner strength in a self-assured exterior. But as time marched on, and the pile of rejected clothing on my bed grew, I knew without doubt that it was actually all part of wanting to present myself that evening as Morgan's equal; physically, as well as intellectually and professionally. I didn't feel great about that urge, but neither did I have the emotional resources to fight it. So, in the end, I gave in to it and, as I stood on my neighbours' doorstep at 8:05 p.m., fox-head knocker in hand, I felt pretty good about how I looked on the outside: in my unfussy but perfectly fitted black linen shift dress, and my barely-there-but-dear-God-it's-taken-hours make-up. The downside, of course, was an all too miserable awareness of the significantly less attractive Dorian Gray intentions and motivations which lurked beneath.

I let the knocker drop and waited, taking several deep breaths in a futile attempt to calm my nerves. After a moment, Elliot opened the door.

'Good evening, Esme,' he said loudly, before adding, his voice lowering to a whisper, 'Hi, Es.'

I looked up at him, suddenly struck by the ridiculousness of the fact that, despite having known each other so well and so intimately for so long, neither of us had made any attempt to deliver either a hug or a kiss on the cheek.

I had seen nothing of him since our evening in the wine bar and our texted communications had been restricted to making arrangements regarding Douglas's vole, which Elliot had then collected from the gallery when I wasn't there. It was an arm's length approach, adopted by mutual unspoken consent, and one which I was able to stick to by reminding myself that the less contact we had, the less we had to hide. Imagining Morgan reading every single one of his texts over his shoulder also aided my resolve.

It was a situation of conscious emotional and social censorship which now, as he stood in the doorway of his home, left me unable to return either his smile or his greeting. In fact, I wondered whether I would even make it into the hallway, let alone through the evening.

'Thanks for coming,' he said gently, his own smile fading a little. 'And you know I mean that.'

I nodded.

'So... coming inside?' he asked uncertainly, as if even at this late stage he wasn't entirely sure that I would.

'Sure,' I said, still not quite managing a smile, but at least somehow accessing the gross motor skills required to step inside. 'And,' I added, holding out a bottle of champagne, 'I brought you this.'

–

The early part of the evening was for me – as I knew it would be – torture. But I must have hidden my misery pretty well, because it didn't seem to impact in any way on either Morgan's or David's mood, as they laughed and joked together, apparently oblivious to the fact that, behind my own forced laughter, I was dying inside.

I realised that until that evening, *dying inside* wasn't a concept that I had ever really fully appreciated. But from 8:10 p.m. to 8:40 p.m., I was aware of my inner-being withering and dimming, until the real me – the actual Esme Green – was barely a flicker within a grinning, nodding husk, as I was forced to listen to Morgan, in response to David's questioning, telling us lots of things I already knew about Elliot, and lots of things about herself and Elliot that I really didn't want to know.

Meanwhile, Elliot had managed to absent himself from the lounge by insisting, so Morgan told us, that he should do all the cooking that evening. Cooking was, she explained, something he enjoyed but rarely had time for, so he was keen to put on an apron whenever possible. This was news to me and I suspected that, on this particular occasion, Elliot might have decided that the less time we spent in each other's company, the better. And while on paper the plan might have seemed a good one, in practice it left me all on my own to deal with the agonies of the situation, and with no one to help direct Morgan's conversation away from a topic which was so painful to me: namely, the topic of Elliot himself.

It was around 8:45 p.m., and Morgan had just begun to tell the *hilarious* story of how she and Elliot had met, when I decided that I had two choices: either I could massively up my alcoholic intake, and get quickly and quietly drunk to the point of unconsciousness, or I could leave – at least the room, if not the house. As the latter option offered a more immediate escape from my current torment, that was the one I plumped for.

'We were in an optician's at the time and Elliot always says that it was good that I saw him *before* I got my new contacts,' laughed Morgan.

David joined in the laughter. 'Brilliant,' he said.

I attempted a chuckle, which even to my own ears sounded more asthmatic than amused. Both David and Morgan stopped laughing and looked at me with concern.

'Sorry,' I said, patting my chest. 'Not sure what happened there. But you know what?' I jerked my head towards the kitchen. 'I'm starting to feel sorry for Elliot stuck in the kitchen all by himself. How about I go and offer some help?'

'He's fine,' said Morgan, her tone upbeat, her expression neutral. 'And you don't want to get splashed with anything. He's an incredibly messy cook.'

I stood up. 'I'm not worried about getting anything on this old thing,' I said, tugging at one of the most expensive dresses I owned.

She blinked rapidly, as if sitting in the path of a sandstorm, and then she too stood up. 'Why don't I go and check if he needs anything?' She walked towards me and, placing a hand on my arm, leaned in conspiratorially as she passed. 'He can be a bit shy about accepting help,' she murmured, before making her way to the kitchen.

I flopped back down into my armchair and heaved a sigh – primarily of relief. OK, so I hadn't escaped the room, but I had, at least for now, escaped the Morgan-and-Elliot love story.

'All OK?'

I started at David's question, having for the moment forgotten that I wasn't alone.

'What? Oh, yes, I just...' I placed a finger on my temple. 'I had a headache when I arrived, but it's easing now.'

He nodded. 'I thought you were quiet.'

'Did you? Oh no. I hope I didn't seem rude.'

'Not at all. You were just quiet – for you. I'm sure Morgan didn't notice.'

'That's good. I'd hate to upset her. She's very...' I left the description hanging, aware that whatever complimentary characteristic I ascribed to Morgan, it wasn't going to make me feel great about myself. 'God, I hate this,' I murmured, my head drooping.

'Why? It's great on you,' said David, causing me to start for the second time in two minutes.

'What? Oh,' I shook my head. 'I didn't mean the dress. I...' I hesitated, fighting a significant urge to ask him to take me home. I felt desperately in need of rescue, and of an opportunity to confide.

He looked at me questioningly, waiting for me to go on.

'All is fine and under control in the kitchen,' announced Morgan brightly, returning to the room, 'and to be honest,' she added, with a wrinkle of her nose and a display of teeth – her current version of a smile – 'I think he'd be a bit flustered if you tried to help.'

I nodded acceptingly.

'Yes, so where was I?' she asked, sitting back down on the sofa next to David.

'At the optician's,' he said helpfully.

'Oh, yes. So I was waiting for my appointment, as was Elliot, and this is where it gets a bit crazy...'

David caught my eye and I hastily adopted a look of amused interest. Then, as he returned his attention to Morgan, I picked up the bottle of wine next to me and filled my glass almost to the brim. It was, I decided, time for Plan B.

–

By the time Elliot, and our food, were ready to join us at the dining table, I was still, sadly, far from drunk. But the large glass of red I'd surreptitiously consumed in between Morgan's Specsavers anecdote and the arrival of dinner had at least begun to dull the pain of an evening that was turning out to be about as much fun as a slow-mo bikini wax.

'So,' she said, taking her seat next to David and leaving the one next to me worryingly empty, 'I know what David did before opening the gallery, but what were you up to, Esme? Have you ever been a full-time artist? Are any of your pictures on sale in the gallery?'

'Esme's actually rather shy about her art,' said David, before I could answer. 'But anything she has ever been persuaded to hang has sold within days.'

'I just prefer promoting other people's work. Besides, David can't talk,' I said, shifting the focus, reluctant to explain that I wasn't very keen on the idea of strangers hanging my innermost feelings on their walls. 'He's a very talented sculptor, but never shows anything at all.'

He shook his head. 'That's completely different. I'm a novice, an amateur.'

'That doesn't make your work any less impressive. Saleable art is saleable art and you,' I insisted, 'produce pieces which would, if only you'd test the water, have broad commercial appeal. Trust me, I know.'

Morgan laughed. 'This doesn't sound like the first time you've had this discussion.'

'It's not,' I said. 'He's too modest. He is his own, and possibly only, business blind spot.'

'We have wild mushroom risotto,' said Elliot, emerging from the kitchen and placing a plate in front of David and a second in front of me, before disappearing again.

I stared down at the plate, which bore what had been my favourite dish from Elliot's repertoire, and heard a small gasp from the other side of the table.

'I didn't think to ask if either of you had any preferences or allergies,' said Morgan. 'I just knew that David was pescatarian. Is there a problem with the risotto, Esme?'

I looked up and shook my head. 'No,' I said. 'I love mushroom risotto.'

Elliot returned with two more plates and, after handing one to Morgan, he sat down next to me without making eye contact.

'Esme loves mushroom risotto, El,' said Morgan.

'That's lucky.' He smiled at her, but still didn't turn towards me.

I picked up my glass and as David asked Morgan something about her time in Edinburgh, I took a large gulp, trying to come up with an over-dinner question for Elliot to which I didn't already know the answer and which was also fit for general consumption.

'So, do you like Bristol, Elliot?'

'I really like the suspension bridge,' he said, staring determinedly at his plate. 'What an engineering marvel. How about you?'

'I also like the bridge and the big metal ship and the balloons.'

He offered me a sidelong glance. 'Anything else?'

'The wine,' I said, as David nodded along to Morgan's comments on regional accents, 'even if it's not actually local.'

'Agreed. I actually got through rather a lot of it in the kitchen,' he added in a murmur.

I smiled and began to feel better; there was something relaxing about a shared tension.

'This is great, Elliot,' said David, pointing at his plate. 'I'm so impressed.'

'Oh, don't be, I've made it a thousand times.'

'He's being modest!' exclaimed Morgan. 'This is his first attempt.'

Elliot looked up at her and smiled. 'I'm just pleased everyone is enjoying it,' he said.

–

'Here, let me take that.' Morgan reached to take the empty dessert bowl from me.

'Thank you, that was so delicious,' I said brightly, free at last from the crippling anxiety with which the evening had started. A combination of innumerable top-ups, courtesy of Elliot, and a conversation diverted away from the personal and onto politics and the arts had helped enormously. There had also been a brief, and wholly uncharacteristic, foray into reality TV by David, during which he had revealed himself to be woefully unaware by describing *Love Island* as a documentary.

'Admit it, David,' I said, 'you've never seen it.'

Morgan's body language expressed disappointment and something else. 'Were you just saying you'd seen it to make me feel better about watching it?' she asked, adding his bowl to the stack in front of her.

'Not at all,' he said. 'My girlfriend was fascinated by it.'

Both Elliot and I looked up simultaneously.

'And how is Sophie?' I asked dryly, a bottle of red freeing me from tactful restraint. 'I haven't seen her for simply *ages*.'

'Oh my goodness, I've got to tell you something so funny, David,' said Morgan, picking up her glass with one hand and placing her other hand on his arm as he frowned at me across the table. 'When I introduced you to Elliot at Douglas's show...'

'Morgan, there's no need to—' began Elliot quietly.

'...and I said that you were Esme's partner,' she continued, apparently oblivious to the interruption, 'he was really shocked, weren't you, Elliot?'

'Shocked is a bit of an exaggeration.' He was smiling, but his amusement didn't seem entirely genuine.

I focused on Morgan, judging – despite my inebriated state – that giving either David or Elliot my attention at that moment might not be the best idea.

'Oh, don't lie. You were all confusion, El,' laughed Morgan. 'Because Elliot prides himself, you see,' she continued, turning to David, 'on being able to match people and he said that he just couldn't see you two together. Then of course I explained that you were business partners, not romantic partners, and order was restored for him.' She rolled her eyes and bared some teeth. 'It made me laugh, because Jasmine had told everyone half an hour earlier that she was seeing you.' She nudged David. 'So I already knew your type.'

I laughed explosively. 'What? Jasmine said that she was seeing David? She is unbelievable.'

Morgan put a hand to her mouth. 'Is that not true?'

'No, but don't worry, the woman is…' I paused and took a breath. 'Well, she is first and foremost an *excellent* artist, of course,' I said, holding up a finger, 'but she does also have a tendency to…' I hesitated, searching my increasingly anaesthetised brain for the right words, 'to extend her creativity beyond the bounds of the canvas.'

'We've been for drinks,' said David calmly, addressing the statement exclusively to Morgan. 'And for dinner.'

'Drinks? Dinner? You and Jasmine?' I exclaimed, screwing up my face into an expression of disbelief to match my tone, while aware that making connections and forming sentences was beginning to require some degree of concentration.

'Me and Jasmine,' confirmed David, reaching for his glass.

'Well,' I said, 'what a revelation. That's astonishing news, David. Oh and brilliant news, obviously. Hey, and sorry if I, you know, doubted Jasmine at all back there. She's an amazing talent and here's to her,' I added, raising my glass, 'and all who sail in her.'

Elliot laughed and stood up. 'Morgan,' he said, pointing at the dessert bowls, 'pass those to me and I'll go and make some coffee.'

'Sounds good,' she nodded.

I looked at David. He appeared far from upset, but a slightly raised eyebrow in my direction was enough to make me feel guilty about my reaction to the news that he was dating Jasmine.

'You know, I think I'm just going to pop to the loo,' I said, standing up while keeping a steadying hand on the table.

'There's one upstairs, or there's the shower room, just beyond the kitchen,' said Morgan.

'Yes, both cottages have the same layout, don't they?' I smiled.

Elliot kept his back to me as I breezed through the kitchen and, once in the loo, I took the opportunity to splash some cold water on my cheeks and my wrists, in an attempt to sober up just enough to politely consume my coffee, make my excuses and leave, hopefully with David in tow, so that I could apologise – more profusely this time – about Jasmine. I couldn't deny that I was feeling astonished, bordering on betrayed, that he was seeing somebody so utterly irritating. But, I told myself, I had to accept that it was his life, his choice, and that I had no right to counsel or criticise – no matter how much I may have wanted to.

Drying my face and my hands, I exited the loo, making my way through the small utility room and back into the kitchen, where Elliot was now standing by the hob, waiting for the whistling kettle to boil.

'Looks great,' he said, pointing to it, 'but takes an age.'

'I know. I've got the same one – except mine's not cream, it's—'

'Red,' he said. 'Or have you bought a new one?'

I looked at him for a moment and then shook my head. 'Same one.' I turned to walk away, but he reached out and caught my hand, gently pulling me to a halt.

'Morgan has taken him outside to see the garden,' he said. 'They've only just gone out.'

'But it's pitch-black out there.'

'They've got torches. Besides, it's all about scent and touch at this time of night – apparently. It's all so ridiculous,' he added quietly.

I nodded. 'It is. All of it.'

Still holding my hand, he moved closer, the fabric of his white shirt now brushing against my bare arm. 'Do you ever think we made a mistake? Back then?' he asked suddenly.

I closed my eyes and shook my head.

'I was jealous, Es,' he whispered, his hands moving to my upper arms, as he gently turned me towards him. 'I was jealous of Owen all those years ago and I'm jealous of David right now because he gets to spend every single day with you. I can't help it.'

I looked up at him, my head swimming a little. It felt good to know that jealousy and insecurity weren't my preserve. Elliot was jealous of David and I was jealous of Jasmine. I frowned and shook my head again, confused by the thought. No, I wasn't jealous of Jasmine. She could have David. David and I worked together, that was all.

'There's no one to be jealous of, Elliot,' I said. 'I'm completely alone.'

I knew that I should walk away, but his hands didn't move and instead of leaving, I looked up at him as he lowered his face towards mine and kissed me.

A moment, or minutes, later – I wasn't sure which – we simultaneously registered the sound of the back door opening and stepped apart, hastily adjusting our clothing.

'I know it's silly, because we won't be here long,' I heard Morgan say, as David led the way into the kitchen. 'But I'm still going to plant them.'

'You should. Don't let anyone persuade you otherwise. It's your legacy,' he said, sounding surprisingly serious about the horticultural suggestion, whatever it had been.

'Kettle's still not boiled,' said Elliot with impressive calm. 'I'm afraid I filled it way too full again.'

I said nothing, staring wide-eyed at the faux-stone floor, as if it were a newly discovered Caravaggio, my heart threatening to burst through my chest wall.

'I keep telling you,' said Morgan, bending to take off her boots and then snaking an arm around Elliot's waist, 'we should get an electric one.'

'I know,' he said, stepping away from her and turning towards the hob, as the kettle at last began to sing, 'but there's something about this one that I love.'

Chapter 24

I awoke the next morning, relieved to find myself in my cottage, with bright summer sunshine streaming in through a crack in the aesthetically unpleasing floral bedroom curtains.

The relief was due to the fact that I had spent the night dreaming that I was in the gallery, hanging my own artwork, with David silently assisting me in the process. I'd kept asking him whether he liked the paintings but, despite his nods, I had a strong suspicion that he disapproved. Then Jasmine had turned up, with a palette of smeared acrylics and a vaseful of brushes, and had proceeded to cancel my paintings by daubing huge corner-to-corner crosses on each one in turn, while falling into raptures over David's beautiful frames. He had then declared her to be a creative genius and they had just started to make out on the deck of a Hebridean longboat, captained by Lloyd, when, thankfully, I woke up.

Hauling myself into a sitting position on the edge of the bed, I positioned a hand on either side of my head in an attempt to keep it in place, as the unmistakable indications of an Esme Green hangover (extreme hunger, middling nausea, mild regret) began to kick in.

I looked around in a slow motion, and ultimately fruitless, search for my phone, before cautiously wobbling my way to the bedroom door and unhooking my dressing gown. After several failed attempts to put it on, I eventually managed to solve the conundrum of an inside-out sleeve and made my way slowly downstairs, towards the kitchen, all the while feeling extremely pissed off with Jasmine for dream-defacing my artwork, and equally pissed off with David for not dream-defending it and, worse still, for *actually* dating such an annoying woman. What was he thinking? I couldn't wait to report back to Cass, just as soon as I found my phone. She would be appalled.

Shaking my head at David's jaw-droppingly dismal taste, I meandered into the kitchen, flopping down at the table and once again positioning my head between my hands. Shaking it had been a mistake. This morning, I decided, was a morning for avoiding all sudden movements and for taking things very slowly indeed. I had already achieved walking downstairs and traversing the lounge. That was way more than enough to justify a little steadying sit-down before filling the kettle.

I frowned, strangely troubled by the thought, before executing a stop-motion, hand-assisted, head-turn in the direction of the hob, and the red… whistling…

Kettle.

My eyes widened and I let out a tiny anguished cry, my hands moving to cover my mouth, as the memory of Elliot's slow-to-boil kettle and, more crucially, his slow-moving tongue, finally surfaced – about as welcome as a floater in a swimming pool, or a shark fin in the surf.

I closed my eyes, forcing myself to excavate the details of an event which my psyche had, until that moment, been doing such an impressive job of burying. Yes, I had definitely snogged Elliot – very enthusiastically, in fact. We had been in the kitchen. Alone. That was something. Because even if it did nothing whatsoever to assuage the crushing sense of guilt, at least there were no witnesses to add to my shame – other than Elliot, of course.

I groaned and collapsed forward onto the table, resting my head on my folded arms, now desperately trying to piece together the post-snog events. I had definitely stayed on, but I couldn't remember taking much part in the over-coffee conversation. Nor could I remember what anyone else had said. Had I dozed off? Or – in the interest of emotional self-preservation – switched off, maybe?

I was certain that David had walked me home and put the key in the front door for me – and maybe with a disapproving sigh. God, I hoped I hadn't said anything more to him about Jasmine. I felt bad enough as it was about my dinnertime reaction to the fact that he was dating her.

But what was any of that compared to what had happened with Elliot? And more to the point, compared to what might happen next? Would he confess to Morgan? Should I be expecting to hear the angry pounding of a hysterical and wronged woman on my door at any minute?

I sat upright, anxiously clutching my dressing gown around me and retying it firmly at the waist, as if that might offer some defence against the justified anger and recriminations of a woman who had done nothing wrong, other than unwittingly invite her partner's ex to dinner.

A sudden buzzing distracted me from this miserable train of thought and I turned to see my phone, vibrating in a mug next to the sink. I leaned back in my chair, reaching for the mug and relieved to discover it clean and empty, save for the phone.

My notifications told me that I had four messages, all from Cass, none from Elliot. My heart sank. I realised that there was unlikely to be any opportunity for him to discreetly text or call, but that didn't stop me wanting him to, as I clung desperately to the unlikely possibility that he might just be able to make me despise myself a little less.

Feeling increasingly despairing and with Elliot silent, I decided to give self-help a whirl, focusing my limited energies on finding a mitigating circumstance, or emotional excuse, which might prove of some comfort. However, after several minutes of intense mental concentration, my hungover brain had managed to trawl up nothing more than an increased sense of self-loathing and self-reproach. The simple inescapable fact of the matter was that I had made a huge mistake, one with the potential to devastate relationships. The only current uncertainty was the precise extent of that devastation, as that was of course dependent upon what all those with a personal interest in the matter, including myself, did next.

In my own case, I quickly decided that doing absolutely nothing was definitely my best bet, on the basis that I couldn't do anything to improve matters, and if I gave into any early, fuzzy-headed impulses to seek comfort from, confide in or apologise to anyone, there was a significant risk of me making things much, much worse.

I picked up the phone and read Cass's texts. They had been sent at half-hourly intervals, starting at 9:30 a.m., and were identical, save for a switch to upper case in the most recently received.

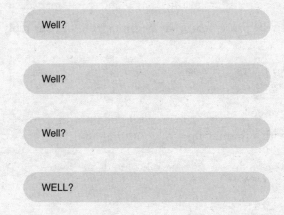

Well?

Well?

Well?

WELL?

I stared miserably at the screen, knowing that I'd have to give her something, or the enquiries would simply just keep coming.

Just woken up. It was a pretty heavy night. Very hungover. Will tell you about it Tue. xx

She began typing immediately and her reply landed within seconds.

> Come on. There must be something to report. I'm bored out of my mind here. Kev's rugby mates have taken him on a mystery away-day to cheer him up. Bet he ends up in the harbour.

I hesitated, knowing again that if I didn't reply, the pestering would continue.

> Hope Kevin's got a bag on his cast. Found out that David is seeing Jasmine. Didn't know that. Wonder if Sophie does.

There was zero pause before she began tapping out her reply.

> Who's Jasmine? The squeaky blonde with the curly hair?

I replied with a thumbs-up.

> What's she like?

Awful. I stared impassively at the screen for a moment before deleting and rewriting my reply.

> Much nicer than me.

Then after adding a laughing emoji and telling Cass that I was off for a shower, I sent the text, placed my phone face down on the table and began to cry.

I spent the remainder of the day waiting for it to end, distracting myself with a rolling programme of surfing the internet, reading and sketching darkly in my journal, with no activity successfully holding my attention for more than around half an hour at a time. I did at one point consider going for a walk, but a lingering nausea, combined with a terror of running into Morgan, caused me to abandon that idea and, with the exception of an unavoidable trip to the shed at seven p.m. to check my bike tyres, I remained firmly behind closed doors all day.

My contact with the outside world was therefore limited to Cass, who texted again just after eight, this time to invite me along to cocktails that she'd arranged for Mandy's birthday the next evening. I knew that she was as keen to check up on me, and give me a chance to offload about my Saturday night, as she was to celebrate Mandy's birthday with me. But Elliot was a conversation I wanted to have with her in person and alone, not by text or at high volume while surrounded by a group of women whose idea of therapy – I knew from experience – would be to book me in for free foils and then attempt to set me up with the guy behind the bar.

So in the end, I'd thanked Cass, but said that I'd see her on Tuesday, as planned. And to give her her due, she must have realised that something was up because – wholly against type – she hadn't pushed the matter and had quickly changed the subject, sending me a dozen pictures of Kevin, apparently attempting to complete an army assault course on crutches.

It was around eight thirty and I had just put my phone down on the sofa following what I thought was the conclusion of my exchange with Cass, when it pinged again. Picking it back up, I experienced a mixture of horror and relief at the sight of Elliot's name on-screen. However, the relief element of the mix evaporated immediately upon reading his message.

Morgan on way. Saw you in garden. Knows
you're home.

Experiencing a fresh wave of nausea, I looked up from my phone and towards the window, just as next-door's gate clanked shut and my own creaked open. The subsequent rapping of the knocker, which followed just a few seconds later, was like gunfire: unnaturally loud after a day spent in solitude and silence.

Traumatised into immobility, I had just begun to consider sliding off the sofa and rolling under the coffee table, when my muscles overrode my fevered brain, and I found myself walking towards the front door and then opening it.

'Hi, Esme! Sorry it's late but I wanted to give you this,' she said brightly, handing me a small cardboard box. 'Amazon called around lunchtime but got no answer from you. Ooh, are you OK?' she continued, her voice falling, her expression remaining unchanged. 'Did I wake you up?'

'Oh… no, you didn't. And thanks,' I said quietly, shaking my head, while focusing determinedly on the package. 'I'm just tired and very hungover. I had way too much to drink last night.' I attempted laughter but achieved only a series of short gasping breaths, which I decided to convert into a cough. 'Excuse me,' I croaked.

She reached out and placed a hand on my arm. 'Poor you. I said to Elliot afterwards that he should learn to let people top up their own drinks, rather than filling up glasses all the time. I hope it didn't spoil your evening.'

There was genuine concern in her voice and I looked up to see her anxiously biting her lower lip.

'God, no, I had a really…' I hesitated, clearing my throat. 'It was a lovely evening. Thanks so much for inviting me and I'm just so, so sorry that I—'

My phone pinged twice in quick succession. I placed a hand on the back pocket of my jeans and Morgan nodded at it. 'Do you have to get that?'

'No,' I said abruptly, attempting to pull myself together. 'But thanks so much for last night. I just hope I was still talking sense at the end of the evening.'

She laughed. 'As if I'd know. I was *so* gone. I was another of Elliot's victims.' She made a drinking gesture with her hand. 'He made sure that my glass was always *at least* half-full. I spent most of today in bed. He answered the door to that,' she said, pointing to the box in my hands. 'I was still in my pyjamas at three.'

I made a second attempt at laughter, this time with greater success. 'Well, that makes me feel better,' I lied.

'Good,' she said, beginning to turn away. 'Will look forward to doing it again very soon, and with David too. He's so lovely,' she added, before suddenly putting a hand to her mouth and turning back towards me. 'That reminds me, I hope I didn't put my foot in it over him and Jasmine. I'd already drunk quite a bit by then, and I was worried about it when I finally woke up today. I actually find it quite difficult sometimes to know if people are joking or not, and when I've been drinking, it's even harder.'

I felt my guilt increase to the level of physical burden and placed a hand against the doorframe for support. 'We were definitely joking,' I said, faking a giggle. 'In fact, we were laughing about it on the phone earlier today. Jasmine's really great, you know – very quirky and so kind that it's impossible not to love her. I'm not surprised he's seeing her,' I said rapidly, wondering if that was the most lies I'd ever fitted into a single breath.

'That's good,' she said, sounding relieved. 'He deserves someone nice.'

'Yes, he does.' It was a relief to finally get to tell the truth.

'He's just so—' she began, before being interrupted by the ringing of her phone. Taking it from her pocket, she looked at it for a moment, as if unsure whether to accept the call, before finally answering it.

'Hi, El,' she said, rolling her eyes at me.

I channelled what little energy I had into hoisting my mouth into a smile.

'Right now?' Morgan frowned into the phone. 'No, no, that's fine. I was coming back anyway.' She hung up and shrugged. 'He needs a hand finding something. Besides,' she added, as my own phone pinged for a third time, 'it sounds like there's someone keen to get hold of you too. Bye.'

I offered her a smile, now genuine with relief, and took a step backwards. 'Thanks again for the parcel,' I said, closing the door and resting against it for a moment, before taking a deep breath and returning to the living room and to the sofa. Flopping down, I took out my phone, experiencing no surprise at discovering three texts from Elliot.

In the first, he said he was sorry that he hadn't been able to text sooner, or to prevent Morgan from coming round. In the second, he said he hoped I was feeling OK and that he was in London until Wednesday. But it was in his final, and briefest, text that he came closest to referencing what had happened the night before.

Don't worry. It's between us and no one else.

The implication was clear: Morgan was in the dark and Elliot had no intention of enlightening her. Of course, I knew that was meant to reassure me – to put my mind at rest that the situation wasn't going to escalate and that no one was going to get hurt. But as I hauled myself off the sofa and headed for the stairs, dragging the unbearable weight of my guilt behind me like a thousand whistling kettles, I was actually feeling worse than ever.

Chapter 25

Despite having been desperate for the weekend to be over – and despite telling myself that my faux pas over Jasmine was the very least of my worries – I was still feeling undeniably anxious about the prospect of seeing David as I unlocked the gallery door on Monday morning.

I knew it was silly, because David was the last person in the world to bear a grudge and was well used to my occasional tendency to put my foot in it. These *unfiltered moments*, as he called them, were something which he always took in his stride: calming me down, helping me to see reason and then moving on. What's more, from his point of view, Saturday evening had, overall, been far from dull or disastrous. He and Morgan had got on brilliantly, again bonding over their mutual love of Edinburgh, and he had approved wholeheartedly of her work on the rear garden of the cottage, praising her loudly and at length on their return indoors. It was obvious that they enjoyed each other's company and, as the evening had drawn to a close, I remembered somewhat drunkenly thinking – although not, thank God, declaring – that it was a shame he wasn't her neighbour instead of me. So I certainly wasn't feeling guilty about making him an unwitting participant in my nightmare scenario.

Nevertheless, a seemingly disproportionate level of anxiety persisted, and as I pushed open the door of the gallery and called his name, I experienced a rush of relief on discovering that he wasn't there.

That relief was very short-lived, however, with the electronic beep of the shop door announcing his arrival before I had even finished filling the kettle.

'Hello!' I called tentatively, my sense of unease rising with the prospect of seeing him. 'I'm just making the coffee!' I switched on the kettle, hoping that the next five minutes would prove my anxiety to be nothing more than baseless, alcohol-related, paranoia.

'Morning,' he said, sticking his head around the kitchen door but not coming in. 'I'm going next door to crack on.' He nodded towards the workshop and offered me a brief smile, which had just a hint of afterthought about it.

'Sure. I'll bring your coffee through when it's ready.'

'No need,' he called, already out of sight. 'I picked one up on the way in.'

'Okaaay,' I murmured, opening the cupboard and putting away the mug I had taken out for him. 'Coffee for one it is, then.'

The kettle switched itself off and I stood for a moment, staring at it and listening to the subsiding bubbles, before turning away on impulse and heading for the workshop, rapping on the doorframe as I arrived. David was sitting on a high stool at his workbench and staring at a dark-wood, pictureless frame, in much the same way as I had been staring at the kettle a moment or two earlier. He started at the sound of my knock and looked up without smiling.

'Yes?'

I took a deep breath. 'Look, I hope this is a case of me being overly sensitive, but are you OK? About Saturday, I mean. I know I drank way too much and, to be honest, I can't remember verbatim everything I said, but I know I was a bit flippant about Jasmine and I feel really bad about that. I wanted to catch you after dinner to apologise properly, but it didn't happen.' I took a second breath and smiled. 'So, you know, I'm really sorry and I hope it didn't spoil your evening.'

He looked at me expressionlessly for a moment, and then turned and reached for the Costa cup on the bench in front of him. 'Don't worry about it. I know she's not someone you warm to. You've made that pretty clear in the past.'

He didn't smile and although he didn't appear angry, there was an edge to his tone that I couldn't recall hearing before. We'd had professional disagreements in the past, but they had always been resolved without resentment or negativity on either side, and the outcome was, more often than not, a compromise superior to either of our original points of view. But we'd never had a personal disagreement, and the fact that we seemed to be on the verge of one now felt alien and not at all good.

'If you're talking about what happened after her show, then you'll recall how sorry I was about my behaviour on that occasion too,' I said stiffly. And then, unwilling to roll over completely, and irked that he'd raised the incident again, I added, 'I shouldn't have allowed myself to be provoked like that.'

He looked up from his coffee and laughed humourlessly. 'OK.'

'What?'

'Nothing,' he said, putting down his cup and picking up a length of moulding. 'Let's leave it there.'

'But you're clearly still unhappy about it.'

'Look, let's just forget about Saturday night and get back to trying to run a business.'

I frowned, dissatisfied with what felt like a brusque and condescending dismissal of both myself and the subject. 'Sorry, David, but I think it would be a mistake to let this hang,' I said, aware of my stress levels rising. 'I hate things hanging and I'm surprised that you're apparently OK with it. I've said that I'm sorry, and I'd like to feel that you've accepted both my apology and the fact that I didn't mean to hurt anyone's feelings.'

He looked at me, with not a hint of acceptance.

'And can I just add,' I continued, frustration now adding to my upset, 'that if you weren't so closed about everything – if you had simply told me about dumping Sophie, and your drinks with Jasmine, like any normal person might have – then *of course* I wouldn't have told her to piss off after her show and *of course* I wouldn't have ridiculed the idea of you seeing her.'

Judging it best to stop talking before my voice reached a pitch that only dogs could hear, I instead stared silently at him, awaiting a response.

'I thought that you knew about Sophie,' he replied. 'She has her hair cut next door and she told me that she'd confided in her hairdresser. I assumed that Cass would tell you and spare me the need to raise something which serves no pleasant or positive purpose for either of us.'

'OK, well that's…' I began uncertainly, before deciding that there was no pleasant or positive purpose in admitting that actually, yes, he was quite right: Cass had told me all about Sophie. 'That's interesting, but let's stick to the point. The real issue here is me not knowing about Jasmine.'

'Because you can only make an effort to find the good in someone if they are personally connected to a colleague or a friend?'

'Hey, now that is just not fair!' I exclaimed, surprised and stung by the deliberately barbed comment, something that up until that moment I had always thought him above. 'You know that I try *very* hard to get along with all sorts of annoying people. This,' I said, waving a finger back and forth between us, 'was caused by me being less than charitable about someone I didn't know you'd been for dinner with. I've said I'm sorry, but if you could try to be more upfront about things in the future, then hopefully it won't happen again and I can…' I took a breath as I felt my emotions getting the better of me. 'I can get back to looking forward to coming to work, instead of absolutely dreading it.'

At that, he nodded slowly. 'OK then, let me be more upfront,' he said quietly, carefully laying the moulding down on his workbench. 'Firstly, for the most part I very much enjoyed

Saturday evening. Morgan and Elliot were very welcoming hosts and even your drunken comments about Jazz didn't really bother me, certainly not for long. I knew that you'd soon regret what you'd said and I didn't want to make you feel worse.'

'And yet you're sitting there doing exactly that!' I exclaimed exasperatedly.

He shook his head. 'No. If you want the truth, Esme, I'm sitting here wondering if I really want to be in business with someone who goes to dinner with her neighbours, wanders into their kitchen and makes a move on the partner of a woman who has invited her into her home – on her birthday – and who clearly wants to be her friend. That's what I'm sitting here doing.'

I stared at him, feeling my face begin to burn, unable to speak and with nothing to say anyway.

He looked back at me with an infuriating degree of calm, his eyebrows twitching upwards in a barely perceptible gesture of enquiry, while every other feature conveyed nothing but cold, hard disapproval.

The beep and creak of the gallery door opening and then slamming shut was followed by an excited, bordering on child-like, cry of, 'Hello! Anyone home?'

I turned and, without saying anything further to David, walked back into the gallery, heading for the counter to retrieve my bag.

Jasmine's smile faltered as she saw me. 'Oh hi, Esme. How are you? I just popped in to see David. He said he'd be in by eight… *when I spoke to him yesterday,*' she added significantly.

'He's in the workshop,' I said. 'Just go on through.' I picked up my bag and began to rifle through it for my phone.

A moment later I looked up, aware that Jasmine hadn't moved.

With enormous effort, I managed to affix an enquiring smile. 'All good?'

She nodded with theatrical uncertainty and I clenched my jaw, which had the dual benefit of maintaining the smile and providing a physical outlet for my suppressed irritation.

'I just want you to know that all past negativity is forgiven and forgotten,' she said, her head tilted to one side, her tone that of a patient care-worker dealing with a particularly obstreperous geriatric. 'I sometimes worry that you're still a little… Well, I'd just hate for things to be difficult between us. Especially as David and I are… well… you know…'

'Thank you for being so generous about it,' I replied, while mentally throwing the contents of my bag at her.

She smiled uncertainly, as if not quite satisfied. But clearly deciding that she couldn't achieve her preferred outcome – whatever that was – in the available time, she turned and headed through the gallery and towards the workshop. There I heard her greeting David in a typically sing-song fashion, like Snow White saying hi to the forest creatures, just before making them do all the washing-up. His response was more muted, but still positively tropical compared to the tundra tone he had reserved for me.

I gazed around the empty gallery and then, checking the time on my newly discovered phone, decided that I had a good thirty minutes before I absolutely had to be back behind the counter and customer-ready.

Quickly picking up my bag, I exited onto the pavement and had just got as far as the sportswear shop, next door to Lloyd's, when I heard Lloyd himself, calling my name. I turned to see him standing on his step and beckoning me back.

After a moment's hesitation, and with considerable reluctance, I returned.

'Hi, Lloyd, I was just hoping to squeeze in a quick walk to clear my head,' I said, looking over my shoulder towards my former direction of travel.

He nodded. 'Yes, I saw you steaming past the window and I said to Andy, "Esme doesn't look herself today, Andy. I wonder if there's something amiss."'

I pursed my lips together and looked down. 'No, no, it's all fine. I just...'

But that was as far as I got before the tears came, and Lloyd put his arm around my shoulders and escorted me into his shop.

–

'So this friend you think you've upset, Esme...'

'I don't just think it: I know it, Lloyd. There's absolutely no doubt about it,' I insisted, while nursing a delicately patterned teacup in the shop's surprisingly cosy kitchen.

Despite my distress, I had been a little wary of accepting Lloyd's offer of hospitality and a shoulder to cry on, in case it meant sitting on a dampish chopping block and resting my mug on half a cow. But instead, I had found myself in a small, spotlessly clean, cream-cupboarded kitchen, being poured tea from a pot with a dormouse on the lid and refusing repeated offers of quality biscuits.

'So this friend you have *definitely* upset,' he continued, 'is he an old friend? Do you know each other very well?'

'The thing is,' I sighed, 'we don't really share our worries and feelings and things like that, but we know each other's characters *very* well. I mean, I could tell you what makes him laugh, what interests him, what disappoints him...' I paused and took a slightly uneven breath. 'I know what he'd say if you asked his opinion on art or politics or ethics or, well, anything, really. But he didn't tell me when he split...' I took another breath. 'We don't really discuss our personal lives or feelings. Is that weird?'

'Not at all.' Lloyd shook his head. 'Friendships come in all shapes and sizes, Esme. You only have to look at Ian Paisley and Martin McGuinness, Sir Patrick Moore and Brian May, Christian the lion and the young men in flares.' He paused and smiled into his tea. 'I love that clip on YouTube. You know, when Christian sees the young men in flares after years and years, and they all have a big hug. Have you seen it?'

'Um… I'm not sure that I…'

He waved a hand. 'Doesn't matter. Google it later. My point is that there are no rules about what works when it comes to friendship. But I tell you this, Esme, what's for sure is that we will all disappoint and upset our friends at times – even our best friends. Just look at me a couple of months ago with Gwen. But we're over that now, aren't we? Thanks to you,' he added, saluting me with his cup.

'I'm afraid this is much worse than a muddle over a birthday gift, Lloyd.'

'It might seem so at the moment, but I know you and I know that whatever happened, you won't have had a thought of upsetting anyone in your head,' he said kindly.

'I don't think I had any thoughts in my head at all.'

'Drunk?'

I nodded. 'Very. But that's no excuse. And I think my biggest problem is that my friend is right to be upset. In fact, I'd be massively disappointed in him if he wasn't upset.'

'So he's a good bloke then?'

'A very good bloke.'

Lloyd smiled. 'Well, I think you need to discuss it with him. Because it's very important to talk about your feelings, you know. Although,' he continued, looking suddenly uneasy, 'if you think it's anything to do with his hormones, don't mention that because, in my experience, it doesn't go down too well.'

'OK.'

'But if he's a genuinely good bloke,' he continued, now smiling again, 'and everything is OK with his hormones, he'll listen to what you have to say, think it all through and I'm sure the pair of you will be back on track in no time.'

'I hope so,' I said, not feeling quite as optimistic as Lloyd, but certainly feeling a whole lot better for the kindness he'd shown me and the tea he'd poured down me. 'Thank you so much for taking time out for me, Lloyd. I know how busy you are.'

He went a little pinker than usual and waved a hand. 'You're always willing to help me out, Esme, and I'm glad to do the same for you.'

I smiled and stood up. 'Well, I'd better get back. David's hard at it in the workshop and I don't want him having to do front-of-house as well. That's hardly going to help matters, is it?' I said, having no doubt that Lloyd knew full well, from the details provided, that we were talking about David.

'I'll see you out,' he said, getting to his feet and following, as I made my way from the kitchen to the shop. 'And can I just say, Esme, well done for not naming names. That's very wise and discreet of you.' He tapped the side of his nose and winked.

'I know it's academic, but I just thought it might make things a tiny bit easier for you. You know, going forward.'

'Indeed. Now why don't you go next door and let David man the till for a while?' He beamed encouragingly. 'He won't mind. Just tell him that you've got a personal matter to attend to and that you need a few hours off. Then you can go and have the conversation that you need to have with your friend. Clear the air. Take my word for it; David will be just as keen to help you out as I am and I bet it'll all be sorted by lunchtime.'

I looked up at him, frowning slightly and wondering whom he thought we'd been discussing for the past half-hour. I thought about asking him, before deciding that his endearing ignorance was probably better for both of us, and definitely for David. And so, after thanking him yet again and giving him a very grateful hug, I headed back to the gallery.

Chapter 26

To my relief, Jasmine had gone by the time I got back. David was still in the workshop and, with just five minutes to go before we opened, I knew that now would not be the time to reopen our discussion regarding Saturday night, even if I had known what to say – which I didn't. Instead, our conversation was restricted to a shouted, 'I'm back!' from me and a suitably high volume, 'OK!' from him, and then we each got on with the day.

Our paths didn't cross for another two hours, until a customer came in to discuss a framing and I had to fetch David. Even though our exchange amounted to just a few sentences, it was obvious that neither of us was comfortable with the other, and equally obvious that we were both resigned to the fact there was simply nothing that could be done about the situation for now.

I prayed for a busy day, but it just wasn't to be, with heavy rain making what was always our quietest day of the week, quieter still. I kept myself as occupied as I could, checking in with some of our artists, placing a few orders and relocating and repricing some pieces that had failed to sell. But it still felt like a very long day, with far too much thinking time. Under normal circumstances, I would have asked David if there was anything I could do or organise for him, or even suggested that he come out front while I whizzed off to have a sneaky peek at what some of the competition was up to. But today, for the first time in our three-year association, any communication at all beyond the strictly essential seemed out of the question.

Nevertheless, as closing time approached, I decided that there was nothing for it but to try talking things through, as Lloyd had recommended, because I really couldn't cope with both home and work being places of fractured relationships and hurt feelings.

My preference would have been to bounce things off Cass first – a process which often helped to clarify my issues, if rarely to solve them. But with the salon closed for the day, I would have had to call her at home and interrupt her preparations for Mandy's birthday cocktails, and I didn't want to do that.

So at five thirty, and without the benefit of a chat with Cass, a stiff drink or beta blockers, I turned the sign on the street door to closed, steeled myself for whatever might be to come and went in search of David.

On reaching the small hallway between the gallery and the back rooms, I heard the clink of cutlery on crockery and headed for the kitchen, arriving just in time to see him placing two mugs of coffee on the table.

'I thought perhaps we should talk,' he said, in a voice that sounded unfamiliarly dispassionate and businesslike, and served as a rare reminder that most of his career to date had been corporate and high-powered.

I glanced down at the coffee, the preparation of which was just a little too presumptuous for my liking.

'Actually, I was coming to suggest the very same thing,' I said, sitting down opposite him. 'Thanks for the coffee, but I'm fine.' I forced what I hoped was a confident-looking smile and pushed the mug away.

He nodded and we sat in silence for several seconds.

'As I did most of the talking this morning,' he said eventually, 'maybe you'd like to start this evening.' His tone was even and untroubled, with no hint of the kind of anxiety that I was currently experiencing.

'Sure.' I cleared my throat, folding my arms in a pre-emptive move aimed at avoiding nail-picking and nervy fiddling in general. 'Well, I think the first thing I would like to say is that if any aspect of my personal life offends you, that's a shame, but I'm thirty-four years old and you're my business partner not my mother, so I don't expect you to lecture me on it. I had no problem with you calling me out over my behaviour to Jasmine after her show. She's one of our artists and I shouldn't be disrespectful to her, or negative about her, as that could impact on our business. But my personal life has nothing whatsoever to do with you, or with the gallery, and it's unacceptable for you to question or criticise me over it, or to raise it as an issue in the workplace.'

It was far from the opener I'd had in mind as I'd brooded miserably over the current tension between us just half an hour earlier. What's more, I wasn't entirely sure where it had come from, although I suspected that what I perceived as David's moves to control the situation – he'd convened the meeting, he'd made the coffees – combined with an innate determination on my part never to start a business meeting from a point of weakness, may have had something to do with it.

He nodded slowly. 'I agree and I apologise. It won't happen again.'

Strangely, this calm, concise, conciliatory and wholly unexpected response was of no comfort whatsoever. If anything, it just made me feel even worse.

He raised his mug to his mouth and blew. 'Anything else we need to talk about?'

I frowned down at the table, feeling like I had painted the floor with shit and was now standing in the corner farthest from the door with my back to the wall. Not two months ago, I had told Cass that I wished David would open up to me about his personal life, primarily because I wanted to be able to share *my* personal angst with him. And *not ten hours ago*, I had berated him for failing to tell me that he had dumped Sophie and was seeing Jasmine. Yet now, thanks to me equating him getting to the kettle first with an attempted boardroom takeover, we had somehow passed a motion that any expression of personal interest or personal criticism – even when completely and utterly reasonable – was simply not on.

'I checked in with Douglas and he's got lots more pieces,' I said, simply for something to say. 'He's worried that they're not good enough to show, but I think it may well be a confidence issue, so he's going to bring some in and we'll go through them.'

'Great,' he said, focusing on his coffee.

'And I thought maybe we should talk to Jasmine about another original. We haven't got any to hang, other than the two that are...' I hesitated. 'I don't think they're representative of her style – or her talent.'

He looked up. 'I'll mention it to her tonight.'

My feelings hiccoughed slightly at this reference to their relationship and I pressed my lips firmly together to prevent the escape of any comment or question related to it, given that – according to my own brand-new rule – it wasn't actually any of my business.

'Anything else?' He looked at me questioningly.

'Not that I can think of.'

He placed his hands flat on the table, as if about to push back his chair and stand up.

'Well, if you've nothing to add, let's end it there,' I said quickly, hurrying to stand up and beat him to the sink.

He waited patiently while I poured away my coffee and washed my mug, before washing his own. Then I picked up my bags and we walked, with me leading the way, into the gallery.

We were almost at the door when Lloyd scurried past. He was clearly in a hurry but, on catching sight of me through the window, he skidded to an abrupt halt and, with a concerned expression on his face, gave me a thumbs-up/thumbs-down gesture. Not wanting to worry him, or to prompt a conversation, I stretched my mouth into a smile and offered him a double thumbs-up in return. He looked relieved, waved and was gone.

'What was that about?' asked David.

'Nothing.'

He looked blankly at me and then nodded acceptingly, continuing past me to the door and extending a hand towards the latch.

'No, wait,' I said, reaching out but stopping short of touching his arm. 'It wasn't nothing. It was something. Something important.'

He lowered his hand and turned to face me. 'OK.'

I hesitated, still unsure whether to ask my colleague about a framing and set all things personal to one side – forever – or, as Lloyd had recommended, to talk things through with my friend.

In the end, I opted for the latter. 'I didn't say everything I meant to say back there, about what happened on Saturday with Elliot, or about our argument this morning, or about how I feel about our amazing gallery.' The words tumbled out as I looked around the room, taking in the artwork on the walls and the curios on the shelves, and feeling suddenly impassioned. 'I love coming to work. I love everything about this place. It feels like a part of me. I should have told you that and made clear to you just how much all this means to me.'

David glanced towards the window. 'And Lloyd was worried that you might *not* love the gallery?' he asked uncertainly.

'No, no.' I shook my head in frustration. 'Just forget about Lloyd for a moment.'

He blinked a little. 'OK.'

'What I want you to understand is how I feel about the gallery – *our* gallery. I know what I said a moment ago about keeping everything strictly business and not sticking our noses into each other's personal stuff. But the truth is, David, that nothing to do with this place is strictly business for me – it's personal too.' I took a breath and placed a hand on my chest. 'Deeply, deeply personal.'

He looked at me, remaining silent, giving no hint of his feelings.

'And our relationship is, of course, part of that,' I added, a little desperately.

At that point, he took a breath, as if about to speak, but I beat him to it.

'Just like the gallery, our relationship isn't purely business for me. I mean, I may not know who you had dinner with last night, or what went wrong between you and Sophie, but I do know that sculpting makes you happy, cats make you sneeze and nothing whatsoever makes you swear. I also know that you're risk-averse, unsure of your own creative talent and more embarrassed than proud of your professional background. And despite what I said in there a moment ago,' I paused for breath and gestured towards the kitchen, '*of course* our personal actions, experiences and opinions are relevant to what we do here, and to each other. I can't simply dismiss your personal opinion of me and pretend that the unhappiness and tension, or confidence and calm, it provokes doesn't have repercussions for our business, because of course it does.' I ended the monologue a little breathlessly.

He raised his eyebrows questioningly. 'Can I speak now?'

'Yes.'

'OK, well, neither of us,' he began quietly, 'has the right to—'

'I know the theory,' I interrupted, shaking my head and ignoring his heavy sigh. 'But if the roles were reversed, I'd be thinking really, *really* badly of you right now, David. I'd be wondering who you really were and questioning your values and, whether I'd want it to or not, that would have an impact here at work.'

He was silent for a moment and then shrugged. 'I don't know what you want me to say.'

'I don't want you to say anything. All you have to do is listen.'

'To be fair, I think I've been doing a pretty good job of that so far.'

'I'm going to close my eyes now,' I said, screwing them shut.

'Because…?'

'I don't want to see your reaction.'

'Esme, whatever the—'

'OK, shush now, because Elliot is my ex,' I continued quickly, a statement which immediately prompted some audible foot-shuffling from David.

I took a breath, before pressing on. 'We were together for three years and split four and a half years ago. To say that we didn't achieve closure would be an understatement. We were horrified to discover that we were living next door to each other and Elliot didn't tell Morgan about our history, because she is anxious and insecure and he thought it would upset her and damage their relationship. Meanwhile, I've been doing my best to avoid her. I invited her to Jasmine's show only because I didn't want to go for a drink with her on my own. I really didn't want to celebrate her birthday with her either, but I couldn't see a way out. Then I had way too much to drink on Saturday night – as did Elliot – largely in an attempt to cope with the situation. Nothing at all had happened before that. But I'm not making excuses for either of us because, drunk or sober, it was inexcusable.' I took another, slightly gasping, breath. 'Unforgivable.'

I stopped talking, my voice having tapered to a whisper, and opened my eyes. David was looking at me with obvious and uncharacteristic astonishment.

'You… are… joking,' he said, his head nodding on each word.

I shook my head at half speed. 'I… am… not,' I replied quietly.

'You've been living next door to your ex-partner since April? And his current partner doesn't know?'

'I have,' I confirmed, now staring at the floor. 'And she doesn't.'

'Why on earth didn't you tell me that before we went to dinner with the pair of them?'

I looked up sharply and frowned. 'Would you have told me?'

'Of course.'

'Would you, though?' I pressed. 'Really?'

He ran a hand through his hair. 'I suppose I may not have wanted to drag you into it.'

'Exactly.'

'I'm sorry. It's just very difficult to put myself in your place, because the situation is so... unusual.'

'I know.'

We stood in silence; him with his hands in pockets and head tilted upwards, me once again studying the floor. I was just beginning to wonder if 'unusual' was to be his final word on the matter, when he spoke again.

'I can see why you didn't feel able to tell me. You were right this morning when you said that I was closed.'

'*None* of this is your fault,' I said, looking up. 'Besides, I did think about telling you, but I like work being a positive, uncomplicated place; somewhere we promote art, think about how to build a business, and escape from our personal and domestic worries – like bathtubs coming through the ceiling and massive pores.'

He broke into a genuine smile for the first time since Saturday evening and I was surprised at the level of relief that brought with it.

'But sometimes,' I continued, 'like, for example, when my ex moves in next door, I do consider drawing you into my chaos. It's just that because you're always so cool, calm and collected, it'd all be one-way traffic and that doesn't seem fair.'

He smiled again, although this time more ruefully. 'I have my chaos. It's just that, as you say, it feels best to leave it at home, rather than drag it all the way in here. But I do understand,' he said, his expression now serious, 'that there are some issues which are difficult to leave behind. I think the lesson here is that it might be better for us to acknowledge those things to each other, rather than try to deny that they exist.'

He took a breath as if he was about to say more, but then appeared to change his mind. I wondered if he might not be as at peace over Sophie as I had thought. 'You're not in denial about anything right now, are you?' I asked.

He gazed thoughtfully at his feet. 'I don't know,' he said eventually. 'A greasy T-zone, maybe. Should I talk to Cass?'

He looked up and I tried hard to smile. 'Sorry,' he said. 'It probably wasn't the moment to attempt humour – and it was a very poor attempt.'

I shook my head. 'No, no. Well done for trying to lighten the mood. I've been to funerals with more of a party atmosphere than this place today. But anyway,' I turned away, taking a step towards the door, 'thanks for listening. I know what I said doesn't make Saturday night OK, but hopefully it makes it a little less... well... random.' I looked over my shoulder at him. 'I'll see you tomorrow – or the day after, actually. You're at the dentist tomorrow, aren't you? Hope that goes OK,' I said, turning again towards the door.

'Wait, Esme.'

'Yes?'

'I want you to know that I meant it when I apologised for my behaviour this morning. You've been very generous about it, but I handled things badly – both as a colleague and as a friend. There's no excuse for that. I had no right to be upset or angry with you. Not only are your personal relationships absolutely none of my business, you're right about us knowing each other – and I know that you would never set out to hurt anyone. I also know that you are a fundamentally good person, and that should have been enough for me. It is enough for me. More than enough.'

I looked at him for a moment, adjusting the position of the satchel and small backpack on my shoulder and then fumbling with the buckle of the former, as an excuse to look down. The idea of crying in front of David was, for some reason, in a completely different league to blubbing all over Lloyd.

'I feel so far from fundamentally good right now,' I said, brushing away a tear. 'Sorry for crying. I'm actually fine,' I added hurriedly. 'It's just been a bit of a strange time, plus, you know, hormones.'

'I'm a martyr to them myself.'

'I'll tell Lloyd.'

'Because?'

I waved a hand. 'It's just a joke, from which you're excluded.'

'Is there any other kind?'

I smiled through my tears, feeling that even if things weren't quite back to normal between us, David and I were at least on the road to normal; or maybe to a new normal – a better one.

Wisely deciding to keep my internal philosophical ramblings to myself, I turned again to leave. 'See you Wednesday.'

'Look, why don't we go for a drink?' he said suddenly. 'Right now, I mean. You don't have to rush home, do you?'

'No, but I thought you were seeing Jasmine.'

'God, that's right, I am.' He glanced up at the clock on the wall and grimaced.

I stepped back from the door. 'You get going. I'll lock up.'

'It's not a problem,' he murmured, taking out his phone and tapping the screen. 'I can rearrange with Jazz.'

'But that's so last minute! She'll go nuts!' I exclaimed, simultaneously appalled and entertained by the thought. 'Look, David, it's really kind of you, but I'm OK – honestly,' I said, pulling a tissue from my sleeve and drying my eyes. 'I've had my mini moment and that's me done. I feel so much better for explaining things to you and now I'm going to go home and draw, maybe watch some mindless TV. Then tomorrow I've got a date to talk everything through with Cass after work. There's absolutely no point in me boring you *both* rigid with this thing.'

'I know you're fine. I just thought unwinding a little after a tense day might be good for both of us. It's not a selfless invite,' he added, looking up from his phone. 'I could do with it as much as you.'

'I know that's not true,' I said, stepping towards him and reaching up to hug him with my bag-free arm. 'But thank you for pretending and I'll see you on Wednesday.'

I'd intended the hug to be a brief one, but after two days of drowning in lonely uncertainty, the physical contact with David prompted a sudden and overwhelming longing to be held and reassured. Consequently, I found myself lingering awkwardly with my left arm around his neck, before raising – with some difficulty and much adjustment – my other, bag-laden arm to complete the gesture. I knew without a doubt that my behaviour was both needy and weird, but I didn't care. Outside, an emotional storm was raging, but inside the gallery, with David, I felt protected from the elements and, just for a moment, I wanted to stay put.

After only a slight hesitation, he reciprocated, gently placing his arms around me.

'Sorry,' I mumbled, somewhat huskily, my face pressed against the soft fabric of his grey-green shirt. 'It's just that after the weekend… and then today…' I inhaled deeply and felt myself relax a little. His shirt smelled like a spring meadow after the rain and it struck me that even his choice of liquid detergent was calming.

'I know, and it's fine,' he said.

'I won't make a habit of emotional farewells.'

'It's honestly not a problem.'

'You're such a good bloke.'

'I'm really not.'

'Don't disillusion me,' I said, my eyes closed and my head still resting against his chest. 'Confess your sins to Jasmine, if you've actually got any.'

'I will when I see her, but that's not going to be this evening.'

I opened my eyes. 'David,' I said, sniffing and releasing him, 'you can't cancel her.'

He frowned down at me and sighed. 'Esme, I've told you, this isn't a pity invite.'

'I wouldn't care if it was, but it's too late to change your plans now,' I said, inclining my head towards the window and dabbing again at my eyes with the tissue. 'She's crossing the road and heading this way at speed.'

He turned to look. 'So she is,' he murmured, reaching out to open the door for her. 'Hi there, Jazz.'

'Hi, you!' she exclaimed, beaming and exposing more teeth than I was pretty sure any single human being should possess. 'Just thought I'd check in on the off-chance that you hadn't left yet. And I see that you haven't, you bad boy,' she added in mock annoyance, wagging a finger at him. 'What's keeping you here?' she asked, with an accusing glance in my direction.

'I'm sorry, but we've had a problem here today,' said David, 'and Esme and I need to—'

'Yes, we had a mix-up with orders,' I said, the temerity of my interruption to their exchange causing Jasmine to frown. 'But it's all straightened out now. So,' I placed a hand on David's back and gently propelled him towards the door, 'you two go and have a great time. I'm going to fetch my bags from the back room. Don't wait for me.'

Jasmine's eyes narrowed, and then lowered to the satchel and backpack hanging from my shoulder.

'My other bags. My tote bags,' I said, increasing the pressure on David's back from *gentle* to *shove*. 'Bye. Have fun.'

As soon as he was over the threshold, I closed the door and locked it, waving cheerily at them from inside.

Neither smiled, David looking at me with concern and Jasmine continuing to eye me with suspicion, until he turned towards her, at which point the sun came out again, as she beamed up at him.

I watched them go, while trying very hard to be happy for David and to find something – anything – to like about Jasmine. However, as they disappeared out of sight down a side road, I gave up, deciding that the exercise was simply too much of a challenge for my currently caffeine-starved brain.

But I would, I decided, try again first thing tomorrow, because as much as I didn't warm to Jasmine, and as difficult as I found David's choices to fathom, I was determined not to get in the way of any more relationships.

Chapter 27

I squinted down at the five folded oblongs of card on the counter in front of me. I could usually at least hazard a guess as to what eighty-five-year-old Nerys Matthews might be attempting to depict on her greeting cards, but these were universally defeating. So, in the end, I decided to resort to the question my mother had always asked me when, as a child, I had presented her with some creative masterpiece or other.

'So, Nerys, why don't you tell me a little bit about these?'

She smiled mischievously. 'I expect you're wondering who the young gentleman is, aren't you, Esme?'

'Um...' I peered again at the cards, scouring them in vain for anything which resembled either facial features or a human figure. 'I am,' I nodded.

'He's William Corbett, my first love. We must have walked a thousand miles in those bluebell woods over the years.' She sighed happily and tapped one of the cards. I, meanwhile, continued to nod, despite being unable to make out William, the woods or a single blue anything at all.

This was the fifth set of hand-painted greeting cards – plus envelopes – that Nerys had brought to us over the past six months and they were definitely the most freestyle. I had been absent from the gallery during her first visit and had returned the next day to discover that David had paid her £6 for a set of four cards, each of which depicted what looked like a melted beach-ball on top of a boulder, but which David had explained was actually Nerys's great-niece, Rebecca.

At the time, I had made lots of jokes – over several days – regarding his lack of business acumen. But when Nerys had appeared again six weeks later, this time with five watercolour portrayals of a shredded washing-up sponge from various angles – or *Margaret's Yorkshire terrier*, as she titled them – I'd handed over £7.50 and decided to say nothing about the matter to David. Because the truth of it was that Nerys Matthews was an unequivocally lovely lady, with few close relatives and a passion for art, and I didn't have the heart to tell her that her cards were unsaleable any more than David did.

'Well, it's a shame that David is at the dentist today, because he'd love these, and it cheers me up just looking at them,' I said truthfully, holding up each of the cards in turn. 'Did you paint them with Ken?' I asked – Ken Stevens being a local artist who taught regular classes at Nerys's retirement home.

'I did,' she replied, smiling. 'He is so very encouraging. We also tried using pen and ink but,' she pulled a face and shook her head, 'I have to be honest and say that I don't think my efforts in that respect were very good at all, Esme.'

'Well, maybe you'll improve with practice,' I said. 'Or maybe it's just not your thing,' I added with a shrug. 'Just stick to whatever you love most, Nerys. Now,' I continued, turning to the till and taking out a note and several coins, 'let me give you your commission.'

'Thank you.' She took the money from me with a broad smile. 'I am meeting a friend for afternoon tea and cake in half an hour, and today it shall be my treat. My friends at Rosefield are so impressed that I am now a paid artist, you know,' she said, unzipping her purse and placing the cash inside. 'More than one of them was considering calling on you with their own paintings, following our art class on Friday.'

'Ooh, and do you think they will?' I asked, anxious at the thought of having to choose between crushing geriatric dreams or crippling the gallery with multiple pity purchases. Maybe I'd suggest to David that from tomorrow he handle all acquisitions from the over-eighties. After all, it was a niche group of suppliers, to which his temperament and approach were perfectly suited, and the experience could be wonderfully developmental for him.

Yes, I'd dump it on David.

Meanwhile, Nerys must have read my concern and was rushing to reassure me. 'Don't worry, dear, I've explained to them that you can't take work from every artist and that your standards are very high. David explained that to me on my very first visit.'

I smiled. So he had, bless him, made at least some attempt to let her down gently, before caving in to his own soft-heartedness. 'That's good. Because we hate having to turn anyone down.'

'Right, well, I shall just have a little browse now,' she said, turning away. 'I'm not meeting Margaret until three and I did rather want to see if you happened to have any of those little hedgehogs and mice at the moment. I won't be buying any today, but I do love to look.'

'I know the ones you mean,' I said, coming out from behind the counter, 'and I'm afraid we don't have anything by Douglas Muirhead at the moment, but we're hoping to have a little exhibition of his work soon, so I'll make sure you get an invite. There'll be drinks and nibbles, and you could bring a friend along with you.'

'Ooh, could I, dear?' She clapped her hands in excitement. 'Margaret would love that.'

'I'll make sure you're on the guest list. In terms of browsing today, I do have some other wildlife pieces over here, in bronze,' I said, leading her to the rear of the gallery. 'There are also some clay pieces over—' I paused, distracted by the gallery door opening and Jasmine struggling to enter while carrying two large, flat packages, each wrapped in brown paper.

'Sorry, Nerys,' I said quickly, 'the clay pieces are in the far corner over there, underneath the collage of the suspension bridge. I just have to go and help Jasmine.'

'You carry on, Esme,' she replied. 'I'm very happy just looking.'

I made it to the door just as it closed behind Jasmine. 'Here, let me help you with those.' I took the packages from her. 'Are these the originals?'

'Yes, that's right,' she said loudly, looking a little flushed from the effort of negotiating the door. 'David mentioned last night that you needed some.'

'Great,' I said, while blinking slightly at the volume of her voice. 'Thank you for getting them to us so quickly. I'm afraid I can't look at them right now,' I gestured over her shoulder as another customer, a grey-haired man in his fifties, entered, 'but I'll look at them after closing and then give you a call. Would that work?'

'That would be *amazing*!' This time she directed her weirdly loud proclamation towards the back of the gallery, causing Nerys to jump visibly and the grey-haired man to throw a disapproving frown in our direction.

'I'm so sorry, I'll be with you in just one moment,' I said to him, before returning my attention to Jasmine. 'Brilliant. I'll call you tomorrow.'

She nodded, a little manically I thought, her eyes widening along with her grin and darting anxiously from side to side. 'Super,' she said, taking a step back, but showing no sign of actually leaving.

'Well, I'll just pop these down here and serve that gentleman,' I murmured, placing her paintings behind the counter and glancing at the customer, who was at that moment putting on his glasses to inspect the base of a vase.

'Why don't I take the paintings to the back room for you?' Jasmine offered hurriedly, appearing even more flustered than on entry, but now with her voice reduced to a desperate whisper. 'I'll say hello to David, while I'm there. He'll think I'm snubbing him if I don't.' She laughed lightly.

'He's not in today. He has a dental appointment. Something major with a molar. But if you could put the paintings in the back room that would be great,' I added hastily, now very keen to get her out of the way so that I could make a sale.

Her face fell, her expression rippling with unmistakable irritation, before recovering into a smile. 'Oh, yes,' she said, tutting. 'I'm so silly. Of course, he told me that last night.'

I moved towards the man with the vase, smiling as he held it up, clearly about to make an enquiry, or possibly a purchase.

'Do you know Sophie Bradbury?' Jasmine asked the question in the manner of someone unable to suppress a hiccough or a fart.

I stopped, sighed and turned towards her. 'Er, yes, she went out with David for...' I hesitated, realising that I had no clue as to precisely when their relationship had either begun or ended. 'For a while.'

I took another step towards the waiting customer.

'It's just that,' Jasmine continued suddenly, placing a restraining hand on my arm, 'I was wondering about her current—'

'Maybe I'll come back when you're less busy,' announced the now clearly pissed-off grey-haired gentleman, as he yanked open the gallery door and left.

'Well, that's just great.' I threw up a hand in exasperation and returned to the till.

'I'll leave you to it then, Esme,' said Nerys, waving cheerily as she, too, exited.

'Bye-bye, everyone,' I said with faux cheeriness, stooping to pick up Jasmine's paintings, with a view to taking them through to the workshop. 'Thank you so much for all the purchases.'

I stood up, expecting to find myself alone, only to discover Jasmine still on the other side of the counter, her position and expression unchanged.

'Sorry, was there something else?' I asked, working hard to keep extreme irritation from my tone.

She looked at me uncertainly for a moment, the corners of her mouth drooping. Oh my God, was the woman going to cry? Maybe not, but she was definitely displaying signs of vulnerability – something I had never seen in her before. I put down the paintings.

'What on earth's wrong?' I asked gently, now wishing I'd been paying greater attention earlier. 'You were asking me about Sophie, weren't you? Is she OK?'

'I don't know,' she said. 'I've never met her.'

'Oh… OK…' I fought to maintain my patience, while hoping for an early explanation.

'I'd just heard her mentioned in passing and wondered if you knew her. It wasn't anything important,' she said, with affected breeziness.

I clenched my teeth and counted to three before speaking. 'OK, well, thanks so much for the paintings, Jasmine. I can't wait to look at them. But right now, I'm going to send a few emails, while the gallery is quiet.' I repositioned the stool behind the counter and reached for my iPad.

'Do you think David might be working a little too hard at the moment? He seems distracted and I wondered if anything was going on that he didn't want to burden me with,' Jasmine said, clearly judging my need to earn a living to be secondary to her need for information.

I frowned at the question. 'Distracted in what way?'

'Well, he keeps going off topic.'

I pressed my lips together as it occurred to me that Jasmine probably considered any topic other than herself to be 'off'.

'I see,' I said, reminding myself that this was a woman in whom I was now trying to identify positives.

'And he just doesn't seem quite as interested as you'd expect him to be,' she said, frowning.

'As interested in what?'

'Me.' She continued to frown, clearly at a loss as to why someone might not find her to be of endless fascination. 'It did cross my mind that maybe he was troubled about work or…' She cleared her throat. 'That someone else might be working to distract or confuse him. What do you think?'

I heaved a sigh, wondering at precisely what point in my existence, females of my own age, such as Morgan and Jasmine, had come to regard me as the wise old woman of the village: in the know, great with relationship advice and, most importantly of all, of no competition whatsoever when it came to their men.

'I'm not aware of Sophie Bradbury, or anyone else for that matter, attempting to lure him back, Jasmine,' I said wearily.

'No, no,' she laughed, placing a hand on her midriff and bending slightly, in an attempt to make her mirth appear more genuine. 'I assure you, I didn't think that for a minute.'

'Good.'

'I'm not at all worried about other women showing an interest in him,' she said, chuckling again.

'Well, that's lucky.' I joined in the laughter and looked down at my iPad.

'Are you saying that lots of women show an interest in him?'

'Only the straight ones.' I looked up, still laughing, only to discover Jasmine now stony-faced. God, she was hard work. 'I'm joking,' I said, 'and exaggerating, of course. But obviously David is an attractive guy, so he's always going to have interest from women who, you know, like that tall, dark, enigmatic, imperturbable Scottish thing he has going on.'

Clearly dissatisfied with the response, her expression remained determinedly serious.

'Look, Jasmine, when it comes to David,' I said, taking a deep breath and trying again, 'it's really important to remember that, as well as being Scottish and good-looking, he is also kind, honest and *very* straightforward – not to mention supportive, loyal and *highly* moral.' I tapped out David's favourable attributes on the counter with my forefinger. 'And all that added together means that there is just *no way* he would ever intentionally play games with your feelings, or with any other woman's for that matter. So you can be completely confident that whatever he has told you about what he's thinking, or how he's feeling, will be the absolute truth. As for him appearing distracted, you have to bear in mind that he is a really deep-thinker, with nothing to prove and no ego whatsoever. He's definitely someone who listens more than he talks and who thinks very carefully about what he's heard before he responds. And, personally speaking, I think they're traits which lots of people would do well to emulate – myself included. In fact, me above all people, actually. I mean, if I was more like David, instead of being all shouty and impulsive, my life would be a helluva lot less messy and stressy than it is right now, wouldn't it?' I addressed my closing comments to a serene-looking watercolour female nude on the far wall, emotion taking my voice up a notch.

There followed several seconds of complete silence, during which the nude remained unresponsive and I remembered that Jasmine was in the room.

'So yes,' I said, clearing my throat, surprised by my own strength of feeling on the matter of David's plus points and now attempting to lighten my tone, 'I hope that sets your mind at rest, Jasmine.'

She looked thoughtful for a moment. 'I suppose he could have been worried about the dentist.'

I stared at her, telling myself – yet again – that I had to try to like this person.

'Yes,' I said quietly and managing a smile, 'I suppose he could.'

Chapter 28

'I can't believe that you snogged Elliot in front of Dave!' exclaimed Cass, her eyes wide, her elbows on the table and her chin resting on her hands.

I turned in my seat, looking anxiously around the early-evening bar of The Cambridge. 'OK, so firstly, can you keep your voice down?' I hissed, leaning across the table towards her. 'And secondly, it's not like we were giving a performance. We didn't say, "Hey, David, stand there and watch what we can do with our tongues." He just happened to walk in on us.' I picked up my lime and soda, and sipped it miserably. 'David. Of all people.'

She sat up. 'Oh, come on, at least it wasn't Morgan leading the way back into the kitchen.'

'God, imagine if she had,' I whimpered, lowering my drink and covering my face with my hands.

'Sorry. Didn't mean to trigger you. But it wasn't her, so never mind. Besides, I don't think you need to worry about Morgan anyway.'

I looked up. 'What do you mean?'

'Well,' she shrugged, 'is she really *that* into Elliot?'

I thought about Morgan's tearful visit to the gallery just two weeks earlier and her utter devastation at the possibility of Elliot cheating on her.

'I think she probably is,' I said grimly.

'What makes you so sure?'

I ran a finger around the rim of my glass, reluctant to share the details of the gallery visit with Cass. Reliving it wasn't going to make me feel better and I couldn't see it improving my standing with her either. Just like Nanna Pat, Cass had never – in my experience – been one to judge. But there was always a first time, and telling her that Morgan had bared her vulnerable soul to me just days before I had snogged the face off her boyfriend wouldn't exactly improve my currently very poor credentials as a supporter of the sisterhood.

'Observation,' I said lightly. 'Why do you think she's *not* into him?'

'Same – observation,' she replied. 'Remember how she went on and on about Dave that evening at your place? I mean, I know it's OK to show an interest and pay a guy a compliment, but I reckon she really likes him. You know...' She stuck out her tongue and panted. '*Really* likes him. She talked about him all the time you were in the loo too.' She pointed at me in a point-proven kind of way.

I nodded slowly, surprised to discover myself wondering if maybe Cass actually had a point. After all, Morgan's tearful gallery visit had included an awful lot of astonishingly good attempts at smiling whenever David was around. And they'd got on very well at Jasmine's show, and again on Morgan's birthday. So perhaps Cass was right. Maybe Morgan's interest wasn't entirely held by Elliot. Maybe, given the chance, she would quite happily swap him out for David.

I sipped my drink uncertainly, knowing that the possibility should make me feel better, but not entirely sure that it did.

'Yes, well,' I said, rubbing my forehead. 'I'm glad nothing's happened to test the theory.'

'But if I'm right, you could at least stop worrying about her quite so much,' Cass said brightly, completing her train of thought. 'And you should definitely stop worrying about Dave, because it sounds like the pair of you have cleared the air.'

'As much as was possible.'

'He's not the kind of person to keep bringing it up.'

'I know.'

'So you can park that bit of it at least.'

I stared at the table and sighed. 'Easier said than done.'

'Why?' she asked. 'You know, Es, from what you've said this evening, it's almost as if you're more upset about the fallout with Dave than the snog with Elliot.'

'Of course I'm not,' I said, aware of sounding more defensive than decisive.

Cass shrugged. 'Well, that's how it's coming across.'

'I just think...' I hesitated, running through my list of Saturday night regrets and attempting to weigh them against each other. Up until now, I'd taken it as read that the snog was the headline act in terms of personal regret. But on further analysis, there was no denying that the subsequent fallout with David was definitely up there with it. There was undoubted relief that he and I had talked everything through, and that we both seemed determined to learn a lesson and move on. But every time I thought about what had happened, I had a quiet but unshakeable sense that my kiss with Elliot had somehow been as much a betrayal of David as it had been of Morgan.

'Look, do you know what you're going to say to him when you see him?' asked Cass.

I looked up. 'I think we said everything there was to say yesterday.'

'Not Dave,' she tutted, sounding frustrated. 'Elliot. Do you know what you're going to say to Elliot? Have you even thought about it?' she pressed.

I slumped in my chair at the thought. 'No.'

'Well, you should,' she said emphatically. 'You need to get your feelings and what you want straight, before he gives you his take on it all.'

There was an unfamiliar edge to her voice and the message, too, was uncharacteristically serious. 'He's as upset about all this as I am, you know,' I said.

She laughed suddenly and relaxed back in her chair. 'Hey, I met the guy for two minutes, at most. I couldn't pick him out of a line-up, thanks to all the alcohol you poured down my throat that night. The only two things I know for sure are that you blame yourself for him walking out on you four years ago and that you could have tried to get him back, but you didn't.' She drained her G&T, placing the empty glass on the table. 'Makes me wonder, that's all.'

I felt suddenly exhausted. 'I'll think everything through, I promise. But, just for now, can you please distract me from my car-crash existence with something else? What's the gossip from Mandy's cocktails?'

She grinned. 'Thought you'd never ask. Guess who we bumped into in Her Majesty's Secret Service?'

I smiled, grateful to have been able to offload onto Cass, but also pleased to be moving on. 'Give me a clue.'

'Great hair, never stops crying.'

'Give me another clue.'

'Her name begins with an *S* and ends in *ophie.*'

'No!' I exclaimed. 'I wouldn't have thought cocktails were her thing. Too much dairy, alcohol and artificial colouring.'

'I know, but she was on a hen night with a bunch of nurses from the BRI and having a great time. She's started seeing a new man and suddenly seems to be well on the way to getting over Dave.'

'Ah, that's happy news. Good for Sophie.'

'Yes and the best bit is, no more discounts,' said Cass, picking up her glass and clinking it against mine.

'Bit mercenary in your focus there, but never mind.'

'Business is business, Es. You know that. Anyway, Sophie and I had a little bit of a heart-to-heart over a margarita.'

'You grilled her mercilessly for info.'

'I did.'

I raised my glass. 'Well done.'

'And she said that it's very early days, but so far she's really happy with her new man. Can't remember too much about him, except that he's a blacksmith and only wears wool from sheep that have died of old age.'

'That's kind.'

'Yes and what was *really* interesting was that Sophie said that she'd expected Dave to move straight on to someone else when they split up. Of course, I didn't tell her that she was bang on and that he was already at it with the curly artist.'

I leaned forward, intrigued. 'Why did she think he'd move on so quickly? I don't think of him as flighty, do you?'

She looked thoughtful for a moment. 'I guess I think of Dave as a bit like a museum: all posh and impressive on the outside – and you can tell there's probably loads of really clever and interesting stuff going on inside – but at the end of the day, can you really be arsed?'

'You're saying he's boring.'

She tutted. 'No, I'm not. I'm just saying that I like it on a plate. No digging and delving required. Take Kev. There's no hidden depths to Kev – no depth at all, really. And that's just one of the many things I love about him.' She paused, smirking to herself. 'I mean, I also love his—'

'Shush,' I said. 'Not before the watershed. Get back to Sophie. What else did she say about David?'

'Just that she thought his mind was on other things.'

'Or another person, maybe?'

'Her thinking exactly. She was one hundred per cent clear he wasn't messing her around, but she said he was definitely distracted towards the end.'

'Ooh and you know what's *really* interesting about that?' I leaned towards her, warming to the gossip.

'Ooh, what?'

'That's pretty much *exactly* what Jasmine said to me about him this afternoon.' I tapped the table. 'Maybe that's his MO, Cass: meets someone, gets distracted by someone else, moves on.'

'Has he done that before?'

I shrugged. 'I've never really tuned in to his relationships before. I mean, sometimes a woman would stop by the gallery and I'd think, you know, they're probably at it. But I was never certain and Sophie was the first one I got to know a little bit. Not that much, though. I don't even know how long he was seeing her for.'

'Thirty-six weeks.'

'Wow, that's impressively precise.'

'Six discounted cuts and colours. One every six weeks. Oh no, hang on,' she said, tapping a thoughtful finger against her lower lip. 'Three of those were after he dumped her. So knock off…' She paused again for thought. 'Knock off between twelve and eighteen weeks.'

'OK,' I said, sipping my soda and not actually bothering with the mental maths.

'Hey!' said Cass, with a suddenness that caused me to slop a little of my drink down my shirt. 'You know what'd be *even more* interesting?'

'What?' I asked, reaching into my bag for a tissue.

'What if Dave is distracted by *Morgan*?' she grinned. 'I mean, obviously it wouldn't be great for the curly painter. But you don't rate her anyway, do you?'

I pulled a face and then shook my head guiltily. 'I'm trying really hard to, but it's a push.'

'There you go then, even better. Sophie's with the blacksmith, Dave gets with Morgan and you—' She stopped abruptly and smiled. 'Well, who knows? But you'd definitely be able to stop feeling bad about Morgan, and Dave would definitely be far too busy showing her around *the museum*…' She delivered a salacious wink. '…to give another thought to you showing Elliot a good time in the kitchen. Win-win,' she concluded triumphantly.

I nodded while wondering how I actually felt about that scenario. Once again, it wasn't delivering quite as much feel-good as I might have anticipated from a win-win. 'Here's hoping,' I said, saluting Cass with my drink.

She raised her glass in return, lifting it to her lips before realising that it was empty. 'Oh,' she said, her face falling, 'where's that gone then?'

'My round,' I said. 'Same again?'

'Go on then. And when you get back, I'll fill you in on Mandy having her brand-new birthday shoes stolen last night.'

'She didn't.'

'Yeah. Some cow in the loo asked to try them on and then legged it out the back way. She was too fast for Mandy. But let's face it, in a race with a wardrobe, you wouldn't bet on Mandy, would you?'

'That's so awful,' I said, getting up. 'Poor thing.'

'Yeah, so next time you're feeling all sorry for yourself,' Cass pointed up at me, her finger wagging, 'just think of poor Mandy, waiting for an Uber, on her birthday, in the rain, in shoes made from a pair of Jiffy bags. If that doesn't put things into perspective for you, nothing will.'

Chapter 29

As I closed the gallery door behind me the next morning and went to hang up my coat, it struck me that I was feeling only a little less edgy about seeing David than I had been two days earlier, although now for completely different reasons.

Then, the tension had stemmed from a sense that something was amiss. Now, it related to a potentially positive shift in our relationship following our Monday evening heart-to-heart. The extent of that shift remained to be seen, but whether it proved to be a sea change or merely a temporary lowering of the guards, it felt to me like we were, in a way, starting over – and consequently I was suffering from something akin to first-day nerves.

Making my way to the kitchen, I filled and switched on the kettle, my thoughts turning to Cass's hypothesising in the pub the night before. I knew that she hadn't been serious, but nevertheless, snippets of our conversation about David, Sophie, Jasmine and Morgan kept returning to me, further increasing the sense of shifting relationships and possible change afoot.

I had just scooped some coffee into the cafetière, when the kettle switched itself off and the gallery door beeped. I called hello to David.

There was a delay of a few seconds before he responded with a: 'Hi,' and a moment later, he walked into the kitchen.

'So, how's the tooth?' I asked, placing a mug of coffee on the table for him.

'Not perfect. I've got a temporary crown, but it's going to need more work,' he said, putting down his backpack. 'Thanks for the coffee. How was your evening with Cass?'

'Well-behaved and alcohol-free – on my part, at least. But we had a good time. She told me all about Mandy's birthday cocktails. Sounded like it was quite lively. Oh, but poor Mandy had her shoes stolen.'

'How is that even possible?' he asked, his brow furrowing.

'Somebody asked to try them on and then ran away in them.'

'Cunning.' He picked up his coffee, looking at it for a moment before taking a breath. 'Look, Esme, there's something I've been thinking about for a while now and I'd like to run it past you. Could we take five minutes?' He checked his watch. 'We're both early.'

'Sure,' I said, my edginess increasing slightly as we each pulled out a chair and sat down. 'Fire away.'

'Right.' He put down his coffee and laid his hands flat on the table. 'As you know, the gallery is doing great.'

'I do know that, yes.'

'So rather than rest on our laurels, I wondered if we should think about expanding.'

'Moving to bigger premises?'

He shook his head. 'I was thinking more along the lines of opening a second gallery.'

'I see.' I picked up my coffee and blew, thinking it through. 'That's a big step.'

'It is.'

'Did you have a location in mind? I still think Clifton rents are too high for the return we'd get, plus it's too close to home. We'd just be transferring some of our current custom.'

'Agreed. I was thinking of Bath. We find a similar area to this – a compromise location in terms of rental and clientele – and take it from there.'

'OK...' I nodded, thoughtfully. The idea of establishing a chain of galleries should have been an exciting one, but for some reason it wasn't setting me alight. 'So we'd locally source all the stock again? Promoting new and emerging Bath-area artists?'

'That'd be the idea. What do you think?'

'What about logistics? You're a quiet control freak and I'm a noisy one. I think we'd have a hard time trusting anyone else to...'

I paused, realising that I already knew the answer to my question.

'You want one of us to be here and the other in the Bath gallery?'

'I think that would work, don't you?'

Was this, I wondered, the consequence of revealing our vulnerabilities and admitting our faults? Not an increased closeness, but a sudden desire for distance. Or maybe this was something David had genuinely been considering for some time, and our Monday evening heart-to-heart had simply provided him with the impetus to open up about it and crack on. Either way, I definitely hadn't seen it coming.

'So, one of us would commute? Or would we alternate locations?' I asked.

'It's not a bad commute, but I'd be happy to relocate,' he said. 'Obviously, you'd take charge of the initial sourcing and stocking, but hopefully once relationships with artists were established, I could bother you less and less with that.'

I thought about his visit to Bath with Jasmine at the weekend. Had he been semi-scouting the area, as well as buying her lunch? That might explain why she thought he was distracted.

'And we'd get someone else in here to do the framing,' I said.

'I'm sure we'd see an upturn in profit. We both know what a very slow and expensive employee I am.'

I laughed, while also feeling just a little bit like crying. Two days earlier, I had told David in impassioned terms how much I loved the gallery and how much it meant to me. What I hadn't told him – and what I now recognised when confronted with the possibility of no longer working alongside him – was how much *he* meant to me and how integral his presence was to my positive experience of the gallery.

In that moment, I realised that David's companionship at work was as important to me as the art on the walls and the sculptures on the shelves. More so, in fact, and I knew, without a doubt, that if I'd had to choose between running Cass's salon with him or running the gallery with someone else, I'd have chosen the salon – and I'd have chosen David. It was quite a revelation.

'You're looking very serious,' he said, lowering his head to make eye contact with me as I gazed down at the table. 'I don't want you worrying about finances. Your investment will be protected and—'

'I'm not at all worried about money. You're the least reckless person I know.'

'OK, so is there another problem?'

'I'd miss working with you,' I said, a surprisingly blunt confession which I hadn't expected to make, but didn't immediately regret making.

He looked at me across the table and smiled. 'Kind of you to say so. But no deal-breakers?'

His tone was light, clearly assuming that it wasn't really an issue for me. I took a breath and considered explaining to him that, actually, working together was something that did matter to me – very much, in fact. I was aware that it wouldn't be a wholly professional or businesslike response, but hadn't we agreed, less than forty-eight hours earlier, to acknowledge issues which were important to us, rather than pretending that they didn't exist?

'Working tog—' I began, before coming to an immediate halt, aware that I was in danger of thinking out loud.

'Yes?'

I shook my head. 'I'm thinking.'

'That's fine. It's a lot to consider and I probably shouldn't have sprung it on you first thing.'

We heard the gallery door beep and David pushed back his chair. 'I'll get that,' he said, leaving the kitchen.

I watched him go, gazing after him, grateful that our discussion had been interrupted, allowing me pause for thought. The concept of a chain of galleries which, no matter how much it grew, always focused on local art and local artists appealed hugely to me, and business-wise I couldn't see a reason to express any doubt at this stage. Furthermore, I knew that from a business perspective, arguing against expansion on the basis that I didn't want to give up working alongside a specific colleague day-to-day was irrational, unprofessional and, actually – depending upon how that colleague took it – bordering on creepy. Yet that was how I felt: I did not want David to leave the Bristol gallery and I did not want him to move to Bath.

But, I pointed out to myself, he did.

Putting down my coffee, I rested my chin on my hand and let that pivotal fact sink in. Whatever my feelings might be regarding working with David day-to-day, they clearly weren't reciprocated. His proposed relocation to Bath was proof positive of that.

So that left me with a choice: either I could tell him that I thought his idea was a sound and exciting one, and that we should progress it, or I could tell him that, regrettably, it was a no-go for me, because I'd rather not be more than twenty metres away from him at all times, Monday to Friday. I could then follow that up with a counterproposal that we diversify into the beauty business and make Cass an offer on the salon that she couldn't refuse.

I smiled sadly to myself. So that was settled. David was moving to Bath.

'It's Douglas,' he said quietly, popping his head around the kitchen door. 'He's brought in a crate of pieces for us to go through and says he's got more in the van. I'm going to go and help him with those.'

'Wow,' I whispered, standing up, 'I wonder where he's been hiding those all this time.'

He smiled and was about to reply, but I shook my head. 'Do not say in the basement.' I pushed him gently back towards the gallery. 'I'm anxious enough about what's in those crates as it is.'

As it turned out, Douglas's crates where full of nothing darker than a slightly disgruntled dormouse, clearly unhappy at being woken from its slumber. The collection as a whole – which consisted exclusively of British wildlife – was whimsical, unchallenging and bursting with bucolic charm.

It was a delivery well-timed in terms of both content and quantity; the former lifted my mood, and the latter kept David and me fully occupied in between customers, as we unwrapped, measured, photographed and then rewrapped each of the pieces. There were over thirty in total and, although I agreed with Douglas that a few of what I guessed to be earlier pieces were slightly less finessed than the rest, the vast majority were up to his current impressive standard and definitely sale-able.

'We could start thinking about his show, you know,' I said to David, holding up a sculpture of a bat. 'There's just so much to choose from.' I looked at the two other pieces, a fox and an otter, currently on the counter. 'What I can't understand is why he has kept all these to himself until now.'

'A lack of self-belief?'

'Maybe. I'll call him as soon as we close and tell him how great they are.' I replaced the bat thoughtfully on the counter. 'I also think I should help him find another gallery or two, a little bit further afield. He deserves to be more widely known and he won't branch out unless we encourage him. I wouldn't feel great about keeping him all to ourselves.' I looked at David questioningly. 'What do you think?'

'I think this is another one of those occasions when we're terrifyingly in tune.'

I nodded, wishing that we were in tune about a few more things – in particular the extent to which we valued each other's company. 'Right, well, I'll just rewrap these,' I said, glancing first at the sculptures and then up at the clock. 'And then we can lock up and I'll call Douglas.'

'You free for a drink this evening? We could talk some more about the Bath gallery.'

I hesitated; keen on the idea of a drink, less so on the proposed topic of conversation. But I knew I couldn't avoid it forever. 'Sounds great.'

'Perfect,' he said, turning to leave. 'I'll just go and finish up in the workshop. Oh, but,' he continued, turning back and smiling, 'of course I'd miss working with you too – you know, if we do go with the Bath idea. I should have said that this morning.'

'Yes, you should,' I tutted, walking behind the counter and beginning to wrap the fox. 'It was appallingly insensitive of you not to.'

'I just assumed that you knew.'

I looked up to find him no longer smiling, his eyebrows raised questioningly.

I took a breath. 'Well, *of course*, I knew,' I said, rolling my eyes. 'Who *wouldn't* want to work with me day in, day out?'

'Only a complete lunatic,' he said, walking away.

I watched him go, feeling for the second time that day like sticking out my lower lip and shedding a few, fed-up tears. But resisting the urge to give in to either self-pity or sentiment, I instead returned my attention to the fox and told myself, with impressive optimism, that a calm, common sense conversation with David over a drink would no doubt leave me feeling much better about everything.

I had just finished wrapping the fox and was searching for a new roll of Sellotape under the counter, so that I could make a start on the bat, when the gallery door opened.

'So sorry, we're just about to—' I began, before straightening up to find Elliot standing opposite me. 'Close,' I concluded quietly and pointlessly.

I said nothing more, taking in the white shirt, unbuttoned at the neck, and experiencing a vivid flashback to Saturday night and of clutching at the fabric of a disturbingly similar shirt — maybe even the same one.

'Hello,' he said, his strained expression doing absolutely nothing — I noted resignedly — to diminish his external appeal. 'I'm on my way home and wanted to see you. I'm sorry for not being in touch. I just felt that at this stage it had to be face-to-face.'

I nodded, acknowledging the truth of what he said.

He took a step forward and, for reasons which I was in no fit state to examine, I felt both grateful for and resentful of the counter between us.

The clatter of wood hitting the floor caused us both to look towards the back of the gallery.

'David's in the workshop,' I said.

Elliot nodded and, after a pause, cleared his throat. 'I wanted to apologise for Saturday. I am genuinely sorry for the situation I have put you in, Es, but I can't make myself regret what happened. I've tried, but I just can't.' He reached a hand across the counter towards me. 'Morgan is away this weekend and I think we—'

'For God's sake, Elliot!' It was a softly spoken explosion of frustration and I took a step back. 'How much more of this do you think I can take? I have feelings too, you know. Why does no one seem to realise that?' I looked towards the workshop. 'I actually have lots and lots of very powerful and very confusing feelings, so I'd really appreciate it if everyone could stop taking a hammer to them!' I covered my face with my hands and gave in to the tears which had threatened earlier.

A moment later, Elliot's arms were around me as he pulled me towards him. 'Es,' he said softly, his cheek pressed to the top of my head. 'Es, please. Of course I know you have feelings. There's nothing more important to me. Nothing.'

I didn't reply, instead leaning against his pristine white shirt and sobbing. 'I feel so irrelevant. I'm just an extra in everyone else's drama and my only stage direction is not to get in the way,' I mumbled. 'No one notices me, unless I inadvertently cock it up for them by losing my temper or getting pissed and becoming a *huge* disappointment to them. The only time they're actually looking at *me*, and thinking about *me*, is when they're telling me that they're leaving me behind. Even then, it doesn't occur to them that I might not want to be left behind.'

He stroked my hair and gently eased me away from him, his hands on my shoulders. 'It's not like that,' he said, looking down at me and smiling. 'I promise you.'

He began to say something more, but at that moment my attention was caught by the sound of footsteps, as David entered the gallery from the hallway. I looked towards him as he stopped dead, and Elliot, following my tearful gaze, turned to face him, lowering his hands to his sides and slipping them casually into his pockets.

'Hey, David,' he said, offering him a relaxed smile. 'How are things? I called in on the way home for a bit of a browse. My PA's leaving on Friday and I want to get her something. I was just asking Esme about this.' He gestured to the otter on the counter. 'It's Dougal's work, isn't it?'

David looked at him stonily. 'The piece is by Douglas Muirhead and it's not for sale,' he said evenly, both his tone and expression entirely corporate. There was not a hint of the creative about him. 'Everything OK, Esme?' he continued, walking towards us and coming to a halt opposite me.

I nodded. 'Yes.'

Elliot turned his back on David and frowned down at me. 'What's with him?' he mouthed, with just a hint of a smile.

'He knows,' I said simply.

'Ah, OK,' he replied at full volume. He turned back to David and sighed. 'Look, David,' he began, his genial smile an appeal for masculine understanding. 'You know how it is. Esme and I go back a long way. We know each other inside out and she's in very safe hands. She's understandably upset right now. We both are, in fact. The past few months have been distressing all round and we just need a bit of time to talk – alone. I'm sure you understand.'

'Do you want me to stay until you're ready to leave?' David addressed the question exclusively to me.

Elliot maintained a smile, with barely any loss of warmth. 'That's kind, David, but I'll stay with Esme.'

'Esme?' asked David calmly. It was as if Elliot wasn't even in the room.

I attempted a smile. 'I'm fine, David, honestly. But thank you.'

He nodded, walked to the door and left.

'Jesus,' laughed Elliot quietly, shaking his head in David's direction. 'That was all a bit William Wallace, wasn't it?'

I took a tissue from a box under the counter and dabbed my eyes. 'He disapproves,' I said, now feeling strangely numb. 'Quite rightly.'

His face fell. 'Yes, you're right – and I'm sorry. His reaction is fair enough. I don't have a problem with him. I have a problem with me. God knows I hear enough from Morgan about what a nice guy he is.'

'He is a nice guy,' I said, loosely bubble-wrapping the bat and the otter, and placing them carefully under the counter. 'I have to get my things and lock up,' I continued, beginning to edge past him.

He took a step to the side, blocking my way. 'We need to talk.'

'I know we do,' I said acceptingly. 'But not now. I'm tired.'

'How about Saturday evening? Anywhere you like. Morgan is away with her parents from midday and not back until Sunday evening. We can talk our feelings through.' He raised his hand to gently brush a thumb across my cheek, before lifting my chin and lowering his head to kiss me softly and briefly on the lips. 'Es...' He looked into my eyes for a moment, heaved a sigh and then straightened up. 'I'll let you go,' he said, walking away. 'Message me about Saturday,' he added, reaching the door and pausing with his hand on the latch. 'Any time and anywhere at all is fine.' And, with that, he opened the door and left.

Chapter 30

I closed up the gallery and pedalled my way home slowly and on autopilot, engaging only those parts of my brain essential to the task, while determinedly firewalling any areas likely to pose tricky questions, such as how I felt or what I thought the future – both immediate and longer term – might hold.

Once home, I wheeled my bike down the side-path to the back garden and then into the shed, making sure to keep my eyes determinedly fixed on the gravel pathways, with not even a sideways glance towards the cottage next door.

My bike safely stowed, I went inside via the utility-room door, and having dumped my helmet, jacket, bags and boots in the kitchen, I schlepped into the living room and flopped down on the sofa. With zero appetite for anything other than a glass of wine and a diet of meaningless TV, I kept the volume low and the curtains drawn, lest Morgan should take it upon herself to pop round with a kind word, a misdelivered package or – worst-case scenario – an axe, having at long last uncovered my despicable penchant for her man.

By 10:30 p.m., having downed just over half a bottle of red and watched ten-minute bites of at least a dozen different TV shows, I decided to take the party upstairs. So, newly replenished glass in hand, I teetered off to my room and changed into my pyjamas, cursing clothing manufacturers for their continued use of fiddly buttons in a post-Velcro age, thus making it almost impossible to get dressed and undressed while holding a brimming glass of wine. I then spent several minutes sitting up in bed, staring into space and thinking very deeply about how to get red wine out of a white pillowcase, a beige carpet and a pair of pale-grey pyjamas.

But although the spillages were unfortunate, they did also mean that my thoughts never once turned to Elliot, to Morgan, to Bath or to myself. And I might have been able to maintain that relatively blissful, distracted state all the way into sleep, had I not been jolted out of it by the vibrating of my phone, just as I reached to switch off the bedside light.

I picked it up, squinted at the screen and answered the call.

'Hi, David,' I yawned. 'Everything OK?'

'Yes. How about with you? I haven't woken you up, have I? I know it's late.'

'No.' I frowned, checking the time on my phone and wondering what was so important that he had to call me at eleven p.m. It was another moment or two before a hazy recollection of the somewhat solemn circumstances of his departure from the gallery earlier that evening, managed to fight its way out of the boozy comfort blanket in which I had so successfully swaddled my consciousness.

A shiver of anxiety ran through me at the memory of my most recent encounter with Elliot, only to be almost immediately counterbalanced by a surge of warmth at the thought of David's kindness and concern. He had called to check up on me, even though we would see each other in less than ten hours' time. That was the behaviour of a true friend. Maybe, I mused as I nestled down under the covers – turning the pillow to avoid several large splashes of red wine and pressing the phone more closely to my face – our feelings for each other weren't as unequal as I had thought after all.

'I'm absolutely fine,' I said, smiling to myself. Where, I wondered woozily, would he take the conversation next?

'Sadly, I'm not fine,' he sighed. 'My crown is cracked.'

I frowned, failing to understand the reference. Was 'my crown is cracked' some sort of Scottish idiom? Did he mean that he was upset, or that he had lost out to a competitor in some way? Was it the north-of-the-border equivalent to having one's nose put out of joint? I thought again of Elliot's visit to the gallery. Could it be that David was angry with, or jealous of, him in some way? Was Elliot the cause of the crack in his crown? The possibility left me a little ruffled, in a not entirely unpleasant kind of way. 'Oh dear,' I said. 'Can I help at all?'

He laughed. 'Kind of you to offer, but I think I'll leave it to the dentist. I've seen you with a drill and it wasn't pretty. We had to get a plasterer in after you tried to hang that pewter piece our first summer, remember?'

I closed my eyes and the corners of my mouth drooped downwards. 'You're telling me that the crown on your tooth has cracked.'

'Yes,' he said, adding after a pause, 'is there a problem with the line? Can you hear me OK?'

'I can hear you just fine. Sorry about your tooth,' I said, feeling thoroughly deflated by the unexpectedly mundane turn the conversation was taking.

'Yes, it's not great, but never mind,' he said. 'I'm afraid I'll now be back in the chair tomorrow. I've got an appointment at ten thirty and I'm not sure how long it'll take, or what it will entail, so I thought it might be easier to take tomorrow and Friday as leave. Are you OK without me?'

No, I'm not, actually, but I guess I may as well get used to it, I thought grumpily.

'Yeah, yeah, that's fine. You enjoy yourself,' I said.

'Well, I'm not sure how much fun the dentist will be, but hopefully the tooth'll be sorted by the weekend. I was thinking of taking a trip. You know, getting out of Bristol.'

'That's nice,' I said, my upper lip curling as I imagined David and Jasmine swanning around London, before retiring to some five-star boutique hotel or other. Or maybe they'd hire a cosy Cotswold cottage, and spend Saturday and Sunday walking hand in hand through sunlit fields, with Jasmine's curls streaming behind her in the breeze, like coiled ribbons of gold.

I rolled my eyes at the thought. I had tried hard – or at least a little bit – to like Jasmine, but it was no good. I just had to surrender to it: I really couldn't stand the woman.

'Yes, London, or maybe the Cotswolds,' David continued. 'What do you think?'

'Either would be *marvellous*,' I replied, hoping that it pissed it down relentlessly on the pair of them all weekend.

'You up to anything?'

I felt my hackles rising further. Was he actually trying to rub it in now, with a forced comparison of his picture-perfect weekends and my own dysfunctional, snog-thy-neighbour ones?

'Yes, I am, actually,' I replied, as curtly as three-quarters of a bottle of wine would allow. 'I'm out for dinner on Saturday night. Going to that new restaurant on Chandos Road. The one the guy with all the hair reviewed in the *Guardian* last weekend. The one you said you really wanted to go to.' It was an exceptionally needy lie, but I didn't care. I might not be able to match David's boutique hotel and fields of gold, but that wasn't going to stop me having a bloody good try.

There was a slight pause before he replied. 'That sounds great. I'm impressed that you got a table.'

'He booked it,' I said quickly. If David could keep his dates mysteriously nameless and in the shadows, then so could I.

Another pause. 'Great.'

'Yes, it is great. We're really looking forward to it.'

'I bet,' he said. 'You have fun and I'll see you on Monday.'

'Yeah, see you. Hope the dentist doesn't slip with his drill, hit a nerve and spoil all your amazing weekend plans,' I said, following up with a passable impression of a light laugh. 'Hey, and fingers crossed it doesn't piss it down the whole time.'

'Thank you so much for all those positive vibes.'

'No prob. Night, then.'

I hung up, staring miserably at the phone for several seconds before replacing it heavily on the bedside chest of drawers. Then I closed my eyes, despite knowing that there was now zero chance of sleep, as I compared the mundanity and emotional chaos of my weekend with the luxury and emotional simplicity of David's, in the company of his cutesy, golden-haired girlfriend.

God, I really couldn't stand Jasmine.

Chapter 31

I limped towards the weekend, my first painful, but purposeful, step being a text to Elliot, sent first thing Thursday, to say that I'd meet him at the village pub at seven p.m. Saturday. He had responded with a thumbs-up and a story about a split in his colleague's trousers, which I had recognised as a brave attempt to keep things light. But, feeling beyond that level of counterfeit cheer, I couldn't bring myself to reply; instead determining that, unless completely unavoidable, I would have no further contact with him until Saturday.

After that, Thursday and Friday passed in a busy but uneventful haze of easy-care customers – keen to buy, rather than barter – and lunch hours spent at the counter, eating sandwiches and sketching in my journal, the latter success-fully diverting my thoughts, in between sales, away from the weekend to come.

My evenings were similarly, and quite deliberately, unchal-lenging, as I repeated the lights-off, TV-on approach of Wednesday night, although now substituting food for alcohol. It was a swap which resulted in a much-improved night's sleep on Thursday, although admittedly less so on Friday, as it became harder and harder to keep Elliot from my thoughts.

I had decided to skip my Friday post-work drink with Cass, keen to engender a sense of calm, and aware that dissecting my feelings over a gin and tonic, and under ruthless cross-questioning, might not be conducive to that. Needless to say, Cass wasn't happy with my decision and, after finally giving up trying to change my mind, she had pressed me by text for an assurance that I had thought everything through and was clear about what I wanted from any future relationship with Elliot. I had reassured her on all counts, being careful to avoid going into any detail, due to actually having thought nothing whatsoever through, and thus remaining utterly unclear as to what I wanted. And although I was pretty sure that Cass knew that to be the case and had merely been trying to prod me into action, she didn't pursue the topic, instead winding up the exchange by suggesting that we catch up on Sunday over brunch – a suggestion to which I had happily agreed.

But as I lay in bed on Friday night, trying and failing to get to sleep, a part of me wished that I had gone for a drink with Cass after all, because I realised that I had a question for her. Namely: what exactly was the point in asking myself what I wanted from my relationship with Elliot? In fact, what was the point in ever examining your feelings and drawing up a list of wants in respect of *any* relationship, when the fulfilment of those wants is always subject to the feelings and wants of somebody else? It's not like a business negotiation, where cards are laid on the table, pairs are matched and compromises are reached regarding anything left over. When discussing personal relationships, vulnerable hearts are worn, like sitting targets, on sleeves – and compromise is impossible when feelings are genuinely and deeply held.

I turned over in bed, restlessly rearranging the covers, unhappy at a sudden recollection of telling David that I would miss working with him. That heart-on-sleeve moment certainly hadn't achieved anything, had it? For the simple reason that David's feelings did not align with my own.

And who was to say that exactly the same thing wouldn't happen with Elliot? That being the case, wouldn't it actually be far less painful not even to think about what I wanted? Wouldn't it be better simply to hear him out and then adjust my wants to the circumstances?

I sighed heavily, hugely dissatisfied with what seemed like an unacceptably passive approach to the situation. But what

237

was the alternative? Try to change someone else's mind? Try to change someone else's heart? That didn't feel right either.

Feeling unsettled, uncertain and very far from sleep, I desperately tried to think of something I could do – some positive action I could take – if not to improve the situation, then to at least make myself feel better about me.

After a moment, it came to me.

Sitting up in bed and reaching for my phone, I tapped out a text.

> Should have messaged sooner, but just wanted to say that I hope the tooth was sorted painlessly. I also hope that wherever you find yourself this weekend, the sun shines on you the entire time! Will look forward to hearing all about it on Monday ☺.

Pressing send, I switched off the light and slipped back down under the covers. I lay awake for a little while longer, listening for the buzz of a response to my message. A reply never came, but that was OK, I told myself as I finally drifted off to sleep, because at least now I did feel a little bit better about me.

Chapter 32

As Saturday dawned, I realised that like some grim parody of a wedding day, I didn't want to see Elliot before our appointed seven p.m. meeting time. Consequently, I spent the day cloistered in the kitchen, catching up on gallery paperwork, before rationalising my wardrobe and driving into Clifton to deposit my cast-offs at a charity shop. Then, after an early tea, and with a TED talk on overcoming anxiety playing through my AirPods, I set off for a walk around the fields bordering the village, with a plan to arrive at the pub at seven.

It was actually 7:10 p.m. by the time I found myself scanning the packed tables outside the pub for Elliot, with an acceptance that I must now finally confront the issues of the past week, the past three months and, let's face it, the past four and a half years.

As there was no sign of him outside, I took a breath and crossed the threshold into the low-ceilinged, low-lit bar. I spotted him immediately, sitting some distance from the door at one of the many free tables – the pub's clientele clearly preferring the evening sun to the light from the sconces, which supplemented the meagre natural light from the small, timber-framed windows.

Elliot's eyes had been fixed on the doorway and he offered me a slightly diffident smile as I entered, gesturing to the table in front of him. On it sat three drinks, two of which were positioned opposite him and therefore presumably meant for me. I managed a smile in return and then walked to join him.

'Hello,' he said, standing quickly and steadying his chair as it threatened to topple backwards. It was an oddly formal, and rather awkward, start.

'Hi.'

We stood facing each other, before he reached out, placed a hand on my waist and leaned in briefly to kiss my cheek. Then he stepped back and we sat.

'A lime soda and a red wine,' he said, nodding towards the drinks intended for me. 'I'm trying to cover all bases and moods.'

'Very thoughtful. I think I'll start with the soda. I've been walking and the evening's warmer than I expected.'

'Yes, I called for you before I set off and then realised you'd gone out. I should have done the same thing. It might have helped to clear my head.'

'Well, if it's any comfort, it did nothing for mine.' I picked up the soda. 'Thanks and cheers.'

He nodded but left his own drink, a beer, untouched. 'So, how was your week?'

'OK,' I said, not in the mood for small talk, but at the same time reluctant to move beyond it. 'We're thinking of opening another gallery. In Bath.' I was surprised, and not entirely happy, that I'd mentioned something over which I was so troubled, but it was a subject which I was struggling to keep from the forefront of my mind.

'Business must be good,' he replied.

'It is.'

'And yet you don't look exactly ecstatic at the prospect of expansion.'

I glanced over the top of my drink to find him looking at me with concerned curiosity.

'It's been quite a week,' I shrugged. 'My focus has been… split.'

'I get that.' He nodded empathetically. 'Mine too. I've been constantly distracted from work by thoughts of how I feel and what I want.'

I frowned, unsure whether to feel resentful that he had been able to prioritise his own feelings in a way that I had not, or just grateful that at least one of us had put in a bit of prep before turning up.

'And what I want, Es,' he continued quietly, 'is you.'

I stared unblinkingly at him, incapable of either speech or movement: physically rigid, but an emotional jelly.

'I've thought everything through,' he said, 'and I know that four years ago, I made a mistake. Not just one, in fact. I made lots of big, big mistakes. And the biggest of all was not coming to find you and trying to put things right. Instead, I've spent years trying to avoid repeating those mistakes with other people. I've expended – wasted – time and energy trying to save relationships that I now see weren't worth saving, when what I should have done was go back and save the only one that was. This one.'

He stopped talking, picked up his beer and leaned back in his chair. Clearly, it was my turn to say something. Fair enough. He had, after all, listed his wants and now, according to my preferred process, it was time for me to adjust to fit.

Deciding that soda just wasn't going to cut it, I reached for the wine glass and looked up at Elliot. He was still, without doubt, a very attractive and highly charismatic man. What's more, he wanted me; after years and years he *still* wanted me. So I should want him back, shouldn't I? If not, then what on earth had all those tears over a crumpled pencil sketch from the bottom of my T-shirt drawer been about?

'You're worryingly quiet,' he said.

'It's been a very strange time.'

'Tell me about it. You know me, I've never believed in anything that I can't hear, touch, taste or see. But when I saw you that first day and realised that you lived next door, I found myself thinking, *Is this fate?* Stupid, I know, but that's what it felt like.' He reached across the table, placing his hand on mine. 'Fate giving us another chance to get it right.'

I didn't reply and he stood, picking up his chair and moving it around the small, square table, so that he was now sitting adjacent to me, with his back to the room. 'I want you,' he said quietly, placing his hand on my cheek and turning my face towards him. 'I always have.' He leaned forward and kissed me, and I felt him relax, his hand moving gently to my neck, as I offered no resistance.

'Let's take this home, Es,' he breathed, moving his lips from my mouth to my ear and then looking at me, his face just inches from mine. 'Let's go home.'

'Whose home? Neither of us has one.'

'You're so pedantic,' he said, laughing softly. 'OK, let's take this back to a rented cottage. Yours or mine. Doesn't matter which.' He leaned towards me again, but I pulled away a little.

'Elliot, how do you see the future?'

He smiled. 'Well, I see us together, and I see a house and kids and a dog and a cat… I hope that's what you see too.'

'Yes, I hope for all those things. Except for the cat,' I added absently, 'because of the allergy.'

He frowned. 'You're not allergic to cats, are you? Is that a new thing?'

'No, sorry, I was thinking about David. We can't have a cat in the gallery because David is allergic to cats.'

'Oh,' he said. 'OK.'

'Anyway.' I shook my head, aware that I was in imminent danger of losing my train of thought, as concerns about David's move to Bath once again began to loom large. 'What I actually meant was, how do you see the more immediate future: tomorrow, for example?'

'Well, I see me bringing you breakfast in bed,' he said, a slow smile spreading across his face, as he reached out to tuck my hair behind my ear. 'Then maybe a walk, so that we can talk some more about our bright, longer-term future.'

'And what about tomorrow night?'

He lowered his hand from my face, appearing puzzled again. 'Tomorrow night?'

'Yes, when Morgan arrives back at the rented cottage.'

His smile faded. 'Obviously, it's not going to be pain-free,' he said soothingly. 'Break-ups never are, but you mustn't worry, Es. Some relationships aren't meant to be, and Morgan will accept that and be OK with it, if handled with care. It's much better to end it than to keep something going, when I know that I'm in love with someone else – with you,' he added gently. 'I just have to manage things so as to cause as little pain as possible.'

I picked up my glass. 'And how are you going to do that?'

He leaned back and sighed. 'Well, she's been talking about us buying a place together and obviously I don't want that. So we'll extend the lease on the cottage, just by another month or so, and I'll use that time to ease out of the relationship and to help her to see that it's not working.'

'You're not going to tell her tomorrow that it's over?'

'No, don't worry. I won't spring anything on her, and in the meantime,' he rested his hand on mine and squeezed it reassuringly, 'we'll be together, or at least not far apart. And now that we know what we want, we can work on spending as much time as possible with each other.' He took my hand and pressed it to his lips. 'We can meet up after work and I'm sure we'll manage some weekends together. It's not perfect, I know, but it's a lot closer to perfect than it has been for the past four years. It won't be for long – just a month, at the very most.' His eyes moved to my mouth. 'You're so beautiful,' he murmured, again leaning towards me. 'There's no one more beautiful.'

I pulled my hand sharply from his grasp. 'Hang on; I would just like to be clear about this. You're saying that you propose to live with your partner, next door to me – your lover – for a month, while we conduct a secret relationship. And you're also saying that you're happy with that arrangement.'

'Oh God, of course I'm not happy about it,' he said, holding out both hands, as if in appeal. 'I just want to do what's best for you. Imagine the consequences if Morgan came home tomorrow evening and I said, "That's it. I'm moving in next door with Esme." At the very best there would be extreme drama and at worst…' His voice trailed away and his shoulders dropped. 'Actually, I don't want to think about the worst,' he said quietly. 'But what I do know is that I don't want the beginning of our relationship to be marred and marked by someone else's hurt and distress. And I know that you don't want that either. That's just not who we are. This way, I ease Morgan into the break-up, making her realise that it's for the best and maybe even making her feel like it's her decision, and we all come out of it OK.' He smiled and took my hand again. 'Then you and I can start thinking about those kids – and the dog *and* the cat. David needn't visit,' he added with a wink.

I gazed at him expressionlessly, saying nothing, but aware of a growing sense of enlightenment and empowerment, as I finally understood why I hadn't called Elliot when he had walked out on me, and on our life together, over four years earlier.

It wasn't stubbornness, pride or stupidity.

It wasn't a fear of rejection, or of having to admit fault.

It was because Elliot was a man who could seduce you, make you fall in love with him, be unfaithful to you and then – when you suspected something was wrong – make you believe that it was all in your head and all your fault.

I hadn't been able to prove that categorically to myself four years ago, but I had known it unconsciously and instinctively. The tears that I had shed then and since were tears of regret for a love lost and a heart broken, but they were never going to make me pick up the phone, because deep down I knew the truth: Elliot Chase was a shit.

Here, finally, I had proof positive of that. He was ready to be unfaithful to Morgan, while telling her that he loved her, that there was nothing going on with anyone else and that he had only her very best interests at heart. And he was at peace with that.

'I don't want a cat,' I said.

He laughed. 'Don't worry, it's not a deal-breaker.'

My heart ached at the phrase. 'Maybe not. But being your bit on the side is.'

His shock and confusion were obvious, as he shook his head, his brow furrowing. He took a breath as if to speak, but I cut him off.

'Actually, Elliot,' I continued quietly, 'that's not true. Because even if you had come here this evening and told me that your relationship with Morgan was over and that she was never coming back, you still wouldn't be bringing me breakfast in bed tomorrow. Because the truth is that, as much as I loved you four years ago, I knew it was for the best when you left. No matter how hard I tried, I couldn't make myself trust you and it was driving me insane. Of course, I didn't want to believe that you had manipulated me and lied to me, so instead I took the blame for what happened. I told myself that I was jealous and paranoid – and I've been telling myself that ever since. But there was always a part of me that couldn't quite accept that, and *that's* why I didn't pick up the phone and call. Because, whatever I told myself, I knew me, Elliot – and deep, deep down, I knew you too.'

'Es, I never once—' he began, but I didn't pause for breath.

'Drop it,' I snapped, enraged by his attempt at denial. 'It's over. It was over a long, long time ago and I'm just grateful that – even if you won't admit what you did to me all those years ago – tonight you did admit to being capable of doing it to someone else.'

At that, his face darkened and I shook my head. 'Oh don't worry, I have no intention of sharing my epiphany with poor Morgan,' I said, scathingly. 'But I hope that, for her sake, you manage to end things with her before you do any more damage.'

He looked up at me as I rose to my feet. 'I'm actually the one working on damage limitation here.' He sounded weary, the anger now gone from his expression. 'Call me when you realise that, Es. I'll always pick up.'

I didn't know whether to laugh, cry or pour both of my drinks over his head in quick succession. But, in the end, I simply said, 'You're unbelievable,' and headed for the door, exiting without stopping and striding purposefully away down the lane, in the opposite direction to the cottages.

After several minutes of walking, I hit the main road and, maintaining my pace, I took out my phone and dialled. Cass answered on the second ring.

'You OK?' she asked.

'No,' I said, my voice breaking, 'I've just left the pub and I'm walking to Clifton.'

'OK,' she replied, a little breathlessly, as if running. 'You keep going. I'm on my way to get you.'

Chapter 33

'So, to sum up: Elliot is a shit,' said Cass, handing me a cup of chamomile tea. I sat, legs tucked under me, on the large grey corner-sofa in her front room. She had spent the previous twenty minutes listening to my account of the evening, having spent the twenty minutes before that listening to me sobbing in her car, after she scooped me up and drove me to her Horfield home.

'I just brought Kev up to speed, while I was waiting for the kettle to boil.' She nodded towards the kitchen, where Kevin had been ensconced since my arrival. 'And he also thinks that Elliot's a shit,' she said, sitting down next to me.

'Cass, I really don't mind Kevin being in here with us, you know.' I took a sip of my tea. 'There's nothing I'm worried about him knowing and I feel awful that his Saturday night is being ruined like this.'

'Oh, he's fine,' she said. 'There's a sofa in there and he's got his digestives, his iPad and his grabby stick, so he doesn't have to move unless he needs the loo. Anyway, are you feeling any better about it all for having relived it? Cos *sharing*,' she uttered the word with mild disdain, 'can go either way, can't it? Sophie being a prime example of that.'

'I'm feeling better,' I confirmed. 'Especially about Elliot. In fact, I probably feel better about Elliot than I have at any time over the past four years. It's just…' I put a hand to my face. 'You know, all the other stuff, like maybe seeing Morgan and having to go back to the cottage. The thought of that makes me feel sick.'

'Well, you don't have to think about any of it right now,' she said briskly. 'You make a list of clothes and anything else you want for Monday, and I'll go round tomorrow and bring it all back here for you.'

'Thanks, Cass.'

'And tomorrow, we can do whatever you fancy. Walk, lunch, slob – or you could do some of your arty stuff, if that makes you feel better. We can clear the kitchen for you.'

I rested my head on her shoulder. 'You're such a good friend.'

'I'm just loving the drama of it all. It's like when Mandy had her shoes nicked: a bit tragic, but it really livens up an evening.' She laughed loudly, and I tutted and sat up. 'Seriously, though, Es,' she said, giving me a nudge, 'you know I don't work Mondays. We could have a day out, if you can take the day off.'

I smiled. 'You don't have to give up your day off to nurse me.'

'I'd love a trip!' she exclaimed. 'We could take a boat to that teashop in Bath. I've always wanted to do that.'

My face fell.

'What's wrong?' asked Cass. 'Is it the boat or the teashop that's the problem? You usually love that kind of thing.'

'I do,' I said. 'It's Bath that's the problem. David's latest idea is to open a gallery there and I'd forgotten about it for a moment, that's all.'

'That's not something you're happy about? Does he want to close the Bristol gallery?' She stuck out her lower lip. 'I bloody hope not.'

I shook my head. 'No, no, nothing like that. It would be a second gallery. David would move to Bath and I'd stay here in Bristol.'

She picked up her glass of wine from the coffee table in front of us and took a sip. 'Are you worried about the business risk? Cos Dave would be on top of all that, wouldn't he?'

'He would. And I'm not worried, really. It's just something I've got to think about. It'll involve some pretty big changes.'

'It'd be weird not having Dave next door,' she sighed. 'I'd miss him and that big Scottish brain of his. God, and who'd calm you down when you go off on one?'

I gazed into my mug and nodded. 'I know.'

'And he's actually moving to Bath?'

I continued to nod. 'So he says.'

She didn't reply and, after a moment, I looked up to find her frowning at me.

'What?' I asked.

'Nothing,' she said lightly, shrugging. 'You just looked really thoughtful. And maybe a little bit sad?' She tilted her head to one side. 'Sad about the thought of not working with Dave and sad about Dave moving to Bath?'

I returned my focus to my drink.

'Well, you know what,' she continued brightly, 'that's another thing you don't have to think about this weekend. So, drink up your tea and let's find a funny movie to take us through to bedtime.' She leaned to one side, retrieving the remote from the arm of the sofa. 'And I'll get Kev in and you can read his cast. You should see what his gran wrote on the bottom of it,' she said, laughing quietly to herself as she switched on the TV. 'Pure filth.'

Chapter 34

I arrived at the shop earlier than usual on Monday, having cabbed it from Cass's, with the plan being that she would pick me up after work and transport me – and the clothes, cosmetics, paints, brushes and paper she had fetched on Sunday – back to the cottage.

'In the kitchen!' David called, before the door had even closed behind me. 'Kettle on!'

'Great!' I made my way through the gallery, reaching the kitchen in time to see him placing two mugs of coffee on the table and sitting down in front of one of them.

I took in his relaxed smile, his easy manner and his casual, but immaculately fitted, grey shirt, as he reached for his coffee, and I realised how much I had been looking forward to seeing him and basking in his aura of calm.

'So, we're both early into work, first thing Monday morning,' he said, picking up his coffee. 'Does that make us keen or...' He looked up and paused, with his coffee halfway to his mouth. 'You look...' He blinked a little. 'You look very nice. As always.'

I looked down at my floral shift dress and mid-heel pink pumps. 'Oh God, don't,' I sighed, flopping down in the chair opposite him. 'I feel like I'm going to a wedding. Cass and I have very different ideas of what constitutes workwear.'

'I don't understand,' he said, now sipping his coffee. 'What does Cass have to do with your workwear?'

'It's actually a rather long, boring and complicated story,' I said, exhausted at the thought of retelling it and reluctant to crash my enjoyment of being in David's company with a conversation about someone as unpleasant as Elliot.

'Does the story involve you getting very angry at any point?' asked David.

'Of course, but I can skip that bit.'

'Great.'

'I stayed with Cass this weekend and, for one reason or another, she had to pick up some clothes from the cottage for me, and *this*,' I tugged at the dress, 'is what she picked out for me to wear today. It was either this or Kevin's palazzo pants, because all of Cass's other stuff is too short for me. I thought about nipping home to swap it but...' I hesitated, the mere thought of returning to the cottage depressing me to the core. 'But I couldn't be bothered and, hey,' I shrugged, 'it's only a dress after all.'

'Impressive pragmatism and, besides, you look great,' he said, reassuringly. 'But I thought you went out for dinner at the weekend.'

'Oh, that.' I grimaced and picked up my coffee. 'Didn't happen.'

I watched as his eyebrows flickered upwards slightly. 'That's a shame.'

I shook my head. 'Not really.'

'Hmm,' he said, leaning back in his chair. 'And now, with our recent frank exchange of views regarding offloading at work in mind, I'm wondering whether I should ask you a series of probing questions regarding your weekend.'

'Don't worry; there's no need. But thank you for asking about asking. The weekend had its moments, but it's over with. I'm sure yours was much more interesting. Anything exciting to report?'

'Well, the sun shone, so thank you for that.'

'What? Oh, the text I sent you, yes.' I managed a smile, despite a slight and selfish dip in mood at the thought of David's weekend with Jasmine. 'You're welcome. So was it London or the Cotswolds?'

'Neither. I stayed in Bristol. Didn't do anything remotely exciting or see another soul.'

With confirmation that Jasmine had played no part in David's weekend, my smile took on a more genuine quality – which, admittedly, did me no credit. 'And was that a shame, or was it not?' I asked.

'It was – and it wasn't.'

I laughed. 'OK, so now *I'm* wondering whether *I* should ask lots of probing questions.'

He put down his coffee and looked steadily at me. 'Why not give it a go?'

For whatever reason, the invitation to question him felt to me like a watershed moment in our relationship and, as my smile fell away and we looked at each other in silence across the table, I was convinced that he felt it too.

And if David was willing to be open with me and answer questions about his life's highs and lows, then I wanted to show our friendship the same respect. The idea of telling him about my toxic evening with Elliot was no less distressing than it had been just minutes earlier – and confiding how I really felt about the prospect of him moving to Bath felt even more terrifying. But, nevertheless, I wanted to share it with him: all of it.

I cleared my throat. 'Actually, I'd like to tell you a bit more about my weekend first, if that's OK?' I hesitated for a moment, before continuing. 'And also my thoughts on you leaving to run the Bath gallery. I want to be completely honest with you, but it might… It might throw up some issues for you.'

He smiled. 'I'm sure I'll cope.'

I took a deep breath, wondering if he would.

'Morgan was away this weekend, and Elliot and I met for drinks on Saturday night,' I said hurriedly, before pausing for another breath and also to scrutinise David's face for any initial reaction. There was none, his features now serious and statue-like. 'We talked about how we felt, and the future and—'

The gallery door beeped and, in sync, we turned towards the noise and then back to each other, neither of us moving for a moment, before simultaneously standing up.

'I'll go. You finish your coffee,' I said, walking towards the door. 'It must be a delivery.'

I walked through the small hallway and into the gallery, only to find it empty. Frowning, I continued to the street door, opening it and peering outside. Still nothing. It was only as I turned, to make my way back to the kitchen, that Jasmine revealed herself.

'Boo!' she said, popping up from behind the counter, grinning from ear to ear, her hands fanned either side of her face, making her look like a supremely annoying daisy.

Her expression changed the moment she saw me. 'Oh, it's you,' she said, clearly irritated and momentarily unable to maintain any pretence of actually liking me.

I removed my hands from my mouth, where I had instinctively placed them in order to suppress a terrified scream as she'd leapt out. 'What on earth are you doing?' I asked, my heart thumping.

'I'm so sorry,' she gasped, now giggling. 'I was hoping to surprise David. He told me yesterday that he had to be in super early this morning.'

'He's in the kitchen,' I said quietly, finding her presence, her interruption to my conversation with David and her current status as his girlfriend immediately and utterly depressing. How on earth could someone like her be with someone like him? What was wrong with the universe? More to the point, what was wrong with me?

'Jazz.'

I turned, along with Jasmine, to see David standing in the doorway between the hallway and the gallery.

'Hello, you,' she said, lowering her head and looking up at him coquettishly.

I looked between them and, in a heartbeat, David's relationship with Jasmine went from being bemusing to impossible to bear. I knew I had to leave. 'We're out of coffee,' I mumbled, turning away, walking to the door and yanking it open. 'Won't be long.'

Once outside, I turned right and began walking to nowhere in particular, before being brought to an abrupt halt by the sound of Lloyd's voice and an overwhelming sense of déjà vu.

'Esme?'

I turned to face him and this time neither of us said anything more before he placed an arm around my shoulders, I burst into tears and we went inside for a cuppa.

–

'So, just to sum up,' said Lloyd, handing me a lilac tissue from a box on the table and topping up my teacup from the dormouse teapot. 'Your feelings for the very good friend who was previously very disappointed in you...' He frowned and his already rosy complexion reddened further. 'They actually tend towards the romantic?'

I stopped blowing my nose and looked up at him. 'Is that how it sounds?'

'Well, I'm no expert in these things, Esme,' he said, his eyes widening as he shook his head somewhat despairingly, 'but from what you've just said about wanting to spend every single day with him, how safe you felt as you rested your head against his chest and...' he paused and cleared his throat, 'how lovely he smells, I'd say that – yes – you probably have some degree of romantic interest in him.'

I stared at Lloyd, reviewing and dissecting all that I had told him about my relationships past and present. 'Oh my God, you're right,' I murmured, placing a hand to my forehead. 'You're right. I don't just enjoy his company. I don't just love him as a friend. I actually *want* him. Emotionally, intellectually physically... I *want* him!'

Lloyd shifted awkwardly in his chair. 'Yes, well, have a biscuit, Esme,' he said, pushing the plate towards me. 'They're Marks & Spencer.'

I picked up the one that looked most like solid chocolate. 'The thing is…' I began slowly, still processing. 'I've liked him – a lot – for years. But I think I've been afraid that if I let myself feel more – let my feelings deepen – I'd get all paranoid and possessive again.'

'Like you thought you were with your ex-boyfriend, four years ago?'

'Yes.'

'Except that now you know that you weren't paranoid, because your ex-boyfriend really wasn't a very nice bloke.'

I nodded, a little taken aback to realise just how much I'd shared with Lloyd over the past twenty minutes. And I had to hand it to him, he'd been listening *really* carefully.

'But what do I do now, Lloyd?' I asked desperately. 'I've already come very close to telling him how much I enjoy his company and value his friendship, and also that I really don't want him to leave Bristol. But is confessing how I feel really such a great idea? I might just be creating a lot of baggage for us both, and for what?' I took a bite from my biscuit. 'These are really nice by the way,' I added quietly.

Lloyd picked up his cup and frowned. 'I wish this was *Who Wants to be a Millionaire?* and I could phone a friend – Gwen, obviously,' he sighed. 'I'm just not very good at this kind of thing, Esme.'

'I think you underestimate yourself,' I mumbled, through a second mouthful of biscuit. 'You gave me perfect advice last time.'

'Really?' He appeared simultaneously humble and proud.

'Really.'

'Well,' he replaced his cup on its bone-china saucer and addressed the ceiling. 'I don't suppose we can go too far wrong if we stick to the facts. So, let's just review those for a moment. Firstly, we know, of course, how you feel…'

'We do.'

'But we don't know how *he* feels.'

'We don't.'

'So we can only guess at his feelings by examining his behaviour.'

'That's right,' I said, nodding approvingly. Lloyd was so much better at this than I ever would have imagined.

'Right, so, still sticking with the facts…' He lowered his gaze back down to me. 'He's known you for several years.'

'Three, yes.'

'And never, in all that time, has he shown any romantic interest in you.'

'True.'

'He has a girlfriend.'

'He does.'

'And she's nothing like you, physically or personality-wise.'

'Correct.' I mouthed the word soundlessly, while reaching for another biscuit.

'And he's just announced that he plans to leave Bristol and he's very happy about that – despite it meaning that you'll see each other much less frequently.'

I stuffed the entire biscuit into my mouth, attempting a smile while plucking another hankie from the box.

Lloyd heaved a sigh. 'I've got to say, Esme, I'm not sure the pair of you are quite on the same page. Or even reading the same book.'

I nodded furiously and dabbed at my eyes. 'I see that now, Lloyd. Thank you so much,' I mumbled, showering him with crumbs.

'But what I would say, and I know this will cheer you up,' he continued kindly, dusting himself off and leaning towards me, 'is that it sounds like you have a wonderful friendship – and physical distance does not at all mean the end of that. Take the young men in flares and Christian the lion, for example. When they were reunited years and years later, it was as if they'd never been apart.'

–

Following a quick visit to Lloyd's bathroom to sort out a bad case of panda eyes, I returned to the gallery. I wasn't feeling great, but I was grateful for the timeout with Lloyd which had prevented me from saying things to David which would have made our friendship awkward, and our business relationship strained, at a time when we needed to be able to work together in complete co-operation.

He was standing behind the counter when I got back and looked up as I walked in. 'Are you OK?' he asked, with just a hint of a frown.

'Hay fever,' I said. 'First day.'

He nodded acceptingly and returned his attention to the iPad on the counter. 'I've got some antihistamines, if you'd like one.'

'No, thanks. It'll settle now that I'm inside again.'

'You decided against the coffee, then?'

'What?'

He looked up and pointed at my hands, empty save for my phone. 'You didn't get any coffee.'

'Oh, I got sidetracked by Lloyd.'

He smiled affably. 'It's fine. We've got loads of coffee.'

'Have we? OK.'

'I'm sorry that Jazz interrupted our conversation.'

'It doesn't matter.'

'It does a bit.' He walked from behind the counter and glanced up at the clock. 'We're not far off opening, but we're the boss, so we can leave the closed sign exactly as it is and continue the conversation now, if you like?' He looked at me questioningly and I felt again that our relationship had shifted, just not quite as I'd hoped. Lloyd was right: David and I were on different pages.

'There's no need for that,' I said. 'I've just been doing some thinking over the weekend, about Bristol and about Bath and about galleries and homes, that's all.'

'And?'

'Well, I had thought that moving back into my flat was going to be really great and make everything perfect.'

'But you don't think that anymore?'

I shook my head. 'Moving back to Redland suddenly feels like a backward step. I realise now that I love Bristol because of who is here, not because of the building I live in – or work in, for that matter. Anyway, to cut a *very* long story short, things have changed for me, and so…' I paused and took a deep breath. 'And so, if it's OK with you, I would like to go and run the Bath gallery. It makes more sense for me to be the one to go and establish it, and the relocation would fit in with everything else that's going on for me right now.'

As usual, his face gave little away, but after several seconds of, no doubt, highly contemplative silence, he said, 'You're right. That does make more sense, and I don't have a problem with it at all. Let's work towards that.'

Chapter 35

To my relief, there were no signs of life at Elliot and Morgan's cottage when Cass finally dropped me home at around nine p.m., having insisted that I have dinner with her and Kevin after work. And their cottage remained deserted over the days that followed, with neither sight nor sound of the occupants.

Consequently, by the time Friday came around, I was feeling relaxed enough about being at home to turn down a kind offer of weekend accommodation from Cass, explaining to her that I was looking forward to staying put and recuperating, both physically and mentally, from what felt like a period of extended emotional turmoil.

What I didn't tell her, of course, was that my emotions had far from plateaued and that, as wonderful as it felt to have closure in respect of Elliot, turmoil still persisted in the form of my newly acknowledged feelings for David.

Recognising those feelings, in the same moment as being forced to confront the fact that they were not in any way reciprocated, was a blow from which it wouldn't have been easy to bounce back, even at the best of times. But almost daily drop-ins from Jasmine, coupled with David continuing to be just the kind of caring, calming, highly attractive man any sane woman would kill to be in a relationship with, made it harder still.

My coping mechanism – the one which made it possible for me to continue to work in the gallery, without intermittently falling to the floor in a despairing heap – was to regularly remind myself that, no matter what, David and I would remain business partners and, more importantly, we would remain friends. Furthermore, I could look forward to starting afresh in a new location, with a new perspective on relationships and a newfound confidence in my own judgement, thanks to my second-time-around encounter with Elliot. It was a mindset which kept me customer-ready and dry-eyed, every weekday, nine-to-five. Sadly, though, I couldn't quite muster the emotional energy to maintain this self-help approach once home, and my time at the cottage was therefore largely passed in gloomy introspection and tearful sketching, as I gave in to all those feelings kept at bay during the working day and allowed my heart to ache for David.

It was five p.m. on the Sunday after my blowout with Elliot, and I had just come inside after several hours of art-ache and heartache in the garden, when there was a knock at the door. Without thinking, I dumped my art paraphernalia on the kitchen table and went to answer it. It was only as I was actually opening the door that I questioned the wisdom of the move, and by then, of course, it was too late.

'Hello, Esme!' exclaimed Morgan. Only the effusiveness of her greeting – a strong and very welcome indication that she still knew nothing about Elliot and me – prevented me from fainting dead away.

'Oh, hi,' I said weakly.

'You look so shocked! Have you been wondering where we were?'

'Yes, I…'

'I'm so sorry.' She reached over the threshold and placed a concerned hand on my arm. 'I should have messaged. That was really thoughtless of me. Actually, do I have your number?' She paused and, if she could have frowned, I was pretty sure she would have. 'I know I have David's…'

I stared dumbly at her and she tutted. 'I feel awful now,' she said, without, of course, managing to look remotely distressed. 'I hope you weren't worried.'

I shook my head.

'I don't suppose,' she said, looking past me and towards the living room, 'that you have five minutes right now, do you? I could quickly explain everything.'

'Oh, sorry, of course, yes,' I replied, finding my voice and my manners, and taking a step back. 'Come in. Can I get you a drink? Tea? Or something cool?'

'No, no, thank you. I really haven't got long. But I did just want to explain and to say goodbye properly.'

'Goodbye?' I motioned her towards the sofa. 'You're leaving?'

She nodded excitedly as I sat down in the armchair opposite her. 'Everything happened so quickly, Esme. You know that I was visiting my parents last weekend. Well, of course you don't. Why would you?' She laughed and shook her head. 'But last Sunday morning, completely out of the blue, Elliot turned up with a suitcase, all packed for me, and whisked me off for a surprise birthday trip to Paris. Even my parents knew nothing about it! And *then*,' she laughed again, 'when we got back to the airport, Elliot said, "I've got another surprise for you. How do you feel about not going back to the cottage?"'

She paused, as if giving me a moment to share in her excitement and to appreciate Elliot's thoughtfulness. Instead, a weak echo of, 'Not going back to the cottage?' was all I could manage as I reflected, without surprise, on Elliot's decision to leave the scene of his crime as soon as at all possible.

'Well, Esme, you know how grateful I am for your friendship, but really, you and David aside, I haven't settled here. Between you and me, I never wanted to come to Bristol and I certainly never wanted to live out here in the sticks. I know I can say that to you, because I know you feel exactly the same way about being out of town,' she added, pausing in her breakneck account for a breath. 'So then Elliot said that he knew I hadn't been happy and that he'd rented a place in Bath – he knows I love Bath. He said that if I liked it, we would stay and that if I didn't...' She shrugged. 'Off we go again. Bottom line is that he says he's absolutely determined to make me happy. No matter what it takes.'

My stomach lurched. 'Bath?' I murmured.

'Yes, I just love it. Do you? David mentioned to me on my birthday that he's a real fan and quite fancied the idea of you both opening a gallery there. Oh, I so hope you do.'

'I think we might,' I said quietly.

'That would be amazing. Bath is just so beautiful and we've got a great little place right in the centre, which knocks time off Elliot's commute. And it's where I wanted to be all along. Oh, but, Esme,' she said, shifting to the edge of the sofa and leaning anxiously towards me, 'have I upset you? I'm sorry, I'm sounding so negative about Bristol, aren't I? And you and David have been so kind.'

'Don't worry.' I shook my head. 'I completely understand. It's just a lot to take in.' I paused, attempting to collect my thoughts. 'And you definitely want this, Morgan? What about your job?'

'That's all fine.' She waved a hand. 'I was only ever filling in and temping. I hadn't taken on any clients of my own.'

'OK.'

'I know that it's all very sudden, but Elliot had seen how unhappy I was – and *you* know how unhappy I was – and he took action. He's lucky: he has access to lots and lots of properties and landlords through the insurance arm of the company, because insurers have to be able to help people to find accommodation at such short notice. Well, of course,' she held out a hand and looked around the room, 'you know that. Did your insurer help you to find this?'

I nodded slowly, wondering for a moment just how much Elliot may or may not have been able to find out about my insurance claim and subsequent movements through his contacts. But actually, I didn't care. Every sentence uttered by Morgan was making me feel more and more grateful to be free of him. I just wished that she could be too.

'Look, I really have to go,' she said suddenly, standing up. 'But Bath isn't far away and I would love to stay in touch.'

'Yes, of course.'

'Great!' She made her way to the entrance hall and opened the front door. 'Oh and we'll be back next weekend with a little van to collect the rest of our stuff, if you're around. I'm just making an emergency dash for some more clothes today. I've been living out of a single suitcase since Sunday. Will you be here next weekend?'

'I'm afraid not,' I said, making a mental note not to risk spending even Friday night at the cottage. 'But Morgan...' I reached out, placing a hand on her arm, wanting to share the truth with her, but aware of a need to pick my time, place and words very carefully. Blurting out the details of my entire experience of Elliot right here, right now, would be out of context to the point of making me appear unhinged, unpleasant and unreliable. But at the same time, I didn't feel able to let her leave without attempting to offer at least some words of caution.

'Yes?'

'Don't doubt yourself,' I began, my voice breaking and my heart pounding in my chest. 'Professionally, personally, *do not* doubt yourself. Your instincts are good, so trust them – one hundred per cent.'

She looked at me for a moment, her beautiful face tragically incapable of conveying whatever she might have been feeling at that particular moment, thus depriving me of any clue as to what more I might, or might not, have been able to say.

'Thank you,' she said. 'You're so kind, and I'll try. I promise.'

She leaned in to bestow a hug that I didn't deserve, and then turned and walked away down the gravel path. 'I'll be in touch once we've settled in,' she called, over her shoulder. 'And tell David I said hi – and bye – and I'll message him. I'll miss him too.'

Chapter 36

Three months later

'So, Douglas, I think we've gone over most of the arrangements for tomorrow night,' I said, as we sat together at the small table in the gallery's kitchen. 'But would you like to cast a final eye over the guest list?' I pulled a piece of A4 paper from the file in front of me and handed it to him. 'Victoria Farrell – see, I've highlighted her name? She's the gallery owner from Reading I mentioned to you. We must make sure to have a little chat with her.'

Douglas picked up the list and looked down anxiously at it. It was, I noticed, shaking slightly in his hands. 'So many people,' he murmured.

'I know it looks like a lot when they're listed like that, but they won't all be here at the same time. There'll be lots of coming and going. It won't be anywhere near as crowded as Jasmine Dean's show and you were fine at that, weren't you?'

He looked at me over the top of his small, round glasses. 'I felt OK by the counter, near the door.'

'Well then,' I smiled, 'how about I make sure that there are a couple of stools behind the counter and then if you need a breather, you and me – or you and David – can go and take a break there. Or you can always relax in here and I can introduce you to people in small bursts. How does that sound?'

'I know you'll look after me, Esme.'

'Of course I will,' I said brightly. 'And so will David. Won't you, David?' I added as he joined us, having just finished shutting up the gallery.

'What's that?' he asked.

'You'll look after Douglas tomorrow.'

'Certainly,' he said, sitting down and placing a reassuring hand on Douglas's shoulder. 'We're all in this together, Douglas.'

'We were just taking a final look at the guest list,' I explained.

David nodded. 'Looking good to you, Douglas?'

'Yes, thank you.'

'And,' I tapped the sheet with my pen, 'don't forget that your parents will be here to support you too. I bet they're really excited about it all.'

'I'm not sure if they'll be here,' said Douglas, shifting slightly in his chair.

'Really?'

He removed his glasses and turned them over in his hands. 'They don't get out much,' he said quietly. 'I should have explained.'

'Oh... I see. Well, never mind. Do you have anyone else you'd like me to add to the list? Any other family members, maybe? It's not too late, you know.'

'Two siblings...'

'Great!'

'But they don't get out much either,' he said, offering me a slow smile, which I wanted to believe was regretful, but which to my mind had just a hint of quiet satisfaction about it. 'Not anymore,' he added in a near whisper.

'Do they not?' I said, with an anxious sidelong glance at David.

'That's perfectly fine, Douglas,' said David calmly. 'Esme and I will be here to support you. I'll come and pick you up at six thirty, as planned, and we'll arrange a taxi to take you home, so that you don't have to hang around waiting for us to clear up. Does that sound OK?'

'Yes, and thank you, David, and thank you too, Esme,' replied Douglas, nodding at me. 'I'm a little anxious about it all, but I know I'll be fine with you two there.'

'Well, we're really looking forward to it, aren't we, David?' I said.

He looked at me and smiled, pausing slightly before answering. 'We are indeed, Esme.'

'Is the butcher's open?' asked Douglas.

'Er…' I stopped smiling at David and instead looked quizzically at Douglas. 'Sorry?'

'I was wondering what time it is and whether the butcher's shop is still open,' he said, pushing back his chair and standing up.

David stood too. 'Well, I'm not sure. Shall we go and see?'

'Thank you so much,' he said, as if David had just offered to give him his own kidney, instead of checking whether there were any still available for purchase next door.

'No problem. Come on,' said David, beckoning him to follow as he turned and left the kitchen.

'Bye, Esme!' Douglas bent low, scooping up his rucksack – which today sounded as if it contained cutlery for ten – and hurried after him.

I raised a hand and then reached across the table to retrieve the guest list, placing question marks next to Douglas's parents and scribbling a few conversational pointers for David next to some of the other names. I was still running through the list when he returned and sat down next to me. 'Well?' I asked, without looking up. 'Was Lloyd still open for browsers?'

'Sadly not, but Douglas took it quite well.'

'That's good,' I said absently, continuing to write.

'I wonder if his parents will make it up the basement steps tomorrow.'

I didn't look up. 'Stop it.'

He laughed. 'Sorry.'

'I think this is a useful crowd. It's a good mix of friendly browsers – who won't frighten Douglas – established fans, who will definitely buy, and then some more serious types. I think they'll be really interested in the darker pieces. I so want this to go well for him.'

'I'm sure it will,' he said, 'and while you've got that list in your hand, I've got another name for you to add to it.'

'Who?'

He didn't reply, and I stopped writing and looked up. 'Who?' I repeated.

'But only if you're OK with it.'

I frowned and then my expression cleared. 'Oh, you mean Jasmine. Of course I'm OK with it,' I said, forcing a smile. 'Jasmine and I are fine now. Or at least *I* am fine with *Jasmine*. Obviously, I can't speak for her. But I make a real effort with her every time she drops by – *which is a lot*,' I added under my breath, returning my attention to the sheet.

'Why would Jazz come to Douglas's show?'

'Because you're dating her, obviously,' I murmured, still focused on the list.

'What?'

'Because you're dating her,' I repeated more loudly.

'But I'm not.'

I stopped writing and put my pen down heavily on the table. 'You mean you're no longer dating?'

'I mean that we were never dating.'

'But you said that you were.'

He shook his head. 'I didn't.'

'You did!' I insisted, my voice going up a notch. 'At Morgan's birthday party.'

He appeared thoughtful for a moment. 'I remember not wanting to belittle Jazz by completely contradicting what she'd said to Morgan, but I didn't say we were dating.'

'You told everyone you'd been for drinks and dinner! And you've been out together since. You even went to Bath for the day!' I exclaimed.

'I've never been to Bath with Jasmine,' he said. 'Or anywhere further than Clifton, actually. I went to Bath recently with my schoolfriend Arthur. He's a commercial estate agent. He was free that day, and the weather was good, so we caught up and he helped me check out some areas,' he said, appearing perfectly untroubled. 'As for Jasmine, we've been out for coffee and drinks a few times recently – but it's entirely platonic and always has been. Our conversations centre exclusively on Jazz and her art. It's all business-focused.'

'But Morgan said Jasmine told her—'

'When Morgan mentioned that Jazz had said we were seeing each other, I realised that Jazz and I had different ideas regarding what the relationship was and where it might be going. Obviously, I was uncomfortable with that, so I met Jazz for drinks the Monday after Morgan's birthday and explained to her that I wasn't looking for a relationship. She said she was fine with that.'

I stared at him, my eyes wide, my mouth ajar. 'But she's here *all* the time, David! And I've been *really* tolerant and *really* nice to her for weeks and weeks! Totally unnecessarily!' I threw my hands into the air. 'I thought we were going to be open and honest with each other about stuff like this.'

'I'm sorry,' he said, his expression a mixture of bemusement and amusement, 'but I'm not sure how I could have been open and honest with you about the end of a relationship which had never begun.'

'You could have tried,' I muttered, picking up the pen. 'You knew full bloody well that I was being fake nice and finding it a strain.'

'Not really. Although, I did wonder why you kept complimenting her hair and her shoes.'

'I was doing that for you! You ungrateful...' I left the sentence hanging as the significance of the situation – and of David's single status – dawned on me. I had made valiant efforts to lock away my feelings for him over the past few months, focusing instead on work and on giving genuine consideration to meeting up with at least one of the men on Cass's growing list of questionable recommendations. But my heart wasn't in it, and I was all too aware that my feelings for David, although suppressed, had by no means gone away.

'So are you saying that you're not at all attracted to Jasmine? Is that because she's not remotely your type?' I asked.

He frowned. 'We seem to have gone off a professional–personal precipice with that question.'

'Sorry, yes, you're right. I was being way too personal there,' I said, looking down again. 'Cass is clearly rubbing off on me.'

'But no, she isn't my type.'

My head flicked back up and I toyed with the idea of asking him whether, under any imaginable circumstances, he might be attracted to a slightly shouty brunette.

But in the end, fearing both the answer and the aftermath, I held up my piece of paper. 'I'd really better finish this.'

'It's Morgan,' he said.

'What is?'

'The other person I'd like to add to the guest list – but only if you're OK with it.'

I blinked in surprise. 'Well, of course I'm OK with it,' I said, feeling far from OK, and horrified at the possibility of her turning up with Elliot. 'My only problem—'

'It'd just be her, of course,' continued David, his tone now businesslike. 'I'm sure you know that she and Elliot have split.'

My jaw dropped.

'You didn't know that?'

I shook my head dumbly.

'Oh,' he said, looking mildly surprised. 'I assumed you knew.'

'When did that happen?'

'A month or so ago. Not long after they moved to Bath.'

I continued to shake my head. 'I haven't heard from her recently,' I murmured.

'I thought Elliot might have told you.'

'Why would you think that?' I screwed up my face in confusion. 'Elliot and I haven't communicated at all since I made it clear that I wanted nothing more to do with him. Why on earth do you think he moved out of the cottage?'

He looked at me for a moment before answering. 'I have no idea why he moved out of the cottage. You didn't tell me.'

'So you thought that I was still in touch with him?'

'Morgan had told me that they were moving to Bath, and as we're hoping to open a gallery there—'

'Oh, so you assumed that I was moving to Bath in order to conduct an affair with my ex-boyfriend, is that it?' I asked, frowning. 'Well, thank you for thinking so very highly of me.'

'I didn't think that at all,' he said simply.

'Well, it sounded like it.'

'I didn't know that you'd argued with Elliot and naturally assumed that you'd stay in touch. That seemed even more likely, as you were again going to be in the same city. I don't think that was an unreasonable conclusion to draw, bearing in mind that you hadn't provided me with any information to the contrary.'

'*I don't think that was an unreasonable conclusion to draw, bearing in mind that you hadn't provided me with any information to the contrary,*' I mimicked, in a high-pitched Scottish accent.

'Repeating my words back to me, in a mocking manner, does not make me wrong,' he said quietly. 'And that accent is, incidentally, an insult to every Scot on the planet – and also to Mel Gibson.'

We smiled at each other and I nodded. 'You're right, my mockery needs work. And I'm sorry for not keeping you in the loop about Elliot. I meant to tell you. You know, I sort of thought that I had. But clearly not.' I sighed heavily. 'The truth is that he's just not a very nice person, David. I suspected that to be the case almost five years ago and now I know it for sure.'

'Well, I'm pleased that you have closure, at least.'

'Me too.'

There was silence between us for a moment, before I said, 'I'm relieved that he and Morgan have split.'

'Apparently, she found some explicit texts he'd sent to his graduate assistant.'

I gasped. 'To Joshua?!'

'I believe her name is Libby.'

'Oh, OK, that makes more sense,' I said, trying to focus on Morgan's horror at finding the texts, rather than my own at the fact that she had managed to access Elliot's phone. 'Poor Morgan.'

'Yes. I got the impression that she wasn't entirely surprised.'

'Sound instincts…' I murmured, thinking about Morgan's escape from Elliot, and envying her the relatively early, unequivocal proof of what kind of man he really was. 'Do you hear from her much?' I asked, suddenly struck by how very well-informed David was.

'More so in the weeks since the break-up,' he said. 'She messaged earlier to say that she's in Bristol for the weekend and asked if it would be possible to see us.'

He said 'us', but I couldn't help wondering if that was merely his inference and what Morgan actually wanted was to see him alone. I also wondered whether he, too, might quite like a one-to-one reunion at some point.

'So I mentioned Douglas's show to her,' he continued, 'and said that I'd double-check numbers with you.'

'She should definitely come. She loves Douglas's work and it'll be nice to see her – without Elliot.'

'Yes, he was never good enough for her.'

The comment, delivered so casually and without any intent to hurt, nevertheless stung. David's certainty that Elliot hadn't deserved Morgan was obvious. But had he ever harboured any doubts about whether Elliot was good enough for me? If he had, he'd kept them remarkably well hidden. But then maybe, deep down, David thought that faithless people who snogged in the kitchen at birthday parties, and ended up in one another's arms behind shop counters, actually rather deserved each other.

I shook my head at the thought, knowing that I was misjudging him and that the only person in the room still condemning me was me. David was merely paying Morgan a well-deserved compliment and stating the truth about Elliot.

'You're right: he was nowhere near good enough for her,' I said, as it occurred to me that maybe Cass had been right after all, when she'd paired David and Morgan. They'd always got on very well when she was in Bristol and had obviously managed to keep in touch even when she wasn't – more so now that she was single.

I sighed resignedly. Quietly elegant blondes were, I had to admit, much more likely to be David's type than slightly shouty brunettes.

'I think I'm done here.' I glanced down at the list. 'Oh, but I'll just add Morgan,' I said, scribbling her name.

'Perfect.' He stood up, taking his phone from his pocket. 'I'll message her to confirm things. She sounded keen on the idea when I suggested it earlier, so I think she'll be really pleased,' he said, turning and heading for the gallery.

'I'm sure she will,' I murmured, getting to my feet, collecting my things and following. 'I'm sure she will.'

Chapter 37

'Come in, come in,' I smiled, unlocking the gallery door and beckoning Cass inside. 'Wow, you look amazing!'

'One does try,' she said, holding out the skirt of her deep-pink, beaded wrap dress, while pouting and striking a pose. 'Freezing, though. Left my jacket in the salon. Hey, but I love what you're wearing too,' she said, looking me up and down. 'I keep telling you that you should wear more dresses like that to work. You've got the figure for them. Is it new? That eggshell colour is so good on you.'

'Yes, it's new,' I said, not bothering to add that it was just one of far too many cheer-up purchases I had made over the past few months.

'You're wasting yourself on singledom,' tutted Cass. 'Chris's hair transplant has started to grow in now and he looks bloody amazing. And have I told you about Max? He works out and owns his own boat. It's got an engine, not oars, before you ask.'

'Is Kevin with you?' I held open the door and peered out into the freezing, lamp-lit street.

'No, he'll be along later. He's working till eight tonight at the er…' She paused, circling a hand. 'You know… at the place… where he does the thing.'

'After ten years, you really should know what his job is, Cass,' I sighed, closing and relocking the door.

'You know he's tried to explain it to me a thousand times, but it's all hard drives and arms shipments, and I get confused. So, do I have to wait until seven for a glass of something?' she asked without pause, eyeing the flutes on the long, cloth-covered table at the back of the gallery.

I checked my watch. 'David's got a bottle open in the kitchen, and Douglas and Lloyd have already made a start on it.'

'Lloyd's here? Is Gwen coming?' she asked, wandering over to one of the temporary glass display cases housing Douglas's sculptures.

'She'll be here in about half an hour, and in the meantime, Lloyd has been an absolute godsend,' I replied, lowering my voice and glancing towards the back of the gallery. 'Douglas is a nervous wreck, but Lloyd has got him talking about butchery, which has *really* calmed him down.'

Cass gave me a sidelong look. 'Butchery?'

'In particular, their shared respect for the sausage-making process.'

'This Douglas guy makes sausages, as well as sculptures?' she asked, her upper lip curling slightly.

'I think he's planning to have a go,' I said. 'I left when they got on to meat grinders. Apparently, Douglas has a manual one. But anyway,' I continued brightly, while suppressing a shiver, 'aren't his little animals amazing?'

'Very clever,' she said, bending down to take a closer look. 'Not my cup of tea, but Kev's mother would buy the lot.'

'They actually have very broad appeal. The fact that they're—'

'OK, OK,' she said, straightening up, 'enough with the spiel. I'm not one of your punters. I'm just here to give the evening an air of sophistication.'

'And for the booze.'

'And for the booze,' she agreed, grinning. 'So why,' she said, threading her arm through mine and guiding me towards the back of the gallery, 'don't you take me into the kitchen, introduce me to the sausage sculptor and pour me a large glass of something alcoholic.'

'Good so far?' asked David, as he came into the kitchen with an empty platter, which had formerly been laden with light bites.

I glanced up from my iPad. '*Really* good,' I said, looking back at the screen. 'We're not even an hour in, with about a quarter of invitees still to show, and we've sold...' I paused to do a quick count. 'Twelve pieces – all at the higher price. Plus, Victoria Farrell loves it all. I knew she would and she's a handy connection for us to have too. She'll remember the favour.'

'Well done.'

'Back atcha.'

'No, I just fetch and carry. You manage these things and you always do a great job.'

I lowered the iPad. 'I hope you're not trying to kick off a 360-degree appraisal, because I haven't got a good word to say about you.'

He smiled. 'It was just a compliment.'

'Well, thank you and, of course, I think you're brilliant too.'

'I know. But tear yourself away from that iPad for a moment. There are some people I'd like to introduce you to.'

'OK, but I bet you a tenner that there's no one out there I don't know,' I said, standing up.

'Well, you owe me a tenner then,' he said, taking a bottle of Prosecco from the fridge and extending an arm, corralling me towards the door.

We walked into the now busy gallery, with David leading me to the front right-hand corner, where Douglas's human figures were displayed, a little set apart from his wildlife pieces. There was a small huddle of browsers surrounding them and, on the periphery of the group, stood Douglas – looking uncharacter-istically calm. To his left was an elderly, grey-haired couple: a petite woman and a man slightly stooped, but still not far off Douglas's height.

'Esme,' said David, as we approached, 'I'd like to introduce you to Pamela and Bill.' He paused and looked at me. 'Douglas's parents,' he added significantly, with a nod and a slight widening of the eyes.

I placed a hand on my chest and gasped. 'Oh, my goodness,' I said, shaking their hands vigorously in turn. 'I can't tell you how relieved and delighted I am to meet you both.' I laughed and shook my head. 'You know, it's so silly, but when Douglas first showed me these sculptures, I thought—'

'Esme was quite upset at the thought that you might not be able to make it this evening,' said David.

I looked up at him, and then back at Pamela and Bill. 'Yes, that's right, I was. I wasn't *at all* worried about your well-being.'

Pamela smiled a little uncertainly. 'We're really happy to be here for Douglas,' she said, looking fondly up at her son.

'His work is quite wonderful, isn't it?' said Bill, proudly. 'You know, he's never really shown it to us before. He keeps it all locked up in his basement, don't you, son?'

'I do, Dad,' said Douglas shyly.

'Far too humble by half.' Bill patted his son on the back. 'We're a quiet family all round, but Douglas is by far the quietest, and while I don't like braggarts, a talent like his should not be kept hidden away in the dark. But you, Esme, and you, David,' he continued, turning to us, 'have shone a light on it, and Pamela and I would like to thank you very much for that.'

'Well,' I began, now feeling rather emotional, 'I just feel it's a real privilege to have Douglas's work in our gallery and I know David agrees.'

'Absolutely,' he said, placing a hand on Douglas's shoulder. 'Now, let me uncork this bottle and top up those glasses for you.'

Bill and Douglas proffered their flutes, while Pamela placed a hand over hers. 'I'm not a big drinker,' she said quietly, turning to me while David, Bill and Douglas started to discuss the possibility of Douglas's work going on sale in other galleries. 'I'm not actually a going-out type, really. Crowds tend to overwhelm me a little bit but, I have to say, I'm so enjoying seeing Douglas's work on display. He'd love nothing more than to make a full-time job of it.'

'I think he could,' I said. 'His wildlife pieces are amongst our most asked for and it's great to be able to introduce people to his other work too.'

She smiled. 'Yes, he does love his wildlife. As a little boy, he was obsessed and our garden is still full of all the feeders, hedgehog houses and such he made as a teen. He would watch the birds for hours on end through his binoculars, sketching and making notes – and now, of course, he has his lawn camera and his night vision goggles, which he uses in the woods. He's just so fascinated by it all.'

'You can see that fascination in the detail of his pieces.'

'Yes, he's never happier than when he's at home in his garden, watching the birds during the day and the other little creatures scurrying around at night. Oh, except, of course,' she continued, her voice lowering and her expression darkening, 'when those dreadful people moved in next door to him.' She put a hand to her mouth. 'I forget what they were called, but they upset him terribly. A family of four. The teenagers would throw stones at the birds on Douglas's feeders and one day he caught one of them shooting at squirrels with an airgun. The final straw was when one of them… Well,' she bit her lip and shook her head, 'no need to distress you with the details, but it was enough to make Douglas – quiet as he is – go round and knock on the door. Apparently, the parents gave him some sort of boys-will-be-boys line. Quite shameful.'

'That's awful, Pamela,' I said. 'What horrible people. Douglas must have been so upset.'

'Oh, he was, he was,' she said, shaking her head. 'He was extremely distressed and actually quite angry too. We'd never seen him like that before, and Bill offered to go round and speak to the neighbours again for him, because we could see how agitated he was becoming. Douglas said he'd think about it.'

'But Bill didn't go round?'

'That's the funny thing,' she said, shrugging. 'He didn't have to because, just three days later, the neighbours had gone.'

'Gone?'

'Disappeared.' She clicked her fingers. 'Just like that. All four of them. Gone without a trace. No one ever saw them again.'

'Er… and did anyone call the—'

'Esme, sorry to interrupt,' said David, now at my side. 'Sorry, Pamela, I just need to borrow Esme's tablet from her for a moment.'

'Not at all,' she said. 'You carry on. I know you're both working very hard on behalf of Douglas this evening and I don't want to interrupt that.' She saluted us shyly with her glass, and then turned to talk to her husband and son.

'Can I swap you the iPad for the Prosecco?' said David. 'We've sold *Father*.'

I looked up at him, opened my mouth, but didn't reply.

'Is everything OK?' he asked quietly.

'I think Douglas killed his neighbours,' I whispered, 'or kidnapped them.'

David remained silent for several seconds. 'Well, that's certainly an interesting new theory.'

'They abused his squirrels.' I gripped his arm. 'A family of four – people, not squirrels – and no one ever saw them again,' I hissed. 'Ever.'

David looked down at my hand and frowned. 'Firstly, you're hurting me.' He gently prised my fingers from his forearm. 'And secondly, why don't you go over there and check on Nerys Matthews – she's waving to you from behind the counter. Meanwhile, I'll take payment for the sculpture of Douglas's dead neighbour—'

'David!'

He laughed. 'Look,' he said, easing the iPad from my grasp, 'go and talk to Nerys and I promise you that as soon as I've made this sale, I will ask some probing questions and find out exactly what happened to Douglas's neighbours.'

'OK,' I said, reluctantly taking the bottle from him, as he pivoted me towards Nerys. 'But I want a full update later,' I added, looking at him over my shoulder.

'Promise.'

Turning away, and forcing an image of a chipped and peeling basement door from my mind, I weaved my way through the small crowd to Nerys and her friend, Margaret, who were sitting on the stools I had positioned earlier in the evening, for Douglas plus one, behind the counter. I held up the Prosecco. 'Any more, ladies?'

'Ooh, no thank you,' said Nerys, beaming up at me. 'We're on our second and that will suffice. We're just waiting for Margaret's grandson to come and take us home. He'll be here any moment.'

'Yes,' said Margaret, 'he passed his test last year and he chauffeurs us all over the place, doesn't he, Nerys?'

'He does,' she replied. 'He's such a good boy.'

I smiled. 'Well, I hope you've had a good evening. I'm afraid it's a bit more crowded than I expected. But then these things always are and that's not a bad thing.'

'We've had a lovely time,' said Nerys. 'Thank you so much for inviting us. As you know, I bought a robin and Margaret bought an otter *and*, of course, we met the sculptor himself. That was rather wonderful. Such a humble young man and he has so inspired us to keep going with our artwork, hasn't he, Margaret?'

'He has, he has,' said Margaret, nodding along.

'Which reminds me, Esme,' Nerys leaned forward, reaching across the counter and placing a hand on my arm. 'I have another batch of cards for you. I shall bring them in on Monday.'

'Marvellous,' I said, making a mental note to share with David my idea about him dealing with our geriatric artists. 'We'll look forward to seeing them.'

'I might bring some in too,' said Margaret, necking the remaining contents of her glass.

'Even better.' I turned, as a small black car pulled up outside the gallery. 'I wonder if this is your ride.'

'No, Joseph's got a red car,' said Margaret. 'Oh, and there he is. On the other side of the road, by the zebra.'

'That's nice,' I said quietly and a little absently, as I watched Morgan emerge from the passenger side of the black car and then lean back in through the open door to talk to the driver.

'Yes, so we'll be off now, Esme,' said Nerys. 'And thank you again. We'll see you next week.'

'Oh, yes, not at all,' I replied, opening the gallery door for them. 'Thank you so much for coming.'

They waved goodbye and I continued to hold the door, waiting for Morgan to finish her conversation and turn around, which she did the next moment.

'Esme,' she said, smiling broadly and walking towards me. 'It's so lovely to see you. How are things?' she asked, now with just a hint of concern in her expression.

I blinked, fascinated by my first encounter with her fully animated face. Her dependency on injectables had clearly gone the same way as her dependency on Elliot and it struck me that it was a liberated Morgan who now stood before me. 'You look beautiful,' I said.

'Aw, thanks so much for that immediate confidence boost.' She stepped inside and gave me a hug. 'You look lovely too – as always. But is everything OK with you?'

The question felt more weighted than a simple 'How are you?' and I found myself wondering what lay behind it.

'Yes, I'm fine.'

She leaned in and lowered her voice. 'It was just that David said you had some things to work through. He didn't say what, but it's why I didn't message you about Elliot and me,' she said, with a sigh. 'I didn't want to burden you with my problems if you had your own issues to deal with.' She paused and placed a hand on my arm. 'Sorry, I'm assuming that David has told you that we've broken up. He might not have.'

'He has – but only yesterday. I'm sorry...' I hesitated, choosing my words carefully. 'I'm sorry that you had to go through all of that and I hope you have come out the other side feeling stronger for it.'

'Well, he hasn't been gone long, but yes, I do feel stronger. And that's partly thanks to you, Esme.'

'Really?' I asked uncertainly, bracing myself for whatever might come next.

'You told me to trust my instincts and if I hadn't, I never would have checked his phone. I would have continued to blame everything on my own paranoia. But I knew there was something not right. I can't explain it and I had no actual proof, but I just *knew* it. Sounds silly, doesn't it?'

'It doesn't sound silly at all.' I took a breath, wondering how much more to say. That there *was* more to say, I knew without a doubt, but as I looked at Morgan, appearing genuinely happy for the first time in our acquaintance, and then over my shoulder at the crowded room, I also knew that now was not the time. And if there ever should be a time, it certainly wouldn't be until I was absolutely sure that I was sharing my history with Elliot for Morgan's benefit, rather than my own.

I turned back towards her. 'I'm really happy for you. I honestly couldn't be happier. But let me get you a drink and you can tell me all about Bath. David is just over there,' I said, nodding my head in his direction. 'If I relieve him of that iPad he's clutching, he'll be free to catch up with you too. I know he'd love that.'

Chapter 38

'Did you get to talk to Morgan?' asked Cass casually, as she continued to sweep the floor of the now deserted gallery.

I looked up from the large wooden tray I was loading with glasses and yawned. 'A little. But it's difficult to talk to anyone for very long at these things. We've agreed to meet for lunch next time I'm in Bath, or she's in Bristol.'

'Well, I had a *really* interesting conversation with her,' she said, adjusting her wrap dress and then leaning on her broom. 'Wanna hear about it?'

I glanced towards the kitchen, and the continuing clatter of glasses being rinsed and boxed by David. '*Of course.*'

'She told me—' began Cass, before coming to an abrupt halt.

'Go on. Why have you stopped?'

'The thing is, Es, I'm pissed. So I can't work out whether this is going to make you feel better, or like shit.'

'Well, it's too late to worry about that now, isn't it?' I exclaimed. 'If you don't tell me, I'll just be imagining all sorts of terrible things.'

'You're right,' she said, with a quick nod. 'OK, so Morgan was telling me all about Elliot and his dodgy texts. *In detail.*'

I bit my lip.

'God, he didn't sext *you*, did he?' She gasped, in mock horror.

'Of course not. But he did message me quite a bit about his day… his commute… stuff like that, and that would have come as a bit of a surprise to Morgan, wouldn't it?'

282

She waved a hand. 'I think she had bigger fish to fry, Es. Besides, you'd know by now if she'd seen anything. Maybe he was deleting them.'

'Maybe.'

'Anyhoo,' she continued, lowering her voice and needlessly checking over both shoulders for eavesdroppers, 'she told me *all* about the texts, but she also told me about one of Elliot's ex-girlfriends.'

'OK,' I said, 'so that's interesting.'

'I know.' She paused, enjoying the unshared nature of the intel for a moment.

I sighed and gestured towards the clock. 'Kevin will be back to collect you at any moment. It's nearly eleven.'

'Good point,' she said, checking her wrist, despite having never, to the best of my knowledge, worn a watch. 'So, in a nutshell, this ex got in touch with Morgan as soon as she found out she was seeing Elliot. She told Morgan that Elliot couldn't be trusted and gave her loads of examples of what a shit he was, *including…*'

I stared at her and waited. 'Yes…?'

'Including the fact that Elliot had got really drunk one night and told her about his break-up with a long-term girlfriend, who he thought he was going to marry. Apparently, he'd had a casual thing going with a woman at work and his partner had got suspicious, but he'd denied it and walked out. The ex who contacted Morgan said that he seemed really broken up about it, but that hadn't stopped him going on to do *exactly* the same thing to her six months later. Morgan wrote it all off as jealousy and sour grapes at the time, but she obviously believes it now and said that it makes her feel even better about ending it.'

I returned to stacking the tray.

'Oh, Es, I'm sorry.' Cass walked hurriedly to me, placing her arm around my shoulder. 'I shouldn't have told you. Sorry.'

'No, no, it's good to know. Well, not *good*, obviously. But it's further proof that I was right at the time – and not certifiably insane. Plus, it was a long time ago, Cass,' I said wearily, giving her a hug. 'We're talking about someone I honestly don't have feelings for anymore. I just feel sorry for the next poor woman.'

She nodded uncertainly.

I smiled and nudged her. 'Thanks for telling me and, more importantly, thanks for helping to tidy up.'

'No problem.' She handed me the broom and pointed to the window. 'That's Kev across the road, so I'd better go. But there was something else that Morgan said, you know.'

'Do I want to hear it?'

'Well, it's too late not to tell you now, isn't it?'

'I suppose it is. Go on then.'

'She was telling me about the guy who gave her a lift to Bristol this weekend. They work together and they're attending some fitness event at the Marriott, which sounded *really* dull, but never mind.'

'Yes, never mind,' I said, gesturing for her to continue.

'She said they have loads in common and she really likes him, but doesn't want to rush anything – not surprisingly. She still sounded really keen, though.'

'Oh, right. So you don't think she's interested in David?' I asked, lowering my voice.

Cass shook her head. 'I mean, she thinks he's a good-looking museum and all that.'

'She didn't say that, Cass.'

'She did, kind of, and she also said she was surprised that the pair of you had never got together. She said she thought you were perfect for each other and that Elliot had been wrong about that – whatever *that* meant.' She looked at me questioningly.

'Elliot had told her that the idea was ridiculous.'

'What a shocker,' said Cass, rolling her eyes. 'Well, he's in a minority, because it's crossed my mind lately too. And Lloyd's.'

I laughed. 'Lloyd?'

'Yes, but he's positive that you're hung up on someone else. Oh, but he also said that might not be a problem because whoever it is doesn't fancy you – not even a little bit. Do you know what he's on about?'

'He's confused.'

'That's a given, but I mean specifically, in this instance.'

'Time to go, Cass. Kevin's waiting for you.'

'At least add Dave to the list, Es,' she said gently. 'Maybe even put him at the top of it. His hair's his own and he could buy a dozen boats, if he wanted to.'

I hesitated, wanting to tell her that I really didn't need convincing – that I was fully and heartbreakingly aware of David's plus points, and that he was actually currently the only name on a very short, and utterly pointless, list of men with whom I wanted to share my life.

Kevin beeped his horn and Cass tutted. 'Gotta go, but add Dave to the list – as a favour to me, eh?'

'I'll give it some thought,' I said.

'Like you haven't already.' She laughed loudly, delivering another hug and then a peck on the cheek. 'Drunk, not stupid,' she called, tapping the side of her head and cackling as she made her way unsteadily to the door. 'Drunk, not stupid!'

I smiled and shook my head, following to lock the door behind her and watching as she climbed into the waiting car, wound down the window and waved. I raised a hand and then, as the car pulled away, I returned to the back of the gallery, picked up the tray of glasses and went into the kitchen.

David was standing by the sink and drying his hands when I entered.

'Oh,' he said, his shoulders sagging slightly, 'I didn't realise there were more.'

'I'll do these. You head home.'

'No, I'll wait and walk you to your car,' he said, refilling the bowl and then turning off the tap. 'But I'll let you sort the glasses. How's that for compromise?' He sat down at the table, leaning back in his chair and gazing up at the ceiling.

'What was all the shouting about?' he asked.

'Cass,' I said, beginning to wash the glasses.

He nodded but didn't say anything more – as comfortable with the silence between us as I was.

A few minutes later, I dried the last of the glasses and turned to him. 'I'll box them when I return everything on Monday.'

'OK, so home now?' he asked. 'Or debrief first?'

'Debrief,' I said, flopping down onto the chair opposite him. 'Although, I may never get up again. I'm so tired.'

'Plans for the weekend?'

'Nothing, except catching up with progress – or lack of it – on the flat, and catching up on sleep too. You?'

'Yet to be confirmed. So,' he said, sitting up and placing both hands on the table in front of him, 'debrief.'

'Loads of sales, booze left over, no breakages.'

'I'll be sure to include all that in the annual report.'

I held out a hand. 'Your turn.'

'Lloyd and Gwen have invited us to dinner, weekend after next – I'm supposed to pass that on. Kevin has booked a surprise getaway to Barcelona for Cass's birthday. Do *not* tell her,' he said, as I put a hand to my mouth. 'And Douglas neither killed nor imprisoned his neighbours. They're in Ipswich.'

'Wow,' I said, 'your debrief was *so* much better than mine.'

'I know.'

'So Kevin is—'

'Do *not* tell her,' he repeated.

'Of course I won't, but she'll be so pleased. So long as,' I held up a finger, 'he makes sure she has enough time and info to pack appropriate clothing. Remember when he told her to pack for lots of walking and she had nothing but a cagoule and hiking boots to wear around Paris? She was *not* happy. Maybe I'll have a word with him,' I said thoughtfully. 'Anyway, what makes you think that Douglas didn't murder his neighbours?'

'What makes me *certain* that Douglas didn't murder his neighbours is that Bill told me that they did an overnight bunk, owing a quarter's rent, but that the landlord eventually tracked them down.'

'But Pamela said he murdered them.'

'Pamela told *me* that they had disappeared without a trace. So maybe you misinterpreted that sentence,' he said patiently. 'Or made up an entirely different one in your head.'

'Well, I bet that when he does murder someone,' I said, prompting a heavy sigh from David, 'he'll make them into sausages. It's the perfect way to dispose of a body and why else would he have done so much research into mincers?'

'OK, but how about until he's arrested, charged and convicted, we just keep selling his work?'

'Agreed.'

I smiled and, as he smiled back at me, I thought about my conversation with Cass and felt the burden of unspoken feelings increase.

'Shall we go then?' he asked, standing up. 'I'm desperate for my bed.'

'Oh… yes, sure,' I said, hurrying from the kitchen to the workshop to collect my bags, before following David into the low-lit gallery.

When I caught up with him, he was standing next to a display case, peering intently at Douglas's sculpture of a fox. 'I wonder if he's going to be incredibly famous,' he said quietly.

'His wildlife work is extraordinarily commercial and if *that* doesn't make him famous—'

He held up a hand towards me, as he continued to study the piece. 'No more sausage talk.'

I made my way to the door. 'I was just going to say that if he *did* do anything criminal, the value and public profile of his work would obviously rocket. So, you know, provided that we always have some of his work in stock…'

'Excellent point,' he said, straightening up. 'And look, if you're not up to anything tomorrow, how about a trip to Bath? I could show you the areas I scouted with Arthur and then maybe we could start taking some more definite steps.'

I turned sharply and frowned, wrong-footed by the sudden-ness of the proposal and by the unavoidable need to confront the issue.

Registering my obvious lack of enthusiasm, David was quick to offer me a get-out.

'It was just an idea,' he said, joining me at the door, 'and a very last-minute one. You probably don't fancy a working Saturday after a heavy week. We can go another time.'

I hitched my satchel and backpack up onto my shoulder, prompting a memory of our last, tense, after-work exchange, on the exact same spot, several months earlier. At least this time the tension didn't revolve around me snogging someone else's partner. Not that that made the current situation any less stressful.

'Look, David, this is really difficult for me – and a bit embar-rassing, actually,' I said, addressing the comment to the nearest display case, which just happened to house Douglas's rather more grim pieces. 'There's something I should have mentioned weeks ago, but I didn't know how to raise it without making us both feel very uncomfortable. But now there's no choice other than to share it with you and I want you to know, before I go on, that I'm fully aware that what I have to say will probably make our working relationship awkward for a while. Also, I want to be clear that I don't expect any business decisions to be made, or any plans to change, on the basis of what I'm going to say. I'd just like you to listen and then try to set it to one side, in terms of this gallery and in terms of any others we may wish to establish going forward.'

I forced myself to look at him and was unsurprised to find his expression calm. Only the slight elevation of a single eyebrow betrayed any trace of uncertainty or intrigue as to what I might be about to say next.

'If you have any concerns at all, you know I'd want to hear them. I trust your commercial judgement completely.'

'I know, but this is a personal matter.'

'We've already agreed that personal issues can sometimes be very pertinent to the business and that it's therefore important to air them, rather than try to deny that they exist.'

'Yes, we did agree that, didn't we?'

He nodded. 'We did.'

'OK then. Well, the truth is, David...' I began quietly, before pausing immediately for breath. 'The truth is that I'm finding it difficult to be enthusiastic about the idea of opening a second gallery in Bath because I really don't like the idea of working apart from you. Over the past few months, I've had a chance to examine why I feel that way and I've realised that it's not only because I enjoy your company as a colleague and a friend – and have done for a very long time – but also because...' I paused for another steadying breath. 'Because I have deeper feelings for you. Obviously, I know that creates an awkward situation for you – for us, really. And actually, I can see that opening a second gallery at another location, and working separately, might help to ease that awkwardness, as well as being a sound business move. But in any case, I just felt that I had to explain things, because I need you to understand why, right now, my heart isn't in the Bath move. That doesn't mean that my head won't be, but I'm sure you would have eventually noticed a lack of excitement about the process on my part, and it's only fair that you know exactly what's behind that. It's definitely nothing to do with losing my passion or enthusiasm for the business.'

He stood, unspeaking, his single raised eyebrow having gradually descended during the course of my monologue to join the other in a slight frown. 'I'm just processing all that,' he said at last.

'OK, well, how about you process it at home?' I spoke rapidly, suddenly anxious to be gone. 'I understand that this isn't easy for you. I know how difficult I would find it in your place, and I'm sure you'd welcome some time on your own to think it through.'

'It's fine,' he said simply. 'I'm grateful for your honesty and professionalism.'

'Oh… OK. Well, thank you, that's… er… great feedback,' I replied uncertainly, aware of a growing sense of both embarrassment and anticlimax. I looked again at Douglas's sculptures, in particular the seated woman with her head buried in her hands. I wondered if she'd just told her work colleague that she fancied him and been congratulated on her professionalism. If so, her attitude of agonised despair was entirely relatable. I turned away, reaching for the door and trying not to think of anything beyond a need for the solitude and sanctuary of the cottage, so that I could curl up into a ball and cry my eyes out.

The gallery door was half open, when I felt David's hand on my arm, gently turning me back towards him.

'Hang on,' he said. 'You can't deliver that kind of news and then just leave. You're developing a habit of unilaterally deciding when it's time to end important conversations. The last time you did it, you suddenly – and quite literally – shoved me out onto the pavement. I regretted allowing that to happen then and I'm not going to let it happen now. There's more to be said.'

I nodded acceptingly, lowering my eyes from his face to the small, repeating leaf pattern of his shirt. 'I just thought you'd want to get home but, of course,' I said huskily, 'you carry on.'

'Thank you for your forbearance,' he replied, with a level of corporate-cool uncomfortably reminiscent of the tone he'd used over the matter of my kitchen snog with Elliot. But when I looked up, I found that this time he was smiling, and I blinked back tears at the prospect of the kindly and calming reassurances I was certain were to come.

'As I've already said, I'm grateful for your honesty and professionalism,' he repeated quietly. 'I'm only sorry that I couldn't match them. Because the truth is, Esme, that I enjoy being here, *with you*, more than I enjoy anything else in life. With only one exception, I have looked forward to seeing you every single working day since we opened Erskine and Green over two years ago. You are funny, fascinating, clever, kind, beautiful and unique. You are life-enhancing and I resent leaving the gallery each evening without you.'

I stared at him, my mouth falling open long before I was ready to speak. 'Beautiful?' I managed eventually.

He nodded slowly. 'Yes, *beautiful* was on the list. I didn't put it at the top, because I didn't want to appear superficial. And in my defence, I have tried very hard, for a very long time, not to notice that you're an incredibly attractive woman. But it's true nevertheless. Oh and can I just apologise for suggesting a business trip to Bath as a cover for spending time with you over the weekend? A sort of date by stealth, which I admit,' he grimaced slightly, 'doesn't sound great. You might want to have a word with HR about that.'

'You think I'm an incredibly attractive woman,' I murmured, my brain on catch-up, my voice barely above a whisper. 'But you tried not to notice?'

'Well, I couldn't actually detect any signs of you being remotely attracted to me,' he shrugged. 'And the fact that I never made it onto the ever-growing list of men that Cass sticks to the till for you whenever she drops by, just seemed to confirm that there really was no hope for me.' He placed his hands in his pockets and heaved a sigh. 'I always thought the baker from Stokes Croft looked like a guy with potential, by the way.'

'This evening Cass said that you should be on the list,' I said quietly. 'At the top of it, actually.'

He smiled. 'At last.'

'Yes, at last,' I thought, calmed and reassured by his shared sense of longing and of falling short – feelings which had become so familiar to me over the past few months. I gazed dumbly up at him, replaying his words and feeling as safe and secure in the moment as I had when we had held each other close, on that very same spot, several months earlier.

'You're thinking, not talking,' said David, 'and that unnerves me at the best of times.'

I looked at the bags hanging from my shoulder. 'I'm thinking that maybe I should put these down.'

'Because…?'

'Because I'm remembering that the last time I hugged you, they really got in the way. My left arm was fine, but my right arm felt very heavy and awkward. At the same time, I'm also thinking that this might not be a hugging moment for you. What if I put the bags down and you say, "It's good that we've finally discussed this, Esme. Let's give ourselves some time to think really deeply about everything that's been said and then talk again." If you say that, then I'll have to quickly bend down and pick up all my bags, and I'll end up feeling as if I've—'

'OK, so maybe *not* talking was the better option,' he said, walking towards me. 'Just go with your first instinct and put the bags down.'

'OK, then,' I mouthed, letting the bags slip from my shoulder and fall heavily to the floor.

He stepped past me and opened the gallery door. 'Great, now let's talk again on Monday.'

We both laughed at that and then – after reclosing the door and asking me if I knew that I was perfect – David put his arms around me, lowered his head towards mine and kissed me.

Chapter 39

It took almost an hour for David to walk me to my car, despite it being parked directly opposite the gallery. But then there was a lot of snogging to be done, and an awful lot to clarify and discuss, such as, for example, exactly how irresistibly and deeply attracted we were to each other, and how sausages were made.

It's true that David didn't seem particularly invested in the sausage topic, reminding me several times that he didn't actually eat meat. Consequently, he kept dragging the conversation back to such subjects as my wonderful personality, my eyes, the sweep of my neck and how he'd wanted to kiss me months ago – just after I told him about Elliot and just before I shoved him out onto the pavement. Not surprisingly, I didn't hugely resent these efforts to divert the conversation away from butchery, and I reciprocated with an admission that I wished he had just gone ahead and kissed me months ago. I also asked a question about liquid detergent: his shirts and jumpers always smelled so great.

But as midnight approached, we'd reluctantly gone our separate ways, with David suggesting that we meet at my cottage at two p.m. the next day for a walk, to which I had agreed.

In the end, he turned up at two thirty, in an uncharacteristic display of lateness.

'Sorry,' he said, as I opened the door to him with an unexpected degree of first-date nerves. 'I had some domestic issues to resolve.'

'Not a problem.' I stepped back to let him inside, loosening the woollen scarf around my neck, 'I've been sketching in the garden to, you know, keep a lid on my nerves.' I took a deep breath and looked up at him anxiously. 'Are you nervous?'

'No.'

'Oh.'

'Well, maybe just a little.'

'Really?'

'No. I'm just trying to make you feel better.'

I tutted, beckoning him into the living room. 'Have a seat while I grab my boots. They're in the utility room.'

A moment later, I returned to find him looking relaxed in the calico armchair. 'Have you had a good morning?' I asked, sitting down on the sofa and bending to slip my feet into my boots. When he didn't reply, I looked up and he smiled at me. 'What?'

'Nothing.' He shook his head. 'I was just thinking how good everything feels today.'

I smiled. 'I know.'

'And before we head off, I have something for you.' He bent down and picked up a cardboard box from beside his chair, leaning forward to hand it to me. 'Instead of first-date flowers.'

'Ooh, thank you.' I rested the box on my lap, prising open the flaps, which had been interwoven to keep them secure. Reaching inside, I took out a wooden sculpture, sanded and polished to an almost glassy finish. It was a woman – head and shoulders only – her head turned to one side and a slight, bordering on mischievous, smile playing across her lips. It was clearly and unmistakably me.

I put a hand to my mouth. 'It's absolutely beautiful,' I said. 'I mean it's beautifully made. I'm not commenting on the subject. You are so, *so* talented, David. How long did it take to make?' I asked, turning it over in my hands.

'A while, and it's not my first attempt. There are three others at home.'

'So you've been studying me for months?'

'When you say it like that, it sounds as dodgy as the stealth date.'

I laughed. 'Not at all. It's wonderful and look, since you've put yourself out there, I'm going to share something with you,' I said, walking to place the sculpture on a bookcase and then continuing into the kitchen. 'It'll make you feel better,' I called.

'Or possibly not,' I continued a moment later, returning with my red leather-bound journal and handing it to him. 'Take a look.'

'Are you sure?' he asked doubtfully. 'This is your diary, isn't it?'

'It's fine. It's all pictures – apart from the dates. Just people and scenes which strike me on a day-to-day basis. For instance,' I leaned towards him and opened it at random, 'here you are on 7 June, hanging Jasmine's oils on the day of her show.'

He looked down and smiled. 'Is my jawline really that strong?'

'I'm flattering you, obviously.'

'Obviously. But this isn't comparable to secretively studying and sculpting one person for weeks on end. It's just brilliantly observed, rapidly and randomly executed art. Not remotely dodgy.'

'Pick another page,' I said. 'From about halfway in. Then pick another and another.'

He flipped through the journal, his eyes widening slightly. 'Oh, OK,' he said. 'So are there any drawings of anyone or anything else except me in here?'

I shrugged. 'I think there might be a horse in there somewhere. And if you turn back to early March, you'll find a rather disturbing image of an upturned bath but, for the most part, for quite a while now, it's just you.'

He nodded. 'Yes, that is dodgy,' he said, before pausing over one particular sketch, his frown deepening. 'I see that you've given this one a title.'

I craned my neck in an attempt to see. 'Have I? I don't usually write anything at all.'

He turned the book towards me and I saw the words *Dingle Dangle Scarecrow* scrawled beneath a sketch of David, sitting at his workbench, his head bowed, as he gazed thoughtfully at a large block of wood.

I laughed. 'I'd forgotten about that one!'

'Hmm,' he said, closing the book and returning it to me.

'You're extremely handsome.'

He held up a hand. 'No reassurance needed. Your unnerving obsession with me is all the ego boost I require.'

'Good. Now, shall we go?'

He nodded and together we made our way to the front door, heading out onto the gravel pathway. We had just stepped into the lane when David paused and looked upwards. 'I think it might rain,' he said.

'Seriously?' I scanned the bright blue sky for any hint of a cloud.

'Yes, I think I'll swap this jacket for a waterproof one,' he replied, executing a sharp left turn, opening next-door's gate, jogging up the path and going inside.

I watched, laughing, as he re-emerged a moment later and returned to join me.

'You've moved in next door!' I exclaimed.

'Just for a couple of nights. It was on Airbnb and I thought it might be nice to share the commute on Monday.'

'Is that why you were late today?'

'I was collecting the keys.'

'I can't believe you did that,' I said, looking up at him and shaking my head.

'Dodgy?'

'No! I think it's really romantic. But then I have been sketching you on an almost daily basis without your knowledge for the past six months, so maybe I'm not the best judge of dodgy. But you haven't swapped to your waterproof.' I tugged lightly at his jacket.

'My things are still in the car. That was pure theatrics,' he said, inclining his head towards the cottage.

I looped my arms around his neck. 'You know, you're way more creative than corporate these days, David Erskine.'

'I like to think so,' he said quietly, putting his arms around me and kissing me softly.

I kissed him back, rather less softly, and when I realised that my hands were beginning to track inside his unbuttoned jacket, I calmed myself by switching to hugging him tightly around the middle, resting my head against his meadow-fresh jumper and inhaling deeply.

'I hate to interrupt,' he said, kissing the top of my head, 'whatever it is that you're doing down there, but are we going for a walk or not?'

'I'm afraid it might rain,' I mumbled into his chest before lifting my head and looking up at him.

He tilted his face towards the sun and sighed. 'You know, it's a shame, but I think you might be right,' he said, prising my arms from around him and nodding towards my cottage. 'Perhaps we should go back inside.'

'And get creative, you mean?' I asked, turning to open the gate.

He laughed. 'Well, that's what got us here, isn't it?' he said, taking my hand as we made our way back up the path. 'So why stop now?'

Acknowledgements

When you're attempting to write feel good fiction, it helps to be surrounded by feel good people, and topping the list of positive influences in my literary life is my agent, Camilla Bolton. My thanks go to her for her endless encouragement and cheerful patience, and to the entire Darley Anderson team, in particular Jade Kavanagh, Mary Darby and Rosanna Bellingham.

I'm fortunate that my publishers, Canelo, are an equally uplifting bunch, and that Emily Bedford has, once again, lent her considerable editing skills, energy and insight to the process of bringing this book to publication. I'm grateful also to Daniela Nava and Alicia Pountney whose kind words and attention to detail were appreciated in equal measure.

I know we shouldn't judge a book by its cover but, let's face it, we often do. So many thanks to Clare Stacey at Head Design for creating such a beautiful and ingenious one for *The Ex Next Door*. I can't stop staring.

Closer to home, thank you to Sharon Marshall, Gerry Platt and Jo Fort, for laughing in all the right places and for repeatedly hammering down my moments of self-doubt in a splat-the-rat fashion. Thank you also to my noisy neighbours, Kathie Butters, Angelique Furey, Claire Sanders and Sophie Welsman, for mood-boosting evenings of raucous conversation and excellent cuisine, and to The Curry Night Crew: Kate Battersby, Wendy Morgan and Linda Hardwick – plus their lovely other halves – for always making grey skies blue.

And finally, my love and thanks to Martin, Ollie and Betty, for sharing my sense of humour and for making me feel like a coper, despite all evidence to the contrary. I've said it before and I'll say it again: you're the best.